Amy Andrews is a multi-award winning, *USA Today* bestselling author who has written over forty contemporary romances for several Mills & Boon imprints. She's an Aussie who loves good books, fab food, great wine and frequent travel – preferably all four together. She lives by the ocean with her husband of twenty-nine years. To keep up with her latest releases and giveaways, sign up for her newsletter at www.amyandrews.com.au/newsletter.html

Kate Hewitt has worked a variety of different jobs, from drama teacher to editorial assistant to youth worker, but writing romance is the best one yet. She also writes women's fiction and all her stories celebrate the healing and redemptive power of love. Kate lives in a tiny village in the English Cotswolds with her husband, five children, and an overly affectionate Golden Retriever.

Three-times Golden Heart® finalist **Tina Beckett** learned to pack her suitcases almost before she learned to read. Born to a military family, she has lived in the United States, Puerto Rico, Portugal and Brazil. In addition to travelling, Tina loves to cuddle with her pug, Alex, spend time with her family, and hit the trails on her horse. Learn more about Tina from her website, or 'friend' her on Facebook.

Tropical Temptation

Tropical Temptation: Exotic Dreams

AMY ANDREWS

KATE HEWITT

TINA BECKETT

MILLS & BOON

First Published in Great Britain 2020
By Mills & Boon, an imprint of HarperCollins*Publishers*
1 London Bridge Street, London, SE1 9GF

TROPICAL TEMPTATION: EXOTIC DREAMS
© 2020 Harlequin Books S.A.

The Devil and the Deep © 2012 Amy Andrews
The Prince She Never Knew © 2013 Kate Hewitt
Doctor's Guide to Dating in the Jungle © 2012 Tina Beckett

ISBN: 978-0-263-29858-1

MIX
Paper from
responsible sources
FSC® C007454

This book is produced from independently certified FSC™ paper to ensure responsible forest management.

For more information visit: www.harpercollins.co.uk/green

Printed and bound in Spain
by CPI, Barcelona

THE DEVIL AND THE DEEP

AMY ANDREWS

For Halle Anne Baxter.
Much loved.

PROLOGUE

*Lady Mary Bingham had never seen such a fine speci-
men of manhood in all her twenty years as she held out
her hand to her unlikely saviour so he could aid her
aboard. Pirate or not, Vasco Ramirez's potent masculinity tingled through every cell of her body. And even had
it not, his piercing blue eyes, the exact colour of warm,
tropical waters that fringed the reefs he was rumoured
to know like the back of his hand, touched a place inside her that she'd never known existed.*

A place she could never now deny.

*She supposed, if she were given to swooning, this
would be as good a time as any. But she wasn't. In fact
she'd always found the practice rather tiresome and
refused to even allow her knees the slightest tremble.
Women who had fits of the vapours and cried for their
smelling salts every two seconds—like her aunt—were
not the kind of women she admired.*

*Her breath hitched as sable lashes framing those in-
credible eyes swept downwards in a frank inspection of
every inch of her body. When his gaze returned to her
face she was left in no doubt that he'd liked what he'd
seen. His thumb lightly stroked the skin of her forearm
and she felt the caress deep inside that newly awakened place.*

Looking at the bronzed angles of his exotic face, she

knew she should be afraid for had she not just gone from the frying pan straight into the fire?

Yet strangely she wasn't.

Not even when his gaze dropped to the pulse beating rapidly against the milky white skin of her neck. Or lower to where her breasts strained against the constrictive fabric of her bodice. His lazy inspection of the agitated rise of her bosom did not elicit fear even when what it did elicit was reason for fear itself.

Her uncle, the bishop, would have declared him an instrument of the devil. A man willing to lead unsuspecting ladies to the edge of sin but strangely she'd never felt so compelled to transgress. The thought was titillating and she sucked in a breath, annoyed that this buccaneer had caused such consternation after such short acquaintance.

After all, was not one pirate just like the next?

Mary looked down at the insolent drift of his thumb. 'You will unhand me immediately,' she intoned in a voice that brooked no argument.

Ramirez's smile was nine parts charm one part insolence as he slowly—very slowly—ceased the involuntary caress.

'As you wish,' he murmured, bowing slightly over her hand, his fingers tracing down the delicate blue veins of her forearm, whispering over the fragile bones of her wrist and the flat of her palm as he released her.

Lady Mary swallowed as the accented English slid velvet gloves over already sensitised skin. 'I insist that you return me to my uncle forthwith.'

Vasco admired her pluck. The girl, who he knew to be barely out of her teens, may well be staring him straight in the eye but he could smell her fear as only a veteran of a hundred raids on the high seas could.

Lord alone knew what had happened to her in the two

days she'd been at the mercy of Juan Del Toro and his ruffians. But something told him this pampered English miss could certainly hold her own.

And virgins fetched a much higher price at the slave markets.

'As you wish,' he murmured again.

Mary narrowed her eyes, suspicious of his easy capitulation. 'You know my uncle? You know who I am?'

He smiled at her. 'You are Lady Mary Bingham. The bishop commissioned me to...retrieve you.'

For the first time in two days Mary could see an end to the nightmare that had begun with her abduction down by the wharfs a mere forty-eight hours before and she almost sagged to the damp floorboards at his feet. She'd heard her former captives talking about slave markets and had been scared witless.

Alas, falling at the feet of a pirate, whether sanctioned by her uncle or not, wasn't something a young woman of good breeding did. 'Thank you,' she said politely. 'I am most grateful for your speedy response. Juan Del Toro's men do not know how to treat a lady.'

'Do not thank me yet, Lady Bingham.' He smiled with steel in his lips. 'There are a lot of miles between here and Plymouth and by the end of it my *men may well care less about you being a lady and more about you being a woman.'*

Mary raised a haughty eyebrow, hoping it disguised the sudden leap in her pulse. 'And you would allow such fiendish behaviour amongst your crew?'

Vasco smiled his most charming smile, his dark tousled hair giving him the look of the devil. 'Amongst my crew? Of course not, Lady Bingham. But captains do enjoy certain privileges...'

STELLA MILLS sighed as she closed down the document on her desktop and dragged herself back from the swashbuck-

ling seventeen hundreds to the reality of the here and now.
She could re-read the words that had flowed effortlessly out
of her last year and made her an 'overnight' sensation until
the cows came home but it didn't change the facts—one book
did not a writer make.

One book did not a career make.

No matter how many publishing houses had bid for
Pleasure Hunt at auction, no matter how many best-seller
lists it had made or how many fan letters she'd received or
how much money competing film companies had thrown at
her for the film rights.

No matter how crazy the romance world had gone for Vasco
Ramirez.

They wanted more.

And so did the publisher.

Stella stared at the blinking cursor on the blank page in
front of her. The same blinking cursor she'd been staring at
for almost a year now.

Oh, God. 'I'm a one-hit wonder,' she groaned as her head
hit the keyboard.

A knock on the door interrupted her pity party and she
glanced up. Several lines of gobbledygook stared back at her
as the knock came again. She grimaced—it seemed she was
destined to write nothing but incomprehensible garbage for
ever more.

Another knock, more insistent than the last, demanded her
attention. 'Coming,' she called as she did what she'd done
every day for the past year—deleted the lot.

She hurried to the door and was reaching for the knob as a
fourth knock landed. 'Okay, okay, hold your horses,' she said
as she wrenched the damn thing open.

Piercing blue eyes, the exact colour of warm, tropical waters that fringed the reefs she knew he knew like the back of
his hand, greeted her. She blinked. 'Rick?'

'Stel,' he murmured, leaning forward to kiss first one cheek then the other, inhaling the familiar coconut essence of her.

She shut her eyes briefly as the smell of sea breezes and ocean salt infused her senses the way they always did whenever Riccardo Granville was close. When she opened them again Rick had withdrawn and her mother came into focus, hovering behind his shoulder. Her eyes were rimmed with red and she was biting on her bottom lip.

Her mother lived in London and Rick called the ocean his home. Why were they here? In Cornwall. Together?

Stella frowned as a feeling of doom descended.

'What's wrong?' she asked, looking from one to the other as her pulse wooshed like a raging torrent through her ears.

Her mother stepped forward and hugged her. 'Darling,' she murmured, 'it's Nathan.'

Stella blinked. Her father?

She looked over her mother's shoulder at Rick, his face grim. 'Rick?' she asked, searching for a spark of something—anything—that would bring her back from the precipice she was balanced upon.

Rick looked down at the woman he'd known almost all his thirty years and sadly shook his head. 'I'm sorry.'

CHAPTER ONE

Six months later...

THE cursor still blinked at her from the same blank page. Although Stella rather fancied that it had given up blinking and had moved on to mocking.

There were no words. No story.

No characters spoke in her head. No plot played like a movie reel. No shards of glittering dialogue burnt brightly on her inward eye desperate for release.

There was just the same old silence.

And now grief to boot.

And Diana would be arriving soon.

As if she'd willed it, a knock on the door heralded Stella's closest friend. Normally she'd have leapt from her seat to welcome Diana but not today. In fact, for a moment, she seriously considered not opening the door at all.

Today, Diana was not here as her friend.

Today, Diana was here as a representative from the publisher.

And she'd promised her chapter one...

'I know you're in there. Don't make me break this sucker down.'

The voice was muffled but determined and Stella resigned herself to her fate as she crossed from her work area in the window alcove, with its spectacular one-eighty-degree views of rugged Cornish coastline, to the front door. She drew in a steadying breath as she unlatched it and pulled it open.

Diana opened her arms. 'Babe,' she muttered as she swept Stella into a rib-cracking hug. 'How are you doing? I've been so worried about you.'

Stella settled into the sweet sisterhood of the embrace, suddenly so glad to see her friend she could feel tears prick at the backs of her eyes. They'd only known each other a handful of years since meeting at uni, but Diana had called most nights since the funeral and this was her tenth visit.

'Pretty rubbish,' she admitted into Diana's shoulder.

'Of course you are,' Diana soothed, rubbing her friend's back. 'Your dad died—it comes with the territory.'

Diana's parents had passed away not long before they'd become friends so Stella knew that Diana had intimate acquaintance with grief.

'I want to stop feeling like this.'

Diana hugged her harder. 'You will. Eventually you will. In the meantime you need to do what you need to do. And I think that starts with a nice glass of red.'

Diana held up a bottle of shiraz she'd bought at an off-licence in Penzance on her way to the windswept, cliff-top cottage her friend had taken out a long-term lease on after her strait-laced fiancé, Dreary Dale, hadn't been able to handle the success of *Pleasure Hunt* and had scuttled away with a stick jammed up his butt.

Sure, Stella had insisted her reasons had more to do with the historic coastline's rich pirate history stimulating her muse but, given that no book was forthcoming, Diana wasn't buying it.

Stella looked at her watch and laughed for the first time today. It was two in the afternoon. 'It's a bit early, isn't it?'

Diana tutted her disapproval. 'The sun's up over the yard-arm—isn't that what you nautical types say? Besides, it's November—it's practically night time.'

Diana didn't wait for an answer, dragging her pull-along case inside the house and kicking the door shut with her four-inch-booted heel. She shrugged out of her calf-length, figure-hugging leather coat and unwound her Louis Vuitton scarf from her neck—all without letting go of the bottle. She wore charcoal trousers and a soft pink cashmere sweater, which matched the thick brunette curls that fell against its pearlescent perfection.

Diana was *very* London.

Stella looked down at her own attire and felt like a total slob. Grey sweats, coffee-stained hoodie and fluffy slippers. A haphazard ponytail that she'd scraped together this morning hung limply from her head in an even bigger state of disarray.

Stella was *very* reclusive writer.

Which would be much more romantic if she'd actually bloody written anything in the last eighteen months.

'Sit,' Diana ordered, tinkling her fingers at her friend as she headed towards the cupboard where she knew, from many a drinking session, the wine glasses were housed.

Stella sat on her red leather sofa if, for nothing else, to feel less diminutive. Diana was almost six feet and big boned in a sexy Amazonian, Wonder Woman kind of way. She, on the other hand, was just a couple of centimetres over five feet, fair and round.

'Here,' Diana said, thrusting a huge glass of red at her and clinking the rims together before claiming the bucket chair opposite. 'To feeling better,' she said, then took a decent swig.

'I'll drink to that,' Stella agreed, taking a more measured sip. She stared into the depths of her wine, finding it easier than looking at her friend.

'You don't have the chapter, do you?' Diana asked after the silence had stretched long enough.

Stella looked at Diana over the rim of her glass. 'No,' she murmured. 'I'm sorry.'

Diana nodded. 'It's okay.'

Stella shook her head and uttered what had been on her mind since the writer's block had descended all those months ago. 'What if I only ever have one book in me?'

The fear had gnawed away at her since finishing the first book. Dale's desertion had added to it. Her father's death had cemented it.

Vasco Ramirez had demanded to be written. He'd strutted straight out of her head onto the page in all his swashbuckling glory. He had been a joy, his story a gift that had flowed effortlessly.

And now?

Now they wanted another pirate and she had nothing.

Diana held up a hand, waving the question away. 'You don't,' she said emphatically.

'But what if I do?'

Stella had never known the sting of rejection and the mere thought was paralysing. What if Joy, her editor, hated what she wrote? What if she laughed?

She'd had a dream ride—from a six-figure auction with a multi-book contract to *New York Times* best-seller to a movie deal.

What if it had all been a fluke?

Diana stabbed her finger at the air in her general direction. 'You. Don't.'

Stella felt a surge of guilt mix with the shiraz in her veins, giving it an extra charge. Diana had championed her crazy foray into writing from the beginning, encouraging her to take a break from being an English teacher and write the damn book.

She'd been the first to read it. The first to know its potential, insisting that she take it to show her boss, who was looking for exactly what Stella had written—a meaty historical romance. As an editorial assistant in a London publishing house Diana had been adamant it was a blockbuster and

Stella had been flabbergasted when Diana's prediction of a quick offer had come to pass.

She smiled at her friend, hoping it didn't come across as desperate on the outside as it felt on the inside. 'Will you get sacked if you return to London empty-handed?'

Almost a year past Stella's deadline, Joy had pulled out the big guns to get her recalcitrant star to deliver. She knew how close Diana and Stella were so she'd sent Diana to do whatever it took to get book number two.

Diana shook her head. 'No. We're not going to talk about this tonight. Tonight, we get messy drunk, tomorrow we talk about the book. Deal?'

Stella felt the knot in her shoulder muscles release like an elastic band and she smiled. 'Deal.'

Two hours later, a storm had drawn night in a little earlier than usual. Wind howled around the house, lashing at the shutters, not that the two women cosied up by the fire were aware. They were on their second bottle of wine and almost at the bottom of a large packet of crisps and were laughing hysterically about their uni days.

A sharp rap at the door caused them both to startle then burst out laughing at their comic-book reactions.

'Bloody hell.' Diana clutched her chest. 'I think I just had a heart attack.'

Stella laughed as she rose a little unsteadily. 'Impossible, red wine's supposed to be good for the heart.'

'Not in these quantities it's not,' Diana said and Stella cracked up again as she headed towards the door.

'Wait, where are you going?' Diana muttered as she also clambered to her feet.

Stella frowned. 'To open the door.'

'But what if it's a two-headed moor monster?' Even through her wine goggles Diana could see the rain lashing the window pane behind Stella's desk. 'It is the very definition of a dark and stormy night out there, babe.'

Stella hiccupped. 'Well, I don't think they knock but I'll politely tell it to shoo and point out that Bodmin is a little north of here.'

Diana cracked up and Stella was still chuckling as she opened the door.

To Vasco Ramirez. In the flesh.

Light from inside the cottage bathed the bronzed angles of his jaw and cheekbones, fell softly against his mouth and illuminated his blue eyes to tourist-brochure perfection. His shoulder-length hair, a relic from his tearaway teens, hung in damp strips around his face and water droplets clung to those incredible sable lashes.

He looked every inch the pirate.

'Rick?' Her breath stuttered to a halt as it always did when he was too close, sucking up all her oxygen. The recalcitrant memory of an almost-kiss over a decade ago flitted like a butterfly through her grey matter.

Rick smiled down at a frowning Stella. 'Now what sort of greeting is that?' he teased as he moved in for his standard double cheek kiss.

Coconut embraced him. Nathan had bought Stella coconut body products every year for her birthday and she'd faithfully worn them. Still was, apparently.

Stella shut her eyes and waited for the choirs of angels in her head to start singing *hallelujah* as the aroma of salt and sea enveloped her. He was, after all, so perfect he had to be heaven-sent.

She blinked as he pulled away. 'Is everything okay?' she asked.

Her heart beat a little faster in her chest. Which had nothing to do with the erotic scrape of his perpetual three-day growth or the brief brush of his lips, and everything to do with his last visit.

Rick didn't just drop by.

Last time he'd arrived unannounced on her doorstep looking bleaker than the North Sea in winter, the news had not been good.

'Is Mum—?'

Rick pressed his fingers against her mouth, hushing her. 'Linda's fine, Stel. Everything's fine.'

She almost sagged against him in relief. Certainly her mouth did. He smiled at her as he withdrew his hand and she smiled back, and with the wind whipping around them and flurries of raindrops speckling their skin it was as if they were kids again, standing on the bow of the *Persephone* as a storm chased them back into harbour.

'So...not a monster from the moors, then?' Diana asked, interrupting their shared reverie.

Rick looked over Stella's shoulder straight into the eyes of a vaguely familiar, striking brunette. She looked at him with frank admiration and he grinned.

God, but he loved women.

Particularly women like this. The kind that liked to laugh and have a good time, enjoyed a flirt and some no-strings company.

'Honey, I can be whatever you want me to be,' he said, pushing off the door jamb, brushing past Stella and extending his hand. 'Hi. Rick. I think we've already met?'

Diana smiled as she shook his hand. 'Yes. When you were here for the funeral. Diana,' she supplied.

'Ah, yes, that's right,' Rick said, stalling a little. He'd been so caught up in his shock and disbelief and being strong for Stella and Linda that he'd not really taken anything in. 'You work for Stel's publishers?'

Diana grinned, her eyes twinkling, not remotely insulted that Rick had struggled to remember her. 'Took you a while.'

Stella watched her bestie and her...whatever the hell Rick was—old family friend? deceased father's business partner?

substitute brother?—flirt effortlessly. Now why couldn't she be more like that? The only time she'd been comfortable, truly comfortable, with a man had been with a fictional pirate.

Even her relationship with Dale had been lukewarm by comparison.

A blast of rain spattered against her neck, bringing her out of her state of bewilderment, and she realised she still had the door wide open. She shook her head at her absent-mindedness.

'To what do we owe the pleasure?' she asked, shutting the weather out and joining the chatty twosome in the centre of the room.

Rick looked down at Stella's cute little button nose. 'Well—' he winked at her before returning his attention to Diana and running his finger around the rim of her glass '—I heard a whisper there was a party going on.'

Diana laughed. She looked at Stella. 'You never told me he had ESP.' Then she scurried to the kitchen to get another glass.

Rick watched her for a moment before returning his gaze to Stella. She stared up at him and the familiar feeling of wanting to wrap her up swelled in his chest. 'How are you doing, Stel?' he murmured.

Rick had felt the loss of Nathan Mills probably even more profoundly than his own father. Nathan had been his guardian and mentor since Anthony Granville had got himself killed in a bar fight when Rick had been seven. The man had been the closest thing to a father he had, had curbed all his hot-headed brashness and he felt his loss in a hundred different ways every day.

He could only imagine how Stella must feel.

Stella shrugged, feeling again the mutual despair that had added an extra depth to their bond. She fell into the empathy that shone in his luminescent gaze. Sometimes it was hard to reconcile the impulsive, teenage bad-boy of her fantasies with the hardworking, responsible, compassionate man in front of her.

'I hate it,' she whispered.

The truth was Stella hadn't seen her father regularly since she'd started university and joined the workforce.

Become a grown-up, as her mother would say.

A flying visit at Christmas, the arrival in the mail of a single perfect shell he'd found on a beach somewhere that always made her smile, an occasional email with pictures of him and Rick and some amazing find at the bottom of a sea bed.

But just knowing he was out there doing what he loved, following his wild boyhood dreams of sunken galleons, had kept her whole world in balance.

And now he was gone, nothing was the same.

'I know,' he murmured, putting his arm around her shoulder and pulling her into his chest. 'I hate it too.'

And he did. He hated doing what he did without the one person who truly understood *why* by his side. He hated turning to tell Nathan something and him not being there. He hated the absence of wise words and Nathan's particular brand of bawdy humour around the dinner table.

Rick shut his eyes against the loss he still felt so acutely and sank into her, enjoying the familiarity of having her close. He liked how she tucked into him just right. How her head fitted perfectly under his chin and how his chest was just the right height to pillow her cheek and how she always smelled liked coconut.

As kids he'd been the pirate and she'd been the mermaid and they'd played endless games revolving around sunken treasure. Not very politically correct these days, he supposed, but they'd amused themselves for countless hours and forged a bond that he still felt today.

Of course there'd been times, during their teenage years, when their games had taken a certain risqué turn and while they'd never indulged, they'd diced pretty close.

Holding her like this reminded him just how close.

'Okay, okay, you two,' Diana teased, pushing a glass of red

wine into Rick's hand. 'No maudlin tonight. That's the rule. Eat, drink and be merry tonight.'

Rick forced himself to step away, grateful that Diana was here to ground them in the present. He'd thought a lot about Stella since Nathan had died, more than usual.

And not all of those thoughts had been pure.

He accepted the wine. 'Good plan,' he said, clinking glasses with them both.

Stella indicated the lounge chairs huddled around the fireplace and watched as Rick shrugged out of his navy duffle coat to reveal well-worn jeans that clung in all the right places and a thick turtle-neck, cable-knit sweater.

Even off the boat the man looked as if he belonged at sea.

Diana lounged back against the cushions, inspecting him dispassionately, her wine goggles making the job a little difficult. She pointed at him over the rim of her glass.

'There's something familiar about you,' she slurred.

Stella didn't like the look of speculation on her friend's face. She'd seen that dogged look before and didn't want to give Diana too much latitude.

'Yes, you met him at the funeral,' she said, hopefully redirecting her friend's thoughts that tended to fancy after several glasses of red.

Diana narrowed her eyes. 'Nope,' she said as she shook her head. 'I have this feeling I know you beyond that.' Even at the funeral all suited and polished he'd looked vaguely familiar to her but now, looking all lone-wolf-of-the-sea, there was definitely something she recognised about him.

Was it his eyes? Or maybe his hair?

Rick chuckled. 'Maybe I look like your great uncle Cyril?'

Diana burst out laughing as she sipped on her drink and Stella even envied her that. She had a jingly laugh that sounded like Tinkerbell waving her magic wand. Stella had no doubt that red wine would be pouring out of her nose had she tried that same manoeuvre.

Diana wagged her finger. 'Good try but *you* don't look like *anyone's* great uncle Cyril.' She narrowed her eyes again and nudged the side of her nose three times with her index finger. 'Don't you worry. I *will* remember. I may just need—' she looked at her almost empty wine glass '—a while.'

Rick saluted. 'I look forward to the final outcome.'

Diana nodded. 'As well you should.'

Rick looked over at Stella sitting quietly watching the byplay. The firelight spun the escaping tendrils of her long blonde hair into golden streams and he was once again reminded of their childhood games when she'd been the mermaid singing his ship onto the rocks. How many times had he snorkelled over reefs with her, her long blonde hair flowing behind her just like the mermaids from ancient mythology?

'So,' he said when the silence had stretched enough. 'Did you get it?'

Stella frowned at him. 'Get what?'

'Your half.'

'My half of what?'

Rick grinned. 'The map?'

Stella shook her head. 'What on earth are you talking about?' she asked.

Rick's eyebrows drew together in a frown to match hers as he placed his half-empty glass on the coffee table. 'You should have received it early last week. I posted it ages ago.'

Diana rolled her eyes. 'She probably has. She's just not been responding to any correspondence.'

Stella blushed at her friend's astuteness as Diana made her way to the hall stand. Unopened mail oozed all over the edges of the sturdy eighteenth-century oak and Stella felt her cheeks grow warmer. She'd been avoiding any attempt at communication with the outside world—particularly from her editor. She didn't open her mail unless it had a window. She screened all her calls. She didn't go to her inbox.

Diana quickly riffled through the mound of mail, letters

and other miscellaneous items that had made it through Stella's front door, some of it spilling haphazardly to the floor. She pulled out a large flat yellow envelope with enough stamps to start a collection.

'This it?' she asked holding it up.

Rick nodded. 'Arrr,' he said in his best pirate accent. 'That be it.'

It was Stella's turn to roll her eyes. Rick had perfected the pirate vernacular as a child, lending an authenticity to their imaginary games.

Diana laughed as she rejoined them, thrusting the envelope at Stella. 'Ooh, you speak pirate?'

Rick grinned. 'Aye, my lovely.'

'Forget it,' Stella murmured absently as she turned the envelope over and over in her hands. There was a variety of colourful postal stamps and airmail stickers adorning the front. 'Diana's a Jack Sparrow fan. You're wasting your time.'

Rick look affronted. 'Are you saying I'm not Captain Jack material?'

It was on the tip of Stella's tongue to say that he was a thousand times sexier than the iconic film character. He was broader and taller with better oral hygiene and more scruples.

'Hmm, I don't know,' Diana mused. 'I'm sure a little more scruffed up...'

But Stella wasn't listening. Her father's distinctive handwriting had drawn her gaze and she touched the letters with great reverence as if they could somehow bring him back.

Rick glanced at Diana as Stella's continuing silence fell loudly around them. She shrugged at him hopelessly and he could tell that Stella's grief touched her too.

'Where did you get this?' Stella asked.

'I finally got around to cleaning out Nathan's desk. It was in a drawer. There was one for me as well.'

Stella nodded absently at his response. It was strange receiving something from her father six months after his death. Like a hand extending from the grave.

'Aren't you going to open it?' he asked quietly.

Stella looked up at him through the blonde stripes of her half-up-half-down fringe. 'Do I want to?'

He grinned and nodded. 'If it's what I think it is you do. You really do.'

Stella doubted it but she turned the envelope over and neatly sliced open the back. A sheath of loose papers lay within and she pulled them out after another encouraging nod from Rick. A brief note from her father was paper-clipped to the front.

> *Stel,*
> *Inigo's treasure is there, I just know it.*
> *You and Rick go find it.*
> *Make me proud.*
> *Daddy.*

Stella swallowed hard and for a moment the bold vertical slashes blurred in front of her eyes. Finding out on autopsy that her father had been riddled with cancer and wondering if the scuba-diving *accident* had really been an accident had been hard to come to terms with.

But this seemed to confirm that he'd known his days were numbered and chosen to go in his own way doing what he'd loved most.

She glanced at Rick. 'You got the same?'

He nodded and she looked back at the documents, leafing through the rest. A hand-drawn map was at the very back.

Or half a map to be precise.

'What's this?' she asked, not quite comprehending her father's frenetic squiggles around the margins.

'The other half of this,' Rick said, pulling out a folded page from his back pocket, unfolding it and laying it on the coffee table.

Diana sat forward. 'Is that a…treasure map?'

Rick grinned. 'Sort of. It shows the potential resting places of Captain Inigo Alvarez's ship, *La Sirena*.'

Diana scrunched up her face, trying to remember her schoolgirl Spanish. 'The…?'

'*The Mermaid,*' Stella supplied.

'Oh my,' Diana said. 'How exciting! Inigo Alvarez…' She rolled the name around her tongue. 'He sounds positively dishy.'

Rick laughed. 'He was. A late-eighteenth-century pirate known as the Robin Hood of the seven seas. Robbing the rich to give to the poor.'

Stella blasted Rick with a *down-boy* glare. 'Robin Hood of the high seas,' she tisked, shaking her head in disgust. 'That's all just anecdotal and you know it. Do not encourage her.'

'Drat,' Diana mused.

'Okay, maybe he was as bloodthirsty and marauding as the rest of them but there's heaps of historical documents citing his and *The Mermaid*'s existence,' he said calmly. 'You used to believe,' Rick reminded her.

They both had. Everyone in the salvaging industry seemed to have a story about the mysterious Captain Alvarez and as children they'd listened to each one until he'd grown large in both their imaginations. Rick picked up the papers that had accompanied the map, the same ones that had been in his envelope. Years of Nathan's research into a character that had captured them both.

'What happened to him?' Diana asked.

Rick looked at a captivated Diana. 'He just disappeared off the face of the earth. There were rumours at the time that *The Mermaid* went down laden with stolen booty during a vicious storm.'

'Where?' Diana whispered, sucked in even if Stella was sitting back in her chair, refusing to be drawn. 'Here somewhere, right?' she asked, picking up Stella's half of the map and joining the two pieces together on the coffee table.

Rick shook his head. 'Nathan obviously thought so. He's drawn this up from his research over the years so I guess it would be hard to be sure. But he was the best damn intuitive treasure hunter I've ever known and if he thinks Inigo's ship is here somewhere, then I'm willing to bet it is too.'

'So why didn't he go after it himself?' Stella demanded, getting up off the chair and heading for the kitchen sink. When she got there she tipped out her almost-full glass of wine. She was suddenly angry with her father.

If he'd known he was dying, why hadn't he told her? Why hadn't he got treatment? Why hadn't he come home?

'When did he have the time, Stel, with so many other projects—sure things—on the books?'

Stella looked up at the reproach in his voice, feeling suddenly guilty. They'd both known Nathan's plans had always involved finding Inigo's treasure…one day…when he retired…

'Why on earth did he give us half a map each? He must have known I was just going to give you my half and let you have at it.'

She'd loved her father and he had given her a magical childhood filled with sunken treasure and tropical waters but it had been a long time since she'd been a little girl who believed in pirates and mermaids. And the romance of that world had always warred with the realities of her life—divorced parents, divided loyalties.

Rick stood and walked towards her. He could tell she was struggling with the same emotions he had when he'd seen Nathan's handwriting again and the memories it had stirred.

'I think he knew his time was drawing to a close and maybe it was his way to keep us connected? I think he wanted us to go and do this together and I think it would be a great way to honour his memory. What do you say? The long-range weather forecast is good. You want to come on a treasure hunt with me?'

Stella glared at Rick as his not-so-subtle guilt trip found its mark. Well, it wouldn't work. 'Are you crazy? I can't go gallivanting around the bloody ocean. My editor would have apoplexy. My book is way overdue and I have probably the worst case of writer's block in the history of written language, don't I, Diana?'

She looked at her friend for confirmation, who did so with a vigorous nod of her head.

'Well, this is exactly what you need.' He grinned, unperturbed. 'Nothing like the open ocean to stimulate the muse.'

Stella stared at him askance. 'Don't you have other salvage jobs on the go?'

Rick shrugged. 'Nothing the guys can't handle. Besides, it won't be a salvage job, just a recon mission, see what we can find. A few weeks, four at the most. Just you and me and the open ocean. Salt, sea air and sunshine. You could get a tan,' he cajoled as he took in her pallor. 'It'll be just like we were kids again.'

Stella shook her head against the temptation and romance of yesteryear, which appealed to her on a primal level she didn't really understand. She dragged her gaze away from his seductive mouth.

They weren't kids any more.

'I can't. I have a book to write.'

'Come on,' he murmured, feeling the longing inside her even if she couldn't. 'You know you want to. You always wrote like crazy whenever you were on the *Persephone*. Remember? You were always scribbling away in that writing pad.'

She remembered. She'd either had her head stuck in a book or she'd been writing something. He'd teased her about it mercilessly. She should have known back then she was destined to be a writer. 'I can't. Can I, Diana?'

Diana looked at Stella. Then at Rick. Then back at her

friend. If anyone needed a change of scenery it was Stella. These four walls were obviously becoming a prison for her despite the view—maybe mixing it up a little would get the juices flowing again.

And if the open ocean was where she was most creative…

Joy would have a fit but Diana had a hunch that this was just what her friend needed. She bloody hoped so because her head would be on the chopping block if Stella returned tanned and still bookless.

She stood and joined them in the kitchen. 'I think you should go. I think it's a great idea.'

Stella blinked. 'What?' she said as Rick's grin trebled.

'*This*,' he said, slipping his arm around Diana's shoulders, 'is a wise woman.'

'Thank you.' Diana beamed at him.

'Come on, Stel. *I dare you.*'

Stella rolled her eyes. As kids their relationship had thrived on dares and one-upmanship, Stella hell-bent on proving she could keep up with a boy.

Dare you to swim through that hole in the wreck. Something expressly forbidden by her father. *Dare you to bring a coin up from the bottom.* Also forbidden. *Dare you to touch that manta ray.* Just plain stupid.

It was a wonder they'd both survived.

She remembered when the dares had stopped. That evening on deck when she'd dared him to kiss her. She wondered if he remembered. His eyes glittered back at her—all bad-boy blue—and she *knew* he remembered.

'Tell you what,' Rick said as he pulled himself back from that ancient memory that still resonated in his dreams, 'don't decide now. Sleep on it first, okay. I bet it won't seem as crazy in the morning.'

Stella was willing to bet that in the cold light of day *and* stone-cold sober it would not only seem crazy, it would actually *be* crazy.

Utterly certifiable.

He leaned forward and kissed her forehead, then winked at Diana. 'Can I crash here?'

Stella felt like a child between two grown-ups. 'What, no girl in this port, sailor?' she asked waspishly. The man had never lacked for company on shore.

Rick chuckled. 'Not one who can make pancakes like you.'

'Ah,' she said, realising she was being churlish and making an effort to get them back to their usual repartee. 'So you only want me for my pancakes.'

'And your half of the map.' He grinned. 'I'm beat. I need a shower. Then I need to sleep for a week. Towels still in the same place?' he asked as he left them, not waiting for an answer.

Diana watched him go. 'Wow.'

Stella nodded. 'Yes.'

She turned to face the sink, leaning her elbows against the cool steel as she looked out of the large bay window into the bleak dark night. Diana joined her, still sipping at her wine.

'Does he wear contacts?' she mused. 'It's quite striking to see a man with such dark colouring have such blue eyes.'

Stella nodded again. She'd been captivated by them for as long as she could remember. 'Yes, it's really quite mesmerising, isn't it?'

'Which room are you in, Diana?'

Both women started guiltily as the voice from behind them had them straightening and whipping around to face Rick. He was naked except for possibly the world's smallest towel around his waist, clutched at the side where it didn't quite meet. His blue eyes looked even bluer with less of anything much to detract from them.

'The one on the left,' Stella confirmed after a quick glance at a gawking, mute-looking Diana.

'Great, I'll doss down in the other.' He smiled at both of them. 'See you in the morning, ladies.'

Stella and Diana watched him as he swaggered away, the towel slipping as he gave up on trying to keep it on. They caught a glimpse of one naked buttock just before he disappeared around the corner.

A buttock adorned with a very sexy, perfectly round, dark brown birthmark, right in the middle of a very sexy dimple.

Diana gasped as suddenly everything fell into place. Bronzed colouring, piercing blue eyes, long shaggy hair, a mouth made for sin and a very cute blemish in a very specific place.

'Oh, my God!' She looked at Stella. 'That's why he's so familiar. It's him—he's Vasco Ramirez!'

CHAPTER TWO

STELLA blushed furiously. 'Shh,' she hissed. 'Don't be pre-
posterous.'

Diana laughed. 'Methinks the lady doth protest too much.'

Stella turned back to the sink, busying herself with washing out her wine glass. 'There are some similarities…' she
admitted.

'Similarities?' Diana hooted. 'I *knew* I knew him…I just
couldn't figure out where from. I mean, hell, let's face it, if
I'd met him somewhere before I'd hardly be likely to forget him—the man's a total hottie. And, I have to say—' she
nudged Stella '—looks like a total sex fiend.'

'Diana!'

She shrugged. 'In a good way.'

'Well, don't look at me,' Stella muttered. 'You know I've
only ever been with Dale.'

Diana tisked. 'I can't believe you've never gone there…
well, I mean you've obviously thought about it because you
wrote an entire three-hundred-and-seventy-five page sexual
fantasy about the man—'

'*I did not,*' Stella denied, picking up a tea towel and briskly
drying the glass.

Diana crooked an eyebrow at her. 'Stella, this is me. Diana.
Who knows you.'

Stella looked into her friend's eyes and could see that she

knew the truth. She sagged against the sink. 'Okay, yes,' she sighed. 'Rick was the inspiration for Vasco.'

Stella hadn't set out to write a book with Rick as the hero but Vasco had taken on Rick's features in a totally organic way. She hadn't even been truly aware of it until she'd written the first kiss.

And then it had been so blindingly obvious she'd wondered why it had taken her so long.

'Hah! I knew it!' Diana clapped delightedly.

Stella rolled her eyes. 'This is between you and me, Diana,' she said, placing a hand on her friend's arm. 'Promise?'

'Don't worry,' Diana said, waving a dismissive hand, 'your secret is safe with me.'

'Thank you,' Stella said, releasing a breath as she shuffled away from the sink and headed towards the fire.

'Well, there's only one thing for it now,' Diana said as she followed Stella and plonked herself down on one of the lounge chairs. 'You have to go with him.'

Stella looked up from her log poking. 'What?'

'The man obviously inspires you to write. You need inspiration. *You need to write.* Problem solved.'

'Joy doesn't want another Vasco Ramirez, Diana.'

'Yes, she does,' Diana said. 'That's exactly what she wants. Vasco sold like hot cakes. Vasco is king. Of course she wants you to do another Vasco.'

Stella gave her friend an impatient look. 'You know what I mean.'

Diana sighed. She didn't want to pull out the big guns. 'Babe, things are going to start to get nasty. And trust me, you don't want to be with a publishing house that plays hard ball. There'll be lawyers. It's time to quit the whole writer's block nonsense and write.'

Stella felt Diana's words slice into her side. 'You think it's nonsense—that I'm making it up?'

Diana shook her head. She knew Stella's instant fame had

compounded her already entrenched second-book syndrome and her father's death had just aggravated everything further. She totally got that Stella's muse had deserted her. But...

'The lawyers will think it is, babe.'

'I just need a little more time,' Stella muttered.

Diana nodded. 'And you should take it. Absolutely. Go with Rick, get inspired. Come back replenished.'

Stella glanced at her friend. She made it sound so easy. She shook her head. 'It's crazy.'

'Why?' Diana challenged. 'Because you have a thing for him?'

'I do not have a thing for him,' Stella denied quickly. A little too quickly perhaps. 'He's an old, *old* friend,' she clarified, not bothering to keep the exasperation out of her voice. 'We've known each other *for ever*. There is no *thing*.'

Diana looked at her friend. Oh, there so *was* a thing.

Even better.

Lord alone knew, if she hadn't had sex for almost a year on top of fairly pedestrian sex for the previous five she'd be looking at a way of fixing that pronto. And if it so happened that the man of Stella's fantasies was there at the precise moment she decided to break the drought, then surely everyone won?

'So it shouldn't be a problem, then?' Diana asked innocently. She held up her hand as Stella went to speak again. 'Look, Rick's right. Just sleep on it. I know it's a lot to consider but, for what it's worth, I think you're mad if you don't.'

'But the book...' Stella murmured in a last-ditch effort to make Diana see sense.

Diana shrugged. 'Whatever you're doing here on good old terra firma ain't working, is it, babe?'

Stella went to bed determined to wake up in the morning and tell both Rick and Diana to go to hell.

But that was before the dream.

She dreamt all night of a mermaid following a pirate ship. No…

She was the mermaid and *she* was following the pirate ship. Inside the hull a lone, rich, tenor voice would occasionally sing a deep mournful song of lost love. It was a thing of beauty and she'd fallen in love with the man even though she'd never laid eyes on him. But she knew he was a prisoner and she knew with an urgency that beat like the swell of the ocean in her breast that she had to save him.

That he was the one for her.

Stella awoke, the last tendrils of the dream still gliding over her skin like the cool kiss of sea water. It was so vivid for a moment she could almost feel the water frothing her hair in a glorious golden crown around her head.

The urge to write thrummed through her veins and she quickly opened the drawer of her bedside table, locating the stash of pens and paper she always kept there. She brushed off the dust and started to scribble and in ten minutes she'd written down the bones of a plot and some detailed description of Lucinda, the mermaid.

When she finished she sat back and stared at the words in front of her. They were a revelation. And not just because she'd written something she didn't have the immediate urge to delete, but because it was a whole new approach.

Stella hadn't imagined for even a minute that the heroine's point of view would take precedence in her head. Vasco had been so strong and dominant, striding onto the page, demanding to be heard, that she'd assumed starting with the hero was always going to be her process.

All this time she'd been beating herself up about not being able to see a hero, getting her knickers in a twist because, no matter how hard she tried to visualise one, no hero was forthcoming.

And he still wasn't. But Lucinda *was* fully formed and she was *awesome*.

Lucinda excited her as nothing had since Vasco had arrived. Lucinda was no Lady Mary waiting around to be saved. The world had gone crazy for Vasco last time, this time they would go crazy for Lucinda.

She could feel it deep inside in the same place that had told her Vasco was special, but she'd been too inexperienced to listen.

Well, she was listening now.

God, Joy was probably going to have a fit at her kick-ass mermaid. She could hear her now saying, *But what about Inigo, Stella?*

Stella gasped as his name came to her. *Inigo.* Of course that was his name. *Inigo.* It had to be Inigo.

It was working.

The buzz was back. *The magic was here.*

Inigo would be strong and noble, a perfect match for Lucinda because a strong woman required a man to equal her. A man secure in himself. A man who would understand the divided loyalties she endured every day and wouldn't demand that she chose between the sea and land.

A subject that Stella could write about intimately.

God, why hadn't she thought to approach her story from this way before? It seemed so obvious now. She kicked off the sheets, reached for her polar fleece dressing gown.

She had to get out of here. Had to get to her computer.

She almost laughed as she tripped over her gown in haste. The revelation had come just in time. It had saved her. There was no time now for seafaring adventures.

There was a mermaid to write. A hero to rescue.

Lucinda was calling.

Inigo too.

Stella padded straight to her computer, notes in hand. She drummed her fingers on the desk as she waited for it to power up. As soon as she was able, she opened a new word document and typed *The Siren's Call* in the header.

She blinked at it. Her fingers hadn't even consulted her brain. The title had just appeared.

It was all happening.

Then the cursor winked at her from a blank page and the buzz and pulse inside shrivelled like a sultana.

What? No...

She took her hands off the keyboard, waited a moment or two, then placed them back on. She waited for her fingers to roam over the keys, pressing randomly to make words on the page. She consulted her notes and desperately tried to recall spunky Lucinda.

But nothing came.

'You're up early,' Rick's voice murmured in her ear as he plonked a steaming hot cup of coffee at her elbow and she almost leapt two feet off the chair.

'Bloody hell, Rick, do you mind?' she griped as she clutched at her chest. Had she been that focused she hadn't even noticed he was up, or smelled the aroma of coffee?

'Whoa there, sorry, didn't mean to startle you.' He grinned. 'What are you working on?'

Stella minimised the document, leaving only her screen saver to view. She glared up at him. Then she wished she hadn't. He was wearing long stripy flannelette pyjama bottoms and nothing on top. The drawstring was pulled low and tight on his hips, revealing way too much skin right at her eye level.

Suddenly Lucinda whispered in her head again, murmuring her story, buzzing through Stella's veins like an illicit drug. Flashes of her childhood felt sweet against Stella's tongue. Lucinda's despair over Inigo tightened Stella's chest.

This was crazy.

Stella turned back to the computer, the need to write an imperative even with Rick hovering. But as suddenly as it had come upon her the flow stopped. Stella blinked—was there a tap somewhere that somebody had just turned off?

Rick let out a long low wolf whistle, ignoring her silence—Stella had never been a morning person. 'Sexy cover,' he murmured, taking the other chair at the desk and straddling it. 'Great rack.'

Stella, still willing Lucinda to come back, took a moment to work out what Rick was referring to. She looked at her computer, the cover for *Pleasure Hunt* her screen saver. Lady Bingham's flowing scarlet dress with the plunging neckline made the best of her assets, pushing her milky breasts practically into the face of the leering Vasco Ramirez.

'Nice.' Stella glared at him as she reopened her blank page, obliterating the screen saver.

Lucinda? Lucinda? Where are you?

'I'm just saying, he seems to be enjoying the view and I can't blame him.'

It would indeed be hypocritical, Rick thought, considering how very much he enjoyed that kind of view himself. The kind of view that Stella was giving him right at this moment as her gown flapped open and the low-cut vest shirt she wore gaped a little to reveal a glimpse of soft female breast.

The view he was trying to ignore.

He'd had a lot of practice at ignoring Stella's breasts, given his treasured honorary position in the Mills family, but that didn't mean it had been easy—then or now. Witness the time he'd lost his head and succumbed to her kissing dare with a heady mix of trepidation, challenge and anticipation.

Anticipation that had been building since the summer she'd arrived on the *Persephone* with curves and a bra.

Being sprung by her father before he'd reached his target and Nathan's little *chat* with him afterwards had set him straight. And he'd never betrayed Nathan's trust.

Not consciously anyway.

'He's practically drooling,' he murmured, gaze firmly fixed on the screen.

Stella turned to Rick to defend Vasco. To say that her hero

was not a salivating pervert, but of course she couldn't because the man *was* a scoundrel of the highest order and she knew damn well he'd appreciated Mary's cleavage as he'd appreciated countless other women's cleavages before he'd met Mary and probably still was, out there in fiction land somewhere.

But it all died on her lips as Lucinda's sweet melodic voice started up a dialogue in her head again, talking about her father disowning her for following a whim and her mother's grief over their rift.

The implications stunk to high heaven.

Oh, God. Please no, not this, Lucinda. I'll do anything, I'll go anywhere else you want, but not this.

Just then Diana entered the room, negating the need for Stella to say anything, for which she was grateful. She yawned loudly and bade them both a good morning as she made her way to the kitchen in her clingy satin Hello Kitty pyjamas and poured herself a coffee from the percolator.

Rick whistled. 'Well, hello Kitty.'

Stella rolled her eyes. Diana grinned as she plonked herself down in a lounge chair.

'So?' she demanded. 'Are you going with Rick or what?'

'Good question, Miss Kitty.' Rick nodded. 'Well?' he asked, seeking Stella's gaze.

Even just looking at him looking at her, Stella could feel the story buzzing through her veins. She could feel Lucinda beckoning her like the siren she was, waving at her from the rocks, drawing her ever closer to her doom.

She looked back at the computer screen with its mocking little cursor and acres of blankness and got nothing.

She sighed as Lucinda won. 'Yes. I'm going.'

'Really?' Rick stood and punched a fist in the air at her curt nod.

How on earth was she going to share a boat with him when she hadn't had sex in ages and he'd always been her private fantasy go-to man?

They were friends.

They were business partners, for crying out loud!

'I've booked us two tickets to Cairns on a flight that leaves Heathrow early this evening.'

'Ooh, cocky, I like that,' Diana murmured, sipping her coffee.

Stella ignored her, as did Rick who, Stella knew from experience, must be biting his tongue to let that one go.

'Australia?' she squeaked.

Rick shrugged. 'The map's Micronesia and I haven't taken the *Dolphin* out since I bought her.'

Stella stood. 'You bought the *Dolphin*?'

Rick had been fascinated with the thirty-foot classic wooden yacht for as long as she could remember. They'd seen it in various ports over the years and it had always been a dream of his to have it for himself.

'When?'

He grinned. 'A few months ago. I finally tracked her down in New Zealand and had her refitted in Cairns. She's ready to go.'

Stella felt a little thrill that had nothing to do with Lucinda. Rick had talked about it so much over the years it had almost become her dream too. 'So we're going to take her?' she clarified.

He nodded. 'If you want to. I could always hire something bigger, whiter, more pretentious if you preferred.'

Stella smiled at the distaste curling his lips. The Mills and Granville salvage fleet was three big white, powerful boats strong and, while she knew Rick was proud of what her father and he had built up, his passion had always been the classic beauty of the *Dolphin*. 'Perish the thought.' She grinned.

Rick grinned back at her and felt a hum of excitement warm his belly. There was something different about Stel this morning. Last night she'd been the Stella he'd always known—slopping around, no airs and graces, no special treatment.

This morning she glowed as if she had a secret that no one else knew. Her olive-green eyes seemed to radiate purpose. Her cheeks seemed pinker. Even her scraped-back ponytail seemed to have more perk in it.

She looked like women did when they were pregnant, as if they were doing something truly amazing and they knew it.

She was *radiant*.

It was quite breathtaking and his stomach clenched inside in a way that, as a man, he was all too familiar with.

But not where she was concerned.

He looked at Diana, all sleepy and tousled with her knowing eyes and cute mouth, and waited for the twinge to come again.

He got nothing.

Hmm.

'Right.' He drained his coffee quickly. There were things to do and not being here for a while was a good option. 'Gotta go get some things sorted. I'll see you both later.'

Stella busied herself in the kitchen until Rick left the house five minutes later. 'How are you going to break it to Joy?' she asked Diana.

'Oh, forget that,' Diana said, waving the query away. 'I'll tell her you've gone off to be inspired. There are much more important things to discuss.'

Stella frowned. 'There are?'

Diana nodded vigorously, her shirt pulling tight across her chest as she leaned over the kitchen bench. 'You two should have sex,' she said.

Stella almost dropped her second mug of coffee. *Was she mad?* 'Ah no.' She shook her head. 'Bad. Idea.'

Diana raised an eyebrow. 'Okay, well, you're going to have to explain that one to me.'

Stella didn't even know where to start with how bad an idea it was. 'Because we're friends. *And* colleagues. I'm his silent partner, for crying out loud! And trust me, I know better than anyone not to get tangled up with a man of the sea. They never choose land. They never choose love.'

Diana rolled her eyes. 'You're just having sex with him, not marrying the man.'

'Which is just as well because men of the sea should not marry. My father chose the sea over my mother. Rick's mother left when he was a baby because his father wouldn't settle on land. We've both seen how that kind of life isn't compatible with long-term relationships.'

'You're. Just. Having. Sex,' Diana reiterated.

'Oh, come on, Diana, you know I'm not good at that. The last guy I was just having sex with I ended up engaged to.'

Diana nodded. 'And the sex was lousy.'

'Hey,' Stella protested. 'It wasn't lousy, it was…nice. Sweet. It may not have been…imaginative but it could have been worse.' Her friend didn't look convinced. 'He was a pretty straight guy, Diana. Not all men want to have sex hanging from the chandeliers. There's nothing wrong with sweet.'

'No, absolutely not,' she agreed. 'Except you did write a book full of hot, sweaty, dirty, pirate sex during your time with Dale.' She shrugged. 'I'm no psychologist but I think they call that transference.'

'*They*,' Stella said, bugging her eyes at her friend, 'call it *fiction*.'

Diana held up her hands in surrender. 'All right, all right. I'm just saying…you're going to be on that boat with him for long periods of time where there'll be nothing to do…it might be worth thinking about, is all…'

Stella shook her head at her incorrigible friend. 'I'll be writing.'

Diana laughed. 'Good answer.'

At two Stella hugged Diana ferociously and thanked her for locking up after them. She was staying on for another night to get some work done far from the distractions of London.

'I promise I'll come back with a book,' she whispered to her friend. 'The ideas are already popping. Tell Joy she's going to love Lucinda.'

Diana laughed. 'Joy will be overjoyed.'

Stella grimaced. She hoped so. She'd added a decade to her very patient editor's life and she *owed* Joy this. Not just a book, but a book to rival Vasco's. She scurried to Rick's hire car with her bag, hoping they made it out of Cornwall before another storm blew in.

Rick pulled up beside Diana and smiled at her. 'See ya later, Miss Kitty. It was nice spending some time with you,' he said.

Diana nodded distractedly, bobbing her head back and forth to see what Stella was up to.

Rick frowned. These two women were hard on his ego. 'I know Stel values your friendship and—'

'Yeh, yeh,' Diana said, cutting him off and dragging him back inside the cottage. She pulled her dog-eared copy of *Pleasure Hunt* from her handbag on the hall stand and thrust it at him. 'Take it. Read it. You won't be disappointed.'

Rick frowned down at the cover he recognised from earlier. 'Er, it's really not my thing.'

'Trust me. It's your thing.' She glanced over Rick's shoulder, knowing that Stella would kill her if she even had an inkling of what Diana was doing. 'It's really quite…illuminating.'

'Okay.'

He ran his fingers over the raised gold lettering that spelt out Stella's name. He felt a surge of pride that Stel had made a path for herself in the world—something that rocked her boat. He knew that Nathan had been immensely proud of his little girl's success.

'Thanks,' he said as he tucked it under his arm and backed out of the cottage.

'Stop,' Diana hissed. 'What are you doing?' She whisked

it out from under his arm, spun him around, unzipped his backpack and shoved it deep inside.

'She's sensitive about it,' Diana explained as Rick gave her a questioning look. 'Do not read it around her. And if she springs you—I will deny all knowledge of how you came by it. Capiche?'

Rick chuckled as he held up his hands in surrender. 'Sure. Okay.'

He took a couple of tentative paces out of the cottage, expecting to be yanked back inside again. It wasn't until he was halfway to the car that he started to relax.

He smiled to himself. *God, but he loved women.*

Five hours later they were airborne and Rick was busily flirting with the air hostess. Stella wasn't sure why she was so annoyed. After all, she'd seen Rick in action with women nearly all of her life.

Maybe it was just the relentless afternoon of it. The woman at the petrol station. The one at the rental desk. Another at the check-in lounge. Oh, and the coffee shop—and she'd have to have been in her sixties. It seemed there wasn't a woman in existence who wasn't fair game for his laid-back style of flirting.

Including her.

But she was used to his casual, flirty banter. She knew it was harmless and she could give as good as she got.

The women of the world were not.

'Champagne?' Rick asked her.

It was tempting but after last night her liver probably needed a break. 'No, thanks,' she said, smiling at the hostess, who she was pretty sure actually didn't give a damn if Stella wanted a drink or not.

Rick watched the swagger of the stewardess's hips in her tight pencil skirt as she left to grab his beer. Stella rolled her eyes at him and he grinned. 'So,' he said, snuggling down further into the comfortable leather seat. 'You haven't asked how the business is going.'

Stella pulled the blind down on her window. 'Well, we're in business class so I'm assuming it's all going okay.'

Rick nodded. 'It is.'

Stella sighed. 'Rick, I told you at the wake that whatever decisions you wanted to make were fine by me. That I only wanted to be a silent partner. You've been half of the business since you were fifteen. It's been *your* blood, sweat and tears that helped to build it to where it is today. Dad should have left his half to you, not me. It should be all yours.'

Rick looked askance, his blue eyes flashing. 'Stel, what is a man worth if he cannot provide for his family?' he said, his voice laced with reproach and sounding remarkably Spanish all of a sudden. 'The business was Nathan's legacy and he knew how much you loved it. Of course he wanted it to go to you. Of course he wanted to leave you with no financial worries.'

She raised an eyebrow. 'Do you have any idea how much money my book has made?'

Rick thought about the contraband copy of *Pleasure Hunt* secreted away in his backpack. 'No. But the business has a multimillion-dollar turnover annually and whether you need it or not—half of it's yours.'

'I know…I'm just saying, I can look after myself.'

He nodded. 'I know that. I've always known that.'

Stella's breath caught in her throat at the sincerity in his tropical eyes. His shoulder-length hair fell forward to form a partial curtain around his face and, with his slight sideways position, she felt as if they were cut off from the rest of the aeroplane.

'Your beer, sir.'

Stella glanced up at the stewardess and was surprised to feel Rick's gaze linger on her face. She looked back at him quizzically and they just looked at each other for a long moment before he smiled at her, then turned to accept the offering.

He started to chat with the stewardess again and Stella turned away. She shut her eyes, not wanting to hear the banter that fell so easily from those wicked Vasco lips.

It was a long flight. She might as well try and get some sleep.

She woke a few hours later feeling miraculously refreshed. Rick was stretched out asleep in his chair, his face turned towards her, those killer sable lashes throwing shadows on his cheeks.

For a moment she just stared at him, at his utter beauty. He'd always been good-looking but age had turned all that brash youthful charisma into a deep and abiding sex appeal.

The urge to push his hair back off his forehead where it had fallen in haphazard array almost trumped the urge to trace his lips with her finger. They looked all soft and slack in slumber but she knew, without ever having experienced it, that they would be just the right amount of hard at precisely the right time—like Vasco's.

She'd come perilously close to knowing it for real. Could still remember the way her pulse had roared, her eyes had fluttered closed as he'd leaned in to make good on her dare and fulfil all her teenage fantasies.

And, courtesy of a crush bigger than the United Kingdom, there'd been plenty of them.

Fantasies that had seen her tick each day down on a calendar as the holidays had approached, her foolish heart tripping every time she'd thought about those blue, blue eyes and all that bare, broad, bronzed skin courtesy of his Spanish mother.

All the time hoping that it would be this summer he'd see her as a woman instead of a girl. That he'd make good on the increasingly confusing signals he sent and act instead of tease.

And the eve of her sixteenth birthday all that breathless longing had come to fruition.

'Sweet sixteen and never been kissed,' he'd teased.

He'd been nearly nineteen and so much more experienced. She'd watched him flirt with girls since he'd been thirteen and been aware of his effect on them for much longer than he had.

She'd screwed up her courage. 'Maybe you should do something about that?' she'd murmured, her heart hammering.

She'd watched as his Adam's apple had bobbed and his gaze had briefly fallen to her mouth. 'Yeh, right,' he'd dismissed.

She'd smiled at him and said the one thing she'd known would work. 'I dare you.'

And it had worked. She'd seen something inside him give as his gaze had zeroed in on her mouth and his lips had moved closer.

Her father's curt 'Riccardo!' had been the bucket of water they'd both needed.

A reminder that there was a line between them that should never be crossed no matter how close they'd danced to it.

And she was glad for it now.

Glad that this magnificent man liked her and enjoyed her company and called her his friend. That he could drop by out of the blue and use her shower and doss down for the night and there was no awkward history, no uncomfortable silences.

Despite what Diana thought, a person didn't die of sexual frustration and she wouldn't sacrifice their friendship and mutual respect for a brief slaking of bodily desires.

No matter how damn good she knew it would be.

He stirred and she froze, hoping like crazy that lazy blue gaze wasn't about to blast her in tropical heat.

It didn't. But it was enough to spur her into action. She was not going to sit here and ogle him as if she were still in the midst of her teenage crush, watching him surreptitiously from behind her dark sunglasses as he went about the business of running a boat.

Without a shirt.

Always without a shirt.

She pulled out her laptop and powered it up.

An hour later the cabin crew came through offering a meal and Rick woke. He stretched, then righted his chair, glancing over at Stella busily tapping away. She seemed engrossed and he smiled at her.

'I thought you were blocked.'

Stella looked up from her notes. 'I've had an idea,' she admitted.

'Hah!' he crowed. 'I told you all you needed was a treasure hunt.'

'Yeh, well, all I'm doing is some preliminary planning, at the moment. It remains to be seen if I can actually write anything.'

Although she knew she could. In fact she itched to. Lucinda and Inigo's story was becoming clearer and clearer.

'So how does that work, then? Writer's block?' he asked.

She shrugged. 'I look at a blank page all day terrified that I'm not good enough, that I'm a one-book wonder, willing the words to come and when, on a good day, some actually do appear, they're all crap and I delete them.'

Rick nodded thoughtfully. He couldn't say that he understood exactly, but he could see the consternation creasing her brow and the look he'd seen in her eyes last night akin to panic. The same look he'd sometimes seen when she'd been a kid and Nathan had been late returning to the surface.

'Maybe you need to give yourself permission to be crap?' he suggested. 'Just get it all down, warts and all. Switch your internal editor off?'

Stella raised an eyebrow at him. 'Did Diana tell you to say that?'

Rick chuckled. 'No.'

'Well, it's easier said than done, believe me.' She sighed.

'I think if I'd had a whole bunch of books rejected before *Pleasure Hunt*, then I'd have known stuff like that. But this crazy instant success didn't give me any time to fail or any time to know who I am as a writer. I think I needed this time to figure that out.'

Rick nodded. 'So…' he said, looking over her shoulder, 'are you going to tell me what it's about?'

Stella shut the lid of her laptop. 'Nope.'

The last time a guy had realised what she'd written it hadn't ended well.

'Excuse me, Ms Mills?'

Stella looked up at a stewardess who had brought her some water earlier. 'Yes?'

'I'm sorry, I hope you don't mind—I saw your name on the passenger list and I just finished reading *Pleasure Hunt*.' She held it up. 'Would you mind signing it for me?'

Stella blushed. 'Certainly,' she murmured as she held her hand out for the book and proffered pen. 'Is there any message in particular you'd like me to write?'

'Just to me, Andrea.' The stewardess smiled.

Stella wrote a brief message to Andrea, then signed her name with a flourish before handing the book and pen back.

'Thank you so much,' Andrea said. 'I shall cherish it.'

'Thank *you*,' Stella replied. 'It's always nice to meet people who like what you do.'

Andrea nodded. 'I better go and serve dinner or my little band of travellers won't be happy.'

Stella and Rick watched her walk away. He turned to her. 'Wow. You're seriously famous, aren't you?'

Stella chuckled. 'Does that threaten your masculinity?' It had certainly threatened Dale's.

'Hell, no.' He grinned. 'I'm a little turned on, actually.'

Stella shook her head. 'If you're thinking threesome, forget it.'

Rick laughed. 'Well, I am now.'

CHAPTER THREE

STELLA had been seven and Rick ten when they'd first laid eyes on the *Dolphin* anchored at St Kitts. They'd both stood on the bow of the *Persephone* with their mouths open, staring at the wooden beauty. Teak, oak, cypress and the original brass fittings had given her an old-world charm hinting at an era when craftsmanship was everything and things were made to last.

Stella still remembered Rick's awed whisper. 'One day she's going to be mine.'

And as they stood on the wharf looking down at her now, the brass gleaming beneath a high Aussie sun, the wooden deck warm and inviting, she looked as grand and majestic as ever.

Lucinda sighed in her head.

'God, Rick,' Stella breathed, that same stirring in her blood she always felt with a stiff sea breeze ruffling her hair. 'She's even more beautiful than I remembered.'

Rick looked down at her, her hair streaming behind her, her pink lips parted in awe. She'd changed into a vest top and cut-off denim shorts and she was so tiny the urge to tuck her under his arm took him by surprise.

'Yes, she is,' he murmured, looking back at his purchase.

Stella looked up at him. The sea breeze whipped his long pirate locks across his face. His strong jaw was dark with stubble. 'She must have cost you a fortune.'

He shrugged. 'Some things are beyond money. And she's worth every cent.'

She nodded, looking back at the superbly crafted boat. 'Why now?' she asked.

He shrugged. 'I listened to your father talk about *The Mermaid* all my life. About how one day he was going to find Inigo's final resting place. And then he died without ever having seen it.'

Rick felt a swell of emotion in his chest and stopped. He slid an arm around her shoulders and pulled her gently into his side. 'I always thought Nathan was invincible...'

Stella snaked an arm around his waist, her heart twisting as his words ran out. She'd always thought so too. Always thought her father would be like Captain Ahab, *The Mermaid* his white whale. They both stood on the dock watching the gentle bob of the *Dolphin* for a few moments.

'I've dreamt about owning this boat since I was ten years old,' Rick murmured, finding his voice again. 'I didn't want to wait any longer.'

Stella nodded, feeling a deep and abiding affinity with Rick that couldn't have been stronger had they been bound by blood.

That wouldn't have been possible had they been lovers.

'Besides,' he grinned, giving her a quick squeeze before letting her go, 'the *company* owns it.'

Stella laughed. 'Oh, really, creative accounting, huh?'

'Something like that,' he laughed.

'So she's actually half mine?' she teased.

Rick threw his backpack on deck and jumped on board. He held out his hand. *'Mi casa es su casa,'* he murmured.

Stella's breath hitched as she took his hand. He spoke Spanish impeccably and with that bronzed colouring and those impossibly blue eyes he was every inch the Spaniard. He might have an English father and have gone to English schools but for his formative years he was raised by his Romany grandmother and she'd made sure her Riccardo had been immersed in the lingo.

As she stepped aboard she checked out the small motorised dinghy hanging from a frame attached to the stern above the water line. Then her gaze fell to the starboard hull where the bold gold lettering outlined in fine black detail proclaimed a change of name. She almost tripped and stumbled into him.

'Whoa there,' he said, holding her hips to steady her. They curved out from her waist and he had to remind himself that the flesh beneath his palms was Stella's. 'You've turned into a real landlubber, haven't you?' he teased.

She stared at him for a moment. 'You changed her name?' she asked breathlessly.

He shrugged as he smiled down at her flummoxed face. 'I promised you.'

Stella thumped his arm and ignored his theatrical recoil. 'I was seven years old,' she yelled.

She stormed to the edge and looked over at the six yellow letters, her eyes filling with tears.

Stella.

'You don't like it?'

She blinked her tears away and marched back to him and thumped his chest this time. 'I love it, you idiot! It's the nicest thing anyone's ever done for me.' Then she threw herself into his arms.

Not even her father had named a boat after her.

Rick chuckled as he lifted her feet off the ground and hugged her back, his senses infusing with coconut.

'I can't believe you did that,' she said, her voice muffled against a pec. She pushed against the bands of his arms and squirmed away from him.

'I told you I would.'

Stella had forgotten, but she remembered it now as if it were yesterday. Rick talking incessantly about buying the *Dolphin*

that summer they'd first seen her and her making him promise that if he did he'd rename it after her.

'I didn't think you *actually* would,' she said incredulously.

'Anything for my favourite girl,' he quipped.

She ignored his easy line as she'd ignored all his others.
'You should have said no. I was a brat.'

He nodded. 'Yes, you were.'

She gave him another playful thump but smiled up at him
just the same. He smiled back and for a moment they just stood
there, the joy of a shared memory uniting them.

'Well, come on, then,' she said after a moment. 'Show me
around.'

A spiral stairway led to a below deck that was far better
than Stella had imagined in her wildest dreams. Polished wood
invited her to run her hands along its surfaces. Brass fittings
gleamed from every nook and cranny. The spacious area was
dominated by ceiling beams, heavy brocade curtains over the
portholes, oriental rugs and dark leather chairs.

It wasn't lavish—she'd seen plenty of lavish interiors in her
time—but it *was* very masculine, the addition of Rick even
more so. He looked completely at home in this nautical nirvana
and for a moment Stella could imagine him in a half-undone
silk shirt and breeches, sprawled out down here, knocking
back some rum after a hard day's seafaring.

She blinked as Rick segued into Vasco.

'Saloon here, galley over there,' he said, thumbing over
his shoulder where she could see a glimpse of stainless steel.
'Engine room…' he stamped his foot '…below us. Forward
and aft cabins both have en suites. I thought you might like
the aft cabin? It's slightly bigger.'

'Sure.' She shrugged, her pulse tripping madly at her bizarre vision. 'That sounds fine.'

Rick, who'd only seen photographs of the finished product himself, sat in a chair. He ran his hand over the decadent
leather. 'Wow, they've done a magnificent job.'

Stella blinked again as she looked down on him for once. If ever there was magnificent it was him, sitting in that chair, captain of all he surveyed. It reminded her of the scene in *Pleasure Hunt* where Lady Mary finally capitulated to his touch. Where she realised, after a particularly harrowing raid, life was short and she didn't want to die without having known the touch of a truly sensual man.

She stood in front of Vasco in the privacy of his cabin as he sat, thighs insolently spread, in his chair, caressing the arm as if it were the breast of a beautiful woman. She looked down at him, waiting. When he leant forward and reached under her skirts she didn't protest, nor when he placed his hands on the backs of her thighs and pulled her onto his lap so she was straddling him, her skirts frothing around her.

'It's so much better than the photos,' Rick murmured.

Stella blinked as his voice dragged her back to the present. She took a step back as the vivid image of Vasco played large in her mind.

'It's amazing, Rick,' she agreed. 'Just…incredible.'

Rick smiled at her as his hand continued to stroke the leather. He was pleased Stella was here to share this moment with him. This boat, more than any of the ones they'd been on over the years, connected them in a way only shared childhood dreams could.

'Let's take her out,' he said, standing. The sudden urge to hoist a sail and go where the wind took him shot through his veins like the first sip of beer on a hot summer day.

'I know we should be provisioning her for our trip but we can do that tomorrow. Let's take her over to Green Island. Give her a good run. We can go snorkelling. We have the basics here…well, we have beer anyway…and we can catch some fish and anchor there for the night. I want to lie on the deck and look at the stars like we used to do when we were kids.'

'Sure,' she agreed readily. Anything, anything to get her out of this saloon and far away from the fantasy.

Where the hell was her filter? She did not fantasise about Rick.

Not in front of him anyway.

'Fabulous idea. Can I take her once she's out of the harbour?'

Stella had learned to sail practically before she could walk. Her father had seen to that. Hell, so had her mother, a keen sailor in her own right, but it had been a lot of years since she'd been on the open sea.

'You still remember what to do?' Rick teased.

She smiled at him. 'I'm sure it'll come back to me. It's just like riding a bike, yes?'

Or having sex.

Diana had assured her you didn't forget how to do that either.

'Don't worry, I'll be there to guide you. Do you trust me?'

Yep…exactly what Vasco had said to Lady Mary.

Do you trust me?

Stella swallowed. 'I trust that you don't want me to run your very expensive boat—sorry, the *company's* very expensive boat—onto a reef,' she quipped.

Rick laughed. 'You have that right. Come on, first mate, let's get this show on the road.'

Within half an hour they were under way, out on the open ocean, and Stella couldn't remember the last time she'd felt this alive. She'd waited patiently while Rick had used the motor to manoeuvre out of the harbour, then helped him with the still familiar motions of putting up the sails. She heard Lucinda sigh as they billowed with the moderate breeze and her pulse leapt as the boat surged forward, slicing across the whitecaps.

Rick, who had taken his shirt off—of course—stood behind her at the wheel for the first ten minutes, giving her a quick refresher. It wasn't needed. Her feel for the boat was instantaneous, like the familiarity of her own heartbeat, and even if it hadn't been they could easily have switched to the sophisticated autopilot system guided by the satellite technology that he'd had installed as part of the fully computerised upgrade.

But it was exhilarating to feel the pulse of the ocean beneath her feet again. She shut her eyes, raised her face to the sun as the big wheel in her hands felt like a natural extension of her being. In her mind's eye she could see Lucinda laughing up at her as she undulated through the waves, riding the bow with the dolphins.

Rick looked up from tying down a loose rope and caught her in her sun-worshipping stance. He'd worried that buying the *Dolphin* on a whim had been a mistake, an indulgence he didn't have the time to realise, a reaction to Nathan's sudden death.

But he didn't any more.

Nathan's *accident* had rocked him to his very core. He'd been there that day. Had seen Nathan's lifeless form, minus his breathing apparatus, bob to the surface. Had frantically dragged him aboard, puffed air into lungs that had been consumed by sea water too many minutes before.

Had demanded that he stay with him.

Stay *for* him.

Stay for Stella.

His own father's memory had faded to nothing over the years. He'd been too young when his father's regular bouts of drunken shore leave had caught up with him. Just a few faded photographs and the oft-repeated stories that got more and more fantastical late into the night after one too many beers.

Anthony Granville had occupied a legendary status amongst the men that knew him but he'd still got himself dead.

It was Nathan who'd been Rick's role model. His stand-in father. And Nathan who had taken on his full-time guardianship when he was a tearaway fifteen-year-old and his grand-mother had washed her hands of him.

Rick had only ever wanted to be at sea managing his half of the business. And Nathan had facilitated it.

But he hadn't made it easy—oh, no.

Nathan had been a tough task master.

Rick had thought his days of schooling and routine were done but Nathan had been worse than his grandmother. Nathan had insisted that he do his schooling by correspondence. And when he was done with that for the day, he'd given him every lousy job possible.

Had worked him like a navvy.

And Rick couldn't be more grateful. In his own way, Nathan had given him a better grounding than if he'd grown up in a loving, two-parent secure home.

He'd been so angry with Nathan when he'd landed in the UK thirty hours after they'd given up trying to resuscitate him.

Angry that Nathan had left him to be the bearer of bad news.

Angry that he'd left full stop.

But he'd known the news had to come from him.

The thought of someone else telling Linda—telling Stella—had been completely unpalatable. Nathan would have wanted it to be him and he hadn't wanted it to come from anyone else.

How could he have let some faceless policeman tell Linda? She and Nathan might have been divorced but even Rick had been able to see the deep and abiding love she still felt for him.

And there was no way he'd have let anyone else tell Stella.

The autopsy results just prior to the funeral had made Nathan's death more palatable. Rick had understood, as a man of the sea himself, that Nathan had chosen the ocean over a hospital.

But it hadn't lessened his loss.

And his very impulsive purchase of the *Dolphin* was so

mixed up in the whole vortex of grief he just hadn't been sure of his motivations.

But, as she opened her eyes and smiled at him as if she were riding a magic carpet instead of some very tame waves, he was one hundred per cent sure.

The *Dolphin* was part of them. Their history. And whatever else happened over the years in their lives, it would always bond them together, always be theirs—his, hers and Nathan's.

It had been quite a few years since Stella had been snorkelling. But as they lay anchor a couple of hours later crystalline tropical waters the exact shade of Rick's eyes beckoned, and she was below deck and back up again in record speed.

'What on earth are you wearing?' Rick demanded as she appeared by his side while he was rummaging around in a storage compartment for some goggles and fins.

Stella looked down at her very sensible one-piece. 'You don't like the colour?' she asked.

He tisked to cover the fact that he didn't give a damn what colour it was. 'It's stinger season, Stel. There should be a wet-suit hanging on the back of your cabin door and a stinger suit in one of the drawers.'

Stella looked at the water, desperate to feel it on her skin with no barriers just as she had in her Lucinda dream.

'Oh, come on,' she protested. 'We'd be pretty protected out here on the reef, surely?'

'I'll be sure to tell them that's what you thought when they're giving you the anti-venin.'

Stella shrugged. 'I'm willing to risk it.'

Rick shook his head emphatically. 'I'm not.'

He worked in an inherently dangerous field—there were a lot of things in the ocean that could kill a man—and his reputation for safety was second to none. He certainly wasn't going to have to explain to Linda that he'd let her daughter die too.

He pointed to the stairs leading to the lower deck. 'Go,' he intoned.

Stella rolled her eyes. 'Yeh, yeh.'

'Don't make me come down there,' he threatened.

Stella felt the flirty threat right down to her toes. What would he say if she challenged him to do just that?

Rick smiled to himself as she slunk away, her one-piece riding up the cheek of one buttock. He looked away. When she reappeared a few minutes later she was zipped into light blue neck-to-ankle Lycra.

'I hate these things,' she complained as she pulled at the clinging fabric. 'I look like a dumpling.'

Rick deliberately didn't look. What Nathan's daughter did or did not look like poured into a stinger suit was none of his business. He was still trying to not think about that half-exposed butt cheek.

'Everyone does,' he said, handing her some flippers and her mask and snorkel.

Stella glared at him. No, not everyone did. Not size-zero six-foot supermodels. Which she wasn't. And certainly not him, half zipped into his, his thighs outlined to perfection, the narrowness of his hips a stark contrast to the roundness of her own. *He* looked like an Yves St Laurent cologne guy or James freaking Bond walking out of the Mediterranean in his teeny tiny swimming trunks.

She fitted her mask to her head and looked at him. 'Aren't you coming?' she asked, staring pointedly at his state of undress.

'Right behind you,' he said.

They snorkelled on and off for most of the afternoon. They stopped a couple of times to grab a drink of water and Rick found his state-of-the-art underwater camera but otherwise they frolicked in the warm tropical waters for hours as if they were kids again playing pirates and mermaids.

She'd forgotten just how magical it was with the sun beating on her back and her head immersed in an enchanted underworld kingdom. Where fish all the colours of the rainbow darted around her and cavorted amongst coral that formed a unique and fascinating underwater garden.

Where the dark shadows of huge manta rays and small reef sharks hovered in the distance.

Where the silence made the beauty that much more profound.

It was after five o'clock when they called it a day. Stella threw on her clothes from earlier; Rick just unzipped his suit to his waist and looked all James Bond again. They threw some fishing lines in to catch their dinner while they drank cold beer and looked at Rick's pictures on her laptop. They laughed and reminisced and Rick showed her the pictures from their latest salvage—a nineteenth-century frigate off the Virgin Islands.

They caught two decent-sized coral trout and he cooked them on a small portable grill plate he'd brought up from below. It melted in their mouths as they dangled their legs over the side and watched the blush of twilight slowly creep across the sky to the gentle slap of waves against the hull.

Stella could feel the fatigue of jet lag catching up with her as the balmy breeze blew her drying hair into a no-doubt completely unattractive bird's nest.

That was the one good thing about hanging out with a guy who'd known you for ever—he'd seen her looking worse.

Rick took her plate away and she collapsed back against the deck, knees bent, looking up at the stars as they slowly, one by one, appeared before her eyes. She could hear the clank of dishes below and by the time Rick rejoined her night had completely claimed the heavens and a mass of diamond pricks winked above them.

A three-quarter moon hung low in the sky, casting a trail of moonbeams on the ocean surface.

'Are you awake, sleepy head?' Rick asked as he approached.

She countered his question with one of her own. 'Is it waxing or waning?' she asked, knowing that a man of the sea knew those things without ever having to look at a tide chart—it was in their DNA.

'Waxing,' Rick confirmed as he took up position beside her, lying back against the sun-warmed wood, also staring towards the heavens. He'd taken his stinger suit off and was wearing just his boardies.

Stella sighed. 'It's so beautiful. I bet you never get sick of this.'

'Nope. Never.'

He'd spent countless hours on deck at night, with Nathan teaching him how to navigate by the stars. He supposed to some, even back then, it had seemed hopelessly old-fashioned with all the sophisticated GPS systems and autopilot technology that had been around in the salvage industry for decades, but it had got him out of trouble more than once when satellites had been down or equipment had failed.

And he'd loved listening to the awe in Nathan's voice as he'd talked about the heavens as if each star were a friend. He hadn't just known their shape or the positions in relation to the horizon, but he'd known all the old seafaring legends about them and told them in such a way that had held Rick enthralled.

Nathan's celestial knowledge had been encyclopaedic and Rick had soaked it up like a sponge.

And then he'd regurgitated it to an awestruck Stella, who'd hung on his every word.

How many hours had they spent as kids lying on their backs on the deck of a boat pointing out different constellations, waiting with bated breath for the first shooting star of the night?

Her arm brushed his as she pointed at the Southern Cross and he realised he'd missed this.

This…companionship.

The last time they'd done it was the summer she'd finished school for good. A year after that near kiss. She'd alternated between giddiness at the freedom of it all and distraction over her impending results. They'd lain together on deck and looked up into the diamond studded abyss and he'd told her if they saw a shooting star it would be a sign that she'd passed.

No sooner had he spoken the words than a white streak trailed its incandescent light across the heavens right above them. She'd gasped and he'd told her to shut her eyes and wish upon it and watched her as she did.

Yep. He'd missed this.

God knew he'd had a lot of women in exactly this position over the years but this was different. For a start he hadn't been remotely interested in looking at the stars with any of them. Although to be fair, as his relationship with Stella had teetered on the brink of something neither of them had been game enough to define during their teen years, he hadn't exactly had his head in the stars with her either.

But he did tonight. Stella somehow seemed to bring out the amateur astronomer in him.

And it was…nice.

No agenda. No pressure. No expectations.

Just two old friends relaxing after the perfect day.

'Hey,' Stella said, extending her neck right back as her peripheral vision caught a moonbeam illuminating a chunk of metal hanging off some kind of a fixed pole at the stern. She squinted. 'Is that a shower head?'

Rick extended his neck too and smiled. 'Yep. I've always wanted to be able to take a shower under the stars.' He grinned, relaxing his neck back to a more neutral position.

She laughed as she also released the abnormal stretch, returning to her inspection of the night sky. 'Well, you've thought of everything, haven't you?'

He nodded. 'I've been thinking about this boat for a lot of years.'

They fell silent for a moment, letting the slap of waves against the hull serenade them as their gazes roamed the magnificence of the celestial display.

Stella's yawn broke the natural rhythm. 'I'm beat.' She shut her eyes. 'All that sun and sea on top of the jet lag is a deadly combination.'

'You can't go to bed before we see a shooting star, Stel. Look.' He nudged her shoulder. 'There's Gemini.'

Stella's eyes flicked open and she dutifully followed the path of a perfectly formed bicep all the way to the tip of his raised index finger. She tutted. 'You always had a thing for Gemini.'

He grinned. 'What's not to like about two chicks?'

They laughed and just as he was lowering his arm it happened: a trail of light shot across the night sky, burning bright for long seconds.

Stella gasped and Rick whispered, 'Quick, make a wish.'

Stella thought about Lucinda and Inigo. And dear Joy with the patience of Job. She squeezed her eyes shut as the light faded into extinction and wished for another blockbuster.

Rick turned his head and watched her eye-scrunching concentration. 'What'd you wish for?' he asked.

Stella opened her eyes, her breath catching in her throat at their closeness. Even with the dark pressing in around them, his blue eyes seemed to pierce right into her soul. 'It's a secret,' she murmured. 'If I tell you it won't come true.'

He shook his head. 'You always were a romantic. I should have known you'd go on to write romance novels.'

His voice was light and teasing and not full of scorn as Dale's had been. Dale had been barely able to say the R word. She smiled. 'Says he who insisted I wait to wish upon a star,' she countered.

He laughed. 'Touché.'

His laugh did funny things to her insides and a part of her wanted to stay out with him all night and watch the sun come up, but her eyelids were growing heavier and she yawned again.

She sat. 'Right. I'm off to bed.' She stood and looked down at him lying on the deck of his boat wearing nothing but a pair of low-slung boardies and still somehow managing to look as if he ruled the entire ocean. 'See you in the morning.'

He nodded. 'I won't be too far behind you,' he murmured.

Stella turned away from him, padding her way across the deck, conscious of his eyes on her. She heard his faint 'Night, Stel' reach her as she climbed down the stairs.

She was too beat to reply as her legs took her past the galley, through the saloon to the aft cabin where Rick must have placed her luggage earlier. She didn't bother to shower, hell, she barely bothered to undress, just kicked out of her shorts, pulled the sheets back and crawled under.

She was dreaming even before her head hit the pillow.

Dreaming of Vasco.

CHAPTER FOUR

It was ten the next morning before Stella woke. The gentle rhythm of the waves had rocked her into a deep, jet-lagged slumber. She had a quick shower and threw on a sarong and T-shirt. Rick wasn't below deck but there was an incredible aroma coming from above and she followed her nose.

He was standing at the grill in his boardies—no shirt—and for a moment she just watched the broad bronzed planes of his back that narrowed the closer they got to his waistband.

Or perhaps hip-band might have been more salient.

But then her stomach outed her by growling loudly and she propelled herself forward. 'Sorry for sleeping so late,' she said as she approached him.

Rick turned and smiled at her. 'It's fine—jet lag's a bitch like that. I've only been up for half an hour myself. But, lucky for us—' his smiled broadened into a grin '—the fish have been up for a while.'

Stella inhaled. 'Hmm. Smells great.'

'Grab some plates—we'll eat, then get back to the marina.'

They ate quickly and were under way half an hour later, Rick again letting Stella take the wheel. It was early afternoon before they were finally on land again and alighting a taxi at Cairns Central Shopping Centre.

'So you think you can remember how to provision a boat for a few weeks?'

Stella nodded. She'd often gone with Sergio to buy supplies just prior to an expedition. Serg, a grizzled veteran of the merchant navy and stalwart of Mills and Granville, usually went out on the longer trips as chief cook and bottle washer. He cooked good plain food in bulk and pastry to die for.

'I checked out the galley properly so I know what storage capabilities there are. I assume we'll buy fresh food where we can along the way?'

'Yep.'

'So I'll get all the usual staples.'

He handed over the company credit card of which she was a signatory. 'Where are you going?' she asked as she slid the plastic into the back pocket of her shorts.

'I'm heading to the Boating, Camping, Fishing store to pick up a few things. Let's meet up back here at that coffee shop,' he said, pointing behind her, 'in about an hour?'

Stella checked her watch. 'Right. See you then.'

Shopping in another country was always a challenge. In Penzance she frequented the local supermarket and she knew what and where everything was. Far from home, it took her much longer to find the things she'd already put on a mental list in her head.

But at least Cairns had first-world shopping facilities and everyone spoke the same language. She and Serg had certainly shopped in much more rudimentary surrounds.

By the time the hour was up Stella had a trolley piled high with provisions and the credit card had taken a hit—if they were going to be limited in what they ate for the next few weeks, then she was going to make damn sure what they did have was of the highest quality. Good chocolate—for her anyway, Rick wasn't fussy—and the most decadent biscuits money could buy—for him.

Serg had told her when she was a teenager that Rick had a sweet tooth that was best kept fed. She hadn't been sure whether that had some double meaning or not, but it had certainly fed *her* hormone-fuelled imagination.

Stella pushed the uncooperative metal beast with two wonky wheels for what seemed like five miles in the giant sprawling shopping centre. She almost crashed into a shop window and earned the wrath of a mother who thought Stella was deliberately trying to run her tantrumming little angel down.

When she finally reached the coffee shop her abdominals, quads and biceps were cramped with the effort of keeping the damn thing on track. Her mood was not great. It didn't improve any to find Rick, with one shopping bag, chatting up a tall, dark-haired waitress who looked as if she were born dancing the Flamenco.

Of course.

The man had a perpetual hard-on.

'Hi,' she said, using the back of Rick's chair as a brake for the trolley.

Rick spun around as the impact interrupted him mid-flirt.

'Oops, sorry, damn thing is impossible to control,' she said, smiling sweetly at the waitress, who looked as if she was about to give Stella a piece of her mind for careening into a customer.

A sex-god customer.

Stella was pretty damn sure if someone had barged into her chair with a dangerous weapon, Ms Flamenco wouldn't have batted an eyelid.

'Hey, Stel.' He grinned. 'Have a seat. You want a coffee? Something to eat? Ramona says they do a mean nachos here.'

Stella smiled at Ramona. 'Nachos and a flat white would be great, thanks.'

Ramona nodded at Rick. 'I'll be back in a jiffy.'

I just bet you will, Stella thought uncharitably as she sat down.

'Whoa, you buy the whole shop?' Rick asked, examining the contents of the missile that had smacked into him.

'You have to cover every contingency,' she said waspishly.

'Ooh, Snickers,' he said, pulling out the packet of fun-sized chocolate bars. 'My favourite.'

Yes. Which was why she'd bought them.

'Can I take your order, sir?'

Stella looked up at another goddess smiling down at Rick as if he'd invented oxygen. Lord, where did this coffee shop source their staff from—www.lookgoodnaked.com?

'We've ordered,' she said tersely.

'Sorry.' Rick smiled and shrugged.

'No worries,' the woman said, her smile not wavering, her gaze not leaving his. 'If you need anything just yell. I'm Holly.'

'Thanks, I'll holler, Holly,' he said and she giggled.

Stella rolled her eyes. 'You're incorrigible.'

Rick grinned. 'I have no idea what you're talking about.'

Stella ignored him, instead choosing to go through the docket with him for anything she might have forgotten while they waited for their meal. It was going to be too late once they'd cast off in the morning. No less than two waitresses interrupted them while they did so.

Their meals finally arrived and Stella almost laughed as yet another woman, a leggy redhead, delivered them.

Were they drawing straws?

This one looked older—older than Rick for sure—and had the calm authority and predatory grace of a woman who knew what she liked. She introduced herself as the owner.

'Ramona was saying you're sailing north for a few weeks. I don't suppose you need a deckhand?' she joked as she placed Rick's meal in front of him.

'I'm the deckhand,' Stella intoned.

Was she invisible?

Was it that ridiculous to think that she could be his girlfriend? It seemed every female employee in the coffee shop thought so, if their quick dismissive gazes followed by their unabashed flirting were any indication.

She wanted to stand up and say, *Hey, I'm a famous author,*

don't you know. But then Rick looked at her and winked and she felt as if he'd just ruffled her hair and slipped her a few bucks to run along and leave him do his thing.

She felt like his kid sister.

'Do you know boats?' Rick asked.

The woman smiled. 'Oh, yes, my ex always owned classic yachts. I hear yours is a beauty.'

Rick nodded enthusiastically. 'You should drop by the marina and see her. The *Stella* is a true class act.'

Stella blinked.

Had he just invited a cougar back to the boat?

Oh, no, don't mind me.

The woman smiled at him. 'I may just do that.'

'Can I get some cracked pepper?' Stella asked.

The redhead gave her a cursory once-over and disregarded her in less than five seconds. 'I'll send Ramona over,' she said and she slunk away.

'God, this looks good, doesn't it?' Rick asked as he turned his attention to his meal.

Stella had suddenly lost her appetite. Sometimes she just couldn't work him out. The man knew he was attractive to women. She'd seen him work that to his advantage too many times to class him as clueless, but she didn't think he truly understood how effortlessly it worked in his favour.

Even when he wasn't trying, women flocked. And of that, he was totally unaware. She was sure of it.

She picked at her meal and was pleased when they managed to leave the coffee shop unmolested forty-five minutes later. He took the trolley, managing it like the flocks of women—effortlessly—and they caught a taxi back to the marina.

Once on board they stocked the galley with the supplies then sat at the dining table drinking beer and plotting their course. Stella felt the jet lag catching up with her again as Rick's deep English voice, sounding even more so in this land of different accents, laid out the first leg from Cairns to Port

Moresby, which would take them about two sailing days. The boat bobbed rhythmically to the melody of a hundred loose halyards clinking against their masts and she yawned.

It wasn't until a voice from outside disturbed them that Stella realised two hours had passed in a drowsy haze and she'd barely taken any of it in.

'Ahoy there! Anyone home?'

Rick frowned. 'Who's that?'

Stella's head cleared as she recognised the sultry tones of the coffee-shop owner. 'I'm guessing it's the leggy, red-headed cougar.'

Rick laughed as he took a swig of his second beer. 'Really? Oh…'

He seemed disappointed, which perversely made her both happy and annoyed and a lot more awake. 'Er…you invited her here. What did you expect?'

'Did I?' Rick frowned. He didn't recall.

Stella blinked. 'You said, you should drop by the marina. Women are literal creatures, Rick.'

He stood. 'That's cool.' He disappeared into the galley and came out with another beer. 'It's never a hardship to spend some time with a beautiful woman. Who appreciates a classic yacht.'

Stella rolled her eyes. 'She's a decade older than you.'

He shrugged, then grinned at her as he cracked the tops on the beers. 'So?' And then she watched him disappear up the winding staircase.

Great.

What the hell was *she* supposed to do while he dallied above deck with a woman about the same age as her mother as if he were some young buck in need of sexual tutelage?

God, no, he wouldn't…surely he wouldn't have sex with her up there where anyone could see him? Surely he'd at least bring her to his cabin?

But then the thought of him bringing her down here was

confronting on other levels. Stella didn't want another woman below deck sullying all that it meant to her—to them.

God, would she be forced to listen to them rocking the bloody boat all night?

Would they be loud?

She didn't think that Rick would be a silent lover. She'd always imagined he'd be quite vocal in his appreciation of a woman.

Just like Vasco.

She could only pray the jet lag still tugging at the peripheries of her consciousness would sink her completely under in a deep sound-proof abyss.

Stella could hear their muffled voices above her and could feel herself getting madder with each passing minute. She tried to concentrate on the weather charts and tide times on the laptop in front of her, but her eyes felt too gritty. She even pulled out her father's research papers and tried to immerse herself in them, but she was just too damn tired and the redhead's deep throaty laugh was just too damn distracting.

She could feel herself getting more and more tense.

How dared he entertain a lady and expect her to just meld into the furniture, stay below deck and pretend she wasn't even here?

It might be his boat but she wasn't going to feel ignored or non-existent. He had his whole life to be with as many women as he liked. To flirt and indulge in whatever hedonistic lifestyle he wanted.

But for the next few weeks he was on this boat with *her* with a job to do and he could bloody well take a break from being Mr Irresistible and keep his head in the game.

Stella was pacing when he joined her five minutes later, aware on some peripheral level she wasn't feeling particularly rational. 'That was quick,' she said testily.

Rick shrugged. Danielle's company had been pleasant

enough but he didn't feel like entertaining tonight. There was a lot of planning to do and he was aware of Stella below deck.

'Big day tomorrow,' he said as he made a beeline for the galley, throwing the empty beer bottles in the bin under the sink.

'You should have brought her down here and shown her around. I bet she was dying to see below deck—a woman with an eye for a classic yacht and all,' Stella said, sarcasm oozing from her pores.

Rick grinned as he washed his hands at the sink. 'Oh, she wanted to. But I told her you had a headache. You know, from the jet lag.'

'How considerate,' she said sweetly. 'She must have been devastated.'

'Nah…I don't really think she was *that* interested in the boat.'

Stella snorted. 'You don't say.'

Rick poked his head out of the galley to look at her. She seemed mad. 'You're bitchy when you're jet-lagged.'

'Yeh, headaches bring out the bitch in me too,' she snapped.

Rick saw a spark of heat turn her olive gaze to an ominous green, like a hailstorm. He knew he was in trouble, he just wasn't sure why. 'What's wrong?' he asked warily, approaching her.

Stella wasn't exactly sure why she was *so* mad all of a sudden, but she knew she was. She shook her head at him. 'You.'

'Okay…?'

'You honestly can't switch it off, can you?'

Rick frowned. 'Switch what off?'

'God, you should come with a flirt alert. How on earth are you possibly going to manage this trip, four bloody weeks, without a woman around to charm?'

Rick, who was used to spending lengthy periods at sea, wasn't worried about it. 'I think I'll manage,' he said dryly.

'Manage?' Stella snorted again. 'You can't go a day without trying to hook up.'

Rick laughed. 'I think you're exaggerating a little.'

Stella stopped pacing and glared at him. 'In thirty-six hours you have flirted with every woman who has crossed your path. Diana, the rental-car woman, the airline check-in chicky, the grandmother who ran the refreshment stall at Heathrow, several air stewardesses, the taxi driver, every waitress in the coffee shop today...'

She ticked off each conquest on a finger. 'And when we get on that boat tomorrow after about twelve hours you're going to start in on me *because you can't help yourself,*' she finished a little shrilly.

Rick blinked. Stel wasn't usually the nagging, hysterical type so it was either jet lag or PMS. Neither of which he was game to suggest, but he hoped it was the former because that surely couldn't last more than another day.

'But I always flirt with you.' He shrugged. 'It doesn't mean anything.'

Stella glared. 'Why the hell not?' she demanded, uncaring that she knew. 'Is there something wrong with me?'

Rick blinked, not quite able to believe he was having this conversation. 'That's not what I meant. There's nothing wrong with you. You're perfectly...' He groped around for a word that was flattering without saying all the things he'd desperately tried not to think about her over the years—curvy, sweet, bootylicious.

A Nathan-approved word.

'Decent.'

Decent?

Good God, she sounded as if she were someone's homely cousin who was all right at a pinch but was hardly likely to be picked to play spin the bottle at a party. Stella doubted she'd ever felt so underwhelmed in her life.

'Gee, thanks,' she snapped.

Rick pushed his hair off his face as he tried to comprehend how this night had gone so rapidly to hell. 'I don't understand… Do you…want me to mean it?' he asked.

Stella's breath hitched in her throat at the illicitness of the suggestion. What would *that* be like? To have all that deliberate blue-eyed charm turned on her? Like when they'd been teenagers and their banter had occasionally wandered into dangerous territory.

But grown up.

Diana's *you should have sex with him* slithered into her brain and she pushed it away.

'Of course I don't!' she said in her very best English-teacher-talking-to-a-student-with-a-crush voice. 'But I don't want you flirting with every other woman you come across either. It really is rather tiresome to watch and completely unproductive.'

Rick cocked an eyebrow. *He'd personally never found flirting to be unproductive.* But she was obviously accusing him of lack of control. 'You think I can't go a few lousy weeks without flirting with a woman?'

Stella crossed her arms. 'Oh, I'm sure of it.'

'Is this a dare?' he asked.

Stella felt the conversation suddenly shift gears. It should have taken her back to their childhood but the silk in his voice took her to another place entirely.

A very adult place.

'Sure.' She shrugged. 'I dare you. I dare you to go through this whole voyage without flirting with a single woman you meet along the way.'

Rick grinned, his gaze locking with hers. 'And what do I get?' he asked, his voice low.

The timbre of his voice stroked along all her tired nerve endings as he stared at her with his Vasco eyes.

What did he want?

Stella swallowed. 'Get?'

Rick held her gaze. 'If I win?'

Stella was lost for words for a moment. They'd never played for stakes before. Several inappropriate suggestions rose to mind but she quashed each one. She was too strung out to play games with him. 'How about my undying gratitude?' she quipped.

Rick shook his head slowly, dropping his gaze to her mouth. 'How about that kiss that we didn't quite get round to?'

Stella blinked as the teenage bad-boy looked back at her. It was a tantalising offer. One she knew he didn't expect her to take. But she'd never been one to back down from a dare and, frankly, the idea was as thrilling as it was illicit.

She smiled. 'Deal.' She held out her hand. He wouldn't be able to manage it, of course, but if the stakes were…interesting…maybe he'd at least try and comply.

Their gazes locked and Rick swallowed as he took her hand, cementing the deal.

Would she taste like coconuts too?

They cast off the next morning at eight o'clock, a good wind aiding their departure. The long-range weather forecast was favourable and Stella was feeling as if her body clock was finally back in sync.

Of course, she was also really embarrassed by her carry-on last night. She tried to apologise to Rick once they were out of the harbour and heading north.

'Are you trying to welch on the deal?' Rick teased. 'Because you know how much I love a challenge.'

She did. God knew how many times she'd come close to drowning while challenging him to a competition to see who could hold their breath underwater the longest.

He'd beat her every time.

Except for that time he'd let her win and she'd been so mad at him he'd promised never to do it again.

'Absolutely not,' she said, shaking her head. 'I stand by it.'

'Good.' He grinned. 'Now go write something.'

And she did. Sitting in a special chair at the bow of the boat, sun on her shoulders, breeze in her hair, laptop balanced on her knees, she found Lucinda flowed from her fingers onto the page. It was as if she frolicked and danced along the keys, slipping magically between Stella's fingers, informing every letter, controlling every mouse click.

The cursor no longer blinked at Stella from a blank page. Instead words, lovely rich words of a bygone era, filled all the white spaces up. When Rick brought her a snack and her hat she realised she'd been writing for two hours solid and the number down the bottom of the page told her she'd written thirteen hundred words.

Thirteen hundred glorious words.

The morning flowed into the afternoon; the perfect calm conditions continued. Rick occasionally called to her, pointing out a pod of dolphins or an island in the distance. She got up and stretched regularly and when she was grappling with a scene she'd take the wheel for a while and magically, like tankers on the horizon, the solution appeared.

By the end of the day she'd written three thousand words and she felt utterly exhilarated. And it wasn't all about the writing.

She'd forgotten how elemental sailing made a person feel. How it connected you to the earth on such a primitive level. How the feel of the waves beneath your feet and the push and pull of the tide drew you into the circadian rhythm of the planet.

How it connected her to her father.

She'd missed Nathan terribly the last six months, but out here he was everywhere. Every turn of the wheel, every flap of the sail, every pitch and roll of the hull.

They anchored just before sundown in the middle of nowhere. Just her and Rick bobbing in the middle of an enormous ocean beneath a giant dome blushing velvet and dappled with tangerine clouds.

Rick grilled steaks this time and Stella was pleased she'd kept a serving out of the freezer. She loved fish, but she knew by the time the voyage was over she'd be all fished out. And with three thousand words to celebrate, nice thick juicy steaks seemed like the perfect food. She tossed a salad and completed the meal with melt-in-your-mouth bread rolls.

It was utterly delicious and they savoured every morsel of the fresh food. Much later in their journey, when their fresh food had run out, the meals wouldn't be this exciting.

Of course, there would always be fish.

Stella took their plates while Rick cleaned the grill and she joined him on deck twenty minutes later after a quick shower. He was lying as he had the night before, flat on his back, stretched out beneath a vast canopy of black and silver.

Although tonight, at least, he'd decided to wear a shirt.

'Are we going to do this every night?' she asked, joining him.

He looked up at her. She was wearing a sarong tied around her neck in some fashion, the corners flapping in the breeze to show a little bare thigh. He looked back at the sky.

'Weather permitting,' he murmured.

Stella settled back, the slap of the halyard against the mast making a delightful clink. The stars seemed so close this far away from the light pollution of land.

'Well, I think I did very well today,' he said after they'd lain in companionable silence for a few minutes. 'Are you ready to concede yet?'

Stella laughed. 'There's only been me here.'

He smiled into the night. 'It won't make a difference.'

'Well, we'll see how it is when you're surrounded by all those Micronesian babes who want to be your own private deckhands.'

He chuckled then and Stella shivered as the delicious noise

slipped down her spine like a feather stroke. She raised her hand to distract herself, just as she had as a child, holding up her thumb to the moon and squinting, obliterating the glowing white orb from her vision.

She dropped her hand. 'They look like you could just pluck them from the sky, one by one, don't they?'

'And that's why you write romance novels,' Rick teased, rolling his head to the side to look at her.

Stella smiled and just as abruptly stopped. Rick seemed so laid-back about what she did.

He frowned. 'What's wrong?'

'Nothing,' she sighed.

'That's kind of a big sigh to be nothing. I thought you were ecstatic about your word count today.'

Stella let her head roll so she was facing him too. 'I am, I'm…beyond ecstatic. I'm just…'

'Just? Are you not happy with what you do?'

'No. I'm very happy with it. Especially now I have words,' she joked. 'I have a great publisher. An editor who's a saint, an agent who's a shark…'

'But?' he asked as she turned her head away to look at the sky. 'You should be proud of what you do. Nathan was. We're all so proud of you, Stel.'

Stella gave a light snort. 'Trust me, not everyone is so… proud of what I do.'

Rick frowned. 'Oh? Someone in particular?'

She looked at him again. 'Dale. He…broke off the engagement when he realised what I wrote.'

Nathan had told Rick about the break-up when it had occurred. Rick hadn't asked why, he'd just assumed it was the usual sort of stuff that broke relationships up. He did remember Nathan being secretly pleased. He'd always thought his daughter's long-term fiancé was a bit of a cold fish.

Rick had to admit to feeling a little pleased himself. He'd

never met Dale but Nathan's instincts about men had usually been spot on.

'He didn't know?'

She shook her head. 'Dale thought I was writing respected historical research on eighteenth-century pirates.'

Rick was confused. 'Didn't you tell him?'

'Of course I did, but he was never good at listening. He's an academic, one of those absent-minded professor types, and all he heard was historical and pirate…'

Rick suppressed a shudder. *He sounded like a total bore.*

'So,' he said, wanting to clarify the situation before he spoke ill of her idiot ex, 'he dumped you when he found out you wrote…'

Stella nodded. 'Trashy, smutty, dirty little books.'

Rick cocked an eyebrow. *He really had to read that book.* 'You write trashy smut?' What the hell was wrong with the man? Didn't he realise that was a really good reason to hang onto a woman?

Stella rolled her eyes. 'No. I write historical romantic fiction for women. Dale called them trashy and smutty.'

Rick sucked in a breath. *What a dufus.* 'How did he find out?'

'One of his students asked him if he was the inspiration for Vasco Ramirez.'

Rick rolled up onto his elbow and looked down at her. 'Was he?'

Stella laughed then. The irony of Rick, Vasco Ramirez personified, asking that question was just too much. 'Most definitely not.'

Rick grinned. 'Ouch.'

Stella felt instantly contrite—not everyone looked like an eighteenth-century pirate. 'No, I'm sorry, I didn't mean it like that. Dale's lovely…was lovely. In kind of a…self-absorbed way. He's just not…buccaneer material.'

'Well,' Rick announced. 'The man's clearly an idiot.'

'Not really...he has an IQ in the hundred and thirties.'

Rick fell back against the deck. 'He can't be too smart if his fiancée is writing smutty novels and he doesn't use that to his advantage.'

Stella burst out laughing. 'His advantage? How?'

Rick shrugged. 'Dress up in breeches and make you read it aloud to him.'

Stella laughed again. The very thought was as wicked as it was absurd. Dale would no sooner have done that than flown to the moon. 'Dale was a little too strait-laced for role playing. In fact I think he considered human desire a little beneath him altogether. Too...messy or something.'

There was just something about laughing with Rick in the night under the stars that encouraged confidences and she felt as if they were kids again, whispering their secrets to each other.

Rick couldn't believe what he was hearing. In fact he was pretty damn sure he didn't want to hear it. And not just because a woman like Stella, or any woman for that matter, should not be having mediocre sex. But because putting sex and Stella in the same sentence was something he'd avoided his entire life.

'Why on earth did you stay with him?' he asked.

Stella rolled her head to face him. That one was easy.

'Because he was a nice guy. A good guy. A kind guy. He made me laugh.' *Not in the ribald way Rick made her laugh but in a lovely, easy way that warmed her up inside.* 'He had a great job. On terra firma. He wanted to get married. He wanted kids.'

Rick almost yawned, it sounded so boring, but the way her voice softened was telling. He looked away. How could someone who had the swell of oceans running in her veins settle for such mediocrity?

'Well, it sounds like you're well shot of him to me,' he said after a few moments star gazing. 'A woman who writes smut needs someone to inspire her.'

Stella laughed. 'You're incorrigible.'

'That's what you like about me.'

She thumped him on the chest. Yeh, it *was* what she liked about him but she wasn't going to admit it.

'I'm going to bed,' she said, sitting up.

He sat also. 'I'm up for that.'

Stella looked behind her at his bad-boy grin and rolled her eyes. 'By myself.'

'I can do smut.'

Stella laughed. 'I bet you can.'

He held up his hand. 'Just saying. The offer's out there.'

Stella shook her head. 'I think this is called flirting, Rick.'

'Hey, you said, with women I meet along the way. I already know you. You're fair game.'

Stella guessed she'd walked right into that one.

'Besides I gotta put the flirt somewhere. It's not good to let it build up. Men,' he said, lowering his voice, 'should never let anything build up.'

Lucky for her she was used to Rick's teasing and was sufficiently over the jet lag to not let it push her buttons. She stood. 'Goodnight, Rick.'

'Sleep tight.' He grinned as he watched her walk away.

Then there were just the stars, the ocean and him, but not even they could keep him from the smutty book he had secreted in his cabin.

He gave her five minutes, then followed her down.

Six hours later, Rick read *The End* and knew he would never be the same again. Diana had been right. It was most illuminating. The hard-on he'd got in chapter two was still there and there was no way it was going away unless he did something about it.

Fortunately now he had plenty of images to help him in that department.

Two things were crystal clear.

Number one—Dale was an idiot of the first order. Hell, if he had a woman that had this sort of stuff in her head— the sheer eroticism of the beautifully scripted love scenes still clung to his loins—he wouldn't let her out of his bed let alone his life.

Number two—the most shocking of all.

She'd written the book about him.

He was Vasco Ramirez.

CHAPTER FIVE

Lady Mary stifled a gasp as Captain Ramirez rose from the tin bath tub with the fluid grace of a stallion. Water sluiced down the long lines of his body as the flickering lamplight gilded his bronzed skin, throwing it both into mysterious shadow and enticing relief.

The mucous membranes of her throat cracked as dry as parchment, her heart skipped frantically in her chest.

She should not be here.

She should not be spying on a man, a nude man, who was unaware of being watched.

But she simply could not stop.

The last time she'd seen flesh this magnificent had been at Lord Ladbrooke's stables and her nostrils flared as she remembered how all that leashed power had felt beneath her jodhpurs as she'd straddled and then ridden the Arabian beauty bareback.

Much to her aunt's chagrin.

Lord alone knew what she'd do now witnessing Mary's scandalous behaviour. There'd be smelling salts for sure.

But, alas, Mary could not take her eyes off the man.

Steam still rose in wisps around his calves as he stood waiting for the excess water to run off. She held her breath as her gaze roamed over the board-taut planes of his shoulders, obscured towards the middle by sleek wet strips of dark hair. Water trekked from the dripping ends and she followed the path of one errant droplet, gleaming in the light, as it slid down the furrow of his spine nestled between the well-defined muscles either side.

She lost it in shadow as it entered the dip of his back, bracketed by enticing hollows, but her eyes roamed south regardless to the rise of his buttocks. Two firm slabs of muscle, potently male even in his relaxed state, greeted her.

Her gaze was drawn to the left where an imperfection snagged her attention. There, in the centre of his left buttock, lay a large smooth brown birthmark.

It was utterly fascinating and Mary stared at it open-mouthed. It was a perfect circle as if some lover, for he looked to be a man who took lovers, had drawn it deliberately to brand him.

Mary's cheeks flamed at the risqué image and she felt the roughness of her breath as it quickened in her lungs.

Just when she thought he'd turned to stone he turned slightly, affording Mary a different view. Her gaze brushed along the flare of a bicep, the jut of a masculine hip, which seemed as savage as it did graceful, and the perfect delineation of a meaty quadricep that seemed to vibrate with barely leashed power.

And then there was his...

Mary swallowed. She had seen illustrations of the nude male anatomy in obscure texts in her uncle's library when she'd been fifteen but they hadn't managed to capture the sheer beauty of the real thing. The long elegant line of the male member in all its potency was a sight to behold.

It was more elongated and the girth more significant than she'd ever imagined. The curls at its base more enticing.

How magnificent would it look standing out proud as she'd seen on the midnight Arabian?

Mary felt a strange sensation take root deep inside her.

How on earth did it fit?

Captain Ramirez suddenly reached for a nearby towel, covering himself as he stepped out of the bath, his fascinating birthmark the last thing she saw before everything was obscured. Just as quickly he'd padded over to the door that led to his private bedchamber and disappeared through it.

Mary let out the breath she'd been holding. It stuttered noisily into the air around her. She knew she should move but she was utterly incapable.

Until now she'd assumed that pirates didn't bathe.

She would be grateful until the day she died that Captain Vasco Ramirez had shattered that rather high-handed illusion.

Vasco was breathing rather heavily himself as he shut the door to his bedchamber, leaning against it, his long sable lashes covering the smoulder in his devil blue eyes. Ever since he'd seen Lady Mary in the looking glass peeking out from behind the curtains he'd been determined to shock her.

But he hadn't been prepared for her thorough appreciation. Nor for his completely involuntary reaction to her fascinated scrutiny.

His fancy did not usually involve gently bred ladies but he'd seen those flared nostrils, heard that muffled gasp.

Maybe beneath all those prim petticoats and haughty eyes beat a passionate heart. Maybe she wasn't as indifferent to him as her demeanour suggested.

Maybe she could be persuaded to make this voyage a lot more bearable for both of them?

Rick shut the book as he finished chapter two.

Again.

He could hear Stella moving around above him and knew he had to get out of bed and get under way but he wasn't sure he could look her in the eye this morning.

And—he looked down at the tented sheet—he needed a little time to compose himself…

He ran his fingers over the glossy cover of *Pleasure Hunt*, the metallic letters boldly pronouncing her name—*Stella Mills*.

This *was not* the Stella Mills he knew.

What on earth had happened to her? The Stella who had played mermaid and pirates? Who liked to snorkel and scuba dive? Who liked to read and watch the stars at night? The Stella who hated carrots and could almost hold her breath as long as he could?

The one who had been devastated when her parents had divorced and had made him promise that whatever happened in their lives they would always be friends.

Of course that Stella had been ten years old.

Just the way he liked her.

Because otherwise he had to think of her as a very different Stella.

A grown-up Stella. Who got engaged.

Who had sex.

Who was twenty-seven and *not* the virgin her father had hoped she would be for ever.

Not if *Pleasure Hunt* was anything to go by anyway.

God, she probably didn't even hate carrots any more.

Rick threw the covers off. This was ridiculous. And not helping his situation down below.

He cut straight to the crux of the issue, or one aspect of it anyway.

She *was not* Lady Mary.

He let it reverberate around his head for good measure.

Lady Mary was a character she'd made up. In that vivid, hot, lustrous, dirty—*God, so dirty*—imagination of hers.

Just because Vasco was him, didn't mean that Lady Mary was her.

It didn't mean she'd been fantasising about him sexually. Or that she'd put herself into a character whose lust for his character bordered on pornographic obsession.

That was just plain crazy.

There was nothing remotely similar about Lady Mary and Stella—nothing.

So he needed to get over himself.

He needed to go and take a shower—a cold one—and get the bloody boat moving.

He was on deck twenty minutes later. And he was in big, big trouble. Suddenly the filter that had always been in place where she was concerned had been stripped away. Those teenage dreams he'd had about her and refused to let himself dwell upon were front and centre.

She was in teeny tiny denim shorts with a frayed edge and a shirt that barely met in the middle. A straw cowboy-style hat, the edges curled up, sat low over her eyes and held her tucked-up hair in place save for a few haphazard wisps that had escaped and brushed her nape.

The girl he always saw, the one he'd trained himself to see, ever since Nathan had sprung them about to kiss, was gone for ever.

Now he saw the ripe bulge of her breasts as the bra he could clearly see through the thin fabric of her shirt pushed and lifted in all the right ways. The wink of her belly button taunting him from the strip of bare skin at her midriff. The killer curve where her hip flared from the tiny line of her waist.

He'd never noticed how curvy she was before. Not consciously anyway. Consciously he'd always thought of her as short and cute.

Like an elf or maybe a munchkin.

But there was nothing cute about those curves—they should come with a yellow warning sign.

And he was stuck on board with them for the next few weeks.

'Well, about time,' Stella said as she caught Rick's advance in her peripheral vision. 'Another gorgeous day for sailing.'

Rick smiled, his gaze drawn to her mouth. The mouth that was nowhere near as innocent as he'd always thought. A mouth he tried and failed not to think about on his body the way Lady Mary's had been on Vasco's.

Stella popped the lid on a bottle of sunscreen and squirted some into her palm. 'If you get us under way,' she said, slapping it on her chest, 'I'll cook some bacon and eggs.'

Rick swallowed as Stella distributed the white liquid to her shoulders and upper arms and across the swell of her cleavage, dipping her fingers beneath the fabric a little.

Do not look at her breasts. Do not *look at her breasts.*
Too late.

He looked at her breasts.

'Sure,' he said distractedly as her hands continued to massage the crème until her cleavage glistened in the sun.

Stella frowned at him as he stood there looking at her. Was he…was he perving at her chest? There were times when they'd been younger, pre her sweet-sixteen debacle, when she'd caught him looking at her, when their gazes had locked and he'd smile at her with wolfish appreciation, but that had been a long time ago.

'Rick?'

Her voice brought him back from the fantasy of licking every inch of the crème off her. He blinked and quickly donned his sunglasses. 'Yes, absolutely, getting under way.' He saluted, turning from her gratefully, his hands trembling as if he were fifteen years old again and trying to undo Sharon Morgan's bra.

He really needed to get a grip.

By the time the sun was high in the sky Rick was half-way to crazy. The boat was travelling along at a steady clip, which left him nothing else to do other than stare at Stella. Even metres away from him in her low chair, doing nothing but writing, she destroyed his concentration. She was almost directly in his line of sight, her legs supporting her laptop, her shirt riding up her spine to reveal a good portion of skin, including the dimples at the small of her back.

With conversation non-existent, he was left with a lot of time to think. A lot of time for his mind to wander.

Standing at the helm, the wheel in his hand, the ocean at his command, it was a little hard not to think of himself as the all-conquering pirate Vasco Ramirez.

The Vasco who decided to turn his treasure hunt into a pleasure hunt. Who actively seduced Lady Mary after the bath scene and whose slow, deliberate dance with her was both clever and cunning.

Rick's mind wandered to those scenes of calculated seduction. Vasco washing Mary's hair on deck. Vasco removing a splinter from her finger with his teeth. Vasco cutting into the juicy flesh of a dripping pear with his jewelled dagger and feeding her slice after slice.

And the sexiest scene of all where Vasco had tied her spreadeagled in her under-things to his bed until Mary had admitted her desire for him.

That one had got Rick hotter than a summer day on the equator.

In fact just thinking about it now was getting him pretty damn hot. Not helped by the fact that she had abandoned her seated position and was doing a sexy little stretch, bending over and touching her toes, then arching her back as she linked her hands above her head and twisted from side to side.

Oh, Lord, kill me now.

She turned then and walked towards him and he was

pleased, as her breasts jiggled enticingly, for the secure placement of his very dark sunglasses.

'You fancy a cold beer and a bite to eat?' Stella asked as she approached.

'Sounds great,' he said.

Stella patted him absently on the arm. 'Be right back,' she said.

Rick stayed very still as the fleeting touch seemed to reach deep down inside and stroke something that it just shouldn't have. Since when had a perfunctory touch from her had such an effect? But he suddenly understood Ramirez's puzzlement over the sensations that Lady Mary had created when she'd clung to his sleeve briefly during some choppy weather.

Rick shook his head at the direction of his errant thoughts. *Bloody hell, had he been emasculated overnight?*

When Stella rejoined him ten minutes later with some ham and salad rolls and two beers, he'd found his testicles and got over himself.

'Put it on autopilot,' Stella said, pressing the beer into his hand. 'Come and sit with me.'

Yeh, that was just what he needed.

But he did it anyway.

'So, how's the book going?' he asked, nodding at the shut laptop as he took a man-sized swallow of beer to dilute the absolute unmanly curiosity over her current romance novel.

Stella nodded. 'Coming along very nicely. I'm just about finished with the first chapter. I've emailed Diana—she's ecstatic. I think Joy had threatened her with editing non-fic if I didn't deliver.' Stella grinned.

Rick smiled too. She seemed relaxed and willing to chat about the book. Maybe, instead of wondering whether Lady Mary was her, which was, quite frankly, driving him nuts, he could just come out and ask. Or at least start a conversation where he could work his way round to it.

'So, what's the book about?' he asked as he took a bite out of his bread roll.

Stella looked up at him from under the brim of her hat. 'You really want to know?'

Rick stopped chewing. 'Of course, why wouldn't I?'

Stella blinked. For as long as she'd known him Rick's tastes had run to non-fiction books on anything to do with the salvage industry and shipwrecks. And *Phantom* comics.

'It's not really your thing.'

Oh, if only she knew how suddenly it was exactly his thing. He looked at her. 'It's yours. I'm interested.'

Stella stared at him for a moment, taken aback by his sincerity. 'Good answer.' She smiled.

He smiled back. She looked so damn sweet, how could she have such a dirty mind? 'So?' He quirked an eyebrow.

She didn't know where to start. She wasn't used to sharing this sort of information with anyone. Only Diana had known about *Pleasure Hunt* and even then Stella had been reticent to share any of the details in the early stages of the book. Non-writers didn't understand how storylines and characters weren't always crystal clear and well defined.

'It's about a mermaid,' she said. 'Called Lucinda.'

And then for some strange reason, under his scrutiny, she blushed. She thought about all the times they'd played pirate and mermaid as kids, swimming through the tropical waters of wherever they happened to be at the time.

'You know I've always had a thing for mermaids,' she said defensively.

Rick's gaze locked with hers. 'I do.'

Stella shrugged. 'She came to me in a dream.'

He nodded, wishing he'd been privy to that dream. Hell, if her dream life was as rich as her on-page fantasy life he wished he were privy to all of them.

'And the hero?' he asked.

Something held Stella back. She straightened the hat on

her head, then whisked it off and let her hair tumble down, stalling for time as she looked towards the horizon. 'I don't know much about the hero this time,' she said with what she hoped seemed like artistic vagueness.

Rick followed the stream of her hair as the stiffening ocean breeze blew it behind her. His palm itched to tangle in it and he kept it firmly planted around his beer. 'Is that unusual?' he asked.

'I don't know. I'm new to this and it's just the way it's happened.'

Rick slid a sideways glance at her. 'Did that happen with your first hero?'

Stella's heart skipped a beat as she glanced at him. 'No,' she said casually. 'He came to me…fairly well developed.'

Rick bit back a smile. *Hell, yeah, honey, no prizes for guessing why.* 'Does he have a name at least, this new guy?'

Stella blushed again. 'Inigo.'

Rick smiled. 'Ah…good choice.'

Stella looked at him and returned his smile grudgingly. 'Thank you.' It was surprisingly hard to talk about the hero with Rick and his Vasco Ramirez eyes staring straight at her even from behind his midnight shades.

Rick knew he had a good opening but was surprised by the pound of his heart as he contemplated the question.

Did he really want to know the answer?

He forced himself to take up inspection of the horizon so the question would seem casual rather than targeted. 'Do you base any of your characters on people you know?' he asked casually.

Stella glanced at him sharply. Did he know? Had he read *Pleasure Hunt*? She'd sent a copy to the *Persephone* for her father, which Rick could have got his hands on, she supposed, but it had been in a box of things that had been cleared from his cabin and sent to her after his death still in pristine condition.

The spine hadn't been cracked and it had been obvious to her that it had been unread.

It was an innocent enough question on the surface—one she'd been asked a hundred times by fans and media alike—but her shoulders tensed as she inspected that inscrutable profile just in case.

He seemed his usual relaxed self, soaking up some rays and downing a beer with the unconscious grace of an Old Spice model.

Besides, she doubted there would be any way he would have read it and not realised immediately who Vasco was. And she knew Rick well enough to know that he wouldn't have been able to resist taunting her mercilessly about it.

'No,' she said faintly, hoping her voice sounded stronger than it felt.

Rick stifled a chuckle. *Liar.* For damn sure Vasco Ramirez was him.

'So they just come to you…like in a dream or something…?' he asked innocently.

'Something like that,' she said vaguely. 'Although if I'm to be honest,' she admitted, trying to divert his attention off the hero, 'I suppose that the heroine is me.'

Rick coughed noisily as he inhaled some of his beer into his windpipe, necessitating her to beat him on the back a few times. He gasped and wheezed and coughed while his airway cleared the irritant.

Vasco probably never did anything so undignified.

'So,' he clarified once he could speak again, 'the heroines are…you?'

Please say no. Please don't let me have to imagine that Lady Mary is really you.

Damn it. He should have left it alone.

Stella blushed as Lady Mary filled her vision. 'Well, to a degree, I suppose, yes. I'm a woman so I can write a female character from my own experiences. In that respect, in very generic terms, I guess they are.'

Rick breathed easier. She was talking in generalisations. Not specifics. 'So Lucinda isn't you?'

Stella shook her head. 'Well, she's more me than Lady Mary,' she admitted.

Rick felt the tension ooze away completely.

Hah! There. She wasn't Lady Mary.

Phew.

'Lady Mary's from the first book?' he asked innocently.

Stella nodded as her embarrassment slipped away. It was actually quite good thinking this sort of stuff out loud. Knowing the differences could only help with her writing process.

Maybe Rick was a good sounding board?

'Lucinda has a strength of character that Lady Mary didn't. She's not waiting around to be rescued—in fact, she's going to rescue the hero, who's being held in chains.'

Rick tried not to think about how that scene would pan out. 'And Lady Mary is weak?'

Because he'd thought, in her own way, Mary had a startling resilience.

Stella shook her head. 'No, she's not weak, she's just more passive. But that's really just a product of the times and her upper-class background.'

Rick thought of the scene where Mary had finally succumbed to Vasco's seduction. There had been nothing passive about her then. And nothing passive about the way she'd totally turned the emotional tables on him.

'Definitely not you, then,' he smiled, relieved.

Stella smiled back. *If only he knew.* Beneath Lady Mary's petticoats and pantaloons lay Stella's every secret desire. She drained her beer, then checked her watch. 'Right, enough time skiving off. Lucinda is whispering sweet nothings in my head.'

Rick frowned. 'They talk to you?'

'Oh, yes.' Stella nodded. 'Most insistently usually.'

He swallowed. 'The heroes as well as the heroines?'

'Yep.'

Rick's mind boggled. 'What do they say?'

Stella shrugged. 'Their thoughts, dreams, desires.'

Good God—had Lady Mary whispered those things to Stella? Had she told Stella she wanted to see Vasco naked in the bath, that she wanted him to suck her finger into his mouth and she wanted to be tied to his bed?

Or had it been Vasco telling Stella what *he* wanted to do to Mary? Describing it in all the erotic detail that it had appeared in the book?

Had Stella been hearing him in her head?

Rick had never been so happy to see terra firma in all his life when they spotted the Papua New Guinea mainland mid-afternoon. His attempt to dissipate the heat of his thoughts hadn't exactly gone to plan and he was pleased to be getting off the boat and distracting himself for a while.

They motored into Port Moresby harbour and docked at the Royal Papua Yacht Club. After seeing to all the official formalities they headed for the club.

'Remember,' Stella said as Rick smiled at a beautiful dark-skinned woman who openly ogled him as she passed by, 'you're on a dare.'

Rick almost groaned out loud. If he had to share quarters with a woman who wrote sexy literature for a living and dressed in next to nothing, then it was vital to put his flirt somewhere!

The fact that he was now bound to a ridiculous dare was just the really rotten icing on a really sucky cake. What was the world coming to when he couldn't negate some totally inappropriate sexual urges with some harmless flirting?

He smiled at her. 'Piece of cake.'

Stella grinned as she fell in beside him. She was so going to enjoy this!

He tried to ditch her first thing in the cool, modern surrounds of the yacht club, but there was no way she was letting him walk around unaccompanied, flirting with no redress. She stuck to him like glue as he organised refuelling and re-stocking of their fresh food supplies and some onwards paperwork for their visit to Micronesia.

They found a nearby craft market and she watched him get crankier as they moved through the stalls thronging with colour and spice and wall-to-wall gorgeous local women. She asked him his opinion about earrings, bikinis and having her hair plaited. None of which he had a strong opinion on other than exasperation.

She bought a sarong and an anklet that had a tiny shell and a little bell on a piece of rope. It was nautical and she was thrilled with her purchase.

He was plain annoyed.

By the time they'd returned to the boat after an evening meal at the club, he was withdrawn and every inch the brooding pirate.

Due to cloud cover and lack of interest there was no star gazing tonight. Just a strictly professional conversation about their onward leg and a discussion revolving around the weather, which wasn't looking good for the next couple of days, but the long-range forecast remained excellent considering they were in the monsoon season.

'You okay?' she asked innocently as she picked up their empty coffee mugs and padded barefoot towards the galley. 'You seem kind of tense?'

Honestly, the man didn't realise how much his very survival depended on his banter with women—he needed it as if it were oxygen.

'The no flirting getting to you?' she queried, suppressing the humour that bubbled in her chest.

Rick heard the laughter in her voice only on a peripheral level as the tinkle of her anklet obliterated all else.

Great.

As if he weren't conscious enough already of her every movement, he was going to *hear* her every movement as well.

He'd probably hear her at night rolling over in bed.

He plastered a smile to his face. 'I'm fine,' he said. It had only been forty-eight hours, for crying out loud—just how oversexed did she think he was? 'I'm going up on deck to plot the course into the sat nav.'

Stella smiled as he departed. She had this dare nailed.

CHAPTER SIX

ON DECK the humid night was quiet and still, clouds obscuring what would almost be a full moon. Not even a light breeze tinkled the halyards. Faint music drifted down from the yacht club but the moorings were otherwise peaceful. No boats had cabin lights on, no one walked about stopping to chat, no low muffled conversations could be heard.

No one around to witness Rick gently belting his head against the wheel.

When he'd embarked on this voyage everything had been clear cut. *The Mermaid* and Inigo's treasure lay out there somewhere and he and his good friend Stella, *whom he'd known for ever, who despite some disturbing dreams was like a sister to him,* were going to find it.

After all, it was what Nathan had wanted.

Now he had a whole other picture going on in his head and he was damn sure there was nothing brotherly about it.

And definitely *not* what Nathan had wanted.

Nathan hadn't told Rick to leave Stella alone that day he'd caught them almost kissing. But he *had* spoken about how special his daughter was and left Rick in no doubt that he'd wanted someone just as special for Stella. Certainly a bunch of transient deckhands and divers on a motley collection of salvage boats had not measured up to Nathan's expectations in any way, shape or form.

Nathan had wanted for his daughter the one thing he'd never been able to give his own wife—stability.

Someone who was going to be there for her always.

And Nathan had made sure every man in his employ had known that his daughter was off-limits.

Himself included.

But that was then. And this was now.

Nathan was dead. And Stella was all grown up.

She had breasts and hips and an imagination that would make a sailor blush.

How on earth was he supposed to ignore that? Particularly when she was downstairs right now—he could hear that bloody bell all the way up here—prancing around, enjoying herself, feeling all smug at his expense.

And it was only day two.

How nuts would he be by the end of it all?

Hell, how nuts would he be in a week?

Unless…

Rick pulled his head off the steering wheel as the cunning of a certain pirate came to his rescue. He sat ramrod straight.

What if he took control of the situation? Turned the tables on her a little?

What if he were to take some of those tantalising scenes from *Pleasure Hunt* and give them life? He'd already established that she wasn't included in their little dare. Maybe he could have some more fun…

Vasco Ramirez had been determined to make the voyage with Lady Mary a pleasure hunt—maybe he should too?

Of course he'd never step over the line, the bondage scene would have to go begging, but what fun it could be seeing if he could get Stella all het up. After all, those scenes were written by her about him. Maybe he could indulge those fantasies for her just a little, give her a taste of the real thing?

It would be fun to see how she reacted.

Would she guess what he was doing or would she be unaware? Would she reject his boundary pushing or would she embrace it with the abandon with which she'd scribed it?

His gaze fell on the shower at the stern of the boat and he smiled.

Stella was putting the supplies away in the galley when she heard a loud splash outside the porthole in front of her. She frowned as she peered out into the night.

Maybe Rick had thrown himself overboard, the dare just too much?

'Rick?' she called, a smile on her face. No answer. 'Rick?'

Still no answer.

Maybe it was one of Moresby's infamous rascals trying to steal from them and he'd knocked Rick unconscious and into the water.

Her smile died as her heart started hammering in her chest. She reached for the nearest weapon, a heavy-based fry pan, and decided to go up and investigate. She climbed the spiral staircase, one tread at a time, an itch up her spine.

She took a deep breath, then popped her head above the deck line, like a meerkat.

'Rick?' she whispered while her eyes took a second or two to adjust from the bright light below to the low cloud-affected moonlight outside.

Still nothing.

She caught a slight movement towards the helm of the boat as the sound of running water defined itself from the gentle slap of sea against hull and the trilling of insects. She squinted to make out the shape, her vision slowly adjusting to its night capabilities.

It was a person…

A man.

Taking a shower.

Taking a shower?

The moon chose that moment to come out from behind the

scudding clouds that had been hampering its brilliance all night and Stella was afforded a side view of the man standing beneath the shower spray as if someone had switched on a spotlight.

Rick.

A one hundred per cent, buck naked, Rick.

She stood there frozen to the spot for a long moment caught between two impulses. To get out now before he discovered she was staring at his naked body or just stop and take in every magnificent inch.

As the celestial spotlight continued to bathe him in milky brilliance the latter won out.

The shower head was behind him, his head tipped back, his face raised to the night as the spray bathed his shoulder-length locks into a sleek, silky sheath. His eyes were shut as if worshipping the moonbeams that painted him in alabaster.

He looked like a statue. A Michelangelo nude.

With all the beautiful symmetry of fluid muscles and the more subtle details of sinews, tendons and veins in living, breathing relief.

Water sluiced over his broad shoulders, his chest, his biceps. It ran down the planes of his back, following the curve of his spine, dipping into those two sexy dimples above the rise of his buttocks. It flowed down firm flanks and rippled like a waterfall across the defined ridges of his abdomen.

Rivulets of water ran down one powerful thigh pressed slightly forward, the knee bent, obscuring her view any lower, and Stella frowned.

Damn it, so close...

Vasco's bath scene had been written over two years ago, and while a lot of it had been scripted out of her imagination some of it hadn't. Having grown up with Rick wearing barely anything at all—boardies or a skin-tight diving suit being his everyday attire—she'd had plenty of inspiration for Vasco's body and had been able to portray it with startling accuracy.

There had been some parts, however, that she'd had to… embellish.

It would be nice to know the truth of it. Had her fevered imaginings accurately represented *all* of Vasco or had it been pure whimsy on her behalf?

And then, as if he'd read her mind, he shifted, twisting his body slightly in her direction, straightening his bent knee and transferring his weight to his other thigh, and she no longer had to wonder if she'd got it right because the evidence that she had was right there.

Riccardo Granville was most definitely Vasco Ramirez in the flesh.

Rick turned so his back was to Stella and smiled to himself as he tilted his neck from side to side, letting the lukewarm water run over muscle that was surprisingly tense. The concentration it had taken to appear unselfconscious and relaxed, as if he were alone and being unwatched, had been much harder to carry off than he'd thought. But to see Stella's head pop up and then feel her avid gaze on him as tangible as the water cascading from the shower head had made the exercise worthwhile.

He was back in control again and that was exactly the way he liked it. Even if he was playing games with someone he had no business playing games with.

But if she was going to secretly put him in a book and not expect him to have a bit of fun with that then she'd completely forgotten about his devilish sense of humour.

As long as he kept it light and remembered who she was—Nathan's daughter, not a single, fully grown woman who wrote dirty books—and where the line was, it would work out just fine.

They'd both have a laugh at the end of the voyage and get on with their lives.

It was win-win as far as he was concerned.

* * *

The second Stella strained to see that birthmark she'd been fascinated with since she'd been five years old she knew that happenstance had turned into voyeurism. She forced herself to cease and desist. With one long last lingering look at possibly the most beautiful rear end in the world, certainly in historical romance fiction, she slunk back down below deck, fry pan still in hand.

She should feel guilty; she knew that. If the positions had been reversed she'd have been mortified. But strangely she didn't. No harm had been committed. He didn't know that she'd been watching him or that he'd just fulfilled a particularly potent fantasy of hers—so potent she'd put it in a book!—and she certainly wasn't going to tell him!

But she would use it.

Late at night when a day of crafting sensual tension or a torrid love scene left her restless and achy and the dictates of her body would not be ignored, a naked Rick bathed in shower spray and moonbeams would come in handy.

Very handy indeed.

Vasco examined the milky white perfection of Lady Mary's hand. He cradled it in the palm of his much bigger, much darker one and admired the contrast for a moment. This was what they'd look like in his bed, their limbs entwined, their stomachs pressed together— coconut and coffee.

He stroked his thumb down the length of her index finger where the long slither of wood had embedded itself and let it drift across her palm. He heard the slight intake of her breath and felt her resistance to his hold.

He looked up into her emerald eyes. 'It's not as bad as it looks,' he murmured.

Mary swallowed. They were seated, her knees primly together beneath her skirts, his legs spread wide in that lord-of-all-he-surveyed way of his, bracketing hers. The fabric of his breeches pulled taut across his thighs as he leaned in over her hand, his head perilously close to her cleavage.

'It really just needs a pair of tweezers,' she said, trying to pull her hand back. He resisted and she resigned herself to the unsettling heat of his touch.

Vasco smiled at her, her pink mouth a tempting bow before him. 'I think I can do better than that.'

His voice was low and silky and Mary felt it in places that she'd only recently, thanks to him, become aware of. Her green gaze locked with the startling blue of his as he raised her finger to his mouth and sucked it inside.

Vasco watched surprise pucker her mouth into a cute little O shape as her pupils dilated. Her breathing was loud in the space between them as she lowered her gaze to where his mouth tasted her. He felt a half-hearted attempt to pull away again but countered it by laving her finger with long strokes of his tongue.

Her whimper went straight to his groin.

Mary felt the throb ease as Vasco ministered to her wound in this most unusual fashion. Her gaze returned to his, finding him watching her with something in those mesmerising eyes she couldn't fathom. She didn't know what it was but she did know she'd seen it there before.

And it was both dangerous and enticing.

Still holding her gaze, Vasco slowly withdrew his lips, his teeth seeking and finding the rough end of the splinter burrowed in at the tip. He nipped at it until he held it firmly, then slowly eased it out, her glistening finger slipping from his mouth altogether. For a moment he held the liberated splinter between his teeth, then turned his head and spat it on the floor.

He smiled as he turned back to face her. 'That's better,' he murmured.

Mary couldn't move. Her finger or anything else for

that matter. She just sat there, hand still in his, finger moist from his ministrations, staring at his mouth. A mouth that had turned her insides to jelly.

'Th-thank you,' she stammered, belatedly remembering her manners.

Vasco lowered his head to her finger again, and pressed a gentle lingering kiss to the exit wound.

He grinned. 'My pleasure.'

Mary felt a sudden urge to call for smelling salts.

After a restless sleep Stella wasn't in any hurry to look Rick in the eye for the first time since her voyeurism of last night. She'd gone straight to her quarters after her little peeping Tom episode, thus avoiding him altogether.

But she couldn't stay in her cabin for ever and it wasn't as if he knew that she'd spied on him. All she had to do was not blush and stammer when she greeted him and pretty soon the awkwardness would pass.

The memory would be emblazoned on her frontal lobe for ever but the awkwardness would pass!

'Hey,' she said to Rick as she wandered into the galley fifteen minutes later. He was sitting at the dining table poring over charts. Fully clothed. She looked away as he looked up at her.

Rick forced himself not to smile like a Cheshire cat, but just give a normal everyday *hey* kind of a smile. Which was kind of difficult when greeted with another pair of brief shorts and some kind of strapless shirt, leaving her shoulders bare and her cleavage…enhanced.

'Morning,' he said. You s*aucy little pervert in barely any clothes.* 'Sleep well?'

He assumed she'd had a pretty fitful sleep if that damn bell jingling was anything to go by.

Stella steeled herself to look at him again and gave a noncommittal shrug. 'Fine,' she murmured.

Rick stifled a smile as she looked away. *Liar.* Good, now they were even. Between the damn book, that silly little bell and an array of teeny tiny clothes, sleep had become a rare commodity.

'You were in bed early last night,' he mused, because he just couldn't resist teasing her a little as she had done over their flirting bet last night. 'Everything okay?'

Stella's breath hitched as she popped two pieces of bread in the toaster. 'Fine,' she replied, her gaze planted firmly on the job at hand.

Rick suppressed a chuckle at her monosyllabic replies. He'd have loved to tease her some more, hell he could have done it all day, but the weather wasn't the best out there and they should be getting under way.

He picked up his plate and glass and headed towards the galley, squeezing behind her to get to the sink. He felt her stiffen a little as he caught a whiff of browning toast and co-conut. Her hair sat in a messy ponytail on top of her head, leaving her neck exposed, and he had the craziest urge to slip his arms around her waist and nuzzle into it.

He stepped away from the temptation—teasing her was one thing, acting as if they'd set up house was another. He placed his plate in the sink and downed the last of his orange juice in one gulp. 'It's going to be a bit choppy out there today so I'll get us under way,' he said.

'Fine,' Stella said again, keeping rigidly still until he'd safely disappeared up the stairs. When the toast popped thirty seconds later she realised she'd been staring out of the port-hole thinking about him naked.

Oh, brother! Would she ever be able to act normally around him again?

As it turned out Rick was fully engaged in keeping control of the boat in the worsening swell so there was no time for conversation, awkward or otherwise. The sky was grey and the wind was brisk, keeping him on his toes. It was far from dangerous but it did require his attention.

She sat up front and worked on her laptop for a bit, but trying to type with the horizon undulating drunkenly played havoc with her equilibrium and wasn't very productive. Even reading through her previous day's work for editing purposes proved impossible to her constitution.

Stella had always possessed an excellent set of sea legs but they'd obviously become rusty from lack of use as nausea sat like a lead sinker in her stomach.

Which at least wiped away the images of Rick showering in the moonlight.

She gave up on the book, shutting her laptop lid.

'Do you want to go down and make sure everything's secured properly below deck?' Rick called out an hour later as she sat very still, keeping her gaze fixed on the horizon, and concentrated on deep breathing.

Stella stood. Good idea. Something to do to keep her mind off the unsettling up and down of the boat.

It started to rain lightly as she passed him and she shivered as the breeze cooled the water droplets on her skin. He'd taken his shirt off at some stage and his chest was speckled with sea spray.

It reminded her of the way water droplets had clung to his naked skin last night and she wondered if they were cool on his skin too. Whether they tasted of salt or of man.

Or some heady mix of both.

If she hadn't felt so rough, she might have been tempted to try. 'Do you want your spray jacket?' she asked, not quite meeting his eyes.

Rick nodded, examining her face. It had gone from pale to white as the sail billowing above their heads. 'Thanks. You okay?' he asked. 'The bureau says it'll only last for another couple of hours.'

Stella gripped the leather back of the high captain's chair

where his butt was parked. He looked totally in his element. Calm and confident. Relishing the inclement weather even, as if it were nothing more than a sun shower. Stella nodded. 'I'm fine.'

He grinned at her, his long hair blowing behind him in true pirate fashion. 'There are some sea sickness pills in the cupboard above the sink,' he offered.

'I'm fine,' she lied.

Rick laughed. 'There's a lot of that going on today.'

Stella was sure if her cheeks weren't so cool they'd be heating up nicely. 'I practically grew up on a boat.'

Rick shrugged. 'Just saying…'

She went below deck and checked every room, securing any items that were lying around. She grabbed her spray jacket and pulled Rick's off the hook on the back of his door and headed to the galley, finding a couple of cans of soup and emptying them into a saucepan. The boat rolled to the side as she placed it over the element and her stomach lurched.

Damn it.

She reached above the sink and threw back two of the little blue pills, praying they'd work in a hurry.

She stood over the soup as it heated, shifting her weight from leg to leg with the motion of the boat. When it was done she puréed it, poured it into thermal mugs, cut off thick chunks of bread from the loaf they'd bought yesterday and loaded it all onto a tray. She shrugged into her jacket and folded his over her arm.

By the time she rejoined him fifteen minutes after taking the anti-emetic she was actually feeling markedly better.

'Thanks,' Rick said, relieving her of the tray and quickly shrugging into the jacket.

She could see water droplets clinging to his eyelashes and spattering his bronzed chest. Just as the shower spray had done last night.

She dragged her eyes away. Must not *think about the shower*.

'Hmm, this is good,' Rick said, watching her face as two pink spots appeared on her pale cheeks. 'I think I'll keep you.'

Stella's gaze flicked to his, to the teasing light in his pirate eyes. Two could play at that game. 'I think I'll let you,' she murmured.

Rick cocked an eyebrow, surprised at her easy comeback, then chuckled. He warmed his hands around the mug, taking another sip of the rich, fragrant pea and ham soup. 'Weather's easing up.'

Stella looked out at the lurching ocean. 'It is?'

He chuckled some more. 'You've become such a landlubber. Can't you feel it beneath your soles?'

Stella felt the laugh reach right inside her and warm her from the inside out. She guessed she had. 'No, Captain Ahab, I can't.'

'Ah, Moby Dick, my favourite book,' he teased, because he knew how much Stella hated it.

She rolled her eyes at him. 'You've never read it.'

'I have,' he protested.

'When?'

'When you dared me to,' he said.

Stella frowned at him, thinking back through the mists of time to that long-ago summer dare. 'I was twelve.'

She'd been going through a classics phase and also trying to read anything nautical to connect with her father, to try and understand why he'd loved the sea more than her mother.

It hadn't helped.

'I never back down on a dare. Besides, I liked it.'

Not as much as the hot pirate sex in Pleasure Hunt...

They had a discussion about its merits while they finished off their lunch and even Stella felt the sea was calmer by the time she reloaded their tray. The wind had definitely dropped. The sprinkling rain had stopped and they shrugged out of their jackets. A bare bicep brushed against her shoulder as he threw his jacket over the back of his chair and she shut her eyes briefly as heat licked at the point of contact.

'I'll get rid of these,' she said briskly, pulling away from him.

Rick watched her go, her hips full and round and swinging enticingly as her gait compensated for the lurch of the boat. Hips that had appeared one summer along with the bra and, no matter how much he'd tried to ignore them in his day-to-day dealings with her, they'd been right there in his fevered teenage dreams.

A sudden gust of wind caused the boat to roll to the side and he watched as she shimmied to counteract the swell. He smiled, admiring the move until he realised she'd overbalanced and was going down.

'Stella!' he called as he sprang from his chair.

Too late. The boat had thrown her sideways and Stella hit the deck hard on her left upper arm, the tray flying as she extended her other hand to buffer the impact, skidding as she grabbed at the wood for purchase.

'Stella,' Rick called again as he threw himself down beside her inert crumpled body, his heart hammering. 'Stella? Are you okay?'

Stella groaned. She couldn't think for the pain in her left arm.

Rick touched her arm, trying to roll her over. 'Stella?'

She moaned and he stopped. 'I'm okay, I'm okay,' she panted. 'Just give me a second.'

'Where are you hurt?' he asked.

'Arm,' she said after a moment. 'Hand.' She looked up at him through her fringe. 'Dignity.'

Rick laughed, relieved that she couldn't be too badly hurt if her sense of humour was still intact. 'Do you think anything's broken?'

Stella zeroed in on the pain in her upper arm where she'd

fallen the hardest. It had initially been excruciating but the intensity had eased quickly. It only felt as if a brick had fallen on it now as opposed to a cement column.

'Let me help you up,' he offered.

Stella acquiesced with a brief nod of her head. With both arms hurting like blazes, she had no idea how she was even going to get up. Rick grabbed her around the waist and gently pulled her into a sitting position. His big warm body was behind hers and for a moment she was so relieved she wasn't destined to spend for ever spread on the deck like a stranded beetle she sagged against him and shut her eyes.

Rick rubbed his cheek against her hair, the scent of coconuts filling his nostrils. He picked up her right hand. The knuckles were grazed and the middle three finger pads were bleeding with splinters embedded in each one.

He tried really hard not to think about Lady Mary and her splinter, but with Stella all warm and pliant against him, smelling like a pina colada, it was hard not to go there.

'Nasty,' he murmured, anticipation already building in his gut, knowing that he was the one who would take them out. Kiss those fingers better just as Vasco had. 'How's your arm? Can you move it?'

Stella gingerly rotated her shoulder. 'Bloody sore,' she bitched.

He smiled into her hair. 'What about your dignity?'

Her arm throbbed and she couldn't even rub it with her opposite hand because it throbbed as well. And was bleeding to boot. 'Unrecoverable, I should imagine.'

He chuckled. 'Nah. You really fell very gracefully.'

'Oh, goody,' she said dryly. 'A critique.'

He laughed again. 'Come on. Let's get you down below and have a look at you.'

'I bet you say that to all the girls,' she muttered.

Stella blinked as the snappy rejoinder loaded with innuendo slipped from her mouth. What the?

He laughed some more. 'Just the ones who fall at my feet.'

Rick helped her up. The boat rolled again slightly and he grabbed her waist and her good arm to steady her as she wobbled against him. He sucked in a breath as, for a moment, every part of her from her soft breasts to her round hips was pressed against him.

He took a step back as his body leapt to life. 'You've got your sea legs?' he asked.

Stella nodded. 'Sorry 'bout that.'

'No worries.' He shrugged. 'Why don't you go on down? I'll fix a few things up here and then I'll join you.'

Stella, despite the throb in her arm and the sting in her fingers, was still stuck back in that moment.

She nodded her head dumbly.

No dignity anywhere in sight!

When Rick joined her half an hour later she'd recovered sufficiently to have taken some painkillers, located the first-aid kit, washed her hand in the sink and was sitting at the table valiantly trying to dig the splinters out. But trying to do it left-handed was a slow enough process without being hampered by a restricted range of movement from the soft tissue damage inflicted by the fall up higher, near her shoulder.

Rick shoved his hands on his hips. 'What are you doing?' he asked.

Stella, who had made more of a mess through pricking herself, was not in the best of moods. It really didn't help that he looked all hot and sexy in that shirtless way of his.

'What do you think?' she demanded. 'I'm trying to get the splinters out.'

Rick smiled down at the petulant set to her mouth. *Oh, goody, this was going to be fun.*

'Here,' he said, scooting her along the bench seat as he moved in beside her. 'Let me.' Rick held out his hand. When she didn't comply he gave her an impatient look. 'Stella?'

Stella was in a quandary as the scene she'd written for *Pleasure Hunt* looked as if it too was about to play out. Well, the G-rated version of it anyway.

She couldn't imagine Rick sucking her fingers into his mouth. Well...she could. And she had. She'd even written it down.

But that was Vasco.

Rick could almost read the thoughts in her very expressive eyes. She was torn between medical necessity and curiosity. 'You don't want them to fester, do you?' he asked innocently.

Stella swallowed as she offered him her palm, hoping that she was submitting purely on medical grounds but knowing there were other less sensible, less pure reasons.

She just prayed he never read her book.

Her palm was warm in his as Rick took an antiseptic swab and cleaned up the site so he had a clearer field of vision. This close, like Vasco, he could see Stella's mouth and the way her teeth dug into her bottom lip.

He raised an eyebrow. 'You ready for this?' he asked.

Stella doubted she'd ever be ready for Rick being this close, his sea-salt-and-ocean-spray aroma wrapping her in a hundred childhood memories that warred with the very adult visions of him naked beneath a shower.

'I promise I'll be gentle,' he murmured.

Stella rolled her eyes at the amused glitter in his tropical gaze. The only way she was going to survive being the sole focus of his stymied flirting reflex was to give as good as she got. 'Maybe I don't like it gentle.'

Rick's heart thunked hard in his chest as he pulled back a little in surprise. She had her eyebrow raised and a small smile playing on her lips.

She was flirting back.

He chuckled. It had been a long time since they'd traded banter like this. It made his plan that much more enticing.

As Vasco had, he ducked his head and leaned over her

hand. Given that his deck was much more polished than that of a pirate ship from the seventeen hundreds, the splinters were much smaller than the one Mary had embedded in her finger. Certainly they were not removable by his teeth and it took some time digging them out.

She didn't whimper or complain although Rick looked up at one stage and she had her eyes shut and face screwed up. Their legs brushed intermittently beneath the table, their upper bodies were almost touching, his head was level with her cleavage and he wondered what she'd do if he claimed that long-awaited kiss early.

Find out if her mouth tasted as sweet as it looked. If it really did taste like coconuts.

Stella opened her eyes and caught him looking at her. Her breath caught in her throat. 'What?' she asked.

Rick took a moment or two to answer. Then he shook his head and said, 'Nothing,' and returned to his ministration, his hand not quite as steady.

Another ten minutes saw the job done. 'There now,' he announced to her closed eyes. 'Isn't that better?'

Stella looked down at her hand, the splinters gone from the pads of her fingers, his thumb lightly brushing her palm— just as Vasco's had done. The instinct to shut her eyes and allow her body to feel the caress everywhere warred with her guilt about indulging another Vasco fantasy with an unsuspecting Rick.

It made her crazy.

And the pain made her bitchy.

'No,' she said testily. 'It bloody hurts, actually.'

Rick felt her trying to withdraw her hand from his but he resisted her attempt, knowing it was too good an opportunity to pass up. 'Fine,' he sighed, 'I'll just have to kiss them better.'

It took a moment for his intention to register and another moment for Stella to open her mouth and lodge a protest. But by then it was too late. He was lifting her fingers to his mouth, holding her gaze as he did so. Her protest stuttered to an inarticulate gurgle as his lips briefly brushed over first one fingertip, then the next. When he got to the third her eyes widened as she felt his tongue press against the pad, laving the wound gently before his lips met then slowly withdrew.

She made some noise at the back of her throat that sounded foreign in the charged atmosphere between them.

It might have been a whimper.

'There,' he said huskily, her dilated pupils not only doing funny things to his groin, but deep inside his chest too. 'Is that better?'

She wanted to shake her head, tell him no. That they burned. That he'd set them on fire. But she was only capable of a nod. A very weak nod.

'Good,' Rick said with difficulty as her mouth hovered so very close and that line became even hazier.

My pleasure.

CHAPTER SEVEN

Lady Mary sat awkwardly on the chair placed in the middle of the sun-drenched deck, conscious of the crew's barely concealed curiosity.

'You'll have to lean back,' Vasco said from behind her.

Mary turned slightly, catching him in her peripheral vision. 'Really, I don't think this is necessary,' she protested primly, her hands folded in her lap.

Vasco placed his hand on her shoulder, urging her back. 'The lady wishes to wash her hair. What the lady wants, the lady gets.'

Mary submitted to the pressure of his hand and turned to face the front again. 'I am perfectly capable of washing my own hair, Captain Ramirez.'

Vasco leaned down, his lips near her ear, inhaling the floral scent of her, so utterly female in this all-male environment. 'Ah, but where would the fun be in that, Mary?'

He smiled at her slight intake of breath at his familiarity. 'Undo your hair,' he ordered in a low whisper. 'Lie back.'

Mary felt her nipples pebble against the fabric of her chemise at the deep vein of risqué in the low command. Another protest rose to her lips but she stifled it. In her week on the ship she'd learned that the Spanish captain always got what he wanted.

And her hair really did need a wash.

Her fingers trembled as she pulled out the pins that secured her hair in an elaborate up do, one by one. She could hear her own breath loud in her ears as he towered above her. When it was all released she shook it out, then furrowed her fingers into the back of the curly mass to loosen any recalcitrant strands.

She became aware that the low chatter from the crew had stopped and she was the object of their blatant attention. 'Captain,' she said, feeling suddenly breathless, 'your men are staring.'

Vasco couldn't blame them. Her hair was like a Titan masterpiece, a flaming torch beneath the blazing sun burnishing the highlights into strands of golden thread.

He gently picked up a long spiral curl from her shoulder and pulled it out to its full length before letting it go, watching it recoil against the scarlet fabric of her frock.

'It's not often they see a woman of such beauty, madam.'

'I would prefer they did not,' she said, reaching for just the right amount of haughty as the low, almost reverent compliment unsettled her.

Vasco preferred they did not as well and he barked some orders at them, more than satisfied with the immediate response.

'Thank you,' Mary murmured as a dozen or so crew got back to their jobs.

'What the lady wants...'

He looked down at her crowning glory and imagined how it would look spread over the milky skin of her breasts. What would she want when he was looking at her like that?

For she would soon be his.

'Tip your head back.'

The command was betrayed by the roughness of his

voice and he expected her to object yet again. When she acquiesced without dissent, her hair falling over the back of the chair in a soft red wave, his anticipation built another notch. It had been many months since he'd last had a woman. And never in all his eight and twenty years had he ever had a creature so stunningly beautiful.

He picked up the bucket and poured the water slowly onto her hair, distributing it evenly, watching as the curls became drenched and the whole glorious mass darkened into a lustrous sheath of the finest satin. The excess pooled around his boots but didn't register as an errant droplet captured his gaze. It trickled onto her forehead and began a slow descent down her face, running over a closed eyelid, down one creamy cheek until it reached her mouth, where her tongue darted out, sipping it up.

Vasco almost threw the bucket down and lowered his mouth to claim those moist, upturned lips on the spot. The desire to kiss her, to ravage that tempting mouth, had been building for days. But even through the savage haze of lust that had set a raging inferno in his loins he knew that she wasn't ready. That the dance wasn't yet complete.

So he picked up the soap and rubbed it over the sodden silky layers. Then he dropped it into the bucket and let his hands take over.

Mary almost moaned as Vasco's hands furrowed into her hair, the pads of his fingers rubbing with sensual ease against her scalp. Her nipples and belly tightened. Goose flesh broke out everywhere. Quite why she had no idea, given she was hotter than she'd ever been.

The sun no doubt.

Nothing to do with his gaze, which she knew without having to open her eyes lay heavily on the pulse drumming a frantic tattoo at the base of her neck.

'How's that?' he murmured.

At some level, Mary knew she should be contained in her reply but the drugging magic of his touch, the aroma of lavender and chives and the warmth of the sun were addling her senses. 'Amazing,' she breathed and Vasco chuckled.

At home this would have been her maid's job, and it would never have felt this...decadent.

And Vasco certainly was nobody's servant.

Her aunt would have an attack of the vapours if she could see the pirate laying his hands on her niece in such a familiar fashion. But Mary, for one, was giving herself up to the experience as she angled her head down to allow him access to where hair met nape.

Vasco's soapy fingers massaged her hairline, dipping down to rub the back of her neck, and he swallowed as a sigh escaped her lips. He noticed how her hands clenched and unclenched the fabric at her lap, the agitated press of her cleavage against the prison of her neckline, and sensed she was feeling things she'd never before experienced.

He worked his way back up to her temples, slowly stroking her there, working his way down to the shell of her ear, drifting his thumb across its ridges, smiling as he heard the rough inward drag of her breath.

He leaned down, replacing his fingers with his lips. 'You are very beautiful, Mary.'

Mary opened her eyes as his words slithered like the serpent into every cell in her body. A dozen retorts came to mind. He should not be talking to her like this. But with his hands creating havoc and her body craving something she didn't understand only one thing came to her lips. She turned her head slightly, their mouths closer than was decent.

'So are you, Vasco, so are you.'
    For he was, quite simply, the most beautiful man
she'd ever seen.

AFTER two more days of similar weather they finally had a calm, sunny day and Stella was able to get out on deck, where she felt most inspired, to do some more writing.

Which was just as well because she was going totally stir crazy.

She'd spent a lot of time down below during the inclement weather, trying to type two-fingered in between doses of pain-killers as her arm swelled up and the bruising came out. Rick, worried that she'd broken her humerus, had wanted to turn back and get her some medical help but Stella had refused.

Yes, she'd fallen heavily and yes, the pain had increased since the swelling and bruising had come out, but she'd broken her radius a few years ago and her current pain was nothing like how excruciating that had been.

She was sure she hadn't broken it. She'd assured him all she needed was a few days for the swelling to go down and she'd be back to normal.

But in the meantime, even the most basic things had been difficult and she was cranky and out of sorts with her limited abilities. Rick, in true Vasco fashion, had gallantly offered to help her dress and bathe, which she declined not quite in the same spirit it was offered.

So she'd battled on by herself, making do with quick showers and dressing in sarongs that required minimal arm lift. More complicated things like shaving her legs and washing her hair seemed like distant luxuries.

It was most frustrating on the writing front. The words were flowing in her head but she just couldn't get them down quick enough and the grazed knuckles and sore finger pads of her right hand made typing slow and laborious. Every twenty minutes she'd had to stop and let her left hand take over, but it caused the throbbing to increase up higher and after about ten minutes she had to take a break.

So, it felt good indeed to have the sun on her face and the feel of a calm ocean beneath her feet again and for the first half hour they got under way she just sat in her low chair with her face turned to the sun, soaking it up.

But it was all downhill from the moment she opened her laptop. It didn't take long for her mood to evaporate as her useless fingers, despite the absolutely exhilarating day, made a hard slog of the writing process. And when her arm started to throb half an hour into the process she shut the lid of the laptop in disgust.

It had felt really good this morning too. The bruising was fading to a greeny-yellow and the swelling had reduced by about half. She could even lift her bent arm almost level with her shoulder before discomfort forced her to stop.

'You okay?'

She turned to see Rick coming up behind her, taking full advantage of the glorious weather by once again going shirtless. She winced as the sudden movement wrenched through her arm. 'Fine,' she said morosely as she blew her fringe out of her eyes on a huffed breath.

Even it was annoying her. It was strawy and scratchy from the rigors of sea salt and the tangling effect of ocean breezes. Conscious of needing to save water on a boat, she hadn't washed it since they'd left Cairns.

Rick chuckled as he sat beside her. 'You don't seem fine.' He laughed again at her responding scowl. 'Come on, what's up? Tell Uncle Rick.'

'The words are coming but my useless fingers can't type them fast enough.'

'I could type them,' he offered. 'You can dictate them to me.' He smiled at her. 'It'll be just like Barbara Cartland.'

Stella rolled her eyes. No way in the world was she ever going to let him anywhere near Lucinda and Inigo.

Rick grinned. 'I'll take that as a no, then. What else?'

'My arm hurts,' she said, aware that it could be interpreted as whining. 'And my head is as itchy as hell because it hasn't been washed in for ever and I can't even scratch it because my fingers are too sore.'

For a moment Rick couldn't believe his luck. He'd read the scene where Vasco washed Lady Mary's hair about a dozen times. He let his gaze run idly over her hair, chunks of it escaping a poorly placed plastic claw. 'Well, now, that *is* something I can help with,' he said, very matter-of-fact.

She glared at him. 'Offering to help me shower was not funny the first time,' Stella said grouchily.

'Oh, I don't know.' Rick shrugged. 'I kind of thought it was but,' he said, holding up his hand to still the protest about to come out of her mouth, 'I didn't mean that. I'll wash it up here, on deck.' He grinned at her. 'You'll be fully clothed, I promise.'

Stella stilled as the implications of his offer slowly sank in. Another Vasco and Mary moment. She searched his tropical blue gaze for a spark of recognition. Something that told her he knew what he was offering was far from innocent. He looked back at her with the same clear, blue-eyed brilliance as always.

She chewed on her lip as the idea teased at her conscience. 'What…you mean with a…bucket?' she asked.

Rick bit the inside of his cheek as he struggled to stay deadpan for her searching gaze. He returned her interest with his best I-have-no-idea-what-you're-talking-about look. 'No…' He pointed to the stern on the boat. 'With the shower.'

She turned gingerly this time to take in the metallic head under which she'd watched him shower the other night. Her cheeks heated as the illicit image revisited.

Rick decided to leap on her indecision and take charge, giving her no quarter. The boat was on autopilot and it was clear sailing today. 'You head on over, I'll get your shampoo. It's in your en suite, yes?'

Stella nodded dumbly, sitting in her chair unmoving, as Rick disappeared. Could she indulge herself for a third time? This voyage was turning into some kind of hedonistic exploration of her fantasies.

It was…immoral, surely?

Debauched, certainly.

Rick came back on deck and smiled to see her still sitting in the same spot, indecision on her face. 'Come on,' he called. 'I don't have all day.'

Stella turned to look at his naked back as he headed towards the stern. She stood automatically to his command, dragging her chair with her. He looked so much like Vasco when she reached him, her conscience piqued.

'I don't think this is a good idea.'

Rick doubted he'd ever heard a more feeble protest and knew he was going to have to hold her hand on this one.

'Are you crazy? It's a brilliant idea. The sun is out, there's a light breeze, it'll dry quickly. And as there's nothing I can do about your arm or help with your writing, you should let me do this.'

Plus, you want to.

He took the chair out of her unprotesting fingers and placed it under the shower head, busying himself with finding the right position. By the time he was done she seemed to have resigned herself to a little piece of *Pleasure Hunt*. She sat when he asked her and even snuggled down low in her chair so just her neck and shoulders were exposed above the canvas and her head could tilt back easily over the edge.

Of course that bent her sarong-clad body into a banana shape with her feet flat on the deck, her thighs bent before him like an offering from the gods. Thighs that her sarong fell away from, leaving them exposed to his view. Not skinny. Firm, rounded like her and smooth with the beginnings of a tan tinting the formerly milky skin.

He turned the water on and doused himself with it first before removing the hand-held head from its cradle, kneeling behind her and directing the spray at her hair. She startled slightly and he swallowed as he noticed her nipples pucker beneath the sarong. 'Too cold?'

Stella reined in her heartbeat as his hand sifted through her hair, wishing she could rein in her other bodily responses as easily. 'No. Just wasn't expecting it.'

'Sorry,' he said, his gaze fixed on the two round points tenting the fabric at her chest. 'Should have warned you.'

Should have warned myself.

He might have been doing this as a tease but he hadn't been immune to that hair-washing scene and already he could feel a tightening in his groin.

Stella shut her eyes tight as his hand sifted and lifted and caressed every strand of her hair to ensure it was waterlogged. His fingers occasionally brushed against her scalp and she squeezed her thighs together as the sensation seemed to travel straight to a point between her legs.

Like acupuncture. Or reflexology.

Whatever…he'd definitely found her sweet spot.

Rick flicked the taps off, determinedly dragging his gaze away from her thighs and nipples and fixing it on her hair, on the job at hand, determined not to get carried away by it.

She was supposed to be turned into a panting mess—not him.

'Shampoo now,' he said as he squirted a healthy dollop into his palm and a waft of coconut—of her—hit him square in the solar plexus. It was like liquid silk in his hands and he spread it over her sodden hair evenly before he started to rub it into a lather with the flat of his palms.

Stella almost sighed at his touch. His movements were brisk at first, but after a few moments they changed, became slower, more defined, the tips of his fingers dragging with languorous subtlety against her scalp. She felt the motion right down to her toes and all the hot spots in between.

Every cell went on high alert. Her back arched involuntarily as she bit back a whimper. The pain in her arm and the sting in her fingers floated away on a sexual high.

Shampoo foamed between Rick's fingers as he watched her shift restlessly in the chair. The image of him sliding his soapy hands onto her shoulders, over her chest, pushing the sarong down off her breasts and lathering them up, teasing the nipples into taut peaks until she orgasmed hit him out of the blue and the tightness became something more.

He was harder than the wood beneath his knees.

He needed to distract himself fast. 'You always had gorgeous hair,' he murmured as the thickness of it filled his palms. He remembered diving with her when they'd been kids and being mesmerised by the way her hair streamed behind her as she swam or floated around her like a crown when she stopped. He'd dreamt of it often during his teenage years. 'Just like that mermaid you always wanted to be.'

Good. That was good.

Reminding himself of why it would be a very bad idea to lean over as Vasco had also wanted to do and ravage her mouth.

Because they were friends. Long-term friends.

He was just having some fun.

Stella opened her eyes, thinking back to those days when she'd truly believed in the imaginary world they'd created. Instead of having to create this faux fantasy life to keep that connection alive.

'Everything was so simple back then,' she murmured.

Rick nodded. Back then he'd been plain Rick, she'd been Nathan's daughter and hadn't had breasts and hips. Now he was Vasco Ramirez, Nathan was dead and she had breasts, hips and a lot of other bits in between.

She bent her head forward, just as Lady Mary had done and he obliged, caressing her hairline, drifting his thumbs over her nape, going lower, kneading his fingers into the muscles of her neck and lower still to her shoulders.

'Mmm,' she groaned. 'That feels good.'

She couldn't help herself, it just tumbled out. Because it did feel good, it felt so damn good *everywhere* she wanted to turn around and French him as she almost had all those years ago, and decades of being buddies and business partners and all those other consequences be damned.

Rick swallowed. 'That's because you're so tense,' he said lightly, feeling pretty damn tense himself but working on the knots in her neck muscles until he had them all ironed out because she kept making these little gurgly noises at the back of her throat that he could really become addicted to.

By the time they were gone and he'd forced himself to turn on the spray he had an erection that could have been used on Vasco's pirate ship as the plank for prisoners to walk to their doom upon.

For his own sanity, he tried to make the conditioning process much faster but pretty much failed. She had her hands stuffed between her thighs and he spent the whole time wondering if she really was just holding her sarong in place or maybe easing a little ache down there.

His imaginings had gone from lathering her breasts to his head disappearing between those amazing thighs and he was fit to burst when he left her, hair brushed and drying off, in the sunshine.

'Thank you,' she called after his disappearing back.

Rick gave her a wave, not turning around because he looked perfectly indecent at the moment and probably would be for quite a while with her squirmy, back-archy thing imprinted on his retinas. 'My pleasure,' he murmured quietly to himself as he descended below deck as quickly as his legs would carry him.

* * *

At midnight Rick gave up trying to sleep and trudged up to the deck to lie under the stars for a while. They'd always had a calming effect and he needed that badly at the moment, when his body was raging with undiluted lust and no amount of diversion tactics seemed to be working.

The ocean was still and the night almost silent as he made his way to the middle of the deck. He could barely feel the bob of the boat beneath his back and his breath was loud in his head. The waning moon threw a narrow beam of light on the surface of the gently rippling water as it fought for space in the crowded sky.

He lay with his knees bent and took a deep steadying breath.

Now, *this* made sense.

Stella and what happened to him every time he looked at her didn't make sense at all.

But this—the ocean—did.

This was like coming home.

He remembered turning up at Dartmouth at the age of fifteen, a rucksack on his back and four pounds in his pocket. He'd hitched from London the previous day. Nathan had looked at him from the deck of the *Persephone* and said, 'Sophia's been on the phone to me.'

He'd looked at Nathan with mutiny in his eyes. He'd loved his grandmother, but she hadn't understood that the ocean ran in his veins. She'd wanted him to study hard and go to university and all he'd wanted was a sea breeze in his hair. He'd chafed against her bonds. Cut classes. Flunked out.

'I'm not going back. This is where I belong.'

Nathan had looked at him for long moments. 'It's not the glamorous life it seems on summer break or from your father's grandiose sea stories, Rick. You should be in school.'

He'd shaken his head. He'd always known from Nathan's quiet restraint that his father's embellishments were romantic sentimentality and that there wasn't a lot of romance or sentiment in salvaging. He'd learned early it was ninety-nine per cent grunt, one per cent glory. 'I should be here. The business is half mine.'

They'd both known that Rick didn't legally inherit until he was of age but Nathan hadn't called him on it.

'That it is. But are you man enough?'

Rick had nodded his head firmly. 'Yes, sir.'

Nathan had crossed his arms. 'You come on board, you answer to me.'

'Aye, aye, captain.'

'And you finish school.' Nathan had raised his hand at the objections that had been about to tumble from Rick's mouth. 'A man knows the importance of education, Rick.' He'd shoved a hand on his hip and said, 'Take it or leave it.'

Rick had bristled at the harshness of it when he'd reluctantly agreed and had done his lessons by correspondence with less than good grace, but he'd been grateful for the many years that Nathan had forced his hand.

It hadn't been until years later that he'd found out Nathan and Sophia had done a deal while he'd been hitching his way to Dartmouth. Nathan had promised to look after Rick and see that he finished school and Sophia had agreed to loosen the reins she'd held on her stubborn grandson.

Nathan had had the utmost respect for Rick's Spanish grandmother, who had selflessly taken care of him when her daughter, Carmela's, tempestuous love affair with Anthony Granville had finished and neither had known what to do with a toddler. Rick knew now that if Sophia had demanded that Nathan bring her grandson back then he would have been back in London faster than he'd been able to blink.

Nathan had always said to never get between a woman and her child but he had still gone into bat for Rick. Had been the father his own father had never been. Had been his family after Sophia had passed away the following year.

So, messing around with Nathan's daughter was not the way he repaid the man, even if it was just a bit of teasing.

That was getting out of hand.

Remembering what made sense—the pulse of the ocean, the business, Inigo's treasure—that was how he repaid him.

It was just a little difficult at the moment with so little to do on a boat that virtually sailed itself and a barely dressed first mate who didn't seem like so much of a mate any more. In a few days they'd be at their destination in Micronesia and then he'd have things to do other than look at Stella all day in hardly any clothes.

They'd both be occupied. Their days filled with diving and poring over charts and Nathan's research trying to pinpoint *The Mermaid*.

In the meantime he really needed to stop reading *Pleasure Hunt*.

Stella kicked at the sheets restlessly, straining to hear any more movement from above deck. She'd heard Rick's footsteps twenty minutes ago after hours of staring at the ceiling, trying not to think about how his hands had felt on her scalp. How if she just shut her eyes she could be Mary and he could be Vasco and how maybe they could skip a few chapters and she could be tied to his bed.

She shut her eyes and erased the image. She was taking shameful advantage of the situation. Indulging her fantasies when Rick was just being himself. The guy she'd always known. A friend. One who would do anything for her. From coming to tell her personally about her father's sudden death to washing her hair because it was scratchy and itchy and she was physically limited.

Still, there was a part of her, egged on by her hormones and a latent wicked streak, that couldn't help but speculate. Just what would he do? How far would he go? Would he cut up those ripe mangoes that they'd purchased in Moresby and that permeated the galley with sweet promise and feed them to her as Vasco had done with a juicy pear? Would he scratch that itch that drove her mad right in the centre of her back that she just couldn't reach with her current injuries?

And what about that other itch that seemed to build and build the longer she spent in his company? The one that tingled between her thighs, that made her breasts feel heavy, that caused an ache down deep and low somewhere behind her belly button?

Would he relieve that if she asked him?

Because she wasn't even capable of that at the moment and God knew she was fit to burst.

Not that helping herself was ever as good as the real thing. But it was better than death by deprivation.

Damn it!

She kicked the sheets off. This was insane. Lying here thinking about Rick like this was pure madness. Neither of them was ever going to do anything that ruined twenty-plus years of friendship so she just needed to get over herself.

She needed to go on deck and normalise their relationship. Lying in her bed, her body throbbing, put images in her head that didn't have any place in reality. Lying on deck, looking at the stars with him as she'd done a hundred times before, would help to put things into perspective.

And God knew, if her body couldn't have passion then it sure as hell needed perspective.

Rick heard the bell before she made it to the top of the stairs. He shut his eyes and prayed to Neptune for restraint.

'Hey,' he said as she tramped over, eyes staring doggedly at the sky.

'Hey,' Stella acknowledged as she drew level and looked down at him. 'Can't sleep?'

'Something like that,' he said as her face appeared in his line of vision. She was wearing some three-quarter-length grey pants, the fabric of which was quite thin, clingy around the thighs, loose around the calves. And what he could only describe as a boob tube.

'Neither can I. Want some company?'

'Sure.'

He was already burning in the fires of hell—what was one more lie?

Stella joined him on her back on the deck, making sure her injured left arm was on the outer and that she maintained some distance between them. Rick and her didn't really do distance so it seemed awkward.

'Any shooters tonight?'

He nodded. 'Saw one earlier.'

'Did you make a wish?' she asked, rolling her head towards him.

Not one that he could repeat in decent company. He turned his head too. 'I wished for—'

'Stop,' Stella said urgently, automatically silencing him with the press of a finger against his lips. A finger that still stung a little and protested the movement. 'You know you're not supposed to say.'

Rick stilled as her fingerprint seared into the DNA of his lips. There were a lot of things he wasn't supposed to say.

Or do.

And every single one of them begged to be ignored.

Stella's eyes widened as a glitter of something distinctly sexual enriched his blue gaze with something distinctly pirate.

Heat flared in her belly and breasts.

Between her legs.

And deep, deep inside.

So deep she doubted anyone had ever touched it.

Her gaze narrowed to his mouth as her finger moved of its own volition, tracing his lips, the sting instantly easing. She could feel the warmth of his breath against it, the roughness of every inhalation and exhalation.

Rick opened his mouth slightly, giving silent permission to that seeking finger. When it had circumnavigated every millimetre he grazed the tip gently with his teeth as he touched his tongue to where the splinter had been.

The way she stared at his mouth as if it were the most perfect creation went straight to his head. The sound of her indrawn breath travelled straight to his groin.

He swallowed as a jungle drum beat in his head and thudded through his chest. 'Stella.'

'Hmm?' she asked absently as she mapped his mouth with her gaze. Vasco's mouth.

Rick tried again. 'I don't think we should—'

This time she didn't cut him off with her finger. This time she used her mouth and Rick was totally unprepared. He'd always dreamt their mythical first kiss would be soft and gentle. Tentative. It was certainly the way he would have kissed her at sixteen. But there was nothing tentative about the way she opened up to him.

In seconds the kiss was wet and deep and hard, leaving no room for finesse or wishing on stars. There was just feeling, reacting. Letting all that suppressed desire bubble up on a wave of coconut and take him to a higher plane.

Stella moaned as fantasy fused into reality on a rush of high octane lust that blasted heat into every cell of her body.

And it was better than she'd ever imagined.

The dare faded as they both collected on the prize early.

Desire coursed through her bloodstream and she gasped against his mouth as Rick rolled up onto his elbow, his face looming over hers, his fingers furrowing into her hair.

She sucked in great slabs of air as the kiss robbed her of breath. They both did. Their breathing loud as they rode the dizzying heat and the high oxygen demand of the incendiary kiss. His lips were demanding against hers and she opened to him wider, revelling in the thrust and tangle of his tongue, her head lifting off the deck trying to match it.

Trying to lead. Trying to follow.

Trying to get closer.

She squeezed her thighs together as the heat there morphed into a tingling that became more unbearable with every second. Her pelvic floor muscles undulated with each swipe of his tongue and she pressed her hips firmly into the deck to soothe the pressure building deep and low.

Was it possible to orgasm from a kiss alone?

God knew she'd fantasised about his kiss often enough both as a teenager and as a writer crafting all those highly sensual, gloriously descriptive love scenes. Maybe it was?

His thumb stroked along her temple and her head spun from the rhythmic caress. Her hips rotated restlessly against the deck as she felt herself edge closer.

Maybe, after all this time, a kiss *was* going to be enough?

Rick had spent a good portion of his life *not* wondering what kissing Stella would be like and now he knew he *never* wanted to stop.

Suddenly it was the *only* thing that made sense. Not the stars or the ocean or Inigo's treasure.

None of it.

Just that little whimpering noise at the back of her throat that reverberated inside his head like a benediction—like his own private cheer squad.

And the sweet aroma of coconuts.

Lying by himself on deck before, Stella hadn't made sense.

Looming over her, pressing her into the deck, feeling the flesh and blood of her, the restless sexuality bubbling in her kiss, the harsh, desperate suck of her breath and the answering rhythm of his own body, she'd never made more sense.

He wanted more. He wanted all. He wanted everything.

His hand fell to her arm, to gather her closer, pull her nearer, imprint her along the length of him.

And then she stiffened against him, cried out, broke away…

CHAPTER EIGHT

R ICK froze as he stared down at her, her right hand supporting her injured left arm, her teeth sunken into her bottom lip, plump and moist from his ravaging. He was dazed for a moment, trying to compute what had brought an abrupt end to the passion.

Trying to compute what the hell had happened in the first place.

'I'm fine,' Stella said, breathing hard through clenched teeth as the jarring settled. She could see his bewilderment and something else, a slow dawning that seemed to closely resemble horror.

No, no, no.

'Just give me a moment,' she scrambled to assure him as she watched his blue gaze lose its drugged lustre and slowly recoil from her. 'Now.' She smiled up at him, the pain in her left arm easing as she slipped her good hand onto his shoulder. 'Where were we?'

Rick shook his head to clear the remnants of a very powerful buzz. *What the hell?* He groaned as he collapsed back against the deck.

'Oh, my God,' he said to the sky, blind to the beauty of the celestial display.

'Rick,' she assured him again, brushing a finger against his hand, 'it's fine.'

'Oh, my God,' he repeated, moving his hand to his face,

covering his eyes and shaking his head from side to side. 'What have I done?'

'Rick—'

'No.' He vaulted upright, then sprang to his feet. 'No, Stella,' he said, looking down at her. 'This is...crazy.'

Stella blinked at his vehemence. It had been shocking and surprising and unexpected. Not to mention unbelievably good.

But crazy?

She sat up gingerly. Obviously this wasn't going any further and she couldn't have this conversation with him towering over her reclined body.

'Why?'

Rick stared at her as her calm response filled him with complicated angst. 'Because,' he spluttered, 'you're Stella and I'm Rick and *we*—' he pointed back and forth between the two of them '—don't do this.'

'We made a kiss a stake in your flirting dare,' she pointed out.

And as far as Stella was concerned it was the best first kiss ever. A kiss that had obliterated Dale's best for eternity. A kiss that would surely ruin her for all other kisses.

Rick shook his head vehemently. 'Not this kind of kiss.' He'd thought about how it might go down and it hadn't been anything like this. It had been slow, sweet, controlled.

And they'd both been vertical.

'Why not?' She wasn't sixteen any more. Did he think she'd be satisfied with something chaste?

He blanched at her simple query. 'How about twenty-plus years of friendship? Or a legal document with both our signatures on that states we own a company together? Your father, for crying out loud.'

Stella frowned. 'My father?'

'Yes,' Rick fumed.

'My father?'

Rick nodded. 'He warned me off.'

'My *father* warned you off?'

Rick hadn't been forthcoming about what Nathan had said to him that day and, with the slight impression that she too had somehow let her father down, she hadn't pursued it.

He glared at her incredulous expression. 'Well, not in so many words, no. But every crew member he employed knew you were off-limits, Stel. Nathan didn't want anyone messing with his little girl.'

It took her a moment to process that. Would Rick have made a move a long time ago had her father not been all Neanderthal about his daughter?

She'd known there was an undercurrent between them as teenagers but it had all ended abruptly that day and she'd figured it was for the best.

But maybe Rick had always pondered the what-ifs too?

Stella used her right hand to push up from the deck, wincing slightly. 'Well, I don't know if you've noticed, but I'm not a little girl any more, Rick. And my father is dead.'

Rick's gaze dropped involuntarily to her boob tube. 'Yeah.' He grimaced as he returned his gaze to her face. 'I noticed.'

Stella laughed at his forlorn reply. 'I got breasts, sorry.'

He looked at them again. 'Yes, you did. It was simpler when you didn't.'

She frowned. 'I've had them for a long time, Rick—what changed this time?'

He looked at her. That damn book. *Pleasure Hunt.* Thanks to Nathan and years of platonic childhood memories he'd managed to keep perspective in his dealings with Stella.

Until the book.

But his perspective was currently shot to hell.

'The moonlight?' he lied. He somehow didn't think she'd approve of him using her book for his own ends. 'I don't know.' He shrugged. 'I guess it's never been an issue before. We've never been alone before. Not like this.'

She thought about it. 'You're right, I don't think we have.'

They looked at each other for a long moment. 'I think we'd regret it, Stel. In the long run. We have all these great memories of growing up together. Summer holidays on the *Persephone.* Bringing up Spanish coins from the ocean floor. Playing mermaid and pirate.'

Although perhaps that wasn't the best memory to bring up now…

'And when I look at you, that's what I see—how you and your father embraced me as part of the family. They are such fond memories, Stel. They mean a lot to me. I don't want to ruin them by giving in to this…crazy thing. It wouldn't be the same between us any more no matter how hard we tried. And I like what we have.'

Stella knew he was making sense but, right now, she liked what they'd been having five minutes ago more. She could still feel the surge of blood tingle through her breasts and between her thighs. Just the bob of the boat was almost enough to push piano-wire-taut muscles into delicious rapture.

God, why was he so bloody gallant? She'd probably only needed another minute or so and she would have been well satisfied. *Embarrassed for sure.* But not going off to bed with her hormones still raging and bitching at her to boot.

Well, if she had to sit on her hands the next few weeks and pretend that he hadn't almost made her come with just a kiss, then she was damned if she was going to play fair.

'Fine,' she huffed, pushing past him, heading for her cabin. 'Glad I packed my vibrator after all.'

Rick blinked. 'You brought a vibrator?' Hell, she *owned* a vibrator?

She stopped and turned. 'I'm a grown woman, Rick. *I have needs.*' She turned and continued on her way.

Rick shut his eyes on a silent groan as a particularly graphic image entered his head. 'Not helping, Stel,' he called after her, his gaze transfixed by the swing of her hips.

She smiled over her shoulder at him. 'Sweet dreams.'

* * *

Rick did not have a good night.

Every time Stella's bell jingled he strained to hear. What, he wasn't sure. A sigh? A moan? Those soft whimpery noises she made at the back of her throat?

Oh, God, those soft whimpery noises were not conducive to sleep.

And what if he *had* heard them? Would it make it any easier lying alone on the moral high ground knowing she was getting off? Knowing that he could have been in there with her, helping out?

Kissing her more.

Touching her more.

No!

It was hard now but at the end of the voyage and for the rest of the years to come, they'd be glad they were sensible. Glad they hadn't gone past the point of no return.

Maybe one day they'd even laugh about it.

Maybe.

Rick got the boat under way by eight the next morning. Stella hadn't put in an appearance and sitting around thinking about all the reasons she might be sleeping late, including a bone-deep sexual satisfaction, was not improving his mood.

It was another glorious day and losing himself in the familiar routine of setting sail seemed like a better alternative than wondering what mischief Nathan's daughter had got up to between the sheets last night.

And it worked to a degree. Until Stella came on deck an hour later.

In a micro bikini.

He stared at her open-mouthed, pleased for the camouflage of his sunglasses. Two tiny triangles barely contained the swell of her breasts and the pants, high on her leg and low on her front, had two tempting little bows at the side keeping them from falling off altogether.

'Morning,' she said airily as she drew level with him, her laptop, some coconut sunscreen and a towel in hand. A smile on her face. 'What a magnificent day,' she murmured, inhaling the sea air deep into her lungs, feeling it resonate with her spirit.

Rick watched as her chest expanded, straining the fabric of her bikini top to indecent proportions. Lord, *was she trying to give him a heart attack?*

'Sleep well?' he asked, his neutral tone almost killing him.

Stella sighed as the air rushed out of her lungs. 'Like a baby,' she purred.

She hadn't, of course. How could she sleep with a fire ravaging every erogenous zone she owned and quite a few she hadn't even known existed?

She'd barely slept a wink.

Perhaps she should have helped herself as she'd led Rick to believe but, after their near miss, she'd wanted strong male arms and a warm solid chest, not just her and Mr Buzzy.

'How's your arm?' he asked politely.

'Good.' She nodded. It was the first morning it hadn't ached when she woke and the bruising was nearly all faded. She could even move it the full range, if a little gingerly. 'I reckon I can hit my word count today.'

'Better get started, then,' he prompted, desperate to get her coconut aroma and bare shoulder out of his direct line of vision.

Stella nodded, knowing it was best to get away from him yet strangely reluctant to do so. It was as if some tropical fever had her in its grip and he was both the cause and the antidote.

'I might catch some rays first, before the sun gets too hot.'

Of course. Why didn't she just roll around in some jelly while she was at it?

'Yell if you need a hand,' she murmured as she pushed past him, heading for the bow.

He watched her sexy sashay from behind his glasses. *Yell if you need a hand.*

* * *

Stella sun-baked for the first two hours. She wasn't entirely sure what she was playing at but it seemed to have something to do with goading a reaction out of Rick. After all, if he was really that into her, he surely wouldn't be able to ignore her best attempts at extreme flirting?

She shifted, she wiggled, she lay on her back, she rolled over, she sat up, she applied liberal amounts of sunscreen, she even retied the bows.

She got nothing.

Last night had obviously been some sort of anomaly for Rick. A mad moment when a balmy night and the moonshine had affected his judgement. This morning he seemed completely indifferent to her. Nothing like the man who had kissed her as if it were his last day on earth.

Nothing like the guy she'd known for ever either—quick to laugh and eager to share his joy of the ocean. He looked like a robot at the wheel, sunglasses on, scanning the horizon for who knew what. The meaning of life? They'd passed several islands in the distance and they'd slipped by without so much as a *land ahoy* and a finger point.

It was already weird between them and nothing had happened.

Well…nothing much anyway.

She gave up trying eventually and drifted off to sleep, exhausted after her long night of tossing and turning. But later she knew she was going to have to make amends. Get things back on track.

Because, one way or another, she needed him in her life. And if that meant going to her grave without carnal knowledge of one Riccardo Granville, then so be it.

After a day of watching Stella prance around in a bikini, it was a relief to finally drop anchor and go below deck. He had a shower. A very cold shower. And lectured himself on the same things he'd lectured himself about all last night.

This was *Stella*. Nathan's daughter. His old, old friend and business partner.

And no one had ever died from sexual frustration.

By the time he got out of the shower he'd almost convinced himself, then his gaze fell on *Pleasure Hunt* and he was lost again. He picked it up to where it was open. The scene where Vasco fed Lady Mary slices of ripe pear jumped out at him. The scene had been rich with visualisation and Rick had almost been able to smell the sweet pear juice that had trekked down Mary's chin and Vasco had lapped up with his kisses.

Rick shut it for his own sanity. He let his fingers linger over the raised gold lettering of her name. How could he reconcile the Stella Mills who'd written the sexy historical with the Stella Mills he'd known practically all of his life?

How could he ever think of her as sweet and innocent again when he'd been privy to her erotic prose?

When he'd been the subject of that erotic prose?

When the taste of her mouth was imprinted onto his?

He meant what he'd said last night. But he'd never thought it would be so hard. He'd never been obsessed by a woman before. Sure, he'd had his usual teenage infatuations and spent some exciting shore leave with some very generous women, but none had played on his mind like this. None had moved into his brain and taken over.

Stella was fast becoming an obsession.

The question was would the obsession end when they went their separate ways? Or was he destined to wonder for ever?

He shoved the book under his pillow.

Out of sight, out of mind.

Although if he had any sense he'd take it above deck and hurl it into the ocean. But it was Diana's so he couldn't.

At least that was what he told himself anyway.

Stella was throwing a line in over the side when Rick reappeared half an hour later. He looked sublimely sexy in his shirt, regulation boardies and bare feet. God knew why—it wasn't as if he were wearing Armani or Ralph Lauren. But there was something about the way he wore them that oozed a special mix of charisma and wonderful outdoorsy sexuality.

'Thought we'd have some fish tonight,' she said.

Rick nodded. She'd put a button-up throw on over her bikini a long time ago but it was as if he had X-ray vision suddenly and it was still *all* he could see. 'I'll set up the grill.'

An hour later the sky was just starting to blush a velvety pink as they sat on deck and ate their fish with the potatoes that Rick had also fried on the grill. A gentle breeze caressed Stella's neck, lifting the tendrils that had escaped her messily constructed bun. The ocean lapped gently at the hull.

'Did you get your word count done?' Rick asked after they'd been eating in silent contemplation for most of the meal.

Stella nodded, grateful for the conversation. She was excruciatingly aware that they'd been avoiding any mention of what happened last night, which seemed kind of ridiculous sitting together and sharing a meal. 'Just over three thousand words today.'

He took a deep swallow of his beer. 'Is that your usual quota?'

She nodded again. 'I try to do three k a day. Some days—' she grimaced '—that's easier to achieve than others.'

'Why's that?' he asked. 'Surely you just sit there until you reach your goal.'

Stella shook her head at him—such a boy. 'Well, it doesn't really work that way unfortunately.'

He gave her a blank look and she knew she was going to have to explain it to this goal-orientated male.

'It's like diving for lost treasure. Sometimes coins are just lying on the ocean floor ready to scoop up, other times they're locked in chests, which are trapped in impossible-to-reach pockets within an aged, treacherous, waterlogged wreck. They're there…you can see them…but they're tantalisingly out of reach. The muse is like that. Some days she comes out to play and the words flow and other days…' She shrugged. 'It feels like every word is locked away in a chest just out of my reach.'

Rick wondered how quickly some of the *Pleasure Hunt* scenes flowed before stopping himself. 'I don't know,' he joked to cover the errant thoughts. 'You arty types.'

Stella laughed. 'Sorry, I suppose that did sound a bit pretentious.'

From her it had sounded just right. 'Not at all,' he dismissed with a smile. 'Do some scenes flow better than others?' The question slipped out unfiltered and couldn't be recalled.

Stella looked away. The sex scenes in *Pleasure Hunt* had flowed like a gushing tap. Years of feverish fantasies let loose had informed the scenes to embarrassing accuracy. She looked away from the piercing intensity of his gaze.

'No, not really,' she lied, standing to clear the plates. 'They can all be as easy or as difficult as each other.' She balanced the plates a little awkwardly, mindful of her injury and thankful for the calm ocean.

'Here, let me take them,' Rick said as he stood.

She shook her head. 'No way, you cooked, plus you've been waiting on me for days. The arm's heaps better so just sit.' Rick sat and she smiled. 'You want another beer?'

He nodded. 'Sure, why not?' Maybe if he was a little cut he'd go straight to sleep.

Stella seemed to take a while. He could hear her banging around down below deck as the sun gradually set above, the evening sky slowly speckling with stars. It felt oddly domesticated and a deep spring of contentment welled inside him, bringing him to his feet.

He frowned as he prowled restlessly around the deck. The boards felt good beneath his bare feet.

His deck, his boat, his ocean.

These were the things that brought him contentment. Not some woman clattering around in his kitchen.

That never made him feel content.

In fact it usually made him want to get away fast. Ditch the chick at the nearest port and sail himself far away. Get back to his true mistress—the ocean.

Like Nathan. Like his father.

But here he was, nonetheless, on the ocean, sharing it with probably the only woman who truly understood the pull of such a demanding mistress.

The tinkle of her bell alerted him to her presence and he turned to see her walking towards him, holding the necks of two beers in one hand and a plate holding two mangoes, a knife and a cloth in the other.

'I'm having a mango,' she said. 'I wasn't sure if you wanted one or not.' She handed him his beer as she sat on the deck, facing the horizon lotus-style, balancing the plate on her crossed knees.

Rick nodded, taking one as he sat beside her. Not too close. 'Sure, thanks. I'll eat mine after the beer.'

Stella raised the large pungent fruit to her face. It was warm against her cheek and she inhaled deeply. It smelled sweet and wild like forbidden berries and exotic like balmy tropical islands.

'Mmm, that smells good,' she murmured. 'The whole galley smells of them suddenly.'

Rick nodded. He'd noticed earlier when he'd gone below but he didn't want to look at her getting all breathy and orgasmic over anything other than him, so he hung his head back and kept his eyes firmly trained on the sky.

Stella placed the mango on the plate, salivating at the thought of the sweet, warm fruit sliding against her palate. She cut into the soft flesh, a pearl of juice beaded around the incision as the strong aroma wafted out to envelop her in its heady fragrance.

She was conscious of Rick beside her not saying anything. Conscious of what happened between them last night when they'd been on this deck. Conscious that it had sat large between them all day, screwing with their usual effortless dynamic. Normally by now Rick would be talking about the stars or prattling on about Inigo and *The Mermaid*.

Instead they sat in silence as they had done for most of their meal.

Stella took a deep breath as she picked up one mango cheek and scored the flesh. They couldn't go on like this. 'About last night…'

Rick's breath seized in his lungs momentarily and he took a moment before looking at her, taking a swallow of beer to calm himself. 'What about last night?'

Stella didn't dare look at him. The weight of his gaze was intimidating enough. 'You were right,' she said, scoring the other cheek. 'We would regret crossing the line. I'm sorry I made it difficult for you.'

Rick swallowed as she picked up a scored mango cheek, inverted it and used her tongue and teeth to liberate a cube of the soft pungent flesh. 'Yes,' he said faintly, trying not to think of the pear scene in *Pleasure Hunt* he'd not long been skimming.

Stella would have sighed as the fruit zinged along her taste-buds if the topic of conversation weren't so damn serious. She turned to face him as she sucked another cube of mango into her mouth and savoured it. 'I mean, of course it would be awkward between us and would negate all the good memories we've ever made.'

She bit into another perfectly square piece of mango flesh.

Rick heard the soft squelch go right to his groin. He zeroed in on her mouth, which glistened with ripe juice. His fingers tightened around the beer bottle. 'Uh-huh,' he said, not really even listening, his reasoning dissolving into a red haze as her mouth and tongue slowly devoured the fruit.

Vasco had fed Lady Mary, taunting her with slithers of pear, inching them closer, stroking them against her moist lips, watching her as she sucked them inside her mouth, her gaze not leaving his face.

He itched to pick the mango up and re-enact the scene. Cut off thin slices and feed them to Stella one by one. Watch her pupils dilate and her breath become shallow just as Lady Mary's had.

Maybe even hear that whimper again at the back of her throat. The whimper that was all Stella.

Stella's breath hitched as Rick's eyes seemed to suddenly glitter like moonbeams on sapphires. She swallowed her mouthful of mango but juice escaped to her lips and she ran her tongue around them to capture the errant moisture.

Rick shut his eyes and groaned as all his noble intentions from last night faded to black with each revolution of her tongue. 'Stella,' he murmured, his eyelids fluttering open to find her staring at him.

Stella blinked at the ache in his voice. Had he edged closer? Or had she? She looked at his mouth, remembered how it had felt against hers. How it had been so much better than she'd ever fantasised. 'This *is* crazy,' she whispered, mango forgotten.

Rick nodded, his gaze fixed on her mouth, inching his own closer to hers, drawn to her as if she were a homing beacon, his heart rate pulsing to the beat of the sea. 'Certifiable.'

Stella felt his pull as a physical force, which seemed only fitting beneath a canopy of stars with the rhythm of the ocean lulling away the insanity of it all. 'What about the memories, Rick?'

Her voice was low and husky in the quiet of the night as she tried to hang onto the one thing that made sense between them, even though her pulse coursed like an ocean squall through every inch of her body.

Suddenly her mouth felt dry.

So dry.

As if she'd been drinking sea water for days and, not only was her thirst unquenchable, it was sending her slowly mad. She swallowed and licked her lips to ease the dry, parched feeling.

Rick's pupils dilated as her tongue darted out. 'Screw 'em,' he muttered as his final shard of resistance melted away. 'Let's make better ones.'

R-rated ones.

And he closed the distance between them, capturing her mouth. There was a moment, ever so brief, when she could have pulled away, could have protested and he would have been capable of letting it slide. But when she opened to him instantly on a deep-in-his-bones moan the moment passed in a blink of an eye and her mango and coconut essence wrapped him in a sticky web of desire that was impossible to break free of.

Even if he wanted to.

Which he didn't.

His heart crashed in his chest, his breath sawed in and out. Her hands crept around his neck and she made that noise at the back of her throat and somehow, some way, he had her on the deck, her breasts pressed against his chest, her hand shoved in his hair.

Where his beer or her mango had ended up he didn't know and he didn't care. All he knew was she smelled like paradise and felt like every erotic dream he'd ever had, and when she moaned into his mouth her desire tasted sweet like mango and he wanted to devour every drop.

He was hard and needy and something in his head insisted that he touch every inch of her, smell every inch of her, know every inch of her.

His hand drifted south to the wild flutter at the base of her throat and she moaned. It moved further to the top button of her wrap, where the swell of her breast was emphasised by the taut fabric of her bikini top, and she gasped.

It fanned down over her ribs and came to rest on the gentle rise of her belly and she arched her back and undulated her stomach and sighed, 'Yes, yes, yes.'

Rick pulled away, breathing hard. Her face was soft and full of wonder. If he were an egotist he might even have called it rapture.

'Let's go to my cabin,' he murmured, kissing her eyes and the tip of her nose and the corner of her mouth.

Stella opened her lashes, seeing nothing but Rick's face crowned by about a million stars—*when had they come out?*

'No.' She shook her head. 'I want it here, on the deck, beneath the stars.'

She'd wanted to write a similar scene with Vasco and Mary but she'd known that it wouldn't have been possible in the middle of the ocean with a boat full of pirates in the eighteenth century.

But now she got to live the fantasy for real and she wasn't going to have it any other way.

He nuzzled her temple, her ear, her neck. 'Kinky,' he murmured as his hand found its way beneath the hem of her throw to trace patterns on her bare abdomen. The same abdomen that had taunted him all day with its cute little perky belly button.

Stella almost moaned out loud as the buzzing of his lips seemed to stroke other places. Lower places. 'Not into kinky?' she asked, smiling against his mouth as his lips brushed hers.

Rick chuckled as his mouth inched down her throat. 'Kinky is my middle name,' he said as his hand crept inexorably north.

'Really?' Stella said as the possibilities swirled around her mind in a sexual kaleidoscope.

'Really,' he repeated as he pushed her shirt up, pulled aside one bikini bra cup, exposing her breast totally to his view. He smiled as she gasped and the nipple puckered beneath his scrutiny. He stared at it fascinated as his hand groped beside her until he found what he was looking for.

Stella was in a sexual haze so heady she doubted even an undersea earthquake could have shifted her. The way he looked at her nipple as if it were his own private property was utterly mesmerising.

This was Rick. Her Rick. Not a fantasy. Not Vasco Ramirez. Riccardo Granville.

He raised his hand above her chest and it took a few seconds for her to focus on what he was doing, and even then it wasn't until the warm sticky mango juice dripped onto her nipple that his actions registered.

But by then he'd lowered his mouth to it and she'd gasped and arched her back and she knew she was totally lost.

Just as Lady Mary had been.

CHAPTER NINE

RICK had never tasted anything so sweet as his tongue lapped at the juice, removing every drop from the hard nub. Stella tasted exotic like forbidden fruit, smelled like an ocean breeze riffling through a stand of coconut palms, and the very unladylike expletive that had fallen from her mouth as he nuzzled her breast played like a symphony in his head.

He pulled away and watched as her wet, puckered nipple dried in the breeze. A little frown appeared between her brows just before she moaned a protest and opened her eyes. There was a feverish glitter to her gaze, which went straight to his groin.

He had put that crazy-drunk look there.

The air felt thick and heavy on her palate as Stella dragged in some much-needed breaths. His hand spanned her ribs beneath her breast exactly where her heart pounded like a gong and she wondered if he knew that he had done that to her. He was staring down at her, his gaze roving over her face and chest, lingering on her mouth and her impossibly taut nipple.

'I have another,' she murmured.

Rick smiled. He relieved her of her throw, then smoothed his hand to her other bikini cup and dragged it aside with his index finger, satisfied as her breast spilled free. 'So you do,' he agreed, watching with fascination as the nipple wrinkled then puckered before his eyes. He groped for the discarded mango cheek.

Her pupils dilated and he heard her breath roughen as he squeezed the cheek again and juice dripped onto her breast, coating her nipple and running in sweet rivulets down her chest. His mouth salivated as he inched his head closer to the gloriously sticky morsel. Her low whimper encouraged him to close the distance and he took it greedily instead of repeating the steady assault he'd used on the other side.

She gasped and he sucked harder, rolling the stiff peak around and around his mouth, grazing the tip with his teeth, pressing it hard between palate and tongue, satisfied only when she arched her back, silently begging for more. His hand found the other nipple, hard and ready. When he brushed it with his thumb she panted. And when he pinched it between his fingers she practically levitated off the deck and cried out so loudly he lifted his head and smothered the husky outcry with his mouth.

Stella, driven by a hunger so insatiable she was blind to everything else, lifted her head off the deck and claimed Rick's lips with indecent vigour. She pushed her tongue into his mouth and when he groaned deep and low and needy she swallowed the sound whole, lapping up his response, wanting to fuse their mouths together, to fuse their bodies together for eternity.

Her pulse pounded through her head, her nostrils flared with each laboured breath. His hand left her nipple and stroked down her belly and she shifted restlessly against the deck as muscles deep inside shivered and undulated. The boards were hard against her back but she didn't care. She wanted him on top of her, pressing down, sinking into her. She wanted to feel his skin on hers, wrap her legs around his waist, have the rock and the sway and the pound of them become one with the rhythm of the ocean.

His hand moved lower, whispering across her skin, skimming the edge of her bikini bottoms. Her hips shifted as heat licked from his fingers and bloomed in her pelvis. An ache took up residence between her legs and she moaned as his hand fumbled with a bow.

She felt the tug as he pulled at it and it came undone.

Then another tug as the other bow ceded to his questing fingers and she shivered as he stripped the tiny triangle of fabric away, leaving her bare to the ocean breeze and the stars and his touch.

'Those damn bows have been driving me nuts all day,' Rick said, lifting his head briefly before moving his lips to her jaw, her ear, her throat. And lower, trailing towards her nipple as his fingers slowly stroked her inner thigh.

Stella whimpered as more heat fanned downwards from his kisses and upwards from his hand, searing and ravaging everything in between with devastating ease.

Suddenly it wasn't enough to be just lying here. She wanted to touch his skin—all of it. Feel it smooth and warm and solid beneath her hands, dance fire across it as he was doing to her.

Wreak a little havoc.

Render him a little crazy.

She grabbed for the hem of his shirt, reefing it up and over his head at the exact time his lips met her nipple. She whimpered as he let go for the briefest second and moaned deep and low when his mouth returned immediately to her breast and his fingers found her thigh again. She sucked in a breath, dug her fingernails into the bare warm flesh of his shoulder as he tormented the sensitive peak.

His flesh shuddered beneath her palm and it vibrated all the way down her arm, stroking gossamer fingers over her neck and her chest and down her belly. Her hands kneaded his shoulders and the defined muscles of his back. Her palms smoothed into the dimples she'd seen all those days ago in the moonlight, slipping beneath his waistband to the firm rounded rise of his buttocks.

When he groaned against her mouth she squeezed them hard.

Rick reared back as his erection surged painfully, bucking

against its confines. 'Stella,' he muttered, seeing stars despite his back being to them.

He recaptured her mouth, plundering its soft sweet depths, getting lost in the taste and the smell and the touch of her. Wanting everything at once, impatient to know the noises she made when she came.

His fingers moved a little north and brushed lightly at the juncture. Her back arched and she cried out as he found her hot and wet and ready. 'God, Stel,' he whispered, his lips hovering above hers. 'You feel so damn good.'

Stella shook her head from side to side, her hips rotating restlessly as his fingers stroked and brushed and sighed against her.

It wasn't enough, she needed more. 'Please,' she whispered.

'Please what?' Rick murmured, licking along the plump softness of her mouth. 'What do you want, Stella?'

Stella arched her back as his finger pressed a little harder, slid through the slick heat of her. 'More,' she said urgently, rotating her hips as she gripped his buttocks convulsively.

Rick slid a finger inside and felt her clamp hard around him. Her gasp echoed around the empty ocean. 'Like this?' he asked, licking down her neck, trailing his tongue down her chest. 'Or this?' He claimed a nipple as he slid another finger home.

'Rick!' Stella clung to him as he stretched her, taunted her. His expert thumb zeroed in on the impossibly hard erogenous zone as if it were fitted with a homing beacon and the stars started to flash in the sky.

A pressure built from deep inside as his thumb fanned and stoked.

God, she was going to come. *Very, very soon.*

'Wait,' she said, removing a hand from his backside to grab his wrist and still his devastatingly rhythmic movements.

Rick lifted his head and frowned. 'What's wrong?' he asked, breathing hard.

If she'd changed her mind, got cold feet, he was toast. He might as well just jump into the ocean now and save himself the slow decline into insanity.

Stella licked her lips. 'It's been a long time,' she panted. 'I swear if you keep doing that it's going to be over very, very quickly.'

It took a moment for her meaning to sink into his lust-addled brain, then everything stopped as he smiled. 'Really? You mean this?' He rotated his fingers deep inside her and grinned at the whimper that rent the air.

'Rick,' she pleaded, squeezing his wrist hard.

'What, Stel?' he murmured. 'You don't like this?' He repeated the manoeuvre, applying pressure to the hard little nub beneath his thumb.

Stella gasped as she shut her eyes. 'Rick, please.'

'What about this?' he asked as he groped awkwardly one-handed for the discarded mango cheek.

Stella opened her eyes as she felt his heat move from her side. His eyes glittered down at her as he half knelt beside her, one hand stroking her intimately, the other paused above the juncture of her thighs.

'You like this, Stella?' he asked as he squeezed the almost spent cheek, wringing the last drops of juice from its now pulpy flesh.

Stella felt the warm sticky ooze mingle with her own slickness as a waft of soft ripe fruit and sex enveloped her. And when he bent over her, his tongue joining the delicious friction, it was too, too much. A sweet wild aroma filled her senses as he stroked and stoked and the pressure accelerated to warp speed.

Rick groaned against her as the salt and the sweet of her slid over his tongue. Her heady aroma surrounded him as he taunted the hard nub, flicking and sucking in equal measure. She bucked and writhed beneath him, begging him to stop, begging him not to stop, as she lifted her hips in silent supplication.

He pinned her down with his hand and his mouth, lapping at her sweetness, refusing to yield. Even when she shattered around him seconds later he gave more, wringing every last tantalising morsel from her as he had done with the mango.

Stella jackknifed up, crying out, 'Stop, stop, stop,' fearing that she might actually die from the intensity of the pleasure.

Rick was breathing hard as he withdrew, rocking back on his haunches, watching as Stella collapsed back against the deck, delightfully naked aside from two pushed-aside bra cups.

He quirked an eyebrow. 'You look like you needed that.'

Stella grunted, which was all she was capable of as strong post-coital aftershocks undulated deep inside her. The stars burst around her like fireworks. 'You have no idea,' she panted.

Diana would be proud.

He ran his eyes over her naked abandon one more time. She lay all loose limbed, her nipples still erect, her legs spread, and his erection twitched painfully in his boardies. 'I think I do.'

Stella saw a flash of carnal hunger glitter in his eyes, aware suddenly that she'd short-changed him. 'I'm sorry,' she said, her breath still laboured. 'I don't know what the equivalent of premature ejaculation is in females but I think I just had an acute attack.'

Rick chuckled. 'It was my pleasure.' He held out his hand to her and pulled her towards him as she took it, kissing her nose. 'Fancy a shower?'

Stella was pleased for the cover of night as an image of a naked Rick, water and moonlight caressing his magnificent body, sprang instantly to mind. Never, all those nights ago when she'd spied on him, had she thought she'd ever be joining him under the deck shower.

He didn't give her a chance to indulge the embarrassing memory or to say no, pulling her to her feet, dragging her towards the bow. He let go of her to flick on the taps and rip at the Velcro on his boardies. In a trice they were gone and he was standing before her, proud and erect, the jut of his sex a tantalising silhouette. An illicit reminder of her peep show with the full embellishment of her fantasy life included for good measure.

Rick felt a tug deep inside as she stared at his erection. Somewhere behind him the water sprayed unattended, his heart pounding just as erratically. The moisture in his mouth dried to dust. 'Your turn,' he murmured.

She frowned for a moment, confused by his comment, then she looked down at her half-on, half-off bikini top and understood. She pulled it off over her head, being careful not to jar her almost recovered arm. It dropped to the deck next to his boardies.

Rick devoured her curvy roundness in one long slow look. 'You're beautiful,' he breathed.

'So are you,' she murmured, her gaze roaming over the perfection of him. This was how she had imagined Vasco. But Rick was more. So much more. He was no figment of her imagination. He was solid flesh and hard muscle and warm blood and he wanted her—*Stella*—not Mary.

She hadn't even realised she'd been jealous of Mary until this moment.

But then Rick held out his hand again and she took it and everything else was forgotten. He stepped backwards into the shower and she followed, watching as the water soaked his hair and ran down his chest, before running free down his obliques.

She stepped closer, raising herself on tippy toe, gliding her hands up his pecs and onto his shoulders. His erection pushed against her belly, thick and rampant, and her hand reached for it as she lifted her mouth to his. She felt the jolt through his body as she palmed the length of him and swallowed his groan as their lips fused.

'Oh...dear...God,' Rick gasped against her mouth as she

increased the intensity of her intimate caress, using the water to her advantage.

Stella couldn't agree with his sentiments more. She could taste mango and sex on his mouth and the water flowing over their heated skin caressed like icicles and he felt good and right in her hand.

But she wanted him good and right elsewhere.

Inside her.

Deep, deep inside her.

'You need to be in me,' she panted, her pulse thrumming so loudly through her ears she was sure she was about to rupture her eardrums.

Rick didn't need a written invitation. He grabbed her around the waist, boosting her up. As she locked her ankles at his waist he turned around in one easy movement. He pushed her against the entirely inadequate pole the shower head was mounted upon and lowered his mouth to hers, plundering hers until nothing but their two frantic heartbeats registered.

Not even the push and pull of the vast, vast ocean.

And when that wasn't enough he dropped his head to her chest, devouring the delicious ripeness of her breasts, revelling in the arch of her back and the crazed keening coming from her throat.

'Now,' Stella begged, her head thrown back, her chest thrust out in pure debauched abandon.

Rick was hard and ready and done with denying himself. He lifted her slightly, aligning her, aligning himself, nudging her entrance, feeling the still slick heat of her.

'Rick!' she begged, lightly pummelling a fist against the muscles of his shoulder as she felt him thick and hard but still not where she wanted him.

Where she needed him.

Rick chuckled at her frustration. 'Easy, Stel, easy. Let's make it last this time, huh?'

Stella whacked him harder. '*Now*, damn it,' she ordered.

Rick grinned. 'Aye, aye captain,' he murmured, smothering the very unladylike bellow that came from her mouth as he pushed into her long and hard and deep.

Stella broke away, gasping for air as he slowly withdrew and steadily pushed his way back in again, hitting exactly the right spot every time. 'Oh, God, yes,' she panted. 'Just there. Don't stop. God, don't stop!'

She squirmed against him, her head lolling back, water flowing down her breasts, her lips parting in a blissful O.

Rick stroked his tongue down her throat, sipping at the rivulets of water as he kept up the slow easy pace. Her whimpers vibrated against his mouth and he pushed deeper as he slowed right down.

Stella moaned as the subtle friction drove her crazy.

In a good way.

In a never-ever-stop way.

The way she'd always imagined it.

Hard and slow and perfect.

But this was better. So much better. Because it was real.

Rick watched Stella's breasts rock as he slowly surged into her again. Water sluiced down her chest, traced the contours of her cleavage, clung in droplets at the ends of her nipples. Stars formed a crown above her head and with her blonde hair plastered in wet strips over her shoulders she looked like a water nymph.

'God,' Rick groaned, his forehead falling against her chest as the tightness in his groin started to tug at his resistance. 'You look great in a shower.'

Stella gasped as he pulled out further this time and thrust all the way in. *So did he.* 'I have a confession,' she murmured.

Rick felt his orgasm drawing nearer and beat it back. 'You do?' he panted.

She nodded as his pulsing became thrusting once again. 'When you had a shower the other night at the yacht club in

Moresby...' her teeth sank into her lower lip and she clenched his shoulder as he picked up the pace '...I was spying on you.'

Rick pulled out all the way this time, pushing back in until she gasped and arched her back. He was a perfect fit.

'I have a confession too,' he said as a more urgent rhythm took over, nudging the slow inexorable build into something much harder to control. He withdrew quickly and just as quickly plunged back in. 'I saw you.'

If she hadn't been about to come Stella might have been angry. *Embarrassed certainly.* But the fact that he'd known, that he'd turned so she could see all of him, was inexplicably arousing. That combined with the continual in-and-out thrust of him was a heady combination.

'Pervert,' she gasped as he hit the spot that made her shudder and quiver and cling.

Rick grunted as her fingernails dug in and everything started to unravel. 'Look who you're calling pervert, my lovely.'

Stella was going to say something else, but all that came out was a gurgly whimper as she let the hypocritical protest fly up and become stardust. 'Ah-h-h,' she cried out as time and space blurred and all that remained was him and her and the silent permission of the ocean.

Rick felt things heat and boil as his belly tensed to an unbearable rigidity. He pulled her into him and crooned, 'Yes, Stella, yes,' directly into her ear as she threw back her head and called out his name, clamping tight around him, falling apart in his arms.

It was all that he needed and he bellowed into her chest, thrusting with none of the finesse of earlier as he rode the savage dictates of his body to their final release.

After a long night of getting acquainted in a way they never had before, Stella woke late the next morning to find Rick propped up on his elbow looking down at her. His eyes seemed even bluer in the morning sunshine slanting through his un-dressed portholes, his eyelashes longer. His hair seemed shag-gier as it hung around his face and brushed his broad bronzed shoulders. His lips fuller.

He should look girly but he didn't.

He looked utterly masculine with nothing but a white sheet riding low on his hips.

'Good morning,' she murmured, blushing as she remem-bered just what lay beneath that sheet and the things he'd done with it.

She'd done with it.

Rick smiled at the pinkness in her cheeks, surprised that someone who knew him so carnally was capable of such mod-esty. 'Good morning to you too,' he replied, dropping a kiss on a bare shoulder.

His smile slackened as a feeling he wasn't familiar with washed over him and took up residence in his gut like a lead sinker. Nothing like how he usually felt the morning after—loose and light with all his kinks ironed out. Stella wasn't some bar hook-up or one of his many port calls. He wasn't sure what came next.

Stella noted his pensive look. 'I hope that's not buyer's re-morse,' she murmured.

Rick shook his head. If she slapped him in the face and swam back home to England right this moment and refused to see him again he would never regret last night. 'Never.'

He lowered his head again and kissed her on the mouth, a long, slow, lingering kiss that tasted of them and left him hard beneath the sheet and aching for more.

Stella sighed as he pulled back, brushing her fingers along the soft bristles of his perpetual three day growth. 'So what's up?' she murmured.

He turned his face, kissing the tips of her fingers. 'I guess,' he said, looking down into her sleepy olive gaze, 'I'm not sure what comes next…'

Stella smiled. 'Breakfast, I think. Unless you want to—' she dropped her hand to his chest, traced her index finger down his belly to the interesting bulge in the sheet '—fool around a bit more?'

Rick captured her hand before it hit her target and thinking wouldn't be possible. 'Stel,' he said. 'I'm serious. Normally I'd kiss you and tell you I had to be somewhere in a couple of hours but…this is you and…I don't have a well-rehearsed morning-after plan for this. Frankly I'm torn between freaking out and ringing Andy Willis to tell him I've seen your boobs.'

Stella laughed, letting her hand fall to the mattress. Andy Willis had been Rick's best friend when he'd been eleven and had spent a couple of weeks one summer on the *Persephone* with them. He'd also had a massive crush on Stella.

Rick frowned down at her. 'It's not funny, Stella.'

Stella sobered, finding his pout irresistible. She lifted her head to kiss it away. He resisted until she tugged on his bottom lip with her teeth and soothed it with her tongue. She smiled when he groaned and kissed her back.

She pulled away when they were both breathing hard, smoothing his brow with her thumb.

'You're not eleven any more, Rick. What's happened with us has taken us both by surprise so I don't have a plan for this either. But do we really need one?'

She remembered what Diana had said—*you're going to be on that boat with him for long periods of time where there'll be nothing to do.* She'd rejected it then as an impossibility but, after last night, maybe Diana had a point.

'You and I both know that we live two very different lives and also know through the bitter experience of two broken families that they're practically mutually exclusive. But for the next little while we're on this boat together—alone—and we're both single and of age and if last night is any yardstick, we're pretty damn good together. Can't that be our plan?'

Rick thought it sounded like possibly the best ever plan

he'd heard. But could things really be that simple between the two of them? If he shut his eyes he could hear Nathan telling him how special Stella was, what she deserved out of life. And what she didn't.

'I don't know, Stel, maybe your father was right—'

Stella shook her head vigorously, interrupting him, annoyed that her father had meddled to the extent he had. She'd always wondered why none of her father's crew had ever spent much time with her once she'd grown breasts and now she knew.

'No, he was wrong. About a *lot* of things but especially this. I understand, Rick. You're like him. I get it. The ocean runs in your veins and the sea is your mistress blah blah.'

She rolled her eyes.

'And I want marriage and one day babies and for the father of those babies to be around full time. I know all that. But that's not what this is. We're not talking marriage and happily-ever-afters here, Rick. We're talking a couple of weeks of hot, sweaty, sandy, frolicking-in-tropical-lagoons sex.'

Rick shut his eyes against the images she evoked as his hard-on voted yes. But…he looked down at her, her blonde hair spread out on the pillow around her, her lovely face so, so familiar…could a woman who immersed herself in happily-ever-afters ever settle for less?

'And then what? We just go back to being friends?'

Stella shrugged. 'Sure. It's not like we see each other much these days, Rick. What…two or three times a year? Probably even less now that Dad's not around. Hell, it'll probably be another year or so before I next see you.'

Rick had to admit she made a good point. 'That's true,' he murmured.

Stella smiled, her hand making its way back to where the sheet still bulged interestingly. 'The truth, the whole truth and nothing but the truth.'

Rick dropped his head to nuzzle along her collarbone. 'It certainly makes sense.'

Her hand dipped under the sheet and she hit pay dirt. Rick swore in Spanish, and she smiled, recognising the word he had taught her when she'd been twelve years old. She wrapped her palm around his girth and revelled in the silky hard length of him and the way he shuddered against her.

She stretched languorously, her free hand slipping under the pillow, grabbing a fistful of sheet as Rick claimed a nipple, sucking it into the heat of his mouth, lashing it with hot wet swipes of his tongue.

Her hand nudged something and it took her lust-drunk brain a moment to ascertain it was a book. Without thinking she pulled it out and looked at it.

The cover of *Pleasure Hunt* stared back at her.

She said a choice swear word of her own, snagging Rick's attention.

'Ah…' he said warily.

'You've read this?'

She frowned as he collapsed back on the mattress and nodded, her worst fears confirmed. She'd wondered when they'd first had that conversation about her writing process if he'd read it, but his comments had set her mind at ease.

His obviously misleading comments.

'This is Diana's copy,' she said as she thumbed through it. She'd have known it without the benefit of her autograph on the title page. She'd know this dog-eared copy anywhere— she'd seen Diana reading it often enough.

'Yes. She gave it to me just before we left your house that day.'

'Oh, did she, now?' Stella murmured, her ire rising as she formulated a rather stinging email rant in her head. But then another thought hit and she sat bolt upright. 'Oh, God,' she said as the most important thing of all occurred to her. She turned her head and looked down at him. 'So you know…'

She couldn't even finish the statement, it was so embarrassing.

Rick grinned at her mortified look as he crossed his ankles and clasped his hands behind his head. 'That I'm Vasco Ramirez?'

The pink she'd gone earlier was nothing to the deep red that currently suffused her cheeks. She opened her mouth to deny it but she couldn't. If he'd read it, he'd know. There was too much of *him* in it. Not just that tantalising birthmark but the essence of him. His mannerisms, his way with words, his sense of humour.

His sense of honour.

She looked away, her fingers absently stroking the raised lettering on the cover. 'Well, there's no need to get too bigheaded about it,' she huffed. 'I needed a pirate of Spanish descent. It made sense to…model him on someone I knew.'

Whatever happened she couldn't let him know that she'd been fantasising about him for a long time before Vasco had come on the scene. That Vasco had walked into her head fully formed because of him. He was already freaked out enough about the development in their relationship.

'But any resemblance to person or persons alive or dead…'

Rick vaulted upright, fitting himself in behind her, his front to her back, covering her mouth with his hand, cutting off the lawyer speak as he kissed her shoulder. 'Shh, Stella,' he murmured. 'I love it that you *modelled* him on me.'

He brushed a string of kisses up higher as he dropped his hand to her shoulder. 'I'm not going to sue you, I'm…flattered. And impressed how…accurate…' he smiled against her skin '…your descriptions are. That bath scene…' He nuzzled her ear; his hands moved to cup her breasts, his thumbs brushing over the already erect nipples. 'It was like you'd painted a portrait of me.'

Stella arched her back and felt her eyes roll back in her head as his mouth and fingers turned her insides to mush.

Rick kissed up her jaw and when she turned her head towards him he feathered kisses along her lips. 'Like you'd actually seen me naked,' he whispered against her mouth as one hand left her breast bearing south.

His words triggered a thought and Stella opened her eyes. 'You knew,' she murmured. 'You'd already read the book when you spied me watching you have that shower.'

He chuckled unashamedly in her ear as both hands stroked her thighs. 'Guilty,' he whispered.

Her brow wrinkled as she remembered how cannily familiar some things on this trip had been. The shower incident. When he'd tended her wounds as Vasco had done. When he'd squeezed mango juice all over her body.

But he'd turned her whole body into an erogenous zone and when he urged her thighs apart she didn't object.

'Have you been deliberately enacting scenes from the book?' she murmured, raising both arms and linking them around his neck, arching her back as his finger slid between her legs.

'What did you expect me to do for fun when you took away all my recreational flirting? Anyway, do you care?' he whispered, his erection pressing into the cleft of her soft round buttocks.

'Yes,' she sighed. 'I'm mad as he…ll.' And she would have sounded much more convincing had he not driven a finger deep inside her.

He chuckled at her breathy whimper. 'Are you telling me you haven't been taking advantage too? That you didn't think about the book when you were spying on me in the shower? Or when I was tending to your wounds? That bringing those scenes to life didn't excite you?'

Stella knew he was right. Knew that it would be hard to take the moral high ground when she'd been using him to indulge a few of her own fantasies.

But she was damned if she was going to let him have it all his way. 'It's just a story,' she panted as he stroked between her legs. 'They're what excited Lady Mary.'

Rick remembered what she'd said about Lady Mary not being her in anything other than a generic female way. Her slickness coated his fingers and he picked up the pace. 'And you're not her, right?' he whispered.

Stella was so close to falling over the edge. So far gone she didn't know which way was up, but even she knew to answer that question truthfully would be madness.

'Right,' she gasped as she squirmed against him and he stroked harder.

She clutched convulsively at the back of his neck as a tiny pulse fluttered deep and low, fanning out in ever-increasing waves. Mary was forgotten, Vasco was forgotten as it pulsed and grew until nothing else mattered but the magic Rick could do with his hands.

'Oh, God,' she groaned, arching her back, tilting her pelvis. 'Don't stop,' she begged. 'Please don't stop.'

Rick felt the tension in his groin tighten to almost unbearable tautness. 'Yes, Stel, yes,' he panted, working her slickness, feeling her ripple around him. 'Come for me. Come.'

Stella bucked as the wave broke over her, undulating with a ferocity that tore the breath from her lungs and, for a moment or two, the beat from her heart.

It gripped her and shook her in endless waves and she knew there was no possible way she could be put back together right, once it ended.

CHAPTER TEN

Mary chafed against the four silken bonds that imprisoned her, legs akimbo, upon Vasco's bed. For no matter how many times she shared it with him she would never regard it as hers. She eyed the big brooding pirate as he prowled back and forth. He was wearing breeches and boots and nothing else save the sunlight slanting through the portholes.

He stopped and turned to face her from the foot of the bed, shoving his hands on his hips. 'I'm waiting, Mary.'

His low rumble set her heart aflutter and her nipples to attention. She watched as his glittering blue eyes took in their state of indecency. How could they not when she was barely covered? When he had stripped her to her undergarments not ten minutes ago this had not been the expected outcome.

Damned stubborn man.

'I insist that you untie me immediately, Captain Ramirez.'

Vasco chuckled, his gaze fanning over the hard peaks tenting her chemise. 'Methinks you like to be tied up, Lady Mary,' he murmured, planting a knee on the bed.

She glared at him both scandalised and titillated at the thought. 'Captain Ramirez.'

He ignored the warning in her voice, slowly advancing onto the bed. 'I do so prefer it when you call me Vasco. Like you did that day on the deck when I washed your hair.' He prowled closer on his hands and knees until he was sitting on his haunches between her spreadeagled legs. 'And when I first touched you here,' he murmured, stroking his finger down the open central seam of her linen drawers.

She sucked in a breath and he smiled triumphantly. 'Like you did last night and the night before that and the five nights before that.' He stroked again.

Mary squirmed against his hand. 'Vasco, please,' she moaned. 'It's the middle of the day. The crew...'

He shook his head and chuckled that she could still keep a sense of propriety while tied to his bed. 'Say it,' he insisted. 'If you want it, Mary, you're going to have to ask for it.'

Lady Mary Bingham had been a willing and eager bed partner but there was part of her he hadn't been able to reach, a part she kept aloof from him even when she was in the throes of her release. It made him feel like a common street urchin and she the lady who was condescending to allow him to use her body while she had nothing better to do.

He needed to know that this fever was burning in her blood too.

Mary shook her head. Gently bred ladies did not talk so.

She'd already taken a pirate as a lover. How much more did he want? 'I will not.'

Vasco smiled at her, watching as she bit down on her bottom lip and fought against closing her eyes. 'You know you want to, Mary, I can feel it right here...' He slipped a finger inside her where it was hot and slick and she gasped. 'I know you, Mary.'

Mary hated how he could addle her senses so quickly.

'You know nothing about me, sir,' she said vehemently as her hips moved against him restlessly.

Vasco grinned. 'I know you like this,' he said, pushing up her chemise with his other hand, exposing a creamy breast and rosy nipple that puckered quickly beneath the stroke of his fingers.

'I know you have this tiny strawberry birthmark just here,' he said, satisfied to hear her whimper as he withdrew his finger, shifting it slightly to the left to the crease where her inner thigh met the very centre of her. 'I know you like it when I lick you there,' he murmured, lowering his head and putting his tongue to where his finger had been, to the mark that had fascinated him right from the beginning.

'Vasco...' Mary cried, arching her back as his finger re-entered her and his tongue swiped in long, lazy, knowing strokes.

He smiled as he pulled away, sitting back on his haunches, his finger still stroking deep inside her. 'I know me tying you up excites you even though I know you're hearing your uncle's voice telling you you're going to hell.'

Mary also hated how he seemed to be able to read her mind. 'Well, I'll be seeing you there first, Captain Ramirez,' she said haughtily.

Vasco threw back his head and laughed. When he stopped his eyes glittered down at her and he started to stroke her in earnest. 'Ah, but what a way to go, Lady Mary,' he taunted as he relentlessly increased the pressure.

Mary especially hated how he could bring her to her peak so effortlessly. 'Vasco,' she whimpered and moved against him, desperate for the rush.

He quirked an eyebrow, easing back a little, refusing to give her what she craved. If she wanted to use him *then she could damn well say the words. 'Yes, Mary, what do you want?'*

Mary rocked her pelvis against his hand as the maddening friction plateaued, divinity frustratingly out of reach. 'Please, Vasco,' she gasped.

Vasco was harder than he'd ever been in his life, watching her lying before him half exposed, fully abandoned, head tossing from side to side, her body begging for that which she would not put into words.

He shook his head. 'Please what, Mary?' he demanded, quickening the pace for a few tantalising seconds, then backing off.

Mary bit into her lip hard, lifting her hips off the bed. 'Vasco!'

'Say it,' he growled.

She opened her eyes and glared at him. 'Damn it, Vasco.' But she knew in that second she'd have given him the world if he'd asked for it. 'I like it when you do this to me,' she said. 'I want you to do it to me. I just plain want you. Now please...please...' her wrists yanked at the bonds '...I beg of you...'

Vasco grinned. 'Of course, Lady Mary, why didn't you just say so?'

But the rebuke that came to Mary's lips was lost as Vasco drove her over the edge in ten seconds. When she was capable of opening her eyes a little while later it was to his smug triumphant smile.

'Okay, Vasco,' she said, her breathing still not quite normal. 'Untie me now.'

Vasco shook his head and the gleam in his eye was positively wicked as he unlaced his breeches.

'I'm just getting started.'

THE next week flew by. Between long nights—and sometimes long days—below deck they made it to Micronesia, sailing into Weno in Chuuk State where they restocked and sorted out the official paperwork.

Chuuk, home to a giant lagoon, the final resting place for over a hundred ships, planes and submarines that had perished during fierce World War Two battles, was a magnate for wreck divers worldwide. Time and warm tropical waters had seen the wrecks bloom into breathtaking coral gardens and artificial reefs sporting a kaleidoscope of colours.

But they headed beyond that to the lesser known outer reefs fringing the deeper waters of the Pacific where Nathan had been convinced Inigo's boat had gone down in bad weather. The islands of Micronesia had once been part of the Spanish East Indies and, Nathan believed, a rich hunting ground for a pirate who wasn't picky or patriotic when it came to loot.

The fact that a veritable maze of two thousand plus, mainly uninhabited islands lay at his disposal, providing the perfect cover to lay low in between raids, had no doubt also been a plus for Inigo Alvarez.

The weather stayed calm and visibility was excellent as, for the first six days, Rick and Stella island-hopped, diving the area Nathan had deduced from his lifetime of research was the most likely resting pace for *The Mermaid*. It was about a hundred nautical miles square so they divided it up into a grid and painstakingly explored each segment from sun up to sundown.

Had they been in the *Persephone* or one of the other boats in the salvage fleet, they would have had all kinds of equipment to help them in their quest. But this was just a basic exploratory—old-fashioned treasure hunting at its best. Like they were kids again, pretending to find Spanish galleons while their fathers undertook their latest salvage operation.

And neither of them would have had it any other way.

The deepest water was ten metres but it still took a couple of dives for Stella to gain her confidence. Ever since she could swim, Stella had dived, and she'd held her open water diving certification for many years, but she hadn't been in a wetsuit for some time now.

Rick, used to diving much, much deeper, enjoyed the slower pace and took time to admire the magnificent underwater scenery, including the curvy little water nymph in a wetsuit that left nothing to the imagination.

At night she wrote, more inspired than ever by being back in the water again, and he reviewed the data from their dives.

And then they burned up the sheets.

On the seventh day they rested. They anchored off one of the many sandy atolls, loaded up the dinghy and motored the short distance, beaching the little runabout high above the tide level. They lolled in the shallows, making love as the water lapped gently around their legs. They sunbathed nude and ate sandwiches and drank cold beer for lunch. They dozed under a stand of coconut palms.

Three other islands could be seen nearby, towering out of the glittering ocean, and in the distance another boat, probably a dive charter, slowly traversed the horizon. It was a reminder that they weren't the only two people in the world, which had been an easy assumption to make these last idyllic days.

'Maybe we could just move here?' Stella said sleepily.

Rick smiled as he rolled his head to look at her. 'Sounds good to me.' If he was going to be stuck on a deserted island with anyone, she would be his preference. 'What happens when the laptop runs out of battery?' he teased.

Stella smiled too. 'Don't be practical,' she murmured as she drifted off again.

When she woke the sun wasn't as high overhead and Rick was lying on his stomach propped up on his elbows beside her. A sea breeze ruffled the papers he was reading. She lay there for a few minutes listening to the swish of the waves against the beach and the rustle of the wind through the palm leaves.

I could get used to this.

She rolled up onto her elbow, dropping a kiss on his bare

shoulder. 'What if it's not here?' she asked. 'What if *The Mermaid* is like Atlantis or El Dorado?'

Rick turned his head and nuzzled her temple before returning his attention to the research material he'd printed off the web just prior to leaving the boat this morning. He'd pored over everything he could get his hands on since deciding to undertake this voyage and he'd come across some more potentially useful information last night.

'It might not be here but I think your father's research definitely supports its existence and his reasonings for *The Mermaid* being in these waters are very sound.'

Stella nodded. She hoped so. It would be good to know that something her father had committed so much of his time and energy to might be realised. They'd both been aware, subliminally, that this voyage had been a pilgrimage of sorts. A way to pay homage to Nathan and his dream.

Neither of them wanted to return empty-handed.

'I'm going for a snorkel,' she said. 'You want to join me?'

Rick shook his head. 'Maybe later.'

Stella kissed his shoulder again. 'Are you sure?' she asked. 'I'm going naked.'

Ah, now that got his attention.

He smiled at her before kissing her hard on the mouth. 'Temptress,' he muttered as he pulled away. 'Be off with you.'

Stella laughed. 'Okay, fine,' she said, standing and stripping off her bikini where she stood, throwing it down on the papers he was reading.

Rick chuckled as he picked it up and looked over his shoulder to find her naked, hips swaying seductively as she sashayed down to the shoreline, a mask and snorkel in one hand. Her skin was a light golden brown from all the sun she'd been getting and as she turned and gave him a wave he copped a magnificent side view of full breast and tiny waist before she waded into the ocean. He levered himself up, turning to sit, papers still in hand, watching as the warm tropical waters slowly swallowed her up.

He realised after looking up for the tenth time in ten minutes he was too distracted to read. The reef was close to the shore so she was only a couple of metres out and he could see the bobbing of her naked bottom as she lazily circled back and forth across the surface, occasionally duck diving and blowing water out of her snorkel when she reappeared.

When a coconut fell beside him, missing him by about an inch, he decided it was time to give up and just enjoy the view. He absently picked up the coconut and shook it, hearing the swish of milk inside. He grabbed his diver's knife out of his backpack and, being an old hand at husking coconuts, quickly did so.

By the time the outer shell was peeled away and he'd removed the stringy bark, revealing the hard smooth surface, Stella was emerging from the ocean like something from a James Bond film.

Except nude. Her blonde hair slicked back from her face, clinging to her naked back like a sheath of honey-gold silk.

Like a mermaid.

He brought the bald nut to his face and inhaled the sweet earthy aroma as he watched her walking towards him. The fragrance was pure Stella.

A fragrance he'd become quite addicted to.

Her bell tinkled as she drew closer, his erection increasing with her every footfall. When she threw the snorkel and mask down beside him his mouth was as dry as the powdery sand beneath him.

'Do women practise that little hip swing or is it just part of their DNA?' he asked, looking up into her face. Water droplets clung to her eyelashes and ran down her body.

Stella laughed as she deliberately reached behind her to wrap her hair around her hand and squeeze out the excess water. 'I don't know what you're talking about.' She grinned.

'Oh, yeah?' he growled as he threw the coconut down and gently tumbled her to the ground.

Stella went down laughing, clinging to his shoulders as she settled against the soft sand. He straddled her, looming above. The grains felt warm and powdery beneath the cool skin of her back, as did the sun on her face, their formerly shaded position now mostly in light as the day grew later.

'I'm going to have sand everywhere,' she grouched good-naturedly.

'That's the plan.' He grinned as he lowered his mouth to hers. Her lips and the curve of her waist were cool to touch. 'Water cold?' he asked as his tongue lapped at the water droplets still clinging and cooling her throat.

Stella shut her eyes and angled her neck to give him wider access. 'A little.'

Rick smiled against her neck. He sat and groped around beside him. 'Let's see if we can't warm you up.'

Stella opened her eyes just in time to see him holding a coconut and his diver's knife over her abdomen. As a teenager she'd often watched him husk a coconut, the muscles of his back and arms way more fascinating than they should have been.

She quirked an eyebrow. 'Been busy?'

He grinned as he struck the coconut with the handle of the knife right between the eyes. It capitulated easily, cracking in half, clear fluid running out over his hand and dripping onto her cool belly.

He eased it apart, gratified to hear her gasp as he poured most of the warm milk over her belly and breasts. Her nipples ruched before him and his erection surged. He groaned as the aroma of ocean and her wafted up to him and he bent his head to her.

'I want to taste you here,' he muttered. His hot tongue swiped over puckered nipples and she arched her back. He removed every trace of the warm juice before moving on.

'And here,' he said, going down, following the trail of liquid that had puddled in her belly button. He heard the suck of her breath as he lapped it up. She tasted sweet and salty. Like the ocean, tropical breezes and the soft sugary nirvana of coconuts.

He sat back on his haunches, watching her, waiting for her to open her eyes. When her eyelashes fluttered open he picked up the half-coconut that still had a little milk remaining.

'And here,' he murmured, trickling it between her legs, as he had done with the mango, supressing a groan as she licked her lips and panted, her thighs parting, the sunlight glistening there so he could see it coating all of her.

He tossed the shell aside, swooping his head down, his hands gliding up her body to cup her breasts, his thumbs brushing across the nipples.

It was then, as he used his elbows to push her open to him more, that he noticed it for the first time. The sun shone like a spotlight and it was suddenly obvious.

A tiny blemish. A pink birthmark.

Exactly where Lady Mary had hers.

He stared at it, as he tried to think past the pounding of his heart.

So...she was Lady Mary?

But the heady aroma of her drowned in coconut juice was rendering his thought processes useless. He wanted to ask her. Needed to know.

He should stop and demand that she tell him the truth.

But she was making those little noises at the back of her throat again and as another waft of coconut headed his way he actually salivated.

Stella rotated her pelvis as the anticipation built to breaking point. Rick liked to tease but this had gone on long enough. She knew the touch of his mouth was coming and every second he made her wait, she could feel herself get wetter.

'Rick!' she begged, unable to bear it any longer. 'Please,' she whimpered, lifting her hips involuntarily. 'Please.'

It was the whimper that did it—just as it always did. There would be time enough for questions later. So he shut his eyes and gave her what she was asking for, licking that cute strawberry mark just as Vasco had done, savouring the sweet coconut essence of her, pinning her to the sand with his tongue and not letting her up until her climax rent the air.

Stella woke the next morning to a tight feeling at her wrists and a strange sense of foreboding. It was immediately allayed when she saw Rick, one knee planted on the edge of the mattress, his face hovering over her, smiling.

'Morning,' he murmured, kissing her.

She kissed him back. It wasn't until she tried to move her arms to hug him that the foreboding returned. It only took a moment to figure out why. She looked behind her. Her wrists were tied with some kind of material to the posts of his bed. As were her feet.

She was naked and spreadeagled.

Her pulse leapt at the illicitness of it all. Was Rick going to enact the scene from *Pleasure Hunt* where Vasco had tied Mary to the bed?

She looked at him. 'You do know that, unlike Mary, I am perfectly willing to ask you for sex and, not only that, but to tell you how, when, where and the number of times I want you to do me, right?'

Rick chuckled as he sat on the edge of the bed. 'I've noticed. You're really not her, are you?' he asked innocently.

Stella nodded as she averted her eyes to her ankle ties. 'Is that one of my sarongs?' she asked.

Rick grinned. 'Sorry. I'm all out of eighteenth-century satin sashes and I thought it'd be gentler on your wrists and ankles than nautical rope.'

Stella pulled against the bonds to test them and had to

agree. Even if she wanted to get out of them, which she didn't, she knew it would be futile—sailors knew how to tie knots.

'How on earth did you manage not to wake me?' she asked.

He shrugged. 'Well, it took me a while and, thankfully, you're a heavy sleeper.'

Stella nodded. That was true. 'So, was there a purpose to this or are you just into bondage suddenly?'

Rick looked at her, naked and spread on his bed like a gift from Neptune himself. He was ragingly hard and pleased he'd decided to put on some boardies instead of being naked as he'd originally thought yesterday when he'd lain in post-coital glory on the beach beside her, formulating this plan to get a confession out of her.

He wasn't sure why knowing whether she was Lady Mary was increasingly important to him.

It just was.

He'd often wondered if she thought about him. Knowing that she might have fantasised about *them* while he'd been training himself not to was beyond tantalising. Maybe it was ego, maybe it was something else he didn't want to examine too closely, but he had to know.

And he'd known that there was only one way to find out.

He smiled down at her as he pushed off his bed. 'Oh, there's a purpose.'

Stella's nipples hardened beneath his incendiary blue gaze as she noticed she was the only one naked. 'You're dressed.' She pouted.

His smile broadened. 'For now.'

Stella's heart beat a little faster at the promise in those two incredible eyes the exact colour of the tropical waters surrounding them.

Rick prowled around the bed as Vasco had done, his gaze boldly running over every delectable inch of her. Blatantly lingering on her breasts and the strawberry mark he couldn't see from this distance but he knew the exact location of—low and to the left of her centre. Their gazes locked as he roamed, dragging out the moment.

He stopped at the foot of the bed, shoving his hands on his hips. 'I discovered something very interesting yesterday,' he murmured.

The timbre of his voice dragged silken fingers across her skin. 'Really?' She hoped she sounded nonchalant, that the vibration of her madly fluttering heart wasn't shaking the entire bed.

He nodded as he planted a knee on the mattress. 'It's intriguing to say the least,' he continued.

'Something to do with Inigo?' she asked as she watched Rick prowl towards her, the light of a fictional pirate in his eyes.

He shook his head. 'No. Something to do with you.'

'Oh?' Her voice sounded high and breathy as he came right in close, his knees brushing her spread inner thighs.

Rick reached out and brushed his fingertips down her exposed centre. Stella gasped and bucked. He smiled. 'You like that, don't you?'

Stella bit her lip and nodded her head as the brush became something more purposeful. 'Yes.'

The hammer of his heart was loud in his head as his finger followed the path of her heat and sank inside her. 'And this?'

Stella whimpered. 'Yes.'

'You want more?' he asked, sliding another finger home, using his thumb to rub the spot that was already tight and hard.

Stella was ready in an instant, balanced on a knife edge of anticipation. 'Yes.'

Rick smiled. 'Don't you want to know what I discovered?'

She arched her back as he picked up the pace. 'Yes, yes.'

Rick swallowed. She looked so bloody desirable at the mercy of his hand that he wanted to rip his boardies off and forget the damn birthmark but it was about more than the blemish.

Had she ever fantasised about them together? As he had despite Nathan's unspoken law? Had she felt something more than friendship for him?

As he had.

He had to know.

He withdrew his fingers from inside her. 'I found that you, too, have a birthmark.'

Stella felt her orgasm recede beyond her reach as her breath stuttered to a halt. She opened her eyes to find his blue ones glittering down at her.

'Strangely enough,' he continued, sliding his finger to the left, locating the blemish immediately, 'in exactly the same spot that Lady Mary has hers. Coincidence, Stel, or are *you* Lady Mary?'

She shook her head vigorously. *This was not what she'd expected.* 'No.'

What would he think if he knew? He'd already guessed too much about her fantasy life from *Pleasure Hunt.*

He quirked an eyebrow as he brushed his finger against the birthmark again. 'Really?'

Stella panted even as she fought not to. 'Really.'

He moved his hand from her completely. 'I think you're lying, Stella. Mary's so very, very familiar to me.'

It was something he'd only just realised, too caught up in the big things to recognise the subtleties of the character. The nuances. The jut of her chin, the turn of her head, the glimpse of her humanity beneath all her starched upper-class Britishness.

Stella glared at him, now torn between telling him to go to hell and lying to him so he'd finish what he'd started.

And she felt vulnerable.

A state that had nothing to do with her nudity.

He wanted her to look at things that she'd never questioned too deeply.

'What the hell does it matter?' she asked in exasperation, yanking against her bonds.

'Because…' He looked into her simmering olive gaze, knowing that if he was demanding the truth from her then the least he could do was return the favour. 'Because despite what your father decreed, I used to fantasise about you. Not consciously, *never consciously*. But in my dreams…that was different. And…'

This bit was the hard part. The bit he'd never admitted to before, not even to himself. 'I guess I'd always wondered… hoped, maybe…that you might have done the same.'

Stella's heart ticked away madly like a thousand halyards tinkling in a stiff breeze. There'd been a vibe between them as teenagers—not spoken about or acted upon. But if she'd known that he used to dream about her she might have ignored her father's silent censure.

He looked so serious kneeling between her legs. Torn, surprised even, as if his words had come as a revelation to him too.

How could she not reciprocate?

Her father was gone and, even if he hadn't been, she was an adult, no longer needy of his approval.

'Yes,' she murmured, their gazes locking. 'Lady Mary is me. Beneath all those layers of clothing she has my heart and soul. *And* my desires.'

The admission was amazingly cathartic. She licked her lips, her mouth suddenly as dry as the ties binding her to the bed.

'When Vasco stormed into my head, I knew he was you. Deep down anyway—it took me a little while to recognise it consciously. And when I knew that, I knew whoever his woman was going to be, she would be me.'

Rick smiled triumphantly as Vasco had done at Mary's capitulation.

Stella rolled her eyes. 'I fantasised constantly about you when I was a teenager. And when I was writing the book…'

She stopped and blushed at the memory. 'Let's just say that Mr Buzzy got quite the working out.'

Rick blinked, relief flooding through his veins. 'So, I wasn't alone?' he murmured.

She shook her head. 'You weren't alone.'

Rick laid both hands over his heart and mouthed, 'Thank you.' Then he leaned forward and brushed his mouth lightly over hers, murmuring, 'Thank you, thank you,' as he dropped a string of tiny kisses before sitting back on his haunches again.

She quirked an eyebrow at him, a smile on her face. 'You going to untie me now?'

Rick shook his head as he ripped at the Velcro fastener on his boardies, a wicked glint in his eyes. 'I'm just getting started.'

The next day Stella and Rick were at six metres and just about to head back to the boat for lunch when Stella spotted a large shape looming below them. Visibility was still excellent but the find was partially obscured by a cascading wall of coral. Rick's breathing and heart rate picked up and he made a conscious effort to control them as they headed down to explore further.

As they neared, the ghostly grey shape of a remarkably intact, large, old wooden ship appeared. It was wedged into some kind of rocky ravine, the outer ledge of which fell away into the deep blue abyss of Pacific Ocean.

They both hovered above it for a moment, their torches aimed at the broken waterlogged beauty, stunned to be finally staring at something they'd both wondered from time to time ever really existed.

Was it *The Mermaid*? They couldn't know for certain—yet. But Rick felt sure in his gut—either that or it was Nathan's presence. They glided slowly through the waters surrounding the ship, trying to find any outward identifying marks but, whatever the origins, Rick already knew from years of salvage experience they had found something truly amazing.

They circled it in awed silence, the coral encrusted ship spooky in its watery grave. Adrenaline buzzed through Rick's veins as he became more certain, the dimensions of the find putting it in *The Mermaid*'s league. They didn't attempt to go in—that would come later when a more detailed survey had been undertaken. Too many divers had got themselves trapped and died in wrecks to be foolhardy.

And, as Nathan had always drilled into him, a shipwreck was a sacred site. The final resting place of the poor souls that had perished along with it and as such was to be treated with respect.

They discovered a figurehead when the bow came into view but it was too decayed and encrusted with weedy growths and coral life to tell if it was the laughing mermaid that had famously spearheaded Inigo Alvarez's ship. The nameplate proclaiming the ship as *La Sirena* was nowhere in sight.

Of course. It was never that easy...

Rick and Stella made their way to where the ghostly shape had settled on rock. He shone his torch, inspecting the damage, trying to ascertain a point of impact. Stella shone hers too, the beam hitting rock, a flash of something reflecting back. Stella looked closer, her heart thumping loudly in the eerie underwater stillness, her hand reaching for the object. She scooped it up, lay it flat in the palm of her hand, shone her torch on it.

A gold coin.

Rick felt a tug on his leg. He turned to find Stella, who was grinning like a loon, holding up what appeared to be a round coin. His heartbeat climbed off the scale as she passed it over.

It was gold and in good nick. Gold coins of good purity usually survived in water unscathed, unlike bronze coins that were degraded by salinity.

It was also Spanish.

It still didn't confirm the ship was *The Mermaid*. Archaeologists were going to have to decide that. But it was another strong indicator.

He grinned back and hugged her tight.

A couple of hours later they were back on board and had finished notifying the necessary people. Rick had organised for the marine archaeology company they used to send a team and had started the application process for a permit to salvage.

Stella was on deck looking at the marker buoy in the distance when Rick came up behind her. She was in a vest top and sarong and he pressed the chilled bottle of champagne they'd brought way back in Cairns for just this occasion against one shoulder as he kissed the other.

Stella jumped at the shock of it, then turned in his arms, and hugged him. 'Thank you,' she whispered.

Rick held her close, the boat bobbing gently. Realising Nathan's dream had meant as much to her as it had to him.

'I've been thinking,' she said, pulling back slightly. 'When they confirm it's *The Mermaid*, I'd like to bring Dad's ashes out here and scatter them.'

Nathan had always wanted them scattered at sea, but until now Stella hadn't felt ready to let him go.

Rick nodded. 'Good idea.' He smiled. 'Let's drink to Nathan,' he said.

They eased apart and he handed her the flutes as he worked the cork. Its pop was lost in the vast ocean surrounds and he quickly filled the glasses, handing her one.

'To Dad,' she said, holding her glass aloft.

Rick nodded, clinking his flute against hers. 'To Nathan.'

He glanced at her as she sipped the frothy nectar and she grinned at him. The breeze caught her drying blonde hair and the sun sparkled on the sea behind her like the champagne bubbles. She looked like a mermaid, a *sirena*, and he felt deep, deep-down-in-his-bones happy.

'What?' Stella asked as the glitter in his gaze became speculative.

'I think I love you,' he murmured.

The words fell from his lips and he didn't even bother to recall them because he knew in that instant that they were the truth. He did love her.

He'd loved her for ever.

Stella blinked. 'Okay...no more champagne for you,' she joked.

He laughed, then sobered, his gaze roaming her lovely familiar face. 'I'm sorry, I know that's sudden but...it's not really. It's just been a long time coming.'

Stella realised he was serious. Her pulse tripped. 'But...I thought the ocean, this...' she threw her arm out, indicating the glory of the scenery around them '...is your great love.'

Rick shook his head. 'This is nothing without you.'

Stella's heart clanged like a gong. She didn't know what to say. The fact that she loved him too was a no-brainer. It was suddenly as clear as the tropical waters fringing the pristine Micronesian reefs. In fact, she couldn't remember a time she hadn't loved him. It had always been there, snuggled inside her. She just hadn't been free to admit it.

Until now.

But she'd already lived through one broken marriage because of the sea and, no matter how much she loved him, she couldn't be with a man who wouldn't put her first.

Stella shook her head sadly, not allowing her love to bloom. 'It's not enough, Rick. Love's not enough. My father loved my mother, after all. I need to know you want me more than the ocean. That you'll put me before it. Something my father and your father *never* did.'

Rick stood firm, understanding her reticence, knowing that what he did for a job was hard on relationships but refusing to be cowed by it. 'You want me to walk away, I'll walk away.'

Stella lifted her hand and stroked his whiskers. 'I can't

ask you to do that, Rick. I'm not going to forbid you from the ocean—I saw how much grief that caused my mother in the long run. That has to be your choice.'

Rick lifted his hand to cover hers with his. 'The sea is not an easy mistress, Stel. She's selfish and addictive. But I've seen what happened with Nathan and Linda, and lived with the consequences of my father's inability to choose between two loves. Believe me, I know the heartache of that just as well as you and I don't want that for you and me. Rest assured, Stel, I will never put the sea before you.' His hands slid to her shoulders. *Never.*

Stella wanted to believe him. His brilliant blue eyes glittered with openness and honesty and she wanted to fall into them for ever. But... 'So tell me how this works?'

He shrugged. 'Up until we decide to start a family—'

'Wait,' she interrupted, the boat suddenly rolling under her feet a little. 'We're starting a family?'

'Sure...one day. Absolutely.' He frowned. 'I thought you wanted kids?'

Stella felt a lump in her throat as she nodded. 'Absolutely. Not soon. But one day.'

'Well, until then,' he continued, gently rubbing his hands up and down her arms, 'we can divide our time between Cornwall and salvage jobs. You have a portable career, Stel, and you love the business as much as I do so...why not?'

Why not indeed? Stella thought. Just because her parents hadn't been able to compromise didn't mean that they couldn't. And he was right—as long as she had a laptop and access to the Internet, her office could be anywhere.

'And when kids come along I'll manage the business from land and get someone in to do the hands-on stuff.'

Stella frowned at him. 'You would do that?'

He nodded. 'For you, I'd do it happily. I guess I'd like to go and spend the odd few days here and there at sea, checking on things, and when the kids get older we can take them on the *Persephone* in the school holidays just like when we were young.'

Stella felt that lump thicken as he painted a picture she'd dreamt about all her life. One that she was supposed to have lived with her own parents, but her father hadn't ever been able to stay on land long enough.

'How do I know you're not just telling me stuff I want to hear?' she asked. 'How many times do you think Dad promised Mum things would be different next time he came home?'

Rick pulled her in close to him. 'I'm not Nathan.'

He held her fiercely for a moment before pulling back to look into her eyes.

'I loved your father, he was like a father to me, you know that, but I was a little jealous of you having Linda. I wished she could have been my mother too. I never got how Nathan had such a terrific woman like Linda and didn't appreciate her. I've seen two male role models in my life blow it with women who loved them with far-reaching consequences, so, trust me, I won't ever make that mistake.'

Stella nodded. She believed him when he said he didn't want to make the same mistakes. Hindsight had put them both on the same page and love would keep them there.

'I love you,' she murmured, freeing her heart, letting her love bloom.

Rick smiled a slow steady smile as she said the three words he'd been waiting to hear nearly all his life.

Better late than never.

'Is that a yes?' he asked.

Stella laughed. 'A yes to what?'

'Embarking on a lifelong pleasure hunt?' he teased.

She smiled and raised her glass. 'That's a *hell* yes.'

Rick lowered his head. 'Then let's get started,' he whispered.

* * * * *

THE PRINCE SHE
NEVER KNEW

KATE HEWITT

To Maisey, Caitlin and Jennie, who first inspired
me with the idea for this story! Love, K.

CHAPTER ONE

TODAY WAS HER wedding day. Alyse Barras gazed at her pale, pinched face in the mirror and decided that not all brides were radiant. As it happened, she looked as if she were on the way to the gallows.

No, she amended, not the gallows; a quick and brutal end was not to be hers, but rather a long, drawn-out life sentence: a loveless marriage to a man whom she barely knew, despite their six-year engagement. Yet even so a small kernel of hope was determined to take root in her heart, to unfurl and grow in the shallowest and poorest of soils.

Maybe he'll learn to love me...

Prince Leo Diomedi of Maldinia seemed unlikely to learn anything of the sort, yet still she hoped. She had to.

'Miss Barras? Are you ready?'

Alyse turned from her reflection to face one of the wedding coordinator's assistants who stood in the doorway of the room she'd been given in the vast royal palace in Averne, Maldinia's capital city, nestled in the foothills of the Alps.

'As ready as I'll ever be,' she replied, trying to smile, but everything in her felt fragile, breakable, and the curve of her lips seemed as if it could crack her face. Split her apart.

The assistant Marina came forward, looking her over

in the assessing and proprietary way Alyse had got used to in the three days since she'd arrived in Maldinia—or, really, the six years since she'd agreed to this engagement. She was a commodity to be bought, shaped, presented. An object of great value, to be sure, but still an object.

She'd learned to live with it, although on today of all days—her wedding day, the day most little girls dreamed about—she felt the falseness of her own role more, the sense that her life was simply something to be staged.

Marina twitched Alyse's veil this way and that, until she gave a nod of satisfaction. It billowed gauzily over her shoulders, a gossamer web edged with three-hundred-year-old lace.

'And now the dress,' Marina said, and flicked her fingers to indicate that Alyse should turn around.

Alyse moved slowly in a circle as Marina examined the yards of white satin that billowed out behind her, the lace bodice that hugged her breasts and hips and had taken eight top-secret fittings over the last six months. The dress had been the source of intense media speculation, the subject of hundreds of articles in tabloids, gossip magazines, even respected newspapers, television and radio interviews, celebrity and gossip blogs and websites.

What kind of dress would the world's real-life Cinderella—not a very creative way of typecasting her, but it had stuck—wear to marry her very own prince, her one true love?

Well, this. And Alyse had had no say in it at all. It was a beautiful dress, she allowed as she caught a glance of the billowing white satin in the full-length mirror. She could hardly complain. She might have chosen something just like it—if she'd been given a choice.

Marina's walkie-talkie crackled and she spoke into it in rapid Italian, too fast for Alyse to understand, even though she'd been learning Italian ever since she'd become engaged to Leo. It was the native language of his country, and Maldinia's queen-in-waiting should be able to speak it. Unfortunately no one spoke slowly enough for her to be able to understand.

'They're ready.' Marina twitched the dress just as she had the veil and then rummaged on the vanity table for some blusher. 'You look a bit pale,' she explained, and brushed Alyse's cheeks with blusher even though the make-up artist had already spent an hour on her face.

'Thank you,' Alyse murmured. She wished her mother were here, but the royal protocol was—and always had been, according to Queen Sophia—that the bride prepare by herself. Alyse wondered whether that was true. Queen Sophia tended to insist on doing things the way they'd 'always been done' when really it was simply the way she wanted them done. And even though Alyse's mother, Natalie, was Queen Sophia's best friend from their days together at a Swiss boarding school, she clearly didn't want Natalie getting in the way on this most important and august of occasions.

Or so Alyse assumed. She was the bride, and she felt as if she were in the way.

She wondered if she would feel so as a wife.

No. She closed her eyes as Marina next dusted her face with loose powder. She couldn't think like that, couldn't give in to the despair, not on today of all days. She had once before, and it had led only to heartache and regret. Today she wanted to hope, to believe, or at least to try to. Today was meant to be a beginning, not an end.

But if Leo hasn't learned to love me in the last six years, why should he now?

Two months ago, with media interest at a frenzied height, her mother had taken her on a weekend to Monaco. They'd sat in deck chairs and sipped frothy drinks and

Alyse had felt herself just begin to relax when Natalie had said, 'You don't have to do this if you don't want to.'

She'd tensed all over again, her drink halfway to her lips. 'Do what?'

'Marry him, Alyse. I know it's all got completely out of hand with the media, and also with the Diomedis, to be frank. But you are still your own woman and I want to make sure you're sure…' Her mother had trailed off, her eyes clouded with anxiety, and Alyse had wondered what she'd guessed.

Did she have even an inkling of how little there was between her and Leo? Few people knew; the world believed they were madly in love, and had done ever since Leo had first kissed her cheek six years ago and the resulting photograph had captured the public's imagination.

Leo's mother Sophia knew, of course, as the pretense of their grand romance had been her idea, Alyse suspected, and of course Leo's father, Alessandro, who had first broached the whole idea to her when she'd been just eighteen years old and starry-eyed over Leo. Perhaps Alexa— Leo's sister, her fiery nature so different from his own sense of cool containment—had guessed.

And, naturally, Leo knew. Leo knew he didn't love her. He just didn't know that for six years she'd been secretly, desperately, loving him.

'I'm happy, Maman,' Alyse had said quietly, and had reached over to squeeze her mother's hand. 'I admit, the media circus isn't my favourite part, but…I love Leo.' She had stumbled only slightly over this unfortunate truth.

'I want for you what your father and I have had,' Natalie had said, and Alyse had smiled wanly. Her parents' romance was something out of a fairy tale: the American heiress who had captured the heart of a wealthy French financier. Alyse had heard the story many times, how her father had seen her mother across a crowded room—they'd both been attending some important dinner—and he had made his way over to her and said, 'What are you doing with the rest of your life?'

She'd simply smiled and answered, 'Spending it with you.'

Love at first sight. And not just an ordinary, run-of-the-mill love, but of the over-the-top, utterly consuming variety.

Of course her mother wanted that for her. And Alyse would never admit to her how little she actually had, even as she still clung stubbornly to the hope that one day it might become more.

'I'm happy,' she'd repeated, and her mother had looked relieved if not entirely convinced.

Marina's walkie-talkie crackled again, and once again Alyse let the rapid-fire Italian assault her with incomprehension.

'They're waiting,' Marina announced briskly, and Alyse wondered if she imagined that slightly accusing tone. She'd felt it since she'd arrived in Maldinia, mostly from Queen Sophia: *you're not precisely what we'd have chosen for our son and heir, but you'll have to do. We have no choice, after all.*

The media—the whole world—had made sure of that. There had been no going back from that moment captured by a photographer six years ago when Leo had come to her eighteenth birthday party and brushed his lips against her cheek in a congratulatory kiss. Alyse, instinctively and helplessly, had stood on her tiptoes and clasped her hand to his face.

If she could go back in time, would she change that moment? Would she have turned her face away and stopped all the speculation, the frenzy?

No, she wouldn't have, and the knowledge was galling. At first it had been her love for Leo that had made her agree to their faked fairy tale, but as the years had passed and Leo had shown no interest in loving her—or love at all—she'd considered whether to cut her losses and break off the engagement.

She never had; she'd possessed neither the courage nor conviction to do something that would quite literally have rocked the world. And of course she'd clung to a hope that seemed naïve at best, more likely desperate: that he would learn to love her.

And yet...we get along. We're friends, of a sort. Surely that's a good foundation for marriage?

Always the hope.

'This way, Miss Barras,' Marina said, and ushered her out of the room she'd been getting dressed in and down a long, ornate corridor with marble walls and chandeliers glittering overhead every few feet.

The stiff satin folds of Alyse's dress rustled against the parquet as she followed Marina down the hallway and towards the main entrance of the palace where a dozen liveried footmen stood to attention. She would make the walk to the cathedral across the street and then the far more important walk down the aisle by herself, another Maldinian tradition.

'Wait.' Marina held up a hand and Alyse paused in front of the gilt-panelled doors that led to the front courtyard of the palace where at least a hundred reporters and photographers, probably more, waited to capture this iconic moment. Alyse had had so many iconic moments in the last six years she felt as if her entire adult life had been catalogued in the glossy pages of gossip magazines.

Marina circled her the way Alyse imagined a lion or tiger circled its prey. She was being fanciful, she knew, but her nerves were stretched to breaking point. She'd been in Maldinia for three days and she hadn't seen Leo outside of state functions once. Hadn't spoken to him alone in over a year.

And she was marrying him in approximately three minutes.

Paula, the royal family's press secretary, approached with a brisk click of heels. 'Alyse? You're ready?' she asked in accented English.

She nodded back, not trusting herself to speak.

'Excellent. Now, all you need to remember is to smile. You're Cinderella and this is your glass slipper moment, yes?' She twitched Alyse's veil just as Sophia had done, and Alyse wondered how much more pointless primping she would have to endure. As soon as she stepped outside the veil would probably blow across her face anyway. At least she had enough hair spray in her hair to prevent a single strand from so much as stirring. She felt positively shellacked.

'Cinderella,' she repeated. 'Right.' She'd been acting like Cinderella for six years. She didn't really need the reminder.

'Everyone wants to be you,' Paula continued. 'Every girl, every woman, is dreaming of walking in your shoes right now. And every man wants to be the prince. Don't forget to wave—this is about them as much as you. Include everyone in the fantasy, yes?'

'Right. Yes.' She knew that, had learned it over the years of public attention. And, truthfully, she didn't mind the attention of the crowds, of people who rather incredibly took encouragement and hope from her and her alleged fairy tale of a life. All they wanted from her was friendliness, a smile, a word. All she needed to be was herself.

It was the paparazzi she had trouble with, the constant scrutiny and sense of invasion as rabid journalists and photographers looked for cracks in the fairy-tale image, ways to shatter it completely.

'I'd better get out there before the clock strikes twelve,' she joked, trying to smile, but her mouth was so dry her lips stuck to her teeth. Paula frowned, whipping a tissue from her pocket to blot Alyse's lipstick.

'We're at thirty seconds,' Marina intoned, and Paula positioned Alyse in front of the doors. 'Twenty…'

Alyse knew she was supposed to emerge when the huge, ornate clock on one of the palace's towers chimed the first of its eleven sonorous notes. She would walk sedately, head held high, towards the cathedral as the clock continued chiming and arrive at its doors when the last chime fell into silence.

It had all been choreographed and rehearsed several times, down to the last second. Everything arranged, orchestrated, managed.

'Ten…'

Alyse took a deep breath, or as deep a breath as the tightly fitted bodice of her dress would allow. She felt dizzy, spots dancing before her eyes, although whether from lack of air or sheer nerves she didn't know.

'Five…'

Two footmen opened the doors to the courtyard with a flourish, and Alyse blinked in the sudden brilliance of the sun. The open doorway framed a dazzling blue sky, the two Gothic towers of the cathedral opposite and a huge throng of people.

'Go,' Paula whispered, and gave her a firm nudge in the small of her back.

Pushed by Paula, she moved forward, her dress snagging on her heel so she stumbled ever so slightly. Still it was enough for the paparazzi to notice, and dozens of cameras snapped frantically to capture the moment. Another iconic moment; Alyse could already picture the headlines: *First Stumble on The Road to Happiness?*

She steadied herself, lifted her head and gave the entire viewing world a brilliant smile. The answering cheer roared through the courtyard. Alyse could feel the sound reverberate through her chest, felt her spirits lift at their obvious excitement and approbation.

This was why she was marrying Leo, why the royal family of Maldinia had agreed to his engagement to a mere commoner: because everyone loved her.

Everyone but Leo.

Still smiling, raising one hand in a not-so-regal wave, Alyse started walking towards the cathedral. She heard a few snatched voices amidst the crowd, shouting her name, asking her to turn for a photo. She smiled, leaving the white carpet that had been laid from the palace to the cathedral to shake people's hands, accept posies of flowers.

She was deviating from the remote, regal script she'd been given, but then she always did. She couldn't help but respond to people's warmth and friendliness; all too often it was what strengthened her to maintain this charade that wasn't a charade at all—for her. For Leo, of course, it was.

But maybe, please God, it won't always be…

'Good luck, Alyse,' one starry-eyed teen gushed, clasping her hands tightly. 'You look so beautiful—you really are a princess!'

Alyse squeezed the girl's hands. 'Thank you,' she murmured. 'You look beautiful too, you know. You're glowing more than I am!'

She realised the clock had stopped chiming; she was late. Queen Sophia would be furious, yet it was because of moments like these she was here at all. She didn't stick to the royal family's formalised script; she wrote her own lines without even meaning to and the public loved them.

Except she didn't know what her lines would be once she was married. She had no idea what she would say to Leo when she finally faced him as his wife.

I love you.

Those were words she was afraid he'd never want to hear.

The cathedral doors loomed in front of her, the interior of the building dim and hushed. Alyse turned one last time towards the crowd and another roar went up, echoing through the ancient streets of Averne. She waved and blew them a kiss, and she heard another cheer. Perhaps the kiss was a bit over the top, but she felt in that moment strangely reckless, almost defiant. There was no going back now.

And then she turned back to the cathedral and her waiting groom.

Leo stood with his back to the doors of the cathedral, but he knew the moment when Alyse had entered. He heard the murmurs fall to an expectant hush, and the roar of approbation that she generated wherever she went had fallen to silence outside. He flexed his shoulders once and remained with his back to the door—and his bride. Maldinian princes did not turn around until the bride had reached the altar and Leo deviated from neither tradition nor duty.

The organ had started playing with sonorous grandeur, some kind of baroque march, and he knew Alyse was walking towards him. He felt a flicker of curiosity; he hadn't seen her dress, had no idea what she looked like in it. Polished, poised and as perfect as usual, he presumed. The perfect bride. The perfect love story. And of course, the perfect marriage. All of it the perfect pretense.

Nothing more.

Finally he felt the folds of her dress whisper against his legs and he turned to face her. He barely noticed the dress. Her face was pale except for two spots of blusher high on her cheekbones. She looked surprisingly nervous, he thought. For the past six years she'd been handling the intense media scrutiny of their engagement with apparent effortless ease, and her attack of nerves now surprised him. Alarmed him a bit too.

She'd agreed to all of this. It was a little late for cold feet.

Conscious of the stares of the congregation—as well as the cameras televising the ceremony live to millions of people—he smiled and took her hand, which was icy and small in his. He squeezed her fingers, an encouragement if anyone saw, but also a warning. Neither of them could make a mistake now. Too much rode on this marriage, this masquerade. She knew that; so did he. They'd both sold their souls, and willingly.

Now he watched as Alyse lifted her chin, her wide grey eyes flashing with both comprehension and spirit. Her lips curved in a tiny smile and she squeezed his hand back. He felt a flicker of admiration for her courage and poise—as well as one of relief. Crisis averted.

She turned towards the archbishop who was performing the ceremony and he saw the gleam of chestnut hair beneath the lace of her veil, the soft glimmer of a pearl in the shell-like curve of her ear. He turned to face the man as well.

Fifteen minutes later it was done. They'd said their vows and Leo had brushed his lips against Alyse's. He'd kissed her dozens, perhaps hundreds, of times during their engagement, always in front of a crowd. A camera.

He kissed her now as he always had, a firm press of lips that conveyed enthusiasm and even desire without actually feeling either. He didn't want to feel either; he wasn't about to complicate what had been a business arrangement by stirring up a hornet's nest of emotions—either in her or himself.

Although now that they were married, now that they would actually consummate this marriage, he would certainly allow himself to feel attraction at least, a natural desire. All his life he'd controlled such contrary emotions, refused to let them dictate his behaviour as they had his parents'. Refused to let them ruin his life and wreck the monarchy, as they had with his parents.

No, he had more dignity, more self-control, than that. But he certainly intended to take full advantage of his marriage vows—and his marriage bed. It didn't mean his emotions would actually be engaged.

Just his libido.

Leo lifted his head and gazed down at her, smiling slightly for the sake of their audience, and saw that Alyse was gazing at him with panic in her eyes. Her nerves clearly had not abated.

Suppressing his own annoyance, he gently wrapped his hands around hers—they were still icy—and pried them from his shoulders. 'All right?' he murmured.

She nodded, managed a rather sickly smile and turned towards the congregation for their recession down the aisle.

And now it begins, Leo thought. The rest of his life enacting this endless charade, started by a single moment six years ago.

Who could ever have known how a paparazzi photographer would catch that kiss? And not just his lips on her cheek but her hand clasped against his cheek, her face uplifted, eyes shining like silver stars.

That photo had been on the cover of every major publication in the western world. It had been named the third most influential photograph of the century, a fact which made Leo want to bark in cynical laughter. A single, *stupid* kiss influential? Important?

But it had become important, because the sight of the happiness shining from Alyse's eyes had ignited a generation, fired their hearts with faith in love and hope for the future. Some economists credited the photograph with helping to kick-start Europe's economy, a fact Leo thought entirely absurd.

Yet when the monarchy's public relations department had realised the power of that photograph, they had harnessed it for themselves. For him, his father King Alessandro and all the future Diomedis that would reign over Maldinia.

Which had led, inevitably, to this engagement and now marriage, he all the while pretending to live up to what that photograph had promised—because for the public to realise it was nothing more than a fake would be a disaster.

Hand in hand with his bride, he walked down the aisle and into a lifetime of pretending.

She was breaking up, splitting apart, all the fragile, barely held parts of her shattering into pieces. She'd held herself together for so long and now…?

She wasn't sure she could do it any more. And it was too late not to.

Somehow Alyse made it down the aisle, although everything around her—the people, the colours, the noise and light—was a blur. Everything but the look that had flashed in Leo's eyes after he'd kissed her, something bordering on impatient annoyance at her obvious unease. Her panic.

She felt Leo's arm like a band of iron beneath her hand. 'Smile as we come out of the cathedral,' he murmured, and then the crowds were upon them, their roar loud in their ears and, still feeling sick inside, she smiled for all she was worth.

The wordless roar turned into a rhythmic chant: *bacialo! Bacialo!*

The crowd wanted them to kiss. Wordlessly, Alyse turned to Leo, tilted her head up at him as he gazed down at her and stroked her cheek with a single fingertip and then, once again, brushed his lips against her in another emotionless kiss.

Even so that cool kiss touched Alyse's soul, whispered its impossible hopes into her heart. She kept her lips mostly slack beneath his, knowing after six years of such kisses he didn't want her to respond, never had. No hot, open-mouthed kisses of passion for them. Just these chaste displays of their mutual love and devotion.

He lifted his head and she smiled and waved to the crowd. It was done.

Still smiling, Leo led her to the waiting carriage, all gilt and scrollwork, like something out of a fairy tale. A Cinderella carriage for a Cinderella bride.

He helped her in and then sat next to her on the narrow leather seat, his thigh pressing against her hip, her dress billowing over his lap. The liveried coachman closed the door and they were off for a celebratory ride through the city, then back to the palace for the reception.

As soon as the door had closed, Leo's smile, his mask, dropped. There was no need for it now; no one was watching. He turned to her, a frown appearing between his brows.

'You're too pale.'

'I'm sorry,' she murmured. 'I'm tired.'

Leo's frown deepened, and then it ironed out and he sighed and raked his hands through his hair. 'It's no wonder. The last few days have been exhausting. I expect it will be good to get away.'

They were leaving tomorrow for a ten-day honeymoon: first a week on a private Caribbean island and then a whistle-stop tour through London, Paris and Rome.

Alyse's insides quaked as she thought of that first week. An entire week alone, without cameras or crowds, no one to perform for, no audience to entertain. A week completely by themselves.

She lived in both hope and fear of that week.

'Yes,' she said now, and thankfully her voice remained steady, strong. 'I expect it will.'

Leo turned to the window and waved at the crowds lining the ancient cobbled streets of Averne, and Alyse turned to her own window and waved as well. Each flutter of her fingers drained her, as if she were lifting a huge weight. Her engagement ring, an enormous emerald surrounded by pearls and diamonds, sparkled in the sun.

She didn't know why everything felt so much harder now. She'd been living this life for six years, after all. She'd come to enjoy her interactions with the public and had learned to live with the media's attention.

Yet today, on her wedding day, with nearly the last words she'd spoken having been vows before the world, before *God*...

She felt the falseness of their masquerade more than ever. They'd only been married a few minutes and already she felt how difficult, how draining, this life of play-acting was going to be. She'd been moving towards that realisation for months as the weight had dropped off and her stomach had churned with nerves, as everything had steamrolled ahead with such frightening implacability that she had known she couldn't call a halt to the proceedings even if she'd wanted to. The pretending.

And the terrible truth was, she *still* didn't want to. She'd still rather hope.

'Alyse?'

She turned from the window where she'd been blindly staring at the crowds, her hand rising and falling in a fluttering wave without even realising she was doing so. 'Yes?'

'You don't look well,' Leo said and he sounded concerned. 'Do you need a few moments to rest before we go into the reception?'

Alyse knew what the reception would entail: hours of

chatting, laughing and pretending to be in love. Of kissing Leo, squeezing his hand and laying her head on his shoulder. She'd done it all before, of course, but now it hurt more. It felt, absurdly perhaps, more fake.

'I'm fine.' She smiled and turned back to the window so he wouldn't see how her smile trembled and almost slid right off her face. 'I'm fine,' she said again, this time for herself, because she needed to believe it. She was stronger than this. She had to be stronger, because she'd chosen this life, knowing how hard it would be.

At times it might have felt as if she had no choice, with the pressure of both the media and the monarchy urging her to agree, but if she'd really wanted to break off the engagement she surely could have. She would have found the strength to.

No, she'd chosen this life, and chosen Leo; she'd believed in the duty she was performing and she'd held out for love.

She still did. Today was a beginning, she reminded herself. Today was the start of her and Leo's life together, days and nights spent with each other in a way neither of them had ever experienced before. Maybe, finally, Leo would fall in love with her.

Leo just wanted this day to be over. Although of course with its end would come a whole new, and rather interesting, complication: the night. Their wedding night.

He glanced again at Alyse; her face was turned away from him but he could still see how pale and wan she looked. And thin. The dress clung to her figure, which had already been slender but now looked rather waif-like. Clearly the strain of the heightened media attention had got to her over these last few months.

Just as it had got to him. He'd lived his life in the spotlight and he certainly should be used to it now. As a child, the play-acting for the media had confused him, but as he'd grown older he'd accepted it as the price he had to pay for the sake of his duty to the crown. At least this time, with Alyse, he'd chosen it. He'd entered this loveless marriage willingly, even happily.

Because wasn't it better to know love was a sham from the beginning, than to live in desperate yearning for it— just as he had done for the whole of his confused and unhappy childhood?

At least he and Alyse agreed on that. She'd always known he didn't love her, and he knew she didn't love him. Really, it was the perfect foundation for a marriage: agreed and emotionless expectations.

Yet he'd found the last few months of intense media speculation and interest wearying. The charade of acting as if they were in love had started to wear thin. And he'd wondered, not for the first time, just why Alyse had agreed to this marriage.

He'd never asked her, had never wanted to know. It was enough that she'd agreed, and she'd gone along with it ever since. Just as he had.

Only, unlike him, she had no incentive to please the press, no duty to repair a badly damaged monarchy and increase the tourist revenue for a small and struggling country. No need to pretend to be wildly in love. So why had she agreed all those years ago? Why had she continued to agree?

He had to assume it was because, like him, she wanted this kind of marriage. Or maybe she just wanted this kind of life—the life of a princess and one day a queen. He didn't fault her for it. She wouldn't be the first person to have her head turned by wealth and fame. In any case, she'd approached their union with a practical acceptance he admired, and she'd embraced the public as much as they'd embraced her.

Really, she was perfect. So why did he wonder? Why did he now feel a new, creeping uncertainty? The questions—and the lack of answers—annoyed him. He liked certainty and precision; he prided himself on both.

He didn't want to wonder about his bride on his wedding day. Didn't want to worry about why she looked so pale and shaky, or why her smile seemed less assured. He wanted things to be simple, straightforward, as they had been for the last six years.

There was no reason for marriage to complicate matters, he told himself.

The carriage came to a stop in front of the palace and he turned to her with a faint smile, determined to banish his brooding thoughts and keep their relationship on the courteous yet impersonal footing they'd maintained for their entire engagement.

'Shall we?' he said, one eyebrow lifted, and Alyse managed just as faint a smile back as she took his hand and allowed him to help her out of the carriage.

CHAPTER TWO

THEY WERE ALONE. Every muscle in Alyse's body ached with exhaustion, yet even so she could not keep a heart-stopping awareness of Leo from streaking through her as he closed the door behind them.

They'd retired to the tower suite, a sumptuous bed-room, bathroom and dressing-room all housed in one of the stone turrets of the ancient royal palace. A fire blazed in the hearth and a huge four-poster bed with silk cover-ings and sheets took up the main part of the room. Alyse stared at the white silk and lace negligee laid out on the bed and swallowed hard.

She and Leo had never talked about *this*.

They should have, she supposed, but then they had never really talked about anything. Their relationship— and she could only use that word loosely—had been little more than a long-term publicity stunt. Conversation had been limited to managing their appearances together.

And now they were married. It felt, at least to her, like a complete game-changer. Until now they'd only expe-rienced manufactured moments lived in the public eye; but here, for the first time, they were alone with no need for pretence.

Would *this* moment be real?

'Relax,' Leo said, coming up behind her. Alyse felt his breath on the back of her neck and she suppressed a shiver

of both anticipation and nervousness. 'We've been waiting
for six years; we don't need to rush things.'

'Right,' she murmured, and then he moved past her to
the window. The latticed shutters were thrown open to
a starlit sky. Earlier in the evening there had been fireworks all over the city; the celebrations of their marriage
had gone on all day.

It was only now that the city's joy was finally subsid-
ing, everyone heading back to his or her home—and Alyse
and Leo to this honeymoon suite.

She watched as Leo loosened his black tie. He'd
changed into a tuxedo for the evening party, and she into
a designer gown chosen by the team of stylists hired to
work on her. It was pale pink, strapless, with a frothy skirt.
A Cinderella dress.

'Do you want to change?' Leo asked as he undid the
top few studs of his shirt. Standing there, framed by the
window, the ends of his bow-tie dangling against the crisp
whiteness of his shirt, he looked unbearably handsome.
His hair was a glossy midnight-black, and rumpled from
where he'd carelessly driven his fingers through it.

His eyes were dark too—once Alyse had thought they
were black but she'd learned long ago from having had
to gaze adoringly up into them so many times they were
actually a very dark blue.

And his body... She might not have seen it in all of its
bare glory, but he certainly wore a suit well. Broad shoulders, trim hips, long and powerful legs, every part of him
declared he was wonderfully, potently male.

Would she see that body tonight? Would she caress and
kiss it, give in to the passion she knew she could feel for
him if he let her?

And what about him? Would he feel it?

In the course of six years, he'd always been solicitous,
considerate, unfailingly polite. She couldn't fault him,

and yet she'd yearned for more. For emotion, passion and, yes, always love. She'd always been drawn to the intensity she felt pulsing latent beneath his coolness, the passion she wanted to believe could be unleashed if he ever freed himself from the bonds of duty and decorum. If he ever revealed himself to her.

Would he tonight, if just a little? Or would this part of their marriage be a masquerade as well?

'I suppose I'll change,' she said, her gaze sliding inexorably to the negligee laid out for both their perusals.

'You don't need to wear that,' Leo said, and he let out an abrupt laugh, the sound without humour. 'There's no point, really, is there?'

Wasn't there? Alyse felt a needle of hurt burrow under her skin, into her soul. What did he want her to wear, if not that?

'Why don't you take a bath?' he suggested. 'Relax. It's been a very long day.' He turned away from her, yanking off his tie, and after a moment Alyse headed to the bathroom, telling herself she was grateful for the temporary reprieve. They could both, perhaps, use a little time apart.

We've basically had six years apart.

Swallowing hard, she turned on the taps.

There were no clothes in the bathroom, something she should have realised before she got in the tub. Two sumptuous terry-cloth robes hung on the door, and after soaking in the bath for a good half-hour Alyse slipped one on, the sleeves coming past her hands and the hem nearly skimming her ankles. She tied it securely, wondering what on earth would happen now. What she wanted to happen.

For Leo to gasp at the sight of me and sweep me into his arms, admit the feelings he's been hiding all along...

Fantasies, pathetic fantasies, and she *knew* that. She wasn't expecting a lightning bolt of love to strike Leo; she just wanted to start building something, something real. And that took time.

Tonight was a *beginning*.

Taking a deep breath, stealing herself for whatever lay ahead, she opened the door.

Leo had changed out of his tuxedo and now wore a pair of navy-blue silk draw-string pyjama bottoms and nothing else. He sat sprawled in a chair by the fire, a tumbler of whisky cradled in his hands, the amber liquid glinting in the firelight.

Alyse barely noticed any of that; her gaze was ensnared by the sight of his bare chest. She'd never seen it before, not in the flesh, although there had been several paparazzi photographs of him in swimming trunks while on holiday—though not with her. They'd never actually had a holiday together in six years' engagement.

Seeing his chest now, up close and in the glorious flesh, was another thing entirely. His skin was bronzed, the fire casting long shadows on the taut flesh and sculpted muscle. She could see dark whorls of hair on his chest, veeing down to the loose waistband of his trousers slung low on his lean hips, and her heart felt as if it had flipped right over in her chest. He was just so beautiful.

He glanced up as she approached, and his lips twitched in sardonic amusement as he took in her huge robe. 'I think that one's mine.'

'Oh.' She blushed, and then as she imagined Leo attempting to wear the smaller, woman's-sized robe, a sudden bubble of nervous laughter escaped her. He arched an eyebrow and she came forward to explain. 'I was picturing you in the other robe. Mine, apparently.'

'An interesting image.' His lips twitched again in a tiny smile and her heart lightened ridiculously. All she needed was a smile. A single smile on which to build a world of dreams.

She sat in the chair opposite his and stretched her bare feet towards the fire. Neither of them spoke for several minutes, the only sound the comforting crackle and spit of the flames.

'This is strange,' Alyse finally said softly, her gaze still on the fire. She heard Leo shift in his seat.

'It's bound to be, I suppose.'

She glanced upwards and saw his face was half in darkness, the firelight casting flickering shadows over the other half. She could see the hard plane of one cheek, the dark glint of stubble on his jaw, the pouty fullness of his sculpted lips. He had the lips of a screen siren, yet he was unabashedly, arrogantly male.

She'd felt those lips on her own so many times, cool brushes of mouths when what she wanted, what she *craved*, was hot, mindless passion—tongues tangling, plunging, hands moving and groping…

She forced the images, and the resulting heat, away from her mind and body.

'Do you realise,' she said, trying to keep her tone light, and even teasing, although they'd never actually teased each other, 'we haven't actually been alone together in about a year?'

He shrugged one bare, powerful shoulder. 'That's not all that surprising, considering.'

She glanced back at the fire, tucking her now-warmed feet underneath the hem of her robe. 'Considering what?'

'Considering we've been living separate lives ever since we announced this sham of an engagement.'

Alyse swallowed. 'I know that.' Neither of them had been in a rush to get married. Leo certainly hadn't, and Alyse had already accepted a place at Durham University. Her parents hadn't wanted her to give it up for marriage at eighteen, and neither had she, although she suspected Queen Sophia could have bullied her into it.

She'd been so young then, so naïve and overwhelmed. She liked to think she'd changed, that she'd grown up, at least a bit. She hoped she had, but right now she felt as gauche as ever.

At any rate, a long engagement had fed the media frenzy, accomplishing the monarchy's purposes of keeping them in positive press for over half a decade. For the last six years she'd been living in England, completing her BA and then her MA in European history—a subject the monarchy had considered acceptable for its future queen, since it could be relevant to her rule. Alyse just loved history.

She'd wanted to have some kind of normalcy in her life, some kind of separation from Leo and the feelings he stirred up in her; from the bizarre intensity of life in the media spotlight and under the monarchy's critical eye.

University had thankfully given her a degree of that normalcy she'd craved. Out of respect, and perhaps even love for her, the paparazzi hadn't followed her too closely.

She'd had a somewhat usual university experience— or as usual as it could be, considering the jaunts to royal functions every few weeks, her carefully choreographed appearances with Leo and the constant curiosity and speculation of the other students and even some of the tutors and lecturers.

Remembering it all now brought a sudden lump to her throat. No matter how normal her life had seemed on the surface, she'd still felt the loneliness of being different from the other students. Of knowing the paltry truth of her relationship with Leo.

It was a knowledge that had sometimes led to despair, and that had once led to a foolish choice and a heartache and shame that even now could bring her to a cringing blush.

She pushed the memory away. It had no place here and now, on her wedding night.

'But we're not going to live separate lives now,' she said and Leo inclined his head in brief acknowledgement.

'I suppose we need to decide how we want to conduct our marriage, now that we'll be under the same roof.' He paused to take a long swallow of whisky, and Alyse watched the movement of the corded muscles of his throat, felt a spasm of helpless longing. 'I don't see any real reason to change things too much,' he continued. Her longing left her in a rush.

She felt the way you did when you thought there was one more step in a staircase, the jolt going right through her bones to her soul. Had she actually thought things would change that much now they were married? That Leo would? It would mean more pretending, not less. Yet how could they pretend *that* much?

'Things will have to change a bit, I imagine,' she said, trying to speak lightly. 'I mean…we're married. It's different.'

'Assuredly, but it doesn't mean we have to be different, does it?' He glanced at her, eyebrows raised, cool smile in place. 'The last six years have worked out quite well, don't you think?'

No. *No, no, no.* Yet how could she disagree with him when she'd been acting like she'd agreed with him all along? Alyse swallowed. 'I suppose, but now we have a chance to actually get to know each other…' She trailed off uncertainly, wanting him to leap in and agree. When would she learn? He wasn't going to do that. He wasn't that kind of man.

Leo frowned, then turned back to the fire. 'We've always had that chance,' he answered after a moment. 'We just chose not to take it.'

'I suppose,' Alyse managed. She tried not to let his

words hurt her; he didn't mean to be cruel; he simply had no idea of how she felt, never had. This wasn't his fault, it was hers, for agreeing to pretend for so long. For never having been honest with him about how she really felt.

'It might get a bit tedious,' she ventured. 'Pretending for so long. We'll have to appear together more often, I mean.'

'Oh, the media will get tired of us eventually,' Leo said dismissively. He gave her a quick, cool smile, his eyes hard and glinting. 'Especially once the next generation comes along.'

The next generation. Their children. Alyse felt her heart start to thud.

He put his glass down, raking both hands through his hair so Alyse's gaze was drawn to the ripple of muscles in his arms and chest, the sculpted beauty of his body. Desire twisted and writhed inside her like some desperate, untamed creature seeking its freedom.

Leo dropped his hands and gave her a measured look. 'I know tonight is bound to be awkward, at least at first.' He nodded towards the huge bed looming behind them. 'I think if we acknowledge that up front, it might be easier.'

Alyse's mouth felt like sandpaper as she stared at him. 'Yes, probably it will be.' She tried for a light tone, or at least as matter-of-fact as his. She wasn't sure she managed either. 'Much better to be upfront and honest with each other from the start.' She forced a smile, knowing her words for lies. 'We pretend enough as it is.'

'Exactly.' Leo nodded in approval. 'It's one thing to pretend to the press, but I hope we can always be honest with each other.'

She nodded back mechanically. 'That…would be good.'

'Don't look so terrified,' Leo said dryly. He nodded once more towards the bed. 'I hope we can find a little pleasure there at least.'

A little pleasure? His words stung. 'I'm not terrified,'

she told him crisply. 'It's just— It's a bit awkward, like you said; that's all.'

'Naturally. I'll do my best to alleviate that awkwardness, of course.'

She heard a thread of amusement in his voice, saw it in his cool smile, and knew that being made love to by Leo wouldn't be awkward at all. It would be wonderful.

Except it wouldn't be making love. It would be cold, emotionless sex. A physical act, a soulless transaction. 'A little pleasure', indeed. She closed her eyes, hating the thought. Hating the fact that she had to pretend, would always have to pretend, not just with the press but with him. It would be so, so much harder now. Why hadn't she realised that?

'Alyse,' Leo said, and she opened her eyes. He was leaning forward, his eyes narrowed in concern. 'If you'd rather, we can wait. We don't have to consummate our marriage tonight.'

'A reprieve?' she said, her voice sounding cynical even to her own ears.

'It might be more pleasant when we're not so tired and there are fewer expectations on us,' Leo answered with a shrug. 'And frankly, no matter what you've said, you do look terrified.'

Yes, she was, but not in the way he thought. She wasn't afraid of sex. She was afraid of it being meaningless for Leo. Did he want her at all? Was this a bore for him, a *chore*?

'I promise you, I'm not afraid,' she said when she trusted herself to speak as neutrally as he had. 'But I am tired, so perhaps this…aspect of our marriage can wait a little while.'

Leo shrugged, as if he didn't care either way, and that hurt too. 'Of course. But we should both sleep in the bed.

Staff see everything, and even palace employees have been known to gossip.'

She nodded, trying not to imagine lying next to Leo, his nearly bare body so close to hers. It was a big bed, after all. And she needed to learn how to manage this kind of situation. They would, after all, be sleeping in the same bed for the next...

Except, no; perhaps they wouldn't. Perhaps they would have separate bedrooms along with separate lives, coming together only for the cameras or to create an heir.

'That's fine,' she said. 'I'll just put some...' She trailed off, because the only clothes in the room were her ball-gown and the negligee. She didn't like either option.

Leo glanced at the lace confection spread out on the bed. 'It's a big bed,' he said dryly. 'And I think I can control myself, even if you wear that bit of nonsense.'

Alyse swallowed, nodded. Even tried to smile, though every careless word he spoke felt like a dagger thrust to her heart. She didn't want him to be able to control himself. She'd always known him to be cool, pragmatic, even ruthless. Yet she wanted him to be different with her, and she was honest enough to recognise that some stupid, school-girl part of her had secretly hoped things might change when they were finally alone.

'Fine,' she said and, rising from the chair, she went to the bed and swept the negligee from it before disappearing into the bathroom once more.

Leo stretched out on one side of the bed and waited for Alyse to emerge from the bathroom. He felt the conversation hadn't gone as well as he would have liked. Alyse had seemed brittle, almost as if he'd hurt her feelings, a possibility which exasperated him. He'd thought she was as pragmatic as he was about their union, yet this new, unexpected awkwardness clearly unnerved her—as well as him.

When had he started caring about her feelings, whether she felt nervous, awkward or afraid? The whole point of this marriage, this pretence, was that he didn't have to care. He didn't have to engage emotions he'd purposely kept dormant for so long.

And while he might be weary of pretending—he'd done enough of it in his life, God only knew—at least this marriage, this pretence, had been his choice. His decision.

He still remembered the negotiation they'd gone through after that wretched photograph had gone viral. His father had asked to see them privately.

Alyse had flown to Maldinia a few weeks after her birthday party; her mother had accompanied her. And, when she'd walked into his father's private study alone, Leo had been jolted by how young and vulnerable she looked, dressed simply in a plain skirt and schoolgirl's blouse, her dark hair held back in a ponytail.

His father hadn't minced words; he never did. Queen Sophia and her mother were friends, he told Alyse, and they'd considered a match between her and Leo. Leo knew that hadn't exactly been true; his mother had wanted someone with slightly bluer blood than Alyse's to marry her son. Leo had gone to that birthday party with only a vague and passing knowledge of Alyse's existence and it was the media hype that had turned it into something else entirely.

'In an ideal world,' King Alessandro had said with a geniality Leo knew his father did not remotely possess, *'you would have got to know each other, courted. Seen if you suited. But it's not an ideal world.'*

Alyse had simply stared.

Leo, of course, had known where this was going all along. He'd talked to his parents already, had received the assignment from on high. *You must marry her, Leo. The public adores her. Think of what it will do for your country, your kingship.*

He'd known what they really meant: what it would do
for them. They'd done enough damage to Maldinia's monarchy with their lies, affairs and careless spending. He was
the only one left to clean up the mess.

He'd understood all that, but Alyse hadn't. She'd just
looked thunderstruck. She'd barely spoken for that whole
meeting, just listened as the King went on about the benefits of a 'decided' marriage—a much more innocuous term
than *arranged,* Leo had thought cynically. Or *commanded.*

She'd only spoken when she'd begun to perceive, dimly,
just what kind of charade they would be perpetuating and
for how long. 'You mean,' she'd said in a voice only a little
above a whisper, 'we have to…to *pretend* we're in love?'

'Feelings come in time, don't they?' Alessandro had answered with that same false joviality, and Leo had looked
away. *No, they didn't.* If Alessandro held up his own marriage, his own family, as an example, it showed they never
came. And you couldn't trust them anyway.

But Alyse had nodded slowly, accepting, and their engagement had been announced the next day along with
them posing for requisite photos.

And the rest, Leo thought now, lacing his arms above
his head, was history. Repeating itself over and over again.

The door to the bathroom opened and Alyse emerged,
wearing the woman's robe. Leo wondered if she'd try to
sleep in that bulky thing. He supposed a little virginal
shyness was natural.

He watched as she skirted the bed and then hesitated
on the far side, her fingers playing with the sash of her
robe. Leo reached for his bedside lamp.

'Shall I turn out the light?'

'If you like.'

Actually, he didn't like. He was suddenly rather curious as to what Alyse looked like in the skimpy negligee.
He'd seen her in plenty of designer dresses and well-

coordinated outfits, hair and make-up immaculately styled, always primped to perfection.

But he'd never seen her like this—wearing a bridal nightgown, her chestnut hair loose about her shoulders, grey eyes wide, about to climb into his bed. He felt an insistent stirring of arousal; it had been a long time since he'd been with a woman. A *very* long time.

He switched the light off, but the moon spilling through the open windows was enough to see by anyway, and as he lay back against the pillows he saw her slip the bulky robe from her body. Dressed as she was in only the slinky negligee, the moon gilded her slender curves in silver.

He could see the shadowy vee between her breasts, the dip of her waist, the hidden juncture of her thighs. Then she slid hurriedly under the covers and lay there, rigid and unmoving.

Leo had never felt so far from sleep and, judging by how she lay there like a board, he suspected Alyse was the same. Perhaps they should have agreed to consummate their marriage tonight. At least it would have given them something to do.

He considered talking to her, but after six years of enacting this parody of love he had nothing of consequence to say, and he didn't think she had either. Which was how he'd wanted it.

Yet in the darkness and silence of that moment he felt a sudden, surprising need for conversation, even connection. Something he'd taught himself never to crave.

And he had no idea how to go about creating it now.

'Goodnight,' he finally said, his voice coming out gruffer than he'd meant it to, and he felt Alyse tense even more next to him.

'Goodnight,' she answered back, her voice so soft and

sad that Leo felt caught between remorse and exasperation at her obvious emotion—and his.

With a barely suppressed sigh, he rolled onto his side, his back to Alyse, and willed himself to sleep.

CHAPTER THREE

ALYSE AWOKE GRITTY-EYED and still feeling exhausted. Lying next to Leo, she hadn't slept well, conscious of his hard, powerful form just inches away from her even when she'd been falling into a restless doze.

Now as sunlight streamed through the windows she wondered what the day would bring. They were meant to fly to St Cristos, a private island in the Caribbean, that morning to begin their honeymoon. A week completely alone, without the distractions of television, telephones, computers or any other people at all. A week, she still hoped, when they could get to know one another properly, or even at all.

A knock sounded at the door and before Alyse could say or even think anything Leo was snaking his arm around her waist, drawing her close against the seductive heat of his body. Shock turned her rigid as she felt the hard contours of his chest and thigh against her backside—and then the unmistakable press of his erection against her bottom.

'Vieni,' he called and then murmured against her hair, 'Sorry, but the staff will gossip.'

Alyse barely took in his words. She'd never been so close to him, every part of her body in exquisite contact with his. The crisp hair on his chest tickled her bare shoulders, and the feel of his arousal pressing insistently against her bottom sent sizzling darts of sensation shooting through her.

She shifted instinctively, although whether she was drawing away or closer to him she didn't even know. She felt a new, dizzying need spiral up inside her as his own hips flexed instinctively back. Leo groaned under his breath and his arm came even more firmly around her. 'Stop wriggling,' he whispered, 'Or I might embarrass myself. I'm only human, you know.'

It took a few seconds for his meaning to penetrate the fog of her dazed mind, and by that time two young serving women were wheeling in a breakfast tray, the smell of fresh coffee and breakfast rolls on the air.

Embarrass himself? Was he actually implying that he wanted her that much? That a mere wriggle of hips could send him over the edge?

Leo let go of her, straightening in bed as he adjusted the duvet over himself. *'Grazie,'* he said and the two women giggled and blushed as they left the room, casting covert looks at the two of them in bed. Alyse realised the strap of her negligee had fallen off one shoulder, and her hair was a tangled mass about her face. Did she look like a woman who had been pleasured and loved? She felt like a mess.

She tucked her tangled hair behind her ears and willed her heart rate to slow. Despite the obvious evidence of his arousal, Leo now looked completely unfazed and indifferent as he slid out of bed and went to the breakfast tray to pour them both coffee.

'Sorry about that. Basic bodily function, at least for a man in the morning. I think we convinced the staff, at any rate.'

Disappointment crashed through her. *Basic bodily function.* So, no, it had had nothing to do with her in particular. Of course it didn't. 'It's fine,' Alyse murmured. She took a steadying breath and forced herself to meet his wry gaze. 'We're married, after all.'

'So we are.' He handed her a cup of coffee and sipped his own, his expression turning preoccupied over the rim of the porcelain cup. 'But I imagine all this pretending will get tiresome for both of us after a while.'

Alyse stared into the fragrant depths of her coffee. 'Like you said, the press will get bored of us now that we're married. As long as we seem happy in public, they won't really care.' It hurt to say it, to imply that that was what she wanted.

'Perhaps.' Leo nodded slowly, and Alyse imagined he was wondering just how soon he could return to his simple, solitary life.

And when he did what would she do? Over the last few months she'd bolstered her flagging spirits by reminding herself that, just like Leo, she had a duty. A role. As princess and later Queen of Maldinia she would encourage and love her people. She would involve herself in her country, its charities and industry, and in doing so bring hope to a nation.

She tried to hold onto that idea now, but it seemed like so much airy, arrogant nonsense when she considered how the majority of her days were likely to be spent: in loneliness and isolation, separated from a husband who was perfectly happy with their business arrangement.

'When do we leave for St Cristos?' she asked, not wanting either of them to dwell on the bleak future they both clearly envisioned.

'We leave the palace at eleven o'clock for a public appearance in the front courtyard. Photo opportunity and all that.' He smiled and Alyse saw the cynicism in the twist of his lips, the flatness in his navy eyes. He never used to be so cynical, she thought. Pragmatic, yes, and even cold, but he'd approached their engagement with a brisk and accepting efficiency she'd tried to match, rather than this jaded resentment.

Was he feeling as she did, that marriage had changed something between them, made it worse? Pretending *after* the vows had been said seemed a greater travesty than before, something she'd never considered as Leo's fiancée. She didn't think Leo had considered it either.

'I'll leave you to get dressed,' he said, putting down his coffee cup. 'I'll meet you downstairs in the foyer a few minutes before eleven.'

Wordlessly Alyse nodded, seeing the practicality of it yet feeling a needling disappointment anyway. Was every interaction going to involve a way to avoid each other? Would her life consist of endless awkward exchanges without any real intimacy or emotion, *ever*? Something would have to change. She couldn't live like this; she wouldn't.

Maybe, she thought with no more than a flicker of weary hope, it would change on St Cristos.

Several hours later they boarded the royal jet and Leo disappeared into a study in the rear of the plane. Alyse had been on the jet before when she'd flown between England and Maldinia, yet the opulent luxury always amazed her. Her own family was wealthy and privileged—her father had built a financial empire and her mother had been an heiress—but they weren't this kind of rich. They weren't royal.

You are now.

It still felt unreal. If she didn't actually feel like Leo's wife, how would she ever feel like a princess? Like a queen?

Pushing the thought aside, she made herself comfortable on one of the leather sofas in the main cabin of the plane. Just as planned, she and Leo had made their appearance outside the palace doors. A crowd had surrounded the palace; posies and bouquets of flowers had been piled up by the gates. Alyse had spent a few minutes chatting, smiling and laughing, while Leo had looked on, his smile faint and a little bit wooden. While the people loved the handsome, enigmatic prince, he didn't engage the crowds the way she did, and never had. This, she knew, was why Maldinia's monarchy needed her. Why Leo needed her.

Nothing else.

Now, with the crowds and reporters gone, she wondered just how she and Leo would spend their time alone. Judging by the way he'd disappeared into the jet's study, *alone* was the operative word.

She felt a sudden stab of annoyance, which at least felt stronger than the misery that had been swamping her since their marriage. No matter how fake their relationship was, Leo's determined ignoring of her was just plain rude.

Fuelled by her outrage, Alyse rose from the sofa and went to find Leo in the study. He sat at a desk, his dark head bent over a sheaf of papers. He was dressed for travel in a crisp blue button-down shirt and dark trousers, but he still looked magnificent, his muscles taut and powerful underneath the starched cotton of his shirt. He glanced up as she approached, his dark brows snapping together.

'What is it?'

'I just wondered if you intended to spend the entire time in your study,' she said, her voice coming out close to a snap, and Leo looked at her in something close to bewilderment.

'Does it matter?'

Impatience warred with hurt. 'A bit, Leo. I understand you don't want things to change between us, but a little conversation could be nice. Or are we going to spend the next week trying to avoid each other?'

He still looked flummoxed, and now also a bit annoyed. 'I'm not trying to avoid you.'

'It just comes naturally, then?'

'We've been on this plane for ten minutes,' he replied, his voice becoming so very even. 'Don't you think you can entertain yourself for a little while longer?'

Alyse shook her head impatiently. She could see how Leo might think she was being unreasonable, but it was so much more than this one journey. 'I can entertain myself just fine,' she said. 'But I don't particularly enjoy living in isolation.'

Leo's mouth thinned into a hard line. 'The plane will take off in a few minutes. I'll join you in the cabin before it does.'

His words seemed so grudgingly given, yet Alyse knew at this point it was better simply to accept them at face value. Now was not the time to force a confrontation, to confess that she didn't think she could live like this for so much as a morning, much less a lifetime. This was, after all, what she'd agreed to all those years ago when King Alessandro had spelled it out so plainly.

Feelings come in time, don't they? She'd built her hopes on that one throwaway remark, clearly meant only to appease her. She'd lived for six years believing it could be true. She might as well have built castles in the air.

Leo had already turned back to his papers, so after a second's uneasy pause Alyse turned around and went to the cabin.

He didn't come out for take-off. Her annoyance turned to a simmering anger as the staff served her sparkling water instead of the champagne left chilling in a bucket, clearly meant for the two of them to toast their marriage.

She avoided their eyes and reached for her e-reader, bitterly glad she'd filled it with newly purchased books before she'd left. Clearly she'd be getting a lot of reading done on her honeymoon.

A few hours into the flight Leo finally made an appearance. 'Sorry about that,' he said, sitting across from her. 'I had a bit of work to catch up on before we go off the grid.'

Despite his casually made apology, Alyse couldn't let go of her anger. 'If you don't want your staff to gossip, perhaps you should be a bit more attentive to your bride,' she answered tartly. 'We've only been married for one day, you know.'

Leo stared at her, nonplussed. 'Even couples wildly in love have work to do.'

'Even on their honeymoon?'

He narrowed his gaze. 'I have a duty to my country—'

'This whole marriage is about duty.' She cut him off and realised too late how shrewish and hurt she sounded. How ridiculous, considering the nature of their relationship.

'Careful,' he said softly, glancing at the closed cabin doors.

'Our whole life is going to be about being careful,' she retorted before she could stop herself. She hated how her hurt was spilling out of her. She'd kept it hidden for so long, why was she weakening now?

'And you always knew that.' The glance he gave her was repressive. 'I think we should save this conversation for another, more private time.'

'At least I have a conversation to look forward to, then.' Leo just stared at her, and Alyse looked away, trying to reclaim some of the cool composure she'd cloaked herself with during the last few years. She'd never lit into him like this, never showed him how much his indifference hurt her or how much more she wanted from him.

'What's wrong with you?' he asked after a moment and he sounded both curious and exasperated. 'You've never acted like this before.'

'We've never been alone like this before,' she answered, her face still averted. 'I just don't want you to ignore or avoid me for the entire week. I'll go crazy.'

Leo was silent for a long moment. 'I don't mean to ignore or avoid you,' he said finally. 'I'm just acting as we always have. I thought you accepted the nature of our relationship—preferred it, as I do.'

Alyse struggled to keep her face composed, her voice even, but his words hurt so much. Too much. 'I've accepted it,' she said carefully. 'But it feels different now. We're married, after all, and we're going to spend more time together. Time alone. It would be nice if we could enjoy it, at least.'

That was so much less than she wanted, but at least it was a start—if Leo agreed.

He didn't answer, just reached for the champagne and poured two flutes, the bubbles fizzing and bursting against the crystal sides. 'I suppose that's not an unreasonable request,' he said eventually, and Alyse didn't know whether to laugh or cry at his grudging tone.

'I'm glad you think so,' she answered, and accepted a glass of champagne.

He eyed her evenly. 'I suppose we should have discussed our expectations of what our married life would look like beforehand.'

'Would it have made any difference?'

'Not to me, perhaps.' He raised his glass. 'To what shall we toast?'

Alyse couldn't think of a single thing. 'To the future,' she finally said, and heard the bleakness in her voice. 'Whatever it may hold.'

Nodding in acceptance, Leo drank.

Leo watched Alyse slowly raise the flute of champagne to her lips. Her face was pale, her eyes wide and dark. She looked rather unbearably sad, he thought, and he had no idea why. What did she want from him? And why, after so long accepting the status quo, did she seem to want things to change?

Shifting in his seat, he turned towards the window. Outside the sky was an endless, brilliant blue. He thought of the week they were to spend on St Cristos, which was apparently the most elite honeymoon destination in the world—chosen, of course, to perpetuate the myth of their relationship. The relationship—a word he didn't even like to use—that he didn't want to change.

But it would have to change in some ways as they spent more time together, he acknowledged. Alyse had a point, even if he didn't like it.

And she seemed to want such change. Want more. Leo felt everything in him recoil at the thought. He didn't do relationships, or intimacy, or emotion, or any of it, yet it seemed Alyse expected a little of all of the above.

He could manage some conversation, he told himself. Some simple pursuits and pleasures…such as the consummation of their marriage. Perhaps he and his wife could find some sympathy with each other in bed. They certainly didn't seem to have much out of it, although he was honest enough to admit he'd never really tried.

He didn't want to get to know Alyse. He didn't want their relationship to be anything than what it was: a carefully managed façade. He never had.

Yet now it seemed she wanted something else. Something more.

Well, she wouldn't get it. He didn't have anything more to give. Suppressing a sigh, he took another sip of champagne. Why did a thought that had once comforted and strengthened him now make him only feel restless and on edge?

By the time they arrived in St Cristos, Alyse was feeling strung out and exhausted. She hated the constant tension she felt in Leo's presence; before today, they'd only seen each other for various occasions, usually formal, and always with other people around. They'd never had more than a few hours in each other's company at a time, and never more than a few minutes alone.

She had hoped that when they were alone properly things would become more natural. They would chat, get to know one another, behave like normal, civil human beings. Except civility, in Leo's world, was a cold-hearted, emotionless thing and Alyse didn't think she could take much more of it.

After their brief exchange on the jet they'd barely spoken, and they'd ridden in silence from the island's tiny airstrip to the exclusive resort. Alyse stared out of the window at the verdant hills on the horizon, the palm trees fringing the narrow track with their fronds drooping to the ground. In the distance the sea glittered under an afternoon sun; it was seven hours behind Maldinia here.

The resort came into view, a gracious grouping of thatched huts that looked both simple yet luxurious. The limo pulled to a stop and Alyse saw that all the staff was lined up outside the main hut, beaming and expectant.

She knew the resort was closed to all other guests this week in order to give her and Leo maximum privacy, yet right now she felt too tired to sparkle and charm the crowd. She wanted to curl up into herself and hide.

'Here we go,' Leo murmured, and with a rather grim smile he helped her out of the limo.

Alyse didn't remember what she said to all the people assembled; she shook hands and murmured pleasantries and Leo put his arm around her, kissing her cheek to the sighs of several chambermaids. After what felt like an hour, but was probably only a few minutes, they were led to their guest quarters in a private cove.

Alyse stood in the middle of the hut on its raised wooden platform and stared at the few, expensive furnishings: a couple of teak bureaux, a rattan chair and a huge bed with soft linen sheets. Mosquito netting was draped over the entrance, tied back now, so she had an unrestricted view of the sea lapping only a few metres away.

There were no electrical outlets, she knew, no computers, televisions, telephones or mobile reception. Nothing to keep her and Leo from spending time with one another.

Except Leo himself.

'I think I'll take a look around,' Leo said. 'Why don't you get settled?'

So much for spending time together. Alyse set about unpacking her cases, even though one of the resort staff had offered to do it for her. Right now she wanted to be alone.

Unpacking her few outfits for their week on the Caribbean island didn't take long, however, and after she'd finished she prowled restlessly around the hut, wishing Leo would return, yet half glad he hadn't. His obvious lack of interest in so much as conversing with her was hard to take.

Since Leo still wasn't around she decided to go for a swim. With a twinge of self-consciousness, she changed into one of the bikinis that had been selected for her; she had not chosen or even seen any of the clothes in her cases, not even the shorts and tee-shirts.

The bikini was a little more revealing than she would have liked but, shrugging aside any self-consciousness— she was alone, after all—she headed for the sea.

The sand was silky under her bare feet, the water lapping her toes clear and warm. Standing there, gazing out at an endless horizon, Alyse felt just a little of the tension she'd been carrying lessen and her shoulders relaxed a fraction.

Maybe when Leo returned they'd have that private conversation he'd resisted on the plane. She'd talk to him properly, explain that she didn't want to act like strangers any more. If they couldn't act as a normal husband and wife, at least they could be friends. Surely that would be more bearable than this horribly stilted awkwardness and avoidance?

Taking a deep breath, she dove into the water, kicking her feet as she swam several metres underwater, enjoying the freedom and the silence of the world below the waves.

When she surfaced, slicking her hair back from her face, she felt a jolt deep inside—for Leo was standing in the shallows, dressed only in board shorts as he gazed out at her.

'I wondered when you'd come back up for air,' he said, his eyes narrowed against the sun's glare. 'I didn't know you were such a good swimmer.'

She stood, for the water was still shallow there, and came up only to her waist. 'There's a lot we don't know about each other.'

Even from this distance she saw the heat flare in his eyes as his gaze roved over her bikini-clad body, rivulets of water coursing down her skin. She felt her own body react—muscles tautening, awareness firing through her, hope flaring. 'Yes,' he said slowly. 'So there is.'

Alyse's heart started thudding even as she strove to sound natural. This was the first time she'd ever seen desire in Leo's eyes, such blatant hunger. It thrilled her to the core, but it surprised and even scared her too, for there was something raw and untamed in Leo's gaze, something she'd never seen from him before. Something she'd craved. When she spoke her voice came out in a husky whisper. 'Do you want to have a swim?'

'I think I might.' He waded into the water, and her breath caught in her chest. He was so beautiful, his body hard, sculpted and *perfect*. He dove neatly into the sea, and she watched with mounting anticipation as he kicked through the water towards her, cutting through the waves to come to stand right next to her, the water lapping at his hips and running down his chest.

He was close enough to feel the heat coming off his skin, to touch him, and she longed to press her hand or even her mouth against his damp chest, to catch the droplets of water with her tongue and taste the saltiness of his skin...

Her heart felt as if it were pounding in her throat. 'It's lovely here, isn't it?' she commented, knowing she sounded inane. She didn't know how to act, what to say. All she could do was *feel*—this overwhelming desire and, even more frighteningly, hope coursing through her. Hope that, if he felt this for her, there could be more. There would be.

Yet now she couldn't think about the more, only about the now. About the reality of the desire kindling in his eyes; her breath went shallow as he lifted one hand as if he would touch her. He'd never touched her without an audience.

'It is lovely,' Leo agreed in a low voice. He reached out then and touched her cheek and, even though she'd been expecting it, craving it, the caress still caught her by surprise so her breath came out in a ragged shudder.

He stroked her cheek gently with one finger. 'You're lovely.' She stared at him, ensnared by the heat of his gaze, the touch of his hand. She saw something hard in his gaze, something cynical in his smile, and she still couldn't keep from wanting him. 'I wonder,' he mused softly, his finger still stroking her cheek, 'How do you make something that's been false, true? What's fake, real?'

Her heart seemed to burst within her like fireworks had gone off in her soul. The very fact that he was even asking the question gave her a hope that was painful in its intensity. 'I want to,' she whispered, her heart beating so hard now that it hurt, the thuds slamming her chest. 'I want this to be real, Leo.'

His lips twisted again, caught between a grimace and a smile. He bent his head, his lips a whisper away from hers. 'This is real enough,' he murmured, and then he kissed her.

It was as different from the chaste kisses he'd pressed upon her for the sake of the cameras and the crowds as could be, as she could possibly want.

His mouth slanted over hers with dark possession and he ran his tongue along the seam of her lips before he went deep into her mouth, and she gasped at the sensations scorching through her. Leo's touch felt so intensely pleasurable it was painful, as painful as the hope that still burst through her and lit her on fire.

Leo fastened his hands on her hips and fitted her against his arousal as he blazed a trail of kisses from her mouth to her cheek and jaw, and then down her neck to the vee between her breasts, his tongue licking the salt from her skin. Alyse shuddered and tilted her head back, allowing him greater access to her body, to everything in her.

'Leo…'

He lifted his head, gave her one of his cool smiles. 'This has all got a bit out of control, hasn't it? I don't want to have our wedding night right here in the sea.' He stepped away and Alyse felt a sudden rush of cold emptiness. 'In any case, I only came to find you and tell you dinner will be served shortly. The staff of the resort are setting up a table here on the beach.'

Alyse's mind was spinning, the hope draining out of her, leaving nothing but that aching, pulsing need. Somehow she forced herself to sound as unconcerned, as unaffected as he seemed to be. 'We could eat in the restaurant.'

'Ah, but this is more romantic.'

Alyse watched Leo swim back to the beach and with a deep, shuddering breath, willing her wayward body back under control, she dove underwater and started back towards the shore.

* * *

As soon as he reached their hut, Leo grabbed his clothes and headed for the shower. He needed a cold one. He hadn't meant lust to overtake him quite so much when he'd joined Alyse in the water, but the sight of her barely clad body had driven all rational thought from his mind. He'd been waiting a long time for his body's basic needs to be fulfilled, and the kiss he'd shared with her had been surprisingly sweet.

No, not sweet—hungry, demanding and raw. It had awakened a deeper need in him than he'd ever acknowledged before, and it had taken nearly all of his willpower to step away from her. She was surely a virgin, and he knew she deserved more than a fumbled grope on the sand. He wanted to take his time, bring them both pleasure and not just release. That was one area of their marriage where, he hoped, they could both find some kind of happiness.

Still, he didn't like how close he'd come to losing control there in the water. He never lost control, never even let it slip—and the last person he wanted to weaken him in that area was his wife.

By the time he'd spent ten minutes in an icy shower he felt his composure return and his libido calm down. He changed into a fresh pair of chinos and a dark green polo shirt, and headed back to their hut.

Alyse had already showered in a separate bathroom and was sitting in a rattan chair, her hair damp and curling about her shoulders. She wore a floaty blue sundress that brought out the blue in her eyes, her legs tanned and endless, her feet bare.

Every time he'd seen Alyse she'd been surrounded by stylists, her clothes carefully chosen, her make-up perfectly done, not a hair out of place. Now he saw her face was make-up-free and the sun had already caused a few freckles to appear on the bridge of her nose. She looked better like this, he decided. More natural. He wondered if she missed all the primping and attention, if she enjoyed the clothes, make-up and jewels.

He didn't know, and decided not to ask. He didn't need to know. He didn't want to care.

Yet even so he couldn't suppress the flicker of interest—and, yes, desire—this new, natural Alyse stirred within him.

The sun was just starting to set, sending long, golden rays across the placid surface of the sea, and Leo could see the staff already setting up their romantic table for two there on the beach. He busied himself unpacking his things while Alyse read, conscious of her nearness, the warmth and softness of her, and even the subtle floral scent of her shampoo or perfume, something he'd never even noticed before.

Even now he remembered the feel of her lips on his, the lush softness of her mouth, her breasts, the hunger of her response. His libido stirred insistently and he blew out an impatient breath. *Control.*

'Dinner's ready,' he said more brusquely than he intended, and nodded towards the table now laid for two on the sand.

Alyse looked up from her e-reader and, tossing it aside, rose from her chair. The sundress she wore clung to her figure, highlighting the small yet perfect roundness of her breasts, her tiny waist, her endless legs. Even though she was thinner than she probably should have been—no doubt due to the stress of the run-up to the wedding—she still had a lovely figure, an amazing figure, and Leo's palms itched to touch her. His body stirred again, insistent, demanding.

Tonight, he decided. They would make their marriage real tonight—real in the only way that mattered, the only way possible.

In bed.

CHAPTER FOUR

ALYSE FOLLOWED LEO out onto the beach, a violet twilight settling all around them as the sun started to slip beneath the sea.

The staff who had set up their table had all melted away, so they were alone with the flickering candlelight, a bucket on the sand with champagne chilling, the first course of crab salad already laid out on exquisite porcelain plates. It was the most romantic dinner Alyse ever could have imagined…and it felt like a minefield.

She had no idea how to act with Leo, especially after that kiss. Already she'd spent far too long reliving it—surely the most wonderful kiss she'd ever known—and thrilling to the undeniable realisation that Leo desired her.

How do you make something that's been false, true? His words had buoyed her soul at that moment, because in all her naïve hope she'd thought he meant their relationship. Their marriage.

This is real.

Watching Leo stride along the shore away from her, Alyse had known then what he'd really meant: the only real thing between them was sexual attraction.

Still, it's something, she told herself as she followed Leo out onto the twilit beach. *It might grow into more.* But only if given a chance…a chance Leo seemed determined not to take.

With a little bow, he pulled out her chair and Alyse sat down. 'Wine?' he asked, and she nodded.

He poured them both glasses and then sat across from her, sipping his wine as he gazed out at the sea, its surface now the inky violet of twilight.

He might not be willing to take that chance, she acknowledged, but she had to be. Taking a deep breath, Alyse gave him as bright a smile as she could manage. 'So, what should we do tomorrow? Snorkel? Scuba? Hike?'

His eyebrows rose, his expression freezing for a second, so she almost laughed. 'Don't look so terrified,' she said dryly, parroting his words from last night back at him. 'I might have suggested macramé.'

'Macramé? I'm not even sure what that is.'

'Weaving with knots,' Alyse explained. 'It's one of my passions. I was hoping you might share it.' Leo looked so nonplussed that this time she did laugh, and the release felt good. Even better was his answering rasp of a chuckle.

'You're having me on.' He shook his head, taking a sip of wine. 'Six years and I had no idea you had a sense of humour.'

Because he'd never had the chance to find out, or the desire. 'Well, we've never had a proper conversation before, not really,' Alyse said. She was trying for light but her voice came out quiet, almost forlorn. She'd have to do better. 'Not one about macramé, at any rate.'

'I must admit, I'm relieved it isn't one of your passions,' Leo answered. He arched an eyebrow, and she was gratified by the lightness of his expression. 'It isn't, is it?'

'No.' A smile twitched at her mouth. 'Definitely not one of them.' Leo just nodded, and despite the obvious opening Alyse knew he wasn't going to press. He would never press, never ask her about herself, what her passions or even her hobbies were. 'So, scuba, then?' she said, keeping her voice bright. 'I'm not qualified, but I read that they have instructors here who can qualify you with a day course.'

Leo made a noncommittal noise and Alyse felt the hurt and anger return, filling the empty places inside her. 'I think you'd enjoy scuba diving,' she said, and heard a new sharp note enter her voice. 'It doesn't allow for any conversation.'

'I have nothing against conversation.'

'Conversation with *me*, then?'

He shook his head, annoyance sparking in his eyes. 'Alyse...'

'I just don't see,' she pressed on in a desperate rush, knowing she needed to say it, to get it out there, 'why we can't be friends. Our marriage is unconventional, I know. I accept that. But we have to live together, Leo. We have to have a life together of some description. And I would like to do that as—as your friend.'

Silence. Leo said nothing, just eyed her over the rim of his wine glass. Why, Alyse wondered, did such a benign offer of friendship make her feel so vulnerable? So needy and demanding?

Because Leo obviously didn't need anyone, and certainly not her. Not even as a friend.

'Say something,' she finally said, just to break the awful silence.

'I don't know what I could say that you'd wish to hear.'

'At this point, anything is better than nothing,' she answered tartly.

'I'm not sure it's possible,' Leo said, each word chosen carefully, 'for us to be friends.'

'Not possible?' She stared at him in confusion. 'Why?'

'Because,' Leo replied, his voice still so terribly careful, 'I have no wish to be friends with you.'

As soon as he said the words, Leo realised how cruel

they sounded. Cruel and deliberately cold…and he hadn't meant it quite like that. Had he?

From the moment Alyse had started teasing and tempting him in turns—asking for things he didn't know how to give—he hadn't known what he meant. How he felt.

And as for the look on Alyse's face… She looked stunned for a moment, and then he saw a flash of hurt darken her eyes before she turned her face away, her expression hidden in the dark.

'Alyse…' he said, although he had no idea how to explain himself, or even if he could. In any case, he didn't get a chance.

With a small sound of distress she rose from the table and walked quickly across the beach, her slight form soon swallowed up by darkness.

Irritation mixed uncomfortably with an already increasing guilt—and a wretched sense of disappointment in himself. He should have handled that better. He should have known how.

He threw his napkin down and rose, his hands braced flat on the table. 'Where are you going?' he called, and from the twilit shadows he heard her muffled response.

'If you're worried I'm going to do something indiscreet, never fear. I just couldn't bear sitting at the table with you.'

His lips twitched with a sudden, macabre humour. 'I'm not surprised.' She didn't answer and he sighed wearily. 'I can't even see you,' he said, taking a few steps towards her. The sand was cool and silky under his bare feet. 'Where are you hiding?'

'I'm not *hiding*,' she snapped, and as he moved closer to the sound of her voice he saw she'd gone to the far side of the little cove, her back to him and the sea as she stood facing the rocky outcropping, her shoulders hunched, her arms wrapped around herself. There wasn't really anywhere else for her to go.

'I'm sorry,' he said after a moment. 'That came out wrong.'

'Was there really room for misinterpretation?'

'I only meant I think it would be easier if we didn't attempt to be friends.'

She let out a harsh bark of disbelieving laughter and turned around. 'Easier? For you, maybe.'

'Yes, for me.' He shifted his weight, his hands digging into his pockets. 'I don't think I need to remind you that this marriage was never meant to be anything but a matter of convenience, Alyse. A business deal.'

'That doesn't mean it can't become something else,' she said quietly. 'Something more.'

Something more? Even though he'd begun to suspect she harboured such hopes, the possibility still appalled him.

'Clearly you find that notion horrifying,' she continued, a hint of mockery in her voice. 'I've reduced you to silence.'

'It's unexpected,' he answered carefully. 'I've thought we've been in agreement about what our marriage would look like.'

'Considering we never discussed it, I don't know how we could be, or why you would think so.'

'Considering we both agreed to play-act at a relationship for six whole years,' he retorted, 'I'm not sure why you think it would suddenly change now, or why either of us would want it to.' He stared at her, her chin tilted in determination or maybe even defiance, her eyes sparking silver. Frustration flared within him; this was so *unexpected*. And he hated how it made him feel—cornered, angry and, damn it, uncertain. He'd been so sure about what he wanted—and what he didn't want.

Why was this woman he'd thought he knew so well—

that was, not at all—changing and, far more alarmingly, making him change?

He straightened, arms folded. 'We both got what we wanted out of this union, Alyse.'

She lifted her chin a notch. 'Which is?'

'To restore the monarchy's reputation and provide an heir.'

'Ah, an heir.' She folded her arms, mirroring his own implacable stance, and stared him down. 'And sex with you is such an appealing prospect, considering you just told me you have no interest at all in getting to know me.'

'I don't know why it would make a difference,' he answered coolly, and she let out a high, wild laugh.

'I should have known you'd say something like that.'

Leo raked a hand through his hair. He needed to perform some damage control, and quickly. 'Look, I told you, I didn't mean it quite like it sounded. I just never thought about—about friendship.'

'Actually, I think you did mean it. You just didn't mean for it to sound as brutal as it really is.' She walked past him back to their table, her dress nearly brushing his legs, and he inhaled the scent of sunshine and sea as she passed.

After a moment Leo followed her back to the table; she'd sat down and was eating her salad with a methodical diligence that suggested no enjoyment in the food at all.

Leo sat down as well, although his appetite had, annoyingly, vanished. Gazing at her pale, drawn face, he still felt guilty, as if he'd disappointed or even hurt her somehow. It was a feeling he'd experienced in varying degrees since they'd said their marriage vows, and he didn't like it.

He didn't want her to be hurt, and more to the point he didn't want to care if she was. Yet somehow he knew both were true, and he wasn't sure what to do about it.

'I honestly didn't mean to offend you,' he finally said,

his tone terse, when Alyse had ploughed through half her salad. His remained untouched.

'I suggest we be friends and you say you have no interest in such a thing,' she returned, not even looking up from her food. 'How is that not going to be offensive?'

'You took me by surprise,' he snapped, goaded into revealing a temper he'd barely known he had. 'For six years we've been as strangers to each other, and you seemed fine with that. Why should I expect anything to change now?'

'Because we're *married.*'

'It's nothing more than a promise and a piece of paper,' Leo said brutally, his temper now well and truly lit. 'It doesn't actually change anything. It doesn't have to.'

She looked up then, her face pale, her lush mouth bloodless. 'Because you don't want anything to change.'

'No, I don't.'

She shook her head slowly, biting those bloodless lips as she looked away. 'Why not?' she asked softly. 'What do you have against me?'

'Oh, for…' He sighed wearily. 'Nothing. I don't have anything against you.'

'Just women in general, then?'

Leo suppressed a curse. 'No, I have no problem with women, Alyse. I don't have a problem with anything. I simply want what I thought we'd agreed on all those years ago—a relationship of convenience, managed and manufactured for the sake of restoring the monarchy.'

'Do you really think I care about the monarchy?' she asked, her voice turning ragged with emotion, reminding him of ripped and ruined things, things torn by desire and broken by need.

He'd felt it once in himself, long ago, that endless ache of disappointment and sorrow. He intended never to feel it again, and he certainly didn't want it coming from his wife. The whole *point* of this marriage had been to avoid such messiness, such pain. That was the benefit of pretending, never mind the cost.

'I suppose you care,' Leo answered evenly. 'Since you agreed to marry me and perpetuate this charade.'

She glanced away, and in the darkness he could not make out her expression at all. 'I've never cared about the monarchy. Or being queen. Or—any of it.'

The bleakness of her tone had the hairs on the back of his neck prickling. He believed her, and he didn't want to. It would be much simpler to believe she'd agreed to their arrangement because of the material benefits she'd enjoy. *So much simpler.* 'Then why did you agree to a pretend engagement? A pretend marriage?' he asked, the words drawn from him reluctantly. It was a question he'd never asked her, never wanted to ask her. It had been enough that she'd accepted. Now, with an increasing sense of foreboding, he braced himself for her answer.

'Why?' Alyse repeated, and her voice sounded far away, her face still averted. She let out a long, shuddering breath. 'It doesn't really matter now.'

And, even though he knew that was no answer at all, Leo chose not to press. He really didn't want to know.

Neither of them spoke for a long moment, the silence strained and somehow sad. Then Alyse turned to him, her expression carefully veiled, yet Leo still felt the hurt emanating from her. It exasperated him, how much he felt now, both from her and in himself. For years he'd managed perfectly well, not feeling anything. Not wanting to.

'I still don't see how friendship will complicate things,' she said quietly. 'I would have thought it would make things easier. We're going to spend the rest of our lives together, after all. We are, God willing, going to have children—' She broke off suddenly, her voice having turned ragged again, and he could feel the need pulsing through her.

That was why friendship would complicate things—because it would open a door he'd kept firmly and forever shut. 'You knew all this before, Alyse,' he said. 'You knew what you were getting into. What you were agreeing to.'

'Knowing something and actually living it are two different things.' She shook her head slowly. 'Do you really not feel any differently, Leo? That actually being married makes a difference?'

He wanted to say no. He should say no, and nip all this talk of friendship and feelings in the bud. Yet he couldn't because, damn it, he did feel differently. He just didn't want to.

Impatiently, he tossed his napkin on the table. He'd barely touched his meal, but he wasn't hungry. 'Look,' he said flatly. 'The reason I said what I said is because I'm not sure I can even be your friend.'

'Why?'

'Because I don't— I've never really had a friend before.' That sounded so utterly pathetic, he realised furiously. He hated, *hated* that she'd driven him to such a confession.

Alyse gaped at him, her jaw dropping inelegantly. 'You've never had a friend?' she said in disbelief, and Leo felt his own jaw bunch, teeth grating.

'Not really.' He was lying, though. He'd had one friend at least—the best friend and brother whom he'd loved more than anyone else. The one person he'd been real with, the one person he'd trusted.

And look how that had turned out. The most real relationship he'd ever had had turned out to be as fake as all the others.

'Why not?' she asked and he just shrugged. She waited: a stand-off.

'When you live your life under the microscope, genuine friendship isn't easy to come by,' he finally said, his voice brusque. *When you lived your life in the spotlight.*

When the only time anyone was interested in affection or emotion was for the cameras...

He wasn't about to explain all that. How could he? He'd hated the glare of the spotlight, yet he'd chosen it for himself and his marriage. Willingly...because at least then he was in control.

Yet he didn't feel much in control at the moment. He felt as if it had been slipping away from him ever since he'd stood next to Alyse in the cathedral and said those vows.

'Even so,' she said, and he heard damnable pity in her voice. 'I would have thought there would be someone—'

'I haven't lived in complete isolation.' He cut her off, his voice coming out in something close to a snap. 'I've had acquaintances, servants, staff...'

'It's not the same.'

'Probably not. But you don't miss what you've never had.' Except he'd had it, and he knew he would miss it if he let himself—which he never did.

Alyse was silent for a long moment. Her expression had turned thoughtful, her head tilted to one side as her quiet gaze swept over him. Leo felt as if he were under a searchlight. 'Do you think,' she finally asked, 'you might be willing to try with me?'

'Try what?'

'Being my friend. Letting me be yours.'

Leo felt his jaw bunch harder and he wiped a hand over his face. 'Next we'll be painting each other's nails and doing—what was it?—macramé?'

A tiny smile hovered on Alyse's lush mouth and despite all the wretched emotion between them Leo felt his libido kick in hard. 'I promise, no weaving. Or nail varnish.'

'Right.' He tried to smile in response but somehow he couldn't. He couldn't take any more of this: not the emotion, not the honesty, not the damn intimacy. He felt as if he was going to burst out of his skin.

He turned resolutely back to his meal. 'Snorkelling sounds like a plan,' he said gruffly. Just as Alyse had said, you couldn't talk with a tube in your mouth. And, from the way her mouth turned down at the corners, Leo had a feeling she'd guessed the exact nature of his thoughts.

CHAPTER FIVE

As soon as they'd finished eating, Leo excused himself to go for a walk. Alyse watched him head down the beach into the darkness with a tired sigh. She didn't ask to join him, knew he'd had enough. Their conversation tonight had been more honest and intimate than anything they'd shared in the last six years, yet it just made her realise how little they actually had. How little they knew each other.

And yet she loved him. How could you love someone you barely knew, someone who purposely kept himself hidden from you and everyone?

It was a question she'd asked herself many times, and with no real answer, and yet she'd never been able to deny or suppress the hopeless longing he made her feel, and had done from the moment he'd come to her eighteenth birthday party. How the sight of one of his rare smiles had made her heart soar, and the barest brush of his fingers had made it leap. She didn't understand why, but she recognized the signs. Just like her parents had.

Love at first sight, and she wouldn't wish it on anyone—at least not when it wasn't returned.

Sighing again, she headed back to their hut. It was the middle of the night in Maldinian time, and she was utterly exhausted.

Yet as she lay between the cool linen sheets and waited for Leo to return, listening to the waves washing onto

the sound and the soothing chirrup of the cicadas, sleep
continued to elude her. Her body still felt tense, her mind
still racing as it replayed tonight's conversation with Leo.

I've never really had a friend before.

Had he meant that literally? How was it possible? Yet if
he'd spoken the truth—which she believed he had—then it
explained so much. His cool containment, his preference
for his own company. His lack of desire for anything intimate, honest or real.

Her own childhood had, in a way, been similarly lonely.
She was an only child of parents who had been rather rap-
turously wrapped up in each other. She'd been tutored by
a taciturn governess and then sent to a boarding school
where she'd been too shy ever to feel as if she really fit
in. At university she'd made friends, at least—*and look
where that had led her.*

And then of course the last six years in the public eye...
Sometimes the connection she'd experienced with the people who thronged the streets to greet her felt like the most
real, honest human interaction in her life, which certainly
said something about the lack of real intimacy in her own
life.

Strange to think both she and Leo had experienced
such loneliness, yet they'd reacted to it in completely different ways. He embraced isolation; she craved closeness.

She wondered if they would ever find a way to compromise, and if such a thing could satisfy either of them.

Leo walked as far down the beach as he could, before a
jagged outcropping of rocks stopped his path. He stopped
and let out a weary sigh. After the excruciating intimacy
of his conversation with Alyse, he'd needed space. Escape.
But, standing here looking at the rocky barrier, he knew
he couldn't outrun his thoughts.

She was asking for something so little, he knew. Something so reasonable: friendship. Friendship wasn't meant to be threatening or scary. It could, in fact, make things easier, just as she'd said. Certainly getting along with one another was better than existing in cold silence, and yet...

His whole life had been about cold silence. About work and duty and *doing*, because those things didn't let you down. Didn't hurt you. They were steady, safe.

And friendship might seem innocent, innocuous, but Leo knew how opening your heart just a little could still allow the pain and need to rush in. And, in any case, he didn't even know how to be a friend. Maybe it seemed incredible and, yes, pathetic, but it was the truth.

He'd lived a solitary life for so long and he didn't want to change.

Yet already, inexorably, impossibly, he felt himself changing. Already he was wondering just how badly he'd hurt her feelings tonight, and hating that he had. Hating even more that he cared that he had.

That's not what this marriage was meant to be about.

Cursing under his breath, he whirled around and began to stride back to the hut.

By the time he returned Alyse was in bed, her slight form draped with the linen sheet. She lay flat on her back, staring at the ceiling and not moving at all.

Leo came in and sat on the edge of the bed. He felt almost unbearably tired, not just from the long flight and the jet lag but from the unexpected roller coaster of emotions they'd both ridden on since their wedding, all of it too much, more than he'd felt in years.

'Are you awake?' he asked quietly and he heard Alyse exhale.

'Funnily enough, I can't get to sleep.'

He half-turned towards her, trying to make out her expression in the moonlit darkness and unable to. 'It's not just an out-of-sync body clock, I suppose?'

She let out a little huff that almost sounded like a laugh and amazingly, absurdly, Leo felt his heart lighten. 'Unfortunately not.'

She shifted in the bed, and he saw the slinky strap of her nightgown fall from one shoulder. His gaze was drawn inexorably to the smooth skin of her neck, her shoulder, and then downwards to the warm curve of her breast. Despite the tension that still vibrated between them, he felt the insistent stirring of arousal. He forced himself to look up into her eyes, and saw she was watching him with a wary expectation.

'I'm sorry,' he said.

'For what, exactly?' He heard a thread of humour in her voice and to his surprise he found himself matching it.

'It must be really bad, if there are options. Have you compiled a list?'

'That sounds like something you would do.'

He let out a tired huff of laughter and raked his hand through his hair. 'Yours is probably a lot longer than mine.'

'Maybe not,' she said softly, and something in him twisted. Yearned.

'I'm sorry for the way I handled our conversation,' he clarified gruffly, pushing away that strange yearning. 'And the unkind things I said to you. They were neither appropriate nor necessary.'

'That's a very formal apology.'

He bristled, instinctively, helplessly. 'I don't know any other way.'

She sighed. 'It's all right, Leo. I accept your apology.' She hesitated, and he heard the gentle in and out of her breath, saw the rise and fall of her chest in the moonlight, her breasts barely covered by a scrap of silky negligee. Had she not packed *any* decent pyjamas?

Of course she hadn't. This was their honeymoon, and they were meant to be wildly in love.

'What now?' she asked after a moment, and he watched as she picked at a thread in the linen sheet with slender, elegant fingers. 'Do you think we can be friends?'

'I can try,' Leo answered, the words drawn from him reluctantly. He hated how weak he sounded. How…incapable. But the truth was trying was all he could do, and he didn't even know if he could do that very well.

Alyse glanced up at him, blinking in the moonlit darkness, a small, wry smile curving her lips. 'I can't ask for more than that.'

'I still want what I wanted before,' Leo told her gruffly, the words a warning. 'A business arrangement, a marriage of convenience.'

Her smile faltered slightly and she glanced away before she met his gaze once more. 'Business arrangements don't have to be cold-blooded. Emotionless.'

Oh yes, they did. For him. Because that was who he was, who he'd determined to be, how to act. Not to feel. Not to want. Not to be disappointed or hurt.

'They can be friendly,' Alyse continued, her voice holding a hint of humour, of hope. And he wondered just what she was hoping for. How much.

Sighing, he pulled his shirt off and reached for his pyjamas. He changed quickly, conscious of Alyse so close to him, and the fact that despite the rather abhorrent intimacy of their conversation, they still hadn't been physically intimate yet. And, hell if he knew now when they would be. Sex and emotion did *not* go together. Yet after tonight he had a feeling Alyse wouldn't be able to separate them. The last thing he needed was her wanting something more than friendship—something ridiculous, like love.

'Look,' he said as he slid between the sheets, knowing he needed to be completely clear, 'I'm not going to love you. I don't love anyone and I never have.'

She was silent for a long moment. 'Is that what you're

worried about?' she asked eventually. 'That, in becoming friends, I might fall in love with you?'

'You might convince yourself you are.'

'You make me sound deluded.'

'Anyone who believes in love is deluded,' Leo said flatly, and he felt Alyse shift next to him, turning to face him.

'Deluded? Why do you think that?'

'Because love isn't real,' Leo stated. 'It's just a hormonal urge, a feeling that changes depending on your mood. It's certainly nothing I've ever pursued or even believed in.'

She was silent for so long Leo, annoyingly, felt a little self-conscious, as if he'd said something he shouldn't have. Revealed more about himself than he'd ever wanted to.

'If you don't think love is even real,' Alyse finally said, 'then you don't need to worry about me feeling it, do you?'

He sighed, shifting away from her tempting warmth. 'I just want to be clear about our expectations. I'm willing to try and be friends, of a sort, but that's all.'

'Of a sort?' She was trying once more for humour but he heard the hurt underneath the wryness. 'What sort is that, Leo?'

He stared up at the ceiling, the ocean breeze causing the palm fronds of the hut to rustle and sway. 'I told you, I haven't had many friends. I'll do my best.'

She turned towards him, and he felt her breasts brush his shoulder. Instantly he was hard. 'That's all anybody can do, isn't it? Your best.'

He breathed in the fresh, floral scent of her and his whole body pulsed with longing. As carefully as he could he moved away from her softness. Sex, he knew, was out of the question for tonight. But soon, damn it. *Very soon*. 'As long as being friends—of a sort—is enough for you,' he answered grudgingly and even through the darkness he saw and felt her sad smile.

'I suppose it will have to be,' she said, and then neither of them spoke again.

CHAPTER SIX

ALYSE WOKE TO the warm spill of sunshine and the gentle *swooshing* of the waves just metres from their bed. She turned to see Leo still asleep next to her, one hand flung over his head, the dark glint of morning stubble visible on his jaw. His lashes, surprisingly long, feathered his cheeks and those all-too-kissable lips were slightly parted. He looked gentler, somehow, in sleep. Softer, almost vulnerable, and so different from the cold, hard man he seemed when he was awake.

She let her gaze move lower and took in his bare chest, the rise and fall of it with each steady breath. Lower still, to the sheet rucked about his waist, his legs tangled beneath it.

Her mouth dried and for a few more seconds she tortured herself by drinking in the male perfection of his body without him knowing. Her gaze was lingering, longing, and completely unrestrained. How would it feel to touch that chest, to slide her hand from shoulder to hip and feel the hot satin of his skin under her seeking fingers?

Desire spiralled dizzily inside her. Never mind wanting to be friends; she just wanted him. For a brief moment she toyed with the idea of touching him. Kissing him awake. But she knew she wasn't bold enough, was too afraid of his surprise or even rejection.

Yet when would they consummate this marriage? When would friendship and desire meld, if ever?

And dared she still hope for more?

Silently she slid from the bed and reached for the robe that matched her nightgown, yet another ridiculous, silky confection. With one last look at Leo, who still seemed deeply asleep, she slipped out of the hut.

The day was already warm although Alyse suspected it wasn't much past dawn, the sun having only just risen over the horizon, its golden light pooling on the placid surface of the sea.

She sat on the beach, tucking her robe around her, and sifted the sun-warmed sand through her fingers as last night's conversation swirled through her mind: Leo's confession that he hadn't had any friends, his grudging acceptance that they might be friends—*of a sort*—and his flat and absolute statement that he would never love her.

Could she really be surprised by that bleak statement? It was no more than what she'd suspected, feared, and had tried to convince herself to believe over the years. And yet…she *had* believed in the miracle. The possibility of a miracle. She'd lied to Leo last night about that, just as she'd lied to herself over the last six years. She'd clung, stubbornly and stupidly, to the hope that he would learn to love her. That things would somehow miraculously change.

And she still clung to it now. Alyse's mouth twisted in a grim smile as she acknowledged the truth. Despite everything Leo had said, she still hoped he might come to love her in time, that physical attraction and possible friendship might deepen into the kind of love he didn't even believe in.

The smarter thing to do would be to let go of that hope, let it trickle away like water in sand, and get on with what was possible. Alyse knew she wouldn't. Couldn't. She'd keep hoping, keep believing, because thin vapour that it was, hope was all that sustained her.

And why shouldn't Leo love her? Why shouldn't it be possible, eventually, ultimately?

I'm not going to love you. I don't love anyone and I never have. The memory of his words made her both wince and wonder. Why didn't he love anyone, not even his parents or his sister? *Anyone who believes in love is deluded.* And what had made him lock up his heart so coldly and tightly that he refused even to believe love could exist, never mind flourish?

Could she—did she dare—be the one to try and unlock it?

'Good morning.'

Alyse turned to see Leo standing on the beach just a little bit away from her. He still wore only his pyjama bottoms and he looked glorious. She hoped her recent thoughts weren't visible on her face, her contrary hope reflected in her eyes.

'Good morning.'

'Did you sleep well?'

'Not particularly.'

He smiled then, a proper grin that set her heart racing. Did he know how attractive he was, how a single smile made her heart turn somersaults and then soar straight up into the sky?

'Me neither.' Leo came to sit beside her, stretching his legs out alongside hers. 'I'm not used to conversations like last night's.'

'I gathered that.'

'It was rather obvious, wasn't it?'

His wry smile tugged at her heart. 'Considering revealing anything of a personal nature seems to be akin to pulling teeth for you, I'd say yes.'

He chuckled softly and shook his head. 'Well. I tried.'

'That's all I'm asking for.'

He turned to her then, his gaze dark and searching, his smile gone. 'Is it?'

She fell silent under that searching and seemingly knowing gaze, for of course it wasn't—and it seemed he knew that, or at least suspected. Did he guess that she was in love with him? The possibility made both humiliation and hope rush through her.

She wanted him to know her feelings, wanted to stop pretending, and yet…the thought of his contempt and horror made everything inside her shrivel. She couldn't risk revealing so much. Not yet, and maybe not ever.

'So, snorkelling,' he said, and she nodded.

'Sounds fun.'

'Why don't we get dressed and go for breakfast, and then we can sort it out after?'

'All right.'

With a brisk nod Leo rose from the sand, brushing off his pyjamas, and headed back to the hut. Alyse watched him go, half-amazed that she was finally, actually going to spend an entire day in Leo's company… And still, as always, hopeful for what this day might bring.

This friendship business, Leo decided, was simple. At least so far. All he had to do was spend a little time with Alyse, *do* things with her. That suited him; he preferred having a plan, preferred action to talking. As long as they kept it to leisure activities, preferably ones that kept them from conversing, he'd be fine. Everything would be fine. The thought brought him a rush of much-needed relief.

Twenty minutes later they were both dressed and heading over to the main resort for breakfast. Alyse wore a pair of body-hugging canvas shorts that made Leo even more aware of her long, slim legs and the curve of her bottom. The tee-shirt she wore, in a pale petal-pink, seemed tight to Leo. Not obscenely so, but he kept finding his gaze being drawn to the high, firm breasts he'd seen on such provocative display in those frothy nightgowns she wore. Her hair was loose and fell down her back in shining, dark waves and her eyes sparkled silver as she fell into step beside him.

He'd always thought her pretty enough but now, seeing her looking natural rather than coiffed, styled and professionally made up, he realised she was actually quite beautiful.

And he wanted her very badly.

There was no reason, he thought, why they couldn't be friends by day and lovers by night. Really, it was the perfect solution.

As long as Alyse didn't confuse the two. As long as she didn't start wanting more.

He'd just have to make sure she didn't.

The restaurant, of course, was empty except for half a dozen staff who scurried to attention as soon as Leo and Alyse entered the pavilion that was shaded from the sun and open to the sea.

They sat at a table in the corner and soon had a pot of coffee and a pitcher of freshly squeezed orange juice in front of them.

'I'm starving,' Alyse confessed. She glanced at the buffet that was spread out along one side of the pavilion. 'I think there's plenty of food.'

Leo followed her gaze, taking in the platters of pastries and bowls of fresh fruit, the personal chef on hand to make omelettes to order and the several silver tureens of bacon, sausage and eggs. 'So it seems.'

'It's a bit of a waste, though, isn't it?' she said. 'When we're the only ones staying here.'

'I'm sure the staff will eat it. The resort is meant to be eco-friendly.'

'That's good to know.' She looked at him curiously. 'Are you very concerned about such things?'

He shrugged. 'I certainly intend to bring my country into the twenty-first century, in environmental matters as well as in others.'

He saw the curiosity flare in her eyes. 'Others? What kinds of things?'

He shrugged again, discomfited now. He wasn't used to talking about himself. He wasn't used to anyone asking. 'Technologically, Maldinia is about twenty years behind the rest of Europe. I've been drafting a proposal for broadband to be accessible to most areas.'

'Is it not now?'

'Really just in Averne and the outlying towns and tourist resorts. Admittedly, most of Maldinia is agricultural, and their methods are about a hundred years out of date, never mind twenty.'

She smiled, her eyes lightening with humour. 'But that must be good for the tourist revenue—very quaint, those farmers in traditional dress herding their sheep along with their wooden crooks.'

He acknowledged the point with a wry nod. 'They do look rather nice on a postcard. But those farmers should be able to check the weather—or the latest football scores—on the Internet when they get back home, don't you think?'

She laughed, the sound silvery and crystal-clear. It was a sound, Leo realised with a jolt, that he liked to hear, and he hadn't heard it very much over the last six years. 'Absolutely. Internet access is practically an inalienable right these days.'

'Inalienable,' he agreed solemnly, and they smiled at each other, the moment spinning out first in simple enjoyment and then in something Leo didn't quite recognise. Something that didn't just skim the surface of his feelings but dove deeper, surprising and almost hurting him with its strange poignancy.

Alyse looked away first. 'I didn't realise you were already involved in governing your country.'

Leo's mouth tightened, the moment evaporating like so much morning mist, gone with the first glare of light. *Good*. It was better that way. 'A bit,' he answered, his tone instinctively repressive.

He wasn't involved, not as much as he wanted to be. He'd been trying to prove to his father for fifteen years that he was capable of being king. That he deserved responsibility and respect. King Alessandro might not be interested in government policy—he was too absorbed in his own selfish pleasures for that—but he didn't want his son cramping his style or seizing his power.

He'd never wanted him to be king at all, and even after a decade and a half as heir Leo never forgot he was second choice. Second best.

Alyse stirred her coffee, her gaze thoughtful. 'There's so much I don't know about you,' she said, and the ensuing, expectant pause made Leo tense. Spending time together was one thing. You couldn't talk while you were snorkelling. But getting to know each other…having Alyse ask him questions…having to answer them… That was an entirely different prospect.

'Don't look so horrified,' she continued dryly. 'I'm not about to ask you for your deepest, darkest secrets.'

'I don't have any secrets. Not too many, anyway.' He tried to speak lightly, but he felt unsettled, uneasy, because for a few moments he'd enjoyed their conversation—the light banter, as well as, God help him, the deeper discussion—and *that* horrified him more than anything Alyse could ask.

Well, almost.

'So no embarrassing moments?' she quipped, a smile

on the lips Leo kept realising were incredibly lush and kissable. He remembered how they had tasted. How *she'd* tasted. Honey-sweet with a tang of salt from the sea. Amazing. 'No secret fears?'

He forced his gaze away from her mouth, up towards her eyes that sparkled with humour. How had he never noticed how silver her eyes were? They weren't grey at all. They were warm and soft, glinting with golden lights, like a moonlit, starry sky…

Good Lord. He was thinking like some sort of besotted fool. Eyes couldn't be *soft*, and he wasn't about to compare them to the night sky.

What was *happening* to him?

'Secret fears?' he repeated, forcing his attention back to the conversation. 'No, I don't have any of those.' None he was willing to share, anyway, and he wouldn't exactly call them *fears*. More like…concerns.

'Oh come on, Leo. There must be something.'

'Why don't you tell me something about you?' he suggested. 'Most embarrassing moment or secret fear or…I don't know…funny dream.'

Her mouth curved wider and she leaned forward. 'Here's something you don't know.'

'Very well.' There had to be a thousand things he didn't know about her, but he felt a sudden, sharp curiosity to hear this one and he leaned forward too.

'That kiss? The photo that started it all?'

'Yes.'

'I only clasped your cheek because I was wearing high heels for the first time and I was about to lose my balance.'

Leo stared at her for a moment, nonplussed, almost disbelieving, and then he burst into laughter. She grinned back and then she started laughing too, and from the corner of his eye he could see several members of the restaurant staff beaming in approval.

This would make a good photo.

The thought was enough to sober him up completely. 'And to think,' he said just a little too flatly, 'if you'd been wearing flats we might not even be married.'

'No,' Alyse agreed, all traces of laughter gone from her face. 'We might not be.' They stared at each other for a moment, and this time Leo felt a certain bleakness in their shared look. Their engagement—their whole lives, entwined as they were—had hinged on something so trivial. So ridiculous.

Why did the thought—which wouldn't have bothered him a bit before; hell, he'd have appreciated the irony— make him feel almost *sad* now? Sad not just for himself but for Alyse, for the way her eyes shuttered and her mouth twisted, and the warmth and ease they'd been sharing seemed to disappear completely.

He needed to put a stop to this somehow. He needed to stop wondering, stop *feeling* so damn much. The trouble was, he didn't know how to stop it. And, worse, part of him didn't even want to.

Alyse knew she shouldn't be hurt by Leo's observation. It was no more than the truth, the truth she'd known all along. Yet the reminder stung, when for the first time they'd actually seemed to be enjoying each other's company.

Not wanting Leo to see how absurdly hurt she felt, she rose from the table and headed for the buffet, filling her plate up with a variety of tempting items. Leo followed, and by the time they were both back at the table her composure was firmly restored.

'So,' she said, spearing a piece of papaya, 'your turn. Secret fear, embarrassing moment, funny dream. Take your pick.'

'I don't have any of those,' Leo answered. She watched him neatly break a croissant in two and rolled her eyes.

'Come on, Leo. You're not a robot. You're a man with feelings and thoughts, hopes and fears. You're *human*. Aren't you? Or am I going to roll over in bed one night and see a little key in the back of your neck, like that *Dr Who* episode with the creepy dolls?'

His eyebrows lifted. 'Creepy dolls?'

'Haven't you ever watched that television programme?'

'I don't watch television.'

She let out a laugh. 'You really are a robot.'

'Ah, you've discovered my one deep secret. And here I thought I hid it so well.'

She laughed again, and his answering smile made everything in her lighten and lift. They'd never, ever joked around before. Teased each other. *Enjoyed* each other. It was as heady as a drug, his smile, his light tone. She craved more, and she knew just how dangerous and foolhardy that was.

Leo had made it abundantly clear last night. *As long as it's enough for you.*

Already she knew it wasn't.

'All right, then,' she said, taking a pastry from her plate. 'No secret fears, funny dreams, or embarrassing moments. How about hobbies, then?'

'Hobbies?' he repeated in something so close to incredulity that Alyse nearly laughed.

'Yes, you have heard of them? Pleasant pastimes such as reading, gardening, stamp-collecting?' He simply stared and she supplied helpfully, 'Tennis? Golf? Pottery?'

'Pottery? I thought macramé was bad enough.'

'You must do something to unwind.'

He arched an eyebrow. 'Do I seem unwound to you?'

'Now that you mention it…maybe I should suggest something? Watercolours, perhaps?'

His lips twitched and he shook his head. 'I play chess.'

'Chess?' She smiled, felt the sweet thrill of a small victory. 'I should have been able to guess that.'

'Oh? How so?'

'Chess is a game requiring patience and precision. You have both in spades.'

'I'm not sure that was a compliment,' he answered. 'But I'll take it as one.'

'Are you very good?'

'Passable.'

Which probably meant he was amazing. She could picture him in front of a chessboard, his long, tapered fingers caressing the smooth ivory shape of the queen… A shaft of desire blazed through her. She really needed to get a grip if she was fantasising about *chess*. Well, really, about Leo.

'Do you play?' he asked.

'I'm passable, but probably not as passable as you.'

'I didn't know there were degrees of passable.'

'There is when I feel your "passable" is a gross understatement.'

'We'll have to have a match.'

'You'll trounce me, I'm sure.' Yet the thought of playing chess—really, of doing anything with him—made her spirits lift. *See?* she wanted to say. *We are friends. This is working.*

But she still wanted more.

'So.' Leo pushed his plate away and nodded to hers. 'Are you finished? I'll just speak to the staff about arranging the snorkelling.'

Alyse watched him stride away as she sipped the last of her coffee. Despite her fledgling hope, she still wished that they were a normal couple. That this was a normal honeymoon. That Leo was striding away with a spring in his step instead of a man resigned to a lifetime of duty. That they'd spent last night wrapped in each other's arms, lost in mutual pleasure, instead of lying next to each other as rigid as two cadavers in a mortuary.

She could go on and on, Alyse knew, pointlessly wishing things had been different before, were different now. She forced herself to stop. *This* was what she had to deal with, to accept and make work. And this morning had been a beginning, a hopeful one. She needed to focus on that and let it be enough, for now at least. Maybe for ever.

Half an hour later they'd changed into swimsuits underneath tee-shirts and shorts and Leo was leading the way along the beach to where a gorgeous catamaran was pulled up on the sand.

Alyse came to a stop in front of the boat. 'Are we going in that?'

'I arranged it with the staff. I thought we'd have a better time if we could go out a bit farther.' He glanced at her, his brows knitted together in a frown. 'Are you all right with boats? I know some people are afraid of open water.'

His thoughtfulness touched her, belated as it was. It really was so confoundedly easy for Leo to affect her, she thought. To make her love him. 'It's fine,' she told him. 'It's great, actually. I love sailing.'

And as Leo navigated the boat out into the sea, the sun bathing them both in warm, golden light, Alyse stretched out on the bridge deck, it *was* great. It was fantastic.

She tilted her head back so the sun bathed her face and felt herself begin to relax, the tension dropping from her shoulders, her body loosening and leaning into the sun. She'd been strung as taut as a bow for far too long; it felt good to unbend.

When they were out on the open water, the sea shimmering in every direction, Leo came and joined her on the bridge deck.

'You look like you're enjoying yourself.'

She lowered her head to smile at him, one hand shading her eyes from the dazzling sun. 'I am. It's good to be away from it all.'

He sat beside her, his long, muscular legs stretched out next to hers, his hands braced behind him. 'The media attention was a bit wild these last few months.'

'I'll say. The journalists were going through my rubbish, and my parents' rubbish, and my friends' as well.'

His mouth twisted in a grimace. 'I'm sorry.'

She shrugged in response. 'I signed up for it, didn't I? When I agreed.'

'That still doesn't make it pleasant.'

'No, but you've been living with it for your whole life, haven't you?'

His eyes narrowed, although whether just from the sun or because of what she'd said Alyse didn't know.

'I have,' he agreed without expression and then he rose from the deck. 'We're out far enough now. We can anchor soon.'

She watched him at the sails of the catamaran, the muscles of his back rippling under the tee-shirt that the wind blew taut against his body. She felt a rush of desire but also a swell of sympathy. She hadn't considered Leo's childhood all that deeply before; she knew as prince and heir he'd lived in the spotlight for most of his life.

Of course, the glare of that spotlight had intensified with their engagement. Did he resent that? Did he resent *her*, for making something he must not like worse? It was a possibility she'd never considered before, and an unwelcome one at that.

A few minutes later Leo set anchor and the catamaran bobbed amid the waves as he tossed their snorkelling equipment on the deck.

He tugged off his tee-shirt and shorts and Alyse did the same, conscious once again of the skimpiness of the string bikini she wore. She hadn't found a single modest swimming costume in her suitcases.

She looked up and there could be no mistaking the blaze of heat in his eyes. 'Your swimming costumes,' he remarked, 'are practically indecent.'

Alyse felt a prickly blush spread not just over her face but her whole body. 'Sorry. I didn't choose them.'

'No need to apologise. I quite like them.' He handed her a pair of fins and then tugged his own on. 'What do you mean, you didn't choose them?'

'All my clothes are chosen by stylists.'

He frowned. 'Don't you see them first? And get to approve them?'

Alyse shrugged. 'I suppose I could have insisted, but...' She trailed off, not wanting to admit how cowed she'd been by Queen Sophia's army of stylists and staff who had seemed to know so much more than her, and had obviously not cared about what she thought.

At eighteen, overawed and more than a little intimidated, she hadn't possessed the courage to disagree with any of them, or so much as offer her own opinion. As the years had passed, bucking the trend had just become harder, not easier.

'I didn't realise you had so little say in such matters. I suppose my mother can be quite intimidating.'

'That's a bit of an understatement,' she answered lightly, but Leo just frowned.

'You were so young when we became engaged.'

She felt herself tense uneasily, unsure what he was implying. 'Eighteen, as you know.'

'Young. And sheltered.' His frown deepened and he shook his head. 'I remember how it was, Alyse. I know my parents can be very...persuasive. And, as the media attention grew, it might have seemed like you were caught in a whirlwind you couldn't control.'

'It did feel like that sometimes,' she allowed. 'At times it was utterly overwhelming. But I knew what I was doing, Leo.' *More or less.* 'I might have only been eighteen, but I knew my own mind.' *And her own heart.* Not that she would ever tell him that. After Leo's revelations about how he didn't even believe in love, never mind actually having ever felt it, Alyse had no intention of baring her heart. Not now, and perhaps not ever.

She forced the thought away. *This is a beginning.*

'Still…' he began, and she thought how easy it would be, to let him believe she'd been railroaded into this marriage. And there was some truth in it, after all. The media attention *had* been out of control, and in those dark moments when she'd considered breaking their engagement she'd known she didn't possess the strength to go against everything and everyone—the monarchy, the media, the adoring public. It had simply been too much.

But it wasn't the whole truth and, while it might satisfy Leo as to why she'd agreed in the first place—a question she hadn't been willing to answer last night—she wouldn't perpetuate another lie.

But neither will you tell him the real reason—that you were in love with him, and still are.

With determined flippancy she adjusted her mask and put her hands on her hips. 'How do I look? I don't think anyone can be taken seriously in flippers.'

His expression lightened into a smile, and Alyse felt a rush of relief. Now she was the one avoiding conversation. Honesty.

'Probably not,' he agreed and held out one of his own flippered feet. 'But they do the job. Are you ready?'

She nodded and a moment later they were slipping over the side of the boat. When Leo put his hands on her bared waist to steady her as she slid into the water, Alyse felt her heart rate rocket. Just the touch of his hands on her flesh sent an ache of longing through her. She wanted to turn to him, to rip off their masks and stupid fins and forget anything but this need that had been building in her for so long, the need she longed to be sated. She wanted to be his lover as well as his friend.

Then he let go of her and with a splash she landed and kicked away from the boat, Leo swimming next to her.

As soon as she put her face in the sea the world seemed to open up, the ocean floor with its twists and curves of coral stretching away endlessly in every direction. Fish of every colour and size darted among the coral: schools of black-and-yellow-striped fish, one large blue fish swimming on its own and a fish that even seemed to change colours as it moved.

Overwhelmed after just a few minutes, Alyse lifted her head from the water. Leo immediately did the same, taking his mask off to gaze at her in concern. 'Are you OK?'

'Amazed,' she admitted. 'I've never seen so many fish before. They're all so beautiful.'

'The snorkelling here is supposed to be the best in the Caribbean.'

She couldn't resist teasing him. 'You sound like a tourist advert.'

'I just do my research. You want to keep going?'

'Of course.'

They snorkelled side by side for over an hour, pointing different fish out to one another, kicking in synchronicity. At one point Leo reached for her hand and pulled her after him to view an octopus nestling in a cave of coral and they grinned at each other at the sight, Leo's eyes glinting behind his mask.

Finally, hungry and tired, they returned to the boat, hauling themselves dripping onto the deck.

'I had the staff pack us a lunch,' Leo informed her. 'They should have left it on the boat.'

Alyse sat drying in the sun while Leo took a wicker basket from one of the storage compartments and began to unpack its contents.

'Champagne and strawberries?' She surveyed the contents of the basket with her eyebrows raised. 'Quite the romantic feast.'

'Did you really expect anything else?'

She watched as he laid it all out on a blanket. 'Do you ever get tired of it?' she asked quietly. 'The pretending? With me?'

His fingers stilled around the neck of the champagne bottle and then he quickly and expertly popped the cork. 'Of course, just as I imagine you do.'

'Why did you agree to it all, Leo? Was it really just to help stabilise the monarchy?'

The glance he gave her was dark and fathomless. 'Does that not seem like enough reason to you?'

'It seems like a huge sacrifice.'

'No more than you were willing to make.'

They were getting into dangerous territory, Alyse knew. She didn't want him to ask her again why she'd agreed. She didn't want to have to answer.

'Does the monarchy matter that much to you?'

'Of course it does. It's everything to me.'

Everything. That was rather all-encompassing; it didn't leave room for much else. 'I suppose you've been preparing to be king since you were born.'

Leo didn't answer for a moment and Alyse felt the tension in his suddenly stilled hands, his long, lean fingers wrapped around the neck of the champagne bottle. Then he began to pour, the bubbles fizzing and popping against the sides of the flute. 'More or less.'

Alyse surveyed him, felt instinctively he wasn't saying something, something important. Perhaps he did have secrets…just as she did.

'Another toast?' she asked as Leo handed her a glass.

'We've had quite a few toasts recently.'

'And quite a lot of champagne.'

'People can be amazingly unoriginal about what they think is romantic,' he said dryly. He eyed her thoughtfully over the rim of his glass. 'How about a toast to friendship?'

Alyse's heart lurched. 'You're coming around, then?' she said lightly, and he inclined his head in acknowledgement.

'A bit.'

'To friendship, then,' she answered, and they both drank, their eyes meeting over the rims of their glasses. Alyse felt her insides tighten and then turn over at the look of heat in Leo's navy eyes. They simmered with it, that warmth seeming to reach out and steal right through her. For such a coldly practical man, his eyes burned. *She* burned.

'So,' she offered shakily. 'What is there to eat besides strawberries?'

'Oh, lots of things,' he said lightly, glancing away from her to fill a plate with various delectable offerings. 'You won't go hungry.'

'No,' Alyse murmured. But she *was* going hungry... hungry in an entirely different, and carnal, way. She knew he wanted her, had thrilled to the taste and feel of his desire when he'd kissed her, when he'd pulled her close to that hard, hard body. Yet she still didn't quite have the confidence to act on it now, to thrust away the plate he'd given her and reach for something far more delicious: *him*.

'Try some,' Leo offered, and she saw the heat flare in his eyes, wondered if he knew the nature of her thoughts.

Wordlessly Alyse put something in her mouth; she didn't even look to see what it was. The burst of sweet flavour on her tongue surprised her and she realised she'd bitten into a plantain fried in orange juice.

'Good?' Leo asked, and now she heard the desire in his voice as well as saw it in his eyes; it poured over her like chocolate, rich and sweet. She'd never heard him sound like this before, never felt so much in herself—or from him.

Somehow she managed to eat most of what was on her plate, the rich flavours bursting on her tongue. Every heavy-lidded look and small, knowing smile from Leo made her more aware of everything: the taste of the food; the feel of the sun on her salt-slicked skin; the heat and desire coursing through her body like warmed honey.

Finally there were only the strawberries left, and the champagne.

'And this is the only way to eat these,' Leo said, dipping a strawberry in his flute of champagne and then raising it to Alyse's parted lips.

Her heart rate skittered and her breathing hitched as she opened her mouth and took a bite of the champagne-sodden fruit. The taste on her tongue was both tart and sweet, but far headier than any champagne she could drink was the look of unabashed hunger in Leo's eyes—and the answering surge she felt in herself.

Strawberry juice dribbled down her chin and Leo's expression flared hotter as he caught it with the tip of his thumb then licked the juice from his own hand.

Alyse let out an audible shudder. Then, filled with a new daring fuelled by this heady desire, she reached for a strawberry and dunked it into her own glass of champagne. Leo's narrowed gaze followed her movements and after a heartbeat's hesitation he opened his mouth.

Her fingers near to trembling, Alyse put the strawberry to his lips. Juice ran over her fingers as he bit down, his gaze hot and hard on hers. She shuddered again, her whole body singing with awareness and need. Then Leo turned his head so his lips brushed her fingers and with his tongue he caught a drip of juice from the sensitive skin of her wrist.

Alyse let out a shocked gasp at the exquisite sensation. *'Leo...'*

And then he was pushing aside the remnants of their picnic, champagne spilling and strawberries scattering, and was reaching for her, finally, *finally* reaching for her.

His hands came hard onto her shoulders and then his mouth was hard on hers, tasting both tart and sweet from the champagne and the fruit.

His tongue swept into her mouth, tasting, searching, and then finding. Pleasure burst inside her like fireworks, like sparks of the sun, heating her all over. Alyse brought her hands up to his shoulders, her palms smoothing and then clutching the hot, bared skin.

Leo's mouth moved from her lips to her jaw and then her neck, his hand cupping her breast with only the thin, damp fabric of her bikini top between the heat of his palm and her sensitive skin.

Alyse moaned aloud, the sound escaping from her, impossible to contain, and Leo drew back.

'I'm sorry,' he murmured, smoothing her hair away from her face. 'I'm rushing like a randy schoolboy and you deserve better than that.'

She blinked, still dazed by the sensations coursing through her. Leo smiled, no more than a quirk of his mouth. 'I don't want your first time to be some hasty grope on the deck of a boat. I do have that much sensitivity, Alyse.'

Alyse blinked again, his words trickling through her, leaving ice in their wake. Her first time. Hers—not *theirs.*

Leo, she realised, thought she was a virgin.

CHAPTER SEVEN

LEO SAW THE emotions flash across Alyse's face like
changes in the weather, sunshine and shadows. Even more
so he felt the change in her, the tensing, the slight withdrawal even though she hadn't actually moved.

'What is it?' he asked quietly. 'What's wrong?'

She gave a little shake of her head. 'Nothing.'

He didn't believe that for a moment. Gently but firmly
he took her chin in his hand, forced her to look at him.
'It's not nothing.'

Her clear grey eyes met his for a moment before she
let her gaze slide away. 'Nothing to talk about now,' she
said, with a not-quite-there smile.

If she was trying to sound light, she'd failed. Leo let go
of her chin and sat back braced on his hands to survey her
thoughtfully. She still wasn't looking at him and a tendril
of hair, curly from the sea air, fell against the soft pale-
ness of her cheek.

'Are you nervous about what will happen between us?'

She looked at him then, a small spark of humour lighting her eyes. 'You sound like something out of a melodrama, Leo. You're usually more blunt than that.'

He felt his mouth curving in an answering smile.
'I'm happy to be blunt. I want you, Alyse.' He gazed at
her frankly, letting the desire that still coursed unsated
through his body reveal itself in his face. 'I want you very

badly. I want to touch you, to kiss you, to be inside you. And I don't want to wait very long.'

He saw an answering flare of heat in her eyes, turning them to molten silver, but her lips twisted and trembled and she looked away again. *What was going on?* 'That's admirably blunt.'

'I'll be even blunter—I think you want me just as much as I want you.' Gently he tucked that curly tendril of hair behind her ear, unable to keep his fingers from lingering on the softness of her skin. He felt her tremble in response. 'Do you deny it?'

'No,' she whispered, but she wouldn't look at him.

Frustration bit into him. *What was going on?* Compelled to make her look at him, make her acknowledge the strength of the desire between them, he touched her chin and turned her to face him. She met his gaze reluctantly but unflinchingly, her eyes like two wide, grey pools Leo thought he could drown in. Lose himself completely.

'I want to make love to you,' he said quietly, each word brought up from a deep well of desire and even emotion inside him. 'But not here, on a hard deck. We have a lovely big bed on a lovely private beach and I quite like the idea of making love to you there.'

Her eyes widened even more, surprise flickering in their depths, and with a jolt he realised what he'd said. Confessed.

Making love. It was a term he'd never used, didn't even like. If love didn't exist beyond a simple hormonal fluctuation, then you couldn't make it. And sex, in his experience, had nothing to do with love. It wouldn't, even with Alyse.

Yet the words had slipped out and he knew that Alyse had noticed. What did she think was happening between them? What *was* happening between them?

Panic, icy and overwhelming, swamped him. Why the hell had he said that? Felt it? This was what happened when you let someone in just a little bit. Friendship be damned.

He dropped his fingers from her chin and rose abruptly from the deck, thankfully shattering the moment that had stretched between them. There would be no putting it together again; he'd make sure of that. 'We should head back,' he said tersely. 'In any case.'

He set sail, his back to her, and wondered just how he could get their relationship—he didn't even like calling it that—back on the impersonal and unthreatening footing he craved. Whatever it took, he vowed grimly, he would do it. He'd had enough of this *friendship*.

Alyse sat on the bridge deck and watched as Leo set sail for their private cove. His shoulders were now rigid with tension, every muscle taut, and she didn't know if it was because of her emotional withdrawal or his. She'd seen the flare of panic in his eyes when he'd said those two revealing words: making love.

But there would be no love in their physical union, just immense, intense attraction. So why had he said it? Had he meant it simply as a turn of phrase that had alarmed him when he'd heard it aloud? Or, for a moment, had he actually felt something more? That alarmed him more than any mere words ever could.

Was she ridiculous to think that little slip might signify something? She knew she had a tendency to read far too much into a smile or a look. She didn't want to make the same mistake now, yet she couldn't keep herself from wondering. From hoping.

And yet, she felt her own flare of panic. What would Leo think—and feel—when she told him, as she must do, that she wasn't a virgin?

Alyse turned to face the sea, hugging her knees to her chest even though the wind was sultry. The coldness she felt came from inside, from the knowledge she'd been hiding from for too long already.

She'd blanked out that one fumbling evening that constituted all of her sexual experience, had consigned it to a terrible, heart-rending mistake and tried to pretend it hadn't happened.

But princesses—future queens—were meant to be pure, unblemished, and she clearly was not. In this day and age, did it really matter?

It would matter, she supposed, to someone like Queen Sophia who, despite having been born into merely an upper-class family, held fast to the archaic bastions of the monarchy as if she were descended from a millennia's worth of royalty. It probably mattered to King Alessandro as well, but she didn't care about either of them. She cared about Leo.

Would it matter to him? Would he be disappointed that he wasn't her first? She had no illusions that *he* was a virgin; he surely hadn't been celibate for the six long years of their engagement, even if he'd been admirably discreet.

Anxiety danced in her belly. Worry gnawed at her mind. She didn't want to give him any reason to withdraw emotionally from her, to feel disappointed or perhaps even angry, yet she knew she would have to tell him... before tonight.

They didn't speak until the catamaran was pulled up on the beach and they were back in their private cove, and then only to talk about when they would have dinner. It was late afternoon, the sun already starting its mellow descent towards the horizon.

Alyse went to shower in the separate bathroom facilities, all sunken marble and gold taps kept in a rocky enclosure that was meant to look like a natural part of the cove.

She washed away the remnants of sea salt and sun cream and wondered what the next few hours would hold.

Something had started to grow between her and Leo, per-haps even to blossom. Friendship—and perhaps something more, until he'd had that moment of panic.

Could they recapture both the camaraderie and passion they'd felt this afternoon?

What if her admission ruined it all?

It doesn't matter, she told herself. *It shouldn't matter. He might be a prince, but Leo's still a modern man...*

Even so, she felt the pinpricks of uncertainty. Of fear.

The staff were setting up another romantic dinner on the beach when Leo came out of the shower, his hair damp and curling slightly by his neck, the sky-blue of his shirt bringing out the blue in his eyes. Alyse had chosen another dress from her stylist-selected wardrobe, this one made of lavender silk, the colour like the last vestiges of sunset. It dipped daringly low in the front and then nipped in at the waist before flaring out around her legs. She left her hair down and her feet bare and went without make-up. It seemed ridiculous to bother with eyeliner or lipstick when they were on a secluded beach and the sea wind and salt air would mess them both up anyway.

Leo seemed to agree, for he took in her appearance with no more than a slight nod, yet she still felt the strength of his response, the leashed desire.

And something else. Something she didn't like—a cool-ness in his expression, a reserve in his manner. He didn't speak as he took her hand and led her to the table set up on the sand.

Still she was achingly aware of him, more now than ever before: the subtle, spicy scent of his aftershave; the dry warmth of his palm as he took her hand; the latent strength of his stride as she fell into step next to him.

'What shall we do tomorrow?' she asked brightly when they'd sat down and begun their starters, slices of succu-lent melon fanned out with paper-thin carpaccio. She was determined not to lose any ground, not to let him retreat back into his usual silence, as much as he might seem to want to. 'Go for a hike?'

Leo's mouth tightened and he speared a slice of melon. 'I need to work tomorrow.'

'Work?' Disappointment crashed over her but with effort she kept her smile in place, her voice light. 'This is your honeymoon, Leo.'

He pinned her with a steely gaze. 'I have duties, Alyse.'

'And what will the staff think of you ignoring your bride on the second full day of our holiday?' she asked, unable to keep herself from it even though she didn't want to bring up the whole pretence of their relationship. She wanted to talk about how it was becoming more real. Or it had seemed to be, this afternoon.

'I'm sure they'll understand. Being in love doesn't mean we live in each other's pockets. The last six years have proved that. We spent most of the time apart and yet no one seemed to have any trouble believing we were wildly, passionately in love.'

That wasn't quite true, Alyse knew. When the media hadn't been celebrating their grand romance, it had been trying to create division: publishing incriminating-looking photos, composing pages and pages of speculation that she'd feared contained more than a grain of truth.

Leo looking for love with Duke's daughter Liana?

The memory still hurt.

'I realise that,' she told him when she trusted herself to speak as evenly as he had. 'But this is our honeymoon.'

'And you know just what kind of honeymoon it is.'

'What is that supposed to mean?'

'We're pretending,' he clarified, his voice cool. 'We always will be.'

'I haven't forgotten.' Alyse stared at him. His face was

as blank as it ever had been, all traces of humour and happiness completely gone.

Today had been so sweet, so wonderful and so full of hope. She hated that they'd lost so much ground so quickly.

And why? Just because of that moment on the boat, when Leo had mentioned the dreaded L-word?

Was he actually spooked? *Afraid?*

The thought seemed ridiculous; Leo was always so confident, so assured. And yet Alyse couldn't think of another reason for his sudden and utter withdrawal.

The friendship—the intimacy—that had been growing between them had him scared.

The thought almost restored her hope. Scared was better than indifferent. Still, she knew there was no point pressing the issue now. That didn't mean she was going to let him off the hook quite so easily.

'I suppose I can entertain myself easily enough for a day,' she said lightly, and saw the flicker of surprise ripple across Leo's features that she was capitulating so easily. 'What work do you have to do?' she continued, and the surprise on his face intensified into discomfort. Alyse almost smiled. 'Are you working on that proposal for broadband?'

'Some paperwork,' he answered after a pause, his voice gruff, but Alyse was determined not to let the conversation sputter out. He would let her in, one way or another. Even if he was scared.

'Will you put the proposal before the Cabinet? That's how it works, isn't it? A constitutional monarchy.'

'Yes. I hope to put it before them eventually. It's not one of my father's priorities.'

'Why not?'

Leo shrugged. 'My father has always been more interested in enjoying the benefits of being king rather than fulfilling his royal responsibilities.'

'But you're different.'

A light blazed briefly in his eyes. 'I hope so.'

'I think you are.' She spoke softly, and was gratified to see something like surprised pleasure lift the corners of Leo's mouth before he glanced away.

'I hope I can match you as queen.' She meant to sound light but the words came out in a rush of sincerity. 'I want to be a credit to you, Leo.'

'You already are. The fact that the public fell in love with you six years ago has been a huge boon to our country. You of all people must know the power of that photograph.'

She nodded slowly. 'Yes, but more than that. I want to do something more than just smile and shake hands.'

'Understandably, but don't sell a smile and a handshake short. It's more than my parents ever did.'

'Is it?'

'One of the reasons they were so keen for our engagement to go ahead is because they'd damaged the monarchy nearly beyond repair,' Leo said flatly. He speared a slice of beef with a little more vigour than necessary.

'How?'

He shrugged. 'Very public affairs, careless spending, a complete indifference to their people. It's hard to say which aspect of their lives was the most damaging.'

And he'd grown up in that environment. 'It doesn't sound like a very happy place to have your childhood,' she said quietly.

'I didn't. I went to boarding school when I was six.'

'*Six?*'

'I didn't mind.' A waiter had materialised on the edge of the beach and with a flick of his fingers Leo indicated for him to come forward. Alyse had a feeling he'd had enough of personal conversation, but at least he'd shared something. More than he ever had before.

Leo hadn't meant to say so much. Reveal so much. How did she do it? he wondered. How did she sneak beneath the defences he'd erected as a boy, had had firmly in place for so long? He never talked about his parents, or himself, or anything. He'd always preferred it that way and yet in these unguarded moments he discovered he almost enjoyed the conversation. The sharing.

So much for getting this relationship back on the footing he'd wanted: impersonal. Unthreatening.

Frustration blazed through him. No more *friendship*. No more conversation. There was only one thing he wanted from Alyse, and he would have it. Tonight.

Over the next few courses of their meal she made a few attempts at conversation and Leo answered politely enough without encouraging further talk. Still, she tried, and he had to admire her determination.

She wouldn't give up. Well, neither would he.

The moon had risen in the sky, sending its silver rays sliding over the placid surface of the sea. The waiter brought them both tiny glasses of liqueurs and a plate of petit fours and then left them alone, retreating silently back to the main resort.

All around them the night seemed very quiet, very still, the only sound the gentle lap of the waves against the sand. In the moonlit darkness, Alyse looked almost ethereal, her hair floating softly about her shoulders, her silvery eyes soft—yes, eyes could be soft, and thoughtful.

Desire tightened inside him and he took a sip of the sweet liqueur, felt its fire join the blaze already ignited in his belly. He wanted her, just as he'd told her that afternoon, and he would have her tonight.

And it wouldn't be making love.

They sat in silence for a few more moments, sipping their liqueurs, when Leo decided he'd had enough. He placed his glass on the table with deliberate precision. 'It's getting late,' he said, and Alyse's gaze widened before she swallowed audibly. Leo smiled and stood, stretching one hand out to her.

She rose and took it, her fingers slender and feeling fragile in his as he drew her from the table and across the sand to their sleeping quarters.

While they'd been eating some of the staff had prepared their hut for the night. The sheets had been turned down and candles lit on either side of the bed, the dancing flames sending flickering shadows across the polished wooden floor.

The perfect setting for romance, for *love*, but Leo pushed that thought away. He stood in front of the bed and turned her to face him; her bare shoulders were soft and warm beneath his hands.

She shivered and he couldn't tell if it was from desire or nervousness. Perhaps both. He knew he needed to go slowly, even though the hunger inside him howled for satiation and release.

He slid his hands up from her shoulders to cup her face, his thumbs tracing the line of her jaw, her skin like silk beneath his fingers. 'Don't be nervous,' he said softly, for now that they were in the moment he still wanted to reassure her, even if he didn't want to engage his emotions.

'I'm not,' she answered, but her voice choked and she looked away.

In answer he brushed a feathery kiss across her jaw before settling his mouth on hers, his tongue tracing the seam of her lips, gently urging her to part for him.

And she did, her mouth yielding to his, her arms coming around him as he drew her pliant softness against him, loving the way her body curved and melted into his.

He kissed her deeply, sliding his hands from her face to her shoulders and then her hips, drawing her close to him, fitting her against the already hard press of his arousal.

Desire shot up through him with fiery arrows of sizzling sensation and he felt her shudder in response.

Gently, slowly, he drew the thin straps of her dress down her shoulders. Alyse stood still, her gaze fastened on him as he reached behind her, and with one sensuous tug had her dress unzipped. It slithered down her body and pooled on the floor, leaving her in only a skimpy white lace bra and matching pants—honeymoon underwear, barely serving their purpose, unless it was to inflame— which it did.

Leo let his gaze travel slowly across her barely clothed body, revelling in the beauty of her, desire coiling tighter and tighter inside him.

He placed one hand on her shoulder, sliding it down to her elbow, smoothing her skin. She drew a shuddering breath.

'Are you cold?'

'No.' She shook her head and, needing to touch her more—everywhere—he slid his hand from her elbow to her breast, his palm cupping its slight fullness as he drew his thumb across the aching peak. Alyse let out a little gasp and he smiled, felt the primal triumph of making her respond.

'I know this is new for you,' he said quietly and he saw a flash of something almost like anguish in her eyes.

'Leo…' She didn't say anything more and he didn't want to waste time or energy on words. Smiling, he brushed a kiss across her forehead and then across her mouth before he unhooked her bra and slid it off her arms. He drew her to him, her bare breasts brushing the crisp cotton of his shirt, and even that sensation made him ache. He wanted her so very much.

'What about your clothes?' she asked shakily and he arched an eyebrow.

'What about mine?'

'They're on you, for starters.'

He laughed softly. 'I suppose you could do something about that.'

Her fingers shook only a little as she fumbled with the buttons of his shirt, the tips of her fingers brushing his bare chest. He stood still, everything in him dark and hot from just those tiny touches. Then she finished unbuttoning it and pulled it off his shoulders, her gaze hungry as she let it rove over him, making him darker and hotter still.

His breathing hitched as she smoothed her hands over his chest, down to his abdomen, and then with a little, mischievous smile her fingers slipped under the waistband of his trousers.

He sucked in a hard breath as with her other hand she tugged on the zip, her fingers skimming the hard length of his erection. 'Alyse…'

'Only fair,' she whispered with a trembling laugh, and Leo's voice lowered to a growl as he answered,

'I'll show you fair.'

He pulled her even closer to him so her breasts were crushed against his bare chest and kissed her with a savage passion he hadn't even known he possessed, the self-control he'd prided himself on for so long slipping away, lost in a red tide of desire.

And she responded, her arms coming up around him, her tongue tangling with his as she matched him kiss for kiss, their breathing coming in ragged gasps as the shy gentleness of their undressing turned into something raw and powerful and almost harsh in its intensity.

He'd never felt like this before. Felt so much before. He wanted and needed her too much to be alarmed or afraid by the power of her feelings—or his own.

Alyse's mind was dazed with desire as Leo drew her to the bed. Ever since he'd led her from the dinner table she'd tried to find a way to tell him the truth, that she wasn't a virgin. His obvious assumption made the need for disclosure all the more vital, yet somehow the words wouldn't come. And when Leo had kissed her, and undressed her, and touched her…

Then she'd had no words at all.

She didn't remember how they ended up lying on the bed, Leo sliding off her underwear and then his own so they were both completely naked. It had all happened so quickly, yet she felt as if she'd been waiting for this moment for ever.

And still she hadn't told him. *Maybe later*, she thought hazily as Leo bent his head to her breast and she raked his shoulders with her nails, her body arching off the bed as he flicked his tongue against her heated, over-sensitised skin. *After*. She'd tell him after.

She felt Leo's hand between her thighs, his fingers sliding deftly to the damp warmth between them and her hips arched instinctively as he found her centre.

'You're lovely,' he murmured as he touched her, brushing kisses across her mouth, her jaw, her throat. 'So lovely.'

'You are too,' Alyse answered, her voice uneven, and he laughed softly.

He slid a finger inside her and she felt her muscles instinctively clench around him. A wave of pleasure crashed over and drowned out any possible attempts at speech or thought. Leo's touch was so knowing, so assured, and her fingernails dug into the bunched muscles of his shoulders as he rolled over her, his clever fingers replaced by the hard press of his erection.

Alyse arched her hips, welcoming this glorious invasion, the sense of completeness she ached to feel with every fibre of her being.

'This might hurt just a little,' he whispered and she closed her eyes against a sudden, soul-quenching rush of shame.

She couldn't lie to him, not even by her silence. Not now, not about this.

'It won't, Leo,' she choked, her anguish all too apparent to both of them. 'I'm—I'm not a virgin.'

She felt him poised above her, could feel the heat and strength of him so close to her; another inch or two and he'd be inside her, as she so desperately wanted. She arched her hips reflexively, but he didn't move.

Alyse let out a shudder of both longing and despair. Clearly she picked her moments well.

Leo swore under his breath and eased back. 'What a time to tell me,' he said, his voice coming out in a groan.

'I didn't—didn't know how to tell you,' she whispered miserably.

Leo rolled onto his back and stared up at the woven-grass roof of the hut, his chest heaving with the effort of stopping at such a critical moment.

'Obviously it's a distressing memory,' he said after a moment, his eyes still on the roof. 'You must have been very young.'

'It was.' She took a breath, hating that they were talking about this now, in such an intimate moment, a moment that had seconds ago promised tenderness and pleasure and perhaps even the first fragile shoots of a deeper and more sacred emotion. 'And I wasn't that young. I was twenty.'

She felt Leo still next to her, every muscle in his body seeming to go rigid. Then he turned his head to stare at her, and everything in Alyse quailed at the sight of the cold blankness in his eyes. *'Twenty?'*

'Yes—at university.'

'You slept with someone at university?' he repeated, sounding so disbelieving that Alyse flinched.

'Yes—do we have to talk about this?'

'I don't particularly relish the conversation myself.' In one fluid movement Leo sat up and reached for his boxers.

Alyse felt her throat thicken as disappointment and frustrated desire rushed through her. 'Leo, I'm sorry. I suppose I should have told you earlier, but we never had any remotely intimate conversations, and frankly I just wanted to forget it ever happened. That's no excuse, I know.' He finished sliding on his boxers and just picked up his shirt. 'Are you—are you angry? That I'm not a virgin?'

He let out a bark of humourless laughter and turned to face her. He looked as cold and remote as he ever had—only worse, because she'd seen his face softened in sleep or with a smile, his eyes warm with laughter and then hot with desire. Now he was reverting once more to the icy stranger she knew, the man who made her despair. 'You think I'm angry that you're not a virgin?'

'Well—yes.'

He shook his head, the movement seeming one of both incredulity and contempt. 'That would be a bit of a double standard, since I'm not one.'

She swallowed, surprised. 'I know, but it's always been different for men, hasn't it? And the whole princess thing…'

'This has nothing to do with the *princess thing*,' Leo answered her shortly. 'And I don't believe in double standards. If I seem angry, Alyse, it's not because you've had sex before. It's because you had sex while you were engaged to me.'

And, before she could even process that statement, he had yanked on his trousers and was heading out into the night.

CHAPTER EIGHT

LEO STRODE ACROSS the beach, knowing that, just like last night, he had nowhere to go and hating it. Damn this island. Damn Alyse. Damn himself, for caring about what she'd done—and who she'd done it with.

He didn't feel merely betrayed, which was what made him so angry. He felt hurt.

Stupid, because it had happened years ago, and it wasn't as if they'd actually loved each other. So what if she'd loved someone else? Given herself to someone else? What did it really matter?

And yet it did.

He knew he was overreacting; knew he should be at most surprised, and a little annoyed, perhaps, by her infidelity during their engagement, but he shouldn't actually *care*.

Not like this. Never like this.

'Leo?'

He turned and saw her slender form framed in the doorway of the hut, now clothed in one of those ridiculously frothy robes, the candlelight silhouetting her slight yet still lush curves, curves he remembered the feel of under his palms. Leo turned his face away.

'Please don't storm off,' she said, the desolation in her voice reaching him in far too many ways. 'Talk to me.'

Leo didn't reply. He didn't want to talk to her, didn't

want to explain the feelings that churned inside him, the feelings he wasn't sure he understood—or wanted to understand—himself.

'Please, Leo.'

Wordlessly he stalked back to the hut, his back to Alyse and the all-too-tempting image she presented in her ridiculous robe. Fine. They would have it out. She could spill all the gritty details and then he would *never* let her close again. Not as a friend. Not as a lover. He'd take her body and use her popularity and their marriage would be exactly what he'd always wanted and intended it to be. Nothing more.

She stood by the bed, the candlelight silhouetting her figure so she might as well have been naked. He tried not to gaze at the dip of her waist, those high, pert breasts, the shadow between her thighs, but still his groin ached. He'd been unbearably close to burying himself so deep inside her he would have forgotten who he was. What he actually wanted.

'I know I should have said something, maybe this afternoon,' she continued, her voice low, her fingers toying with the sash of her robe. 'But I didn't want to bring it up, to ruin what was between us—'

'There was nothing between us,' Leo cut her off harshly, too harshly. His words were loud and ragged in the hushed stillness of the night. They were *emotional*, he thought furiously.

Alyse stared at him, her eyes wide. 'Please don't say that.'

'I knew this would happen,' he continued relentlessly, remorseless now. 'A single day of barely enjoying each other's company and you're building castles in the air. Friendship never would have been enough for you.'

He saw the hurt flash across her face but she lifted her chin and managed a small smile that touched him with its bravery; he didn't *want* to be touched. 'Maybe not,' she said quietly. 'And I admit, I have a tendency to build those kinds of castles. I've been doing it ever since I met you.'

He stilled, every nerve tautening with sudden apprehension, even alarm. 'What are you talking about?'

Alyse drew a shuddering breath. 'I've been in love with you since I met you, Leo. Since my eighteenth birthday party.'

She *really* didn't choose her moments well. Alyse saw the shock blaze in Leo's eyes, followed quickly by something that looked almost like fury.

She shouldn't have told him now, should *never* have told him. Yet how could she keep the secret of her feelings any longer? How could she make him understand what had driven her recklessly into another man's arms—if only for one unfortunate night—if he didn't know how much she loved him?

'You love me,' he repeated, and she heard derision.

'I do,' she answered steadily. 'I fell in love with you at my party…'

He arched an eyebrow, his mouth twisting unpleasantly. 'Did you fall in love with the way I danced? Or perhaps the way I drank champagne?'

'I just fell in love with you,' she answered helplessly. 'I can't explain it. Trust me, I've tried to explain it to myself many times.'

'Such a conundrum,' he drawled, his contempt evident in every taut line of his face.

He didn't believe her, Alyse realised. She hadn't expected that. Surprise, perhaps, or even horror—but incredulity? She spread her hands. 'Why do you think I agreed to the engagement? To our marriage?'

'Not because you *loved* me.'

'I couldn't imagine life without you,' Alyse blurted, the words spilling out of her. 'And I knew—of course, I've always known—you didn't love me back. But I hoped, like your father had said, that love or at least affection might come with time. That's why I kept at it, at the pretending—because I *hoped*—'

'And did that hope lead you into another man's bed, Alyse?' Leo cut her off, his voice wintry. 'Because I can do without that kind of love, thank you very much.'

'It was a mistake,' she whispered. 'A terrible mistake.'

His expression only grew colder. 'Clearly.'

She swallowed, hating that she had to rake this all up, yet knowing she needed to come clean. She'd hidden this heartache and shame for too long already. Maybe confession would help her—and Leo—to move on. 'It was one night, Leo. One awful night. That's all.'

'Is that supposed to make it more excusable?'

She felt the first flicker of anger. 'For someone who doesn't believe in double standards, you're sounding like a bit of a hypocrite.'

'A hypocrite?' He raised his eyebrows. 'How do you reckon that?'

'It's not as if you've been celibate for the last six years,' she answered, and she watched his mouth form a smile that held no humour or happiness at all.

'Haven't I?' he asked softly, his words seeming to reverberate through the room, through the stillness of the night and of her own soul. *He couldn't actually mean...?*

'But—but six *years*...' she stammered, and his smile turned hard.

'Yes, I'm well aware of how long a period of time it was.'

She shook her head slowly. 'I never thought—or expected— The engagement wasn't *real*...'

'On the contrary, our engagement has always been real. So is our marriage. It's the emotion you insist you've been feeling that isn't, Alyse. You don't love me. You don't even

know what love is. A schoolgirl crush? A shaft of desire?'
He shook his head, the movement one of both dismissal
and derision. 'That's all love ever is. And, in any case,
you don't even know me. How on earth could you think
you loved me?'

She shook her head again, drew in a shuddering breath.
She still couldn't believe he'd been celibate for so long.
For her. 'But the magazines—they said you were with
Liana Aterno.'

'You believed them? You know how they stir up gossip. You've experienced it yourself.'

'I know, but I thought— I expected you'd have some
discreet liaisons. The Queen—' She stopped abruptly and
Leo narrowed his eyes.

'The Queen,' he repeated softly. 'What did my mother
say to you?'

'Only that I shouldn't expect you to—to be faithful.'

'Only?'

Alyse gave him a watery smile. 'She did the whole
"men have needs" spiel, and how I was to turn a blind eye.'

'My mother was basing her experience on my father,'
Leo answered shortly. 'And their marriage, which has been
nothing but unpleasant and acrimonious. I wouldn't ever
listen to marriage advice from her.'

'I was only eighteen. I didn't know any better, I suppose.'

Leo nodded, his expression still cold. He hadn't softened in the least towards her, or her indiscretion, no matter what his mother might have said. 'Well, you clearly
used my mother's advice as a justification for your own
behaviour.'

'It wasn't like that, Leo.'

'I don't really want to hear.'

'And I don't want to tell you, but you've got to understand.' She was stumbling over her words in her haste to

explain, to reach him. 'It was one awful night. A friend from university. I was drunk.'

'I really don't need these details.'

She stared at him miserably. 'I know, but I just want you to understand. I'd seen a photo of you with that duke's daughter, Liana, in a magazine. There were articles all over the place about how you were dumping me for her.'

'And you never thought to ask me about it?'

'I never asked you about anything! We never talked. I didn't even have your mobile or your email address.'

'I think,' Leo said coldly, 'you could have got in touch if you'd wanted to. In any case, it doesn't even matter.'

She blinked, stared. 'It—doesn't?'

'No. Admittedly, I'm disappointed you thought so little of the agreement we'd made, the vows we would say. I know we've been pretending to be in love, Alyse, but we weren't pretending that we were going to get married. The rings on both our fingers is a testament to that.'

'I know,' she whispered. She felt the first sting of tears and blinked hard. 'I wish it had never happened.'

'Like I said, it doesn't matter. Naturally, I expect you to be faithful to me during our marriage. What happened in the past we can forget about. Thank God the press never found out.' He turned away from her, towards the bed, and Alyse watched him miserably. She'd never felt as far away from him as she did now...and it was her own fault.

'I'm sorry,' she said quietly.

'Like I said, it's in the past. Let's go to bed.' His meaning was clear as he slid beneath the sheets, his back to her: they would not be consummating their marriage tonight.

Swallowing, Alyse slid into bed next to him. They lay there silently, the only sound the ragged draw and tear of their breathing and the whoosh of the waves on the sand. She could feel the heat of his body, inhaled the scent of his aftershave, and her body still pulsed with longing. Yet she'd never felt farther away from him, or from hope, than she did in this moment.

She knew it was her own fault. She thought of that single night four years ago and closed her eyes in shame. It had been a terrible lapse of judgement, a moment of weakness she'd tried to block out since.

She'd been revising for exams and had caught sight of that awful photograph of Leo laughing with Liana, a gorgeous icy blonde, in a way he never had with her. Jealousy had sunk its razor-sharp claws into her soul, bled out her heart.

She'd been just twenty years old, engaged to Leo for two years, having seen him only a handful of times and spoken to him even less—yet firm, so firm, in the belief she loved him. And in that moment she'd felt certain he would never love her. Never even laugh with her.

It was the closest she'd ever come to breaking off the engagement, but even at her lowest point, halfway to heartbroken, she'd known she couldn't do it. Didn't possess the strength to call a halt to a romance that had captivated the world and still didn't want to.

Yet her despair at feeling that Leo would never love her, never even like her, had led her to go out with a casual friend—Matt—and get far too drunk on cheap cider.

Even now the details of the evening were fuzzy; they'd gone back to her flat and started talking. She'd been drunk enough to be honest, too honest, and she'd said something about how Leo didn't actually love her.

Matt had laughed and said that was impossible; everyone knew how they loved each other madly. Alyse had been just sober enough to keep from insisting on the truth, but she'd stared at that picture of Leo with the lovely Liana—she'd bought the magazine, if only to torture herself—and something in her had broken.

Without thinking about what she was doing, she'd

reached for Matt and kissed him clumsily. She still didn't know what had driven that impulse, perhaps just a desperate need for someone to want her.

He had responded eagerly, both alarming and gratifying her, and somehow it had all got out of control. In her drunken state she hadn't been able or even willing to stop it.

The next morning Matt had been sheepish and she'd been stricken. She'd felt ashamed and dirty, yet also strangely defiant, imagining Leo with the lovely Liana. Hating the thought of it, and hating what she'd done too.

Just as Leo hated it. He believed her one indiscretion showed her love for the flimsy fairy tale he thought it was—and lying there, wide awake and restless, she felt the first seed of doubt burrow deep into her heart, its shell cracking apart all her certainties.

What if Leo was right?

Too restless to lie still any longer, Alyse slid from the bed and headed out to the beach. The sand was cool and soft beneath her bare feet and the sky above was inky black and spangled with stars. The air was cooler now, and in only her nightdress she felt goose bumps rise on her arms.

She sat on the sand, as miserable as she'd ever been when she'd believed herself to be hopelessly in love with Leo. And this time it was because she had a sudden, sneaking fear that she wasn't, and perhaps never had been.

What did that say about her? Could she really have been so childish, so deluded, so *wrong* to convince herself she loved a man she barely knew? And to have kept believing it for so long?

Resting her chin on her knees, Alyse thought back to that first fateful night when Leo had come to her birthday party. Her mother had been almost as excited as she was, telling her that she'd been friends with Sophia in school, and how Leo was such a handsome prince... She'd reminded her too, of course, of the way she'd fallen in love with Alyse's father Henri at a party just like that one, across a crowded room…

Just like she'd convinced herself she had with Leo.

Had she wanted her parents' fairy tale for herself? Was that why she'd convinced herself of her love for Leo, because in her loneliness and uncertainty she'd longed for something more, had half-believed she could have it with Leo?

Everyone else had seemed to think she could, and in her innocence and immaturity she'd allowed a girlish attraction to become something so much bigger and deeper in her own mind and heart. And had continued to believe it, because as time went on and the media frenzy had grown, *not* to believe it took more strength and courage than she'd ever possessed.

Alyse let out a soft groan and pressed her forehead against her drawn-up knees. She didn't want to believe she'd been so deluded, didn't want to let go of her love so easily, so awfully.

And yet the derision on Leo's face had cut her to the bone, to the soul. *You don't even know me.*

No, she didn't, although she was starting to know him now. And, despite her parents' love-at-first-sight story, she wasn't sure she could believe it for her and Leo.

But that didn't mean she couldn't love him now. Learn to love him, the real him, the man she still wanted to believe hid underneath that mask, that armour of cold purpose and ruthless efficiency. He was there; she'd seen glimpses over the years and even more in the last few days. Glimpses that had stole through her soul and touched her heart.

He was there…and farther away from her than ever.

Sighing, her body cold and aching now, Alyse rose from the sand and headed back to the hut. She didn't know what tomorrow, or any of her tomorrows, would now hold. How Leo would feel or act. How they could get back just a little bit of the camaraderie they'd shared.

And as for love?

Her mouth curved in a humourless smile. She didn't dare even think about that now.

She must have slept, although she didn't remember doing so as she'd lain next to Leo's hard body. But when she next opened her eyes sunlight was flooding the little hut and Leo was gone.

Alyse rose and dressed quickly, tossing the lavender silk dress Leo had stripped from her body into one of her cases with a wince. If only the night had ended differently and she'd woken up in Leo's arms…

'Good morning.'

She glanced up, her heart rate skittering as he came into the tent. He was showered and dressed and he looked coldly impassive, no expression at all lightening the navy of his eyes or softening those impossibly stern features. Even so all Alyse had to do was look at him to remember the way his lips had felt on hers, hard and soft at the same time, and how his hands had felt on her body…tormenting her with such exquisite pleasure.

She swallowed hard and looked away. 'Good morning.'

'Sleep well?' he queried, his voice holding a slight, mocking edge, and Alyse shook her head.

'No.'

'Pity. Breakfast is in the pavilion again. I've already eaten.'

'You have?' He'd turned away from her and she stared at his broad back, the stiff set of his shoulders. 'People will talk, you know,' she said, even though she hated using that excuse. She didn't care what people said. She cared only what Leo thought. What he felt…or didn't feel.

'I told them you were having a lie-in after a busy night, and made all the waitresses blush.'

'You didn't.'

'No, I didn't.' He turned around then, his eyes snapping with suppressed anger. 'I've developed a distaste for lying, even to the staff. But they assumed it anyway, so don't worry, our cover isn't blown.'

'Leo, I want to talk to you—'

'And I want to talk to you,' he cut her off coolly. 'But you might as well eat first.' And, reaching for the newspaper he'd brought from the pavilion, he settled in a chair and snapped it open, managing to ignore Alyse completely.

Without another word she left the hut.

Leo stared unseeingly at the newspaper in front of him, amazed at the amount of rage that poured through him in a scalding river. Why on earth was he so angry? He couldn't remember feeling this much emotion before, and it infuriated him—and frightened him. He was honest enough to admit that at least to himself.

No matter what he'd just told her, he wasn't about to admit it to Alyse.

And, when she returned from breakfast, he'd tell her exactly what he had in mind: a return to Maldinia and to their earlier arrangement, an arrangement that had satisfied him exactly. Their marriage would be a matter of business and convenience, nothing more. He'd been a fool to allow her to entertain ideas of friendship or affection. Both were pointless and had only raised ridiculous hopes in Alyse.

And in himself.

That annoyed and angered him most of all—that he'd actually enjoyed their time together, their banter, and of course their kisses… Just remembering how close he'd been to being inside her made Leo shift uncomfortably in his chair, a persistent ache in his groin.

He still wanted her, and he'd have her, perhaps even tonight. There was no longer any need to wait. He wasn't going to concern himself with her feelings, her fears. They'd return to the firm footing he had thought they'd been on when they'd both said those wretched vows.

To have and to hold, from this day forward...

Yes, from this day forward he would know exactly what to expect. And so would Alyse.

She returned to their sleeping quarters half an hour later and Leo glanced up as she approached, forcing himself not to notice the tender, bruised-looking skin under her eyes or the way her lush, pink mouth turned down at the corners. She wore a silky tee-shirt in pale green and a swishy skirt that blew around her long, slim legs. He yanked his gaze upwards, found it settling on the rounded curve of her breasts and determinedly moved it up to her face.

'Leo, I wanted to—'

'Let me tell you what I want to say,' he cut her off, his voice clipped. He had no wish to hear her stammered, desperate apologies or excuses. Neither mattered. 'This whole idea of friendship was a mistake,' he stated flatly. Alyse stilled, her face carefully blank so he couldn't tell at all what she was thinking or feeling.

Not that he cared.

'It was against my better judgement in the first place,' he continued. 'It just complicates matters. It was much simpler and easier before.'

'When we pretended all the time?' Alyse filled in.

'We'll always be pretending,' he answered, his tone deliberately brutal. 'The public expects to see us wildly in love—and, as I've told you before, that will never happen.'

'And here I thought you'd developed a distaste for lying.'

He had. Lord, how he had. He'd been doing it his whole life, just as his parents had been doing it with him. And he'd hated it all, hated how it hurt him, yet he'd thought with Alyse it would be different. It had been his choice and he would be in control.

And so he would. Starting now.

'Sometimes needs must,' he said brusquely. 'But at least we won't lie to each other.'

'So what exactly are you proposing, Leo? That we ignore each other for the length of our honeymoon? Our marriage?'

'Our honeymoon is over,' he answered, and he watched her pale.

'Over?'

'We head back to Maldinia this morning.'

'This morning.' Alyse stared at him, her face white. Then she rallied, a spark of challenge firing her eyes so Leo felt a reluctant surge of admiration for her spirit. 'So we had a honeymoon of all of two days. How do you think the public—the press—will react to that?'

'It's up to us, isn't it? If we return to Averne with faces like a wet weekend then, yes, they might suspect something. But if we smile and present a united front—royal duty must come first, after all—then I don't think we should have a problem.' He raised his eyebrows and smiled coolly. 'I trust that after six years your acting ability is up to the challenge.'

'And what about our scheduled visits to London? Paris? Rome?'

'We can fly from Maldinia. They're not until next week.'

Alyse just shook her head. 'Why do you want to return to Maldinia?' she asked quietly.

'Because I'd like to get our marriage on its proper footing,' Leo answered, his voice coming out in something close to a snap. He strove to level it. 'And that doesn't involve romping around on the beach or playing at being friends on a boat.'

Alyse gazed at him thoughtfully and it took all of his effort not to avert his gaze, to hide from it. 'You're scared,' she finally said, and Leo let out an abrupt, incredulous laugh.

'Scared? Of what?'

'Of me—of what was happening between us. Intimacy.'

'Please.' He held up one hand. 'Spare me your fanciful notions. I had enough of them last night, when you tried to convince me you loved me.'

'I thought I loved you.'

'You've since been disabused of the notion? How convenient.' He felt a flash of hurt and suppressed it. 'I'll go tell the staff to come fetch our bags.' And without a backward glance he stalked out of the hut.

CHAPTER NINE

ALYSE SAT ON the jet across from Leo. In the seven hours since they'd left St Cristos he hadn't spoken to her once. They'd flown overnight, sleeping in separate beds, and now it was morning with the sky hard and bright around them, and cups of coffee, a platter of croissants and fresh fruit set on the coffee table between them.

Leo was scanning some papers, his expression calm and so very collected, while she felt as if she'd swallowed a stone, her insides heavy and leaden, her eyes gritty with exhaustion, both emotional and physical.

They hadn't spoken since that awful exchange in their hut, when Leo had told her they were returning to Maldinia. She had no illusions about what would happen there; in a huge palace, with all of his royal duty beckoning, he would find it entirely easy to ignore her. They would see each other only for royal functions and occasions, and live separate lives the rest of the time.

Just like their engagement.

She swallowed, a hot lump of misery lodging in her throat. She couldn't go back to that. She couldn't live like that, not in Averne, where she wouldn't even have the comfort of her studies and her own circle of friends to bolster her, the way she'd had in Durham—a little bit, at least.

She supposed, like Leo, she could focus on her royal duty. She had a service to perform as a princess of Maldinia, a duty to the country's people, and she'd enjoyed and looked forward to that aspect of her royal life. Yet the thought of making it her entire purpose depressed her beyond measure.

She wanted more.

You've always wanted more. You gambled on this engagement, this marriage, in the hope of more—and now it looks like you'll never have it.

She felt a hot rush behind her lids and blinked hard. She would *not* cry. There had to be some way to salvage this, some way to reach Leo again, to make him understand and open up to her once more. But how?

Closing her eyes, she pictured his unyielding face, the grim set of his mouth and eyes as he'd spoken to her that morning. He'd seemed colder than he ever had before, almost as if he *hated* her.

How had it all gone so disastrously wrong so quickly? They'd been making steps—baby steps, true, but still *progress:* drawing closer to each other, enjoying each other's company. And then in one terrible moment everything had splintered apart. Everything had become worse than before because, instead of being merely indifferent to her, Leo was now angry.

Emotional.

Alyse stilled, realisation and hope trickling slowly, faintly through her. Why would Leo be so angry, so emotional, unless…?

Unless he cared?

Thoughts tumbled through her mind, a kaleidoscope of emotions and hopes. Maybe he'd enjoyed their brief time together more than he wanted to admit. Perhaps he was angry because he'd been hurt—and of course he wouldn't like that. He'd hate it.

Knowing Leo—and she was knowing him more and more every day—he'd fight against feeling anything for her. She didn't understand exactly why he resisted emotion and denied love so vehemently, but she knew there had to be a deep-seated reason, something most likely to do with his family and upbringing. And, when things got sticky, difficult and painful, of course he would revert back to his cold, haughty self. His protective persona, his only armour.

So how could she slip underneath it, touch the heart hidden beneath? How could she breach his defences, crack open his shell?

Sighing, Alyse opened her eyes and stared at the man across from her, his focus still solely on the papers in front of him.

'Leo,' she said, and reluctantly he lifted his gaze from the papers, his expression chillingly remote.

'Yes?'

'Are you really going to ignore me for the rest of this flight? For our entire lives?'

His mouth tightened and his gaze swept over her in unflinching assessment. 'Not ignore, precisely,' he answered coolly. 'I don't, for example, intend to ignore you tonight.'

Shock blazed through her, white-hot. 'Are you saying,' she asked in a low voice, 'that you intend to—to consummate our marriage tonight?'

Leo's expression didn't change at all. 'That's exactly what I'm saying.'

Alyse licked her dry lips. Even now she could not keep a tide of longing from washing over her. She still wanted him, cold and angry as he was. She would always want him. 'Even though you can barely summon the will to speak to me?' she observed and he arched an eyebrow.

'Speaking won't be involved.'

She flinched. 'Don't be crass. No matter how cold this business arrangement is, we both deserve more than that.'

An emotion—she couldn't quite tell what—flickered

across his face and he glanced away. 'As long as you realise that's exactly what this is,' he answered. 'A business
arrangement.'

'Trust me,' she replied. 'I'm not likely to forget.'

Nodding in apparent satisfaction, Leo returned to his
papers. Alyse sank against the sumptuous sofa, closing
her eyes once more. So, she thought with a swamping
sense of desolation, the only thing he wanted from her
now was her body.

*But what if, along with her body, she gave him her
heart?*

She stilled, opened her eyes and gazed blindly ahead.
She'd just realised herself that she'd never actually loved
him; her feelings for him had been part schoolgirl infatua-
tion, part desperately wishful thinking. So how could she
now offer this cold, proud, *hurting* man her heart?

Because that's what I want for my marriage. Because
even if she hadn't loved him all of these years, she knew
she could love him now. She could fall in love with him
if he let her, if she got to know him as she had done over
the last few days.

And that could begin tonight.

Five silent hours later they had landed in Maldinia on a
balmy summer morning and returned by royal motorcade
to the palace, unspeaking all the while.

The reporters had managed to get word of their early
arrival and were waiting both at the airport and in front
of the palace. They posed for photographs in both places,
smiling and waving, Leo's arm snug around her waist. She
glanced at him out of the corner of her eye and saw that,
despite the white flash of his smile and his seemingly relaxed pose, his body was rigid next to her, his eyes flinty.
He might be willing to pretend, but he certainly wasn't
enjoying it. And neither was she.

Once they were back in the palace, Leo disappeared to his study and Alyse was shown to the bedroom she would have as her own—and it was clearly her own, not hers and Leo's; it was a feminine room in pale blues and greys, gorgeous and utterly impersonal.

She sank onto the bed, feeling lonely, lost and completely miserable. A few minutes later, still lost in her own unhappy thoughts, a knock sounded on the door and, without waiting for a response, Queen Sophia swept in.

Alyse stood up, a wary surprise stealing through her. She'd had very few interactions with her haughty mother-in-law and she preferred it that way.

Now Queen Sophia arched one severely plucked eyebrow and swept a thoroughly assessing gaze over Alyse. 'Why have you returned from the honeymoon so early?'

Alyse licked her dry lips. 'Leo— He had work to do.'

'Work? On his honeymoon?' Sophia's mouth pinched tight. 'How do you think the public will react to that? They want to see a young married couple in love, you know. They want to see you celebrating. The monarchy still depends on you.'

Alyse thought of what Leo had said about his parents: their affairs, careless spending and utter indifference to their own people. In light of all that, Sophia's insistence on royal decorum seemed hypocritical at best. 'I would think,' she answered, her voice wavering only slightly, 'the monarchy depends on you just as much.'

Sophia's mouth tightened further and her pale-blue eyes flashed ice. 'Don't be impertinent.'

'I wasn't. I was being honest.'

'I can do without your honesty. The only reason you've risen so high is because we decided it would be so.'

'And the only reason you decided it would be so is because it benefitted you,' Alyse retorted, a sudden anger and courage rising up inside her. 'With Leo and I in the spotlight, you could continue to do as you pleased—which it seems is all you've ever done.' Two spots of bright colour appeared on Sophia's high cheekbones. 'Oh, I know it grates on you,' Alyse continued, her temper now truly lit. 'To see your precious first-born married to a commoner.'

'Precious first-born?' Sophia's mouth twisted. 'Has Leo not even told you about his brother? But then I suppose he doesn't tell you anything.'

Alyse stared at her, nonplussed. 'His brother…?'

'Alessandro. His older brother. My husband disinherited him when he was twenty-one and Leo was eighteen. He would have been King.' For a second, no more, Alyse thought she heard a faint note of bitterness or even sorrow in Sophia's voice. Had she loved her son Alessandro? Loved him, perhaps, more than Leo?

'We don't talk about him,' Sophia continued flatly. 'The media stopped raking his story up over and over again years ago. But, if you wondered why the monarchy needed to be stabilised and restored, why we needed *you*, it's because of the scandal of Sandro leaving the way he did.' Sophia's eyes flashed malice. 'I'm surprised Leo never told you.'

Alyse didn't answer. She didn't sound at all surprised. Had Sophia guessed her schoolgirl feelings for Leo; had she perhaps used them against her all those years ago when she'd suggested their engagement? It seemed all too possible. She was shrewd and calculating and those ice-blue eyes missed nothing.

'Be careful,' Sophia continued softly. 'If the sorry truth of your relationship with Leo comes out now, the scandal will consume us all, including you. You might have enjoyed all the attention these last few years, but it won't be quite so pleasant when everyone starts to hate you.' Sophia's mouth curved in a cruel smile. 'Besides, you'd be no use to us then. No use to Leo.'

Alyse just stared, her mind spinning sickly, and with a click of her heels Sophia was gone, the door shutting firmly behind her.

Alyse sank back onto the bed. Had the Queen's parting shot been a threat? *No use to Leo.* If the media ever turned on her, if she became a liability to the monarchy rather than an asset, would Leo still want to be married to her?

It was a horrible question to ask herself, and even worse to answer. Knowing just what he thought of their marriage, she had a terrible feeling he wouldn't.

And what about his brother? She could hardly be surprised that Leo had never told her about Alessandro; he had told her barely anything personal about himself.

And yet, it could explain so much. She'd suspected his sense of cold detachment stemmed from his upbringing; with parents like King Alessandro and Queen Sophia, how could it not?

But a brother? A brother who had perhaps been the favourite, who had gone his own way, leaving Leo to try and make up for his absence? To prove himself through his endless royal duty?

She knew she was making assumptions, trying to understand the man who still seemed so much of an enigma to her.

The man who would come to her tonight...

She felt a shiver of anticipation for what lay ahead. Was it wrong—or perhaps just shameless—of her actually to be looking forward to tonight, at least in part? No matter how little Leo felt for her now, she still wanted him. Desperately.

Alyse didn't see Leo until that evening, when the royal family assembled for a formal dinner. He looked stunning in black tie, which was the standard dress for these cold family dinners. King Alessandro and Queen Sophia preferred this kind of rigid formality, and as she sat down across from Leo she wondered how it had affected him. How it had affected his brother.

It still surprised her that she'd never even known about him, not from Leo, not from his family, not even from any of the articles she'd read about the Maldinian royal family. *Her* family.

Her and Leo's engagement, and the accompanying scrutiny and excitement, must have taken the attention away from Leo's brother, almost as if everyone had forgotten it. Him.

Everyone but Leo. Somehow she didn't think he had forgotten his brother. She wanted to ask him about it, wanted to learn more about this man and what made him the way he was, and yet…

From the cool expression on Leo's face, he didn't want to have much conversation—not with anyone, and especially not with her.

The dinner was, as Alyse had expected, stilted and mainly silent. Alessandro and Sophia both made a few pointed references to their early return from honeymoon, but Leo was indifferent to any criticism, and Alyse just murmured something about looking forward to settling into life in the palace.

As if.

Alexa shot her an encouraging look when she made that remark, her dark-blue eyes—the same colour as Leo's—flashing both spirit and sympathy. Alyse knew Alexa was engaged to marry a sheikh of a small Middle Eastern country next year, and she had a feeling her new sister-in-law didn't relish the union. At least, Alyse thought with a sigh, Alexa hadn't had to pretend to be in love with her fiancé. As far as Alyse knew, she'd only seen him a handful of times.

By ten o'clock the dinner was finished and Sophia was

about to rise first to escort everyone out to the salon where they would have coffee and petits fours. It was another part of the formal ritual, and one Leo forestalled as he rose before his mother.

'It's been a very long day. Alyse and I will retire.'

Alyse felt herself blush even though there had been no innuendo in Leo's words, just a statement of fact. Sophia looked frostily affronted but Leo didn't even wait for her acquiescence as he took Alyse by the hand and led her from the dining room.

'Your mother doesn't like her order interrupted,' Alyse murmured as they headed upstairs. Her heart was pounding hard and her head felt weirdly light.

'My mother doesn't like anyone to do anything except what she commands,' Leo answered shortly. 'She'll have to get used to disappointment.'

They'd reached the top of the stairs and he drew her down the hallway to a wood-panelled door, opening it to reveal a luxurious and very masculine bedroom. The duvet on the canopied king-sized bed had been turned down and a fire blazed in the huge stone hearth.

Alyse swallowed in a desperate attempt to ease the dryness of her throat. 'This all looks very romantic.'

'Are you being cynical?'

'No, Leo.' She turned to him, tried to smile. She wasn't going to let this evening descend into something base and soulless, or even just physical. 'I was just stating a fact. Don't worry, I don't think you had anything do with it.'

Leo gazed at Alyse, graceful, slender and so achingly beautiful. She looked both vulnerable and strong, he thought and he felt a blaze of something like admiration for her presence, her self-possession. Then he pushed that feeling away, hardened his heart—if that was indeed the organ that was being so wayward—and said coolly, 'I cer-

tainly didn't.' She stood a few feet away from him and he
beckoned her forward. 'Come here.'

'Is that a command?'

'A request.'

She let out a shaky laugh. 'Rather ungraciously made,
Leo.' Yet she moved towards him, head held high, her eyes
flashing with spirit.

Leo made no reply, because in truth he didn't know
what to say, how to act. He didn't want sex between them
to be romantic. He didn't want either of them engaging
their emotions. Ever.

He wanted it to be nothing more than a necessary—
and, albeit physically, pleasurable—transaction, yet he
was already afraid it couldn't be. Already be realised that
his feelings for Alyse had changed too much for this to be
simple—or sordid.

With the tiniest, trembling smile on her lips, she took
another step towards him. Leo watched her hips sway
under the silky fabric of her evening dress, a halter-top
style in ivory that hugged every slender curve. 'Why don't
you take that off?' he said, his voice already thickening
with desire.

'Oh, Leo.' She let out a soft laugh. 'Why don't you take
it off me?' And, despite the sorrow in that laugh, he heard
a hint of a challenge in her voice and he knew she wasn't
going to make this easy for either of them. 'Just because
this is necessary doesn't mean we can't enjoy the experience,' she continued quietly. 'You desire me, Leo, and I
desire you. That's something.'

He didn't answer, because he couldn't. Somehow his
throat had thickened; his blood pounded and his fingers
itched to touch her. He'd thought at first she'd make it
awkward by resisting, or at least not responding to his
touch—a show of defiance.

Compliance, he realised then, was far more dangerous. Still he tried to keep himself emotionally distant, if physically close, knowing how difficult a task it was that he'd set himself.

Wordlessly he reached behind her and undid the halter tie of her dress. The garment slithered off her shoulders, and with one sinuous shrug it slid from her body and pooled at her feet. She gazed at him steadily, a faint blush tingeing her cheeks pink even as she kept her head held high.

She was magnificent. He'd seen her naked before but tonight it was different; tonight it was more. She wore a strapless lacy bra and matching pants, both skimpy items highlighting the lithe perfection of her body.

'I don't think I'm the only one who's meant to be naked,' Alyse said, and he heard both a smile and a tremble in her voice. She reached for the buttons on his shirt and, mesmerised, Leo watched as she undid them, her fingers long and elegant. Her hands smoothed over the already heated skin of his chest and shoulders as she pulled the tie and then the shirt off him.

She'd undressed him last night, had unbuttoned his shirt just like this and, while it had inflamed him then, it moved him now. Touched him in ways he wasn't prepared for, didn't want.

He pushed the emotion away and reached for her, needing to obliterate his thoughts—his *feelings*—with the purely physical. And at first the taste and touch of her lips against his was enough to accomplish his goal. He plundered her mouth, slid his hands through the luxuriant softness of her hair, brought her nearly naked body in achingly exquisite contact with his. All of it was enough to stop the unwanted feeling, the impossible emotion.

Almost.

Her response undid him. She wasn't just unresisting, she was more than compliant. She answered him kiss for kiss, touch for touch, and he could feel the surrender in her supple body, the giving of herself. The offering.

With Alyse sex would never be a soulless transaction. Already it was something else, something he couldn't want and yet desperately needed. He deepened the kiss.

Alyse matched him, her body molding and melting into his, her head tilted back as she emitted a low moan from deep in her throat, the sound swallowed by his own mouth. Desire consumed him in a white-hot flame; thoughts and feelings blurred and coalesced into one.

He was barely aware of unhooking her bra, sliding off her pants; distantly he felt her hands fumble boldly at his zip and then his trousers sliding down his legs. He kicked them off in one abrupt, impatient movement and, sweeping her up in his arms, her skin silken against his, he brought her to the bed.

Even now he fought against all he was feeling. She lay back on the pillows, arms spread, thighs splayed, everything about her open and giving. She gazed up at him without embarrassment or fear; even her gaze was open to him, open and trusting. Kneeling before her, his own body naked and vulnerable, his desire on obvious and proud display, Leo felt humbled.

Humbled and ashamed that he had been attempting something he now knew was impossible: emotionless sex with Alyse. With his wife.

She held out her arms to him. 'Make love to me, Leo,' she said softly, and he let out a sound that was something between a near-sob and a laugh. How had this woman reached him—reached him and felled him—so easily? His jaded cynicism fell away and his cold, hard heart warmed and softened into pliant yielding as he came to her, enfolded her body into his and buried his face in the warm, silken curve of her neck.

In response she curled around him, arching her body

into his, giving him everything she had. Leo took it as his mouth claimed hers and his hands explored her warm, supple curves; then his body found hers as he slid inside and they joined as one—one flesh, one person. It felt holy and sacred, infinitely pleasurable, and so much more than he'd ever expected or thought he wanted.

His last cold reserve broke on the sweetness of her response as he drove into her again and again, losing himself, blending into her until he didn't know where he ended and she began. And, even more amazingly and importantly, such a distinction no longer mattered.

Alyse lay back on the pillows, her whole body thrumming with pleasure. Leo had rolled onto his back next to her, one arm thrown over his face. As her heart rate began to slow from a thud she felt the perspiration cooling on her skin, the slight chill of the night air from the open windows…and the fact that she couldn't see Leo's expression. She had no idea what he was thinking or feeling at all.

Just moments ago when he'd been touching her—been *inside* her—she'd felt so close to him, in such glorious union that all of her fears and doubts had been blown away, scattered like so much cold ash.

Now they returned, settling inside her, unwelcome embers fanning into painful flame.

She'd given everything to Leo in that moment, everything she had in her to give… But perhaps even now he'd turn away from her, slide off the bed and stalk to the bathroom, as coldly indifferent as ever. Even as she braced herself for it she knew she couldn't keep herself from being hurt, or even devastated. She might not love him—yet—but she'd still given more to this man than to any other.

She felt Leo stir next to her and still she was afraid to say anything, to break whatever delicate bond held them together in this moment, the remnants of their love-

making. Words would, she feared, sound like challenges
to Leo, perhaps accusations or even ultimatums. For once
she wanted simply to let this moment be whatever it was,
and not demand or yearn for more.

Slowly he moved his arm from covering his face and
swung up so he was sitting on the edge of the bed, his feet
on the floor, his back to her.

'I'll get us something to drink,' he said and, slipping
on his boxer shorts, he went to the *en suite* dressing room.

Alyse lay there for a moment, increasingly conscious
with every cooling second of her own nakedness, yet she
was loath to cover herself, to leave the intimacy of what
had just happened behind—or, worse, pretend it had never
happened… Just as Leo, perhaps, was pretending.

Or maybe he wasn't pretending. Maybe, for him, it had
been just sex and she was the one, as always, who was con-
structing castles in the air—castles made of nothing, as
insubstantial as smoke or mist, dissipating just as quickly.

He returned a few minutes later while she still lay there
on the bed, naked and fighting against feeling exposed.
She pushed her hair away from her eyes and struggled
to a sitting position, still resisting the urge to cover herself. She'd promised herself—and, without his knowledge, Leo—that she would be open to him tonight. That
she wouldn't dissemble, guard or prevaricate. Not even
now, when every instinct she possessed screamed for self-
protection.

'Here.' His voice sounded alarmingly brusque as he
pressed a bottle of water into her hands.

'Where—?'

'There's a mini-fridge in the dressing room.' The corner of his mouth quirked in what Alyse couldn't be sure
was a smile. 'They put champagne in there as well, but I
thought we'd had enough of that.'

'Ah. Yes.' *Because this wasn't a champagne-worthy moment?* She took a sip of the chilled water.

Leo drained half of his own before he lowered it from his lips, twisting the bottle around in his hands, his gaze averted from hers. Alyse just waited, sensing he intended to say something, but having no idea what it was.

Finally he lifted his gaze to meet hers, and even then she couldn't gauge his mood, couldn't fathom what he intended to say, or how he felt at all. He took a deep breath and let it out slowly. Alyse braced herself.

'I don't know,' he began haltingly, 'how much I have to give.'

Ayse just stared at him, his words slowly penetrating the dazed fog of her mind. *I don't know how much I have to give.* She felt a smile spread across her face—a ridiculously huge smile, considering what he'd said was a far, far cry from a declaration of love.

And yet it was something. It was a lot, for a man like Leo, because he was saying—at least, she hoped he was saying—that he still had *something* to give. And, more importantly, that he wanted to give it.

'That's okay,' she said softly and Leo glanced away.

'I'm sorry,' he said after a moment. 'For treating our marriage—our relationship—like an imposition.'

'That's what it was for you,' Alyse answered. She didn't add what everything inside her was hoping, singing: *until now.*

'I've never tried a real relationship before,' he continued, his gaze still averted. 'At least, not for a long while.'

'Neither have I.'

He glanced at her then, a slow smile curving his mouth. 'Then that makes two of us.'

She smiled back, her hopes soaring straight to the sky. 'I suppose it does.'

Neither of them spoke for a few moments and Alyse

couldn't keep the lightness, the giddy relief, from swooping through her. She tried to tell herself that really this was very little, that she wasn't even sure what Leo was saying or offering. Yet still, the hope. The joy. She couldn't keep herself from feeling them, from wanting to feel them.

Eventually Leo took her half-empty water bottle as well as his own and put them away. Alyse slipped to the bathroom and returned to find him in bed, the firelight flickering over his bronzed body, his arms above his head. She hesitated on the threshold, still unsure how to act, and then Leo pulled aside the duvet and patted the bed.

'Come here,' he said softly and, smiling, she came.

She slid into the bed and felt her heart lurch with unexpected joy once again when he gently pulled her to him and cradled her body against his own, her head pillowed on his arm. She breathed in the scent of him, a woodsy aftershave and clean soap, and listened to the crackle of the logs in the fireplace and the steady beat of his heart against her cheek. She felt almost perfectly content.

Neither of them spoke, but the silence wasn't tense, strained or even awkward at all. It was a silence of new understanding. And, instead of pressing and longing for more, Alyse let this be enough. Lying in Leo's arms, it felt like everything.

CHAPTER TEN

When she woke Leo was still stretched out beside her, a slight smile curving his mouth and softening his features. Alyse gazed at him unreservedly for a moment and then, feeling bold, brushed a kiss against that smiling mouth.

Leo's eyes fluttered open and his hands came up to her shoulders, holding her there against him.

'That's a rather nice way to wake up,' he said, and before she could respond he shifted her body so she was lying fully on top of him, the press of his arousal against her belly.

'I think you might have an even nicer way in mind,' she murmured as Leo slid his hand from her shoulder to her breast, his palm cupping its fullness.

'I certainly do,' he said, and neither of them spoke for a little while after that.

Later, when they'd showered and dressed and were eating breakfast in a private dining room, Alyse asked him what his plans were for the day. Despite their morning love-making, in the bright light of day she felt some of her old uncertainties steal back. Perhaps Leo was content to enjoy their intimacy at night while still keeping himself apart during the day, consumed with work and royal duty.

Sitting across from him, sneaking glances at his stern profile, she was conscious of how little he'd said last night.

I don't know how much I have to give. Really, in most relationships—if they even *had* a relationship—that would
have been a warning, or at least a disclaimer. Not the
promise she, in her naïvely and ridiculous hope, had believed it to be.

Leo considered her question. 'I have a meeting this
morning with some Cabinet members about a new energy
bill. But I'm free this afternoon. I thought—perhaps—I
could give you a tour of the palace? You haven't actually
seen much of it.'

Alyse felt a smile bloom across her face and some of
those uncertainties scattered. Some, not all. Leo smiled
back, a look of boyish uncertainty on his face.

'That sounds wonderful,' she said, and his smile widened, just as hers did.

They talked about other things then, a conversation
that was wonderfully relaxed and yet also strangely new,
exchanging views on films and books; relating anecdotes
they'd never thought to share in the last six years. Simply
getting to know one another.

After breakfast Leo excused himself to get ready for
his meeting and Alyse went upstairs to unpack. She spent
the morning in her room, catching up on correspondence
and tidying her things before she went down to lunch.

Sophia had gone out for the day, thankfully, and Alessandro was otherwise occupied, so it was just her, Leo and
Alexa at the lunch table.

'So how is married life, you two?' Alexa asked after the
footman had served them all and retired. 'Bliss?'

Leo smiled faintly and shook his head. 'Don't be cynical, Lex.'

'*You're* telling *me* not to be cynical?'

'Wonders never cease,' Leo answered dryly, and Alexa
raised her eyebrows.

'So marriage has changed you.'

Alyse held her breath as Leo took a sip of his water, his face thoughtful and yet also frustratingly blank. 'A bit,' he finally answered, not meeting anyone's gaze. Although she knew she shouldn't be, Alyse felt a rush of disappointment.

She took a steadying breath and focused on her own lunch. She knew she needed to be patient. Last night had changed things, but it was all still so new. She had to give it—*him, them*—time to strengthen and grow. Time for Leo truly to believe he *could* change.

Believe he could love.

After lunch Leo took her on a grand tour of the palace. They wandered through a dozen sun-dappled salons, empty and ornate, their footsteps echoing on the marble floors.

'This must have been great for hide and seek,' Alyse commented as they stood in one huge room decorated with portraits of his ancestors and huge pieces of gilt furniture. She tried to picture two dark-haired, solemn-eyed brothers playing in the room. Had Leo and his brother Alessandro been close? Had he missed him when he'd left? She had so many questions, but she knew Leo wasn't ready for her to ask them.

'I didn't really play in these rooms,' Leo answered, his hands shoved into his pockets, his gaze distant as he let it rove around the room. 'We were mostly confined to the nursery.'

'We?' Alyse prompted, and his expression didn't even flicker.

'The children. And of course, as I told you before, I went to boarding school when I was six.'

'That's rather young, isn't it? To go away.'

He shrugged. 'It was what my parents wanted.'

She thought of the remote King, the haughty Queen. Not the most loving of parents. 'Did you miss them?'

'No. You don't miss what you've never had.' She didn't

think he was going to say anything more, but then he took a deep breath and continued, his gaze focused on the sunshine spilling through the window. 'If you've ever wondered how my parents got the idea of having us pretend to be in love, it's because that's all they've ever done. They were only interested in me or my— Or any of us when someone was watching.' His mouth twisted. 'A photo opportunity to show how much they loved us. As soon as it passed, they moved on.'

'But…' Alyse hesitated, mentally reviewing all the magazine inserts and commemorative books she'd seen about Maldinian's golden royal family: the posed portraits, the candid shots on the beach or while skiing. Everyone smiling, laughing.

Playing at happy families.

Was Leo really saying that his whole family life had been as much a masquerade as their engagement? She knew she shouldn't be surprised, yet she was. It was so unbearably soulless, so terribly cold.

No wonder Leo didn't believe in love.

Her heart ached for Leo as a boy, lonely and ignored. 'That sounds very lonely,' she said and he just shrugged.

'I'm not sure I know what loneliness is. It was simply what I was used to.' Yet she didn't believe that; she couldn't. What child didn't long for love and affection, cuddles and laughter? It was innate, impossible to ignore.

But not to suppress. Which was what it seemed Leo had done for his whole life, she thought sadly. Now her heart ached not just for Leo as a boy, but for the man he'd become, determined not to need anyone. Not to love anyone or want to be loved back—only to be let down.

'Anyway.' He turned from the window to face her, eyebrows raised. 'What about you? You're an only child. Did you ever want siblings?'

She recognised the attempt to steer the conversation

away from himself and accepted it. He'd already revealed more than she'd ever anticipated or even hoped for. 'Yes, I did,' she admitted. 'But my parents made it clear there wouldn't be any more from a rather early age.'

'Why was that? Did they have trouble conceiving?'

'No. They just didn't want any more.' She saw the flicker of surprise cross his face and explained, 'They were happy with me—and mainly with each other. They were a real love match, you know. They may not be royalty, but they've still been featured in magazines. Their romance was a fairy tale.' Her voice came out a little flat, and Leo noticed.

'Your mother's some kind of American heiress, isn't she?'

'Her father owned a chain of successful hotels. My uncle runs it now, but my mother was called the Brearley Heiress before she married.'

'And your father?'

'A French financier. They met at a ball in Paris—saw each other across a crowded room and that was it.' She gave him a rather crooked smile. 'You might not believe in love at first sight, but that's how it was for them.'

Leo didn't speak for a moment and when he finally did it was to ask, 'And growing up in the shadow of that... how was it for you?'

And with that telling question he'd gone right to the heart of the matter. 'Hard, sometimes,' Alyse confessed quietly. 'I love my parents, and I have no doubts whatsoever that they love me. But...it was always the two of them and the one of me, if that makes sense. They've always been wrapped up in each other, which is how it should be...'

She trailed off, realising belatedly how whingy she must sound, complaining about how much her parents loved each other. Leo had grown up in a household of bitterness and play-acting, and here she was saying her own home had had too much love? She felt ridiculous and ashamed.

'But it was lonely,' Leo finished softly. 'Or so I imagine, for a little girl on her own.'

'Sometimes,' she whispered. She felt a lump rise in her throat and swallowed hard. Leo reached for her hand, threading her fingers with his, and the simple contact touched her deep inside.

'Strange, how we grew up in two such different families and homes,' he murmured. 'Yet perhaps, in an odd way, our experience was just a little bit the same.'

'I can't complain, not really.'

'You weren't complaining. I asked a question and you answered it.' He drew her towards him, his one hand still linked with hers while the other tangled itself in her hair. 'But perhaps now we can put our families behind us. We'll start our own family, one day.' His smile was knowing and teasingly lascivious as he brushed her lips against his. 'Maybe today.'

'Maybe,' Alyse whispered shakily. They hadn't used birth control, hadn't even discussed it—and why should they? An heir was part of the package, part of her responsibility as Leo's bride and Maldinia's future queen.

Leo's baby.

She wanted it: him, the promise of a new family, a family created by love. Leo broke the kiss. *Patience.* This was still so new, still just a beginning.

But a wonderful one, and with a smile still on her lips she leaned forward and kissed him back.

Alyse gazed at her reflection in the mirror, smoothing the silver gown she was to wear for tonight's reception in one of London's most exclusive clubs. It had been four days since they'd returned from St Cristos, four wonderful days—and nights.

She still had to guard herself from leaping ahead, from longing for more than Leo was ready to offer. *I don't know how much I have to give.* And yet he *was* giving, and trying, and with every new conversation, every shared joke or smile, every utterly amazing night, she knew she was falling in love with him. Falling in love with the real him, the Leo she'd never even known.

She loved discovering that man, learning his habits, preferences and his funny little quirks, like the fact that he had to read the *entire* page of a newspaper, even the adverts, before turning to another; or that he liked chess but hated draughts.

And she loved learning the taut map of his body and hearing the shudder of pleasure that ripped through him when she kissed or touched him in certain places...

Just remembering made longing sweep through her body in a heated wave.

It hadn't all been perfect, of course. The strictures of palace life, of their royal appearances, had created moments of unspoken tension and Leo's inevitable emotional withdrawal. Just that morning they'd appeared in front of the palace to fly to London, and at the sight of the cheering crowds they'd both frozen before Alyse had started forward, smiling and waving.

'How is married life?' one young woman had asked her.

'More than I'd ever hoped for,' she'd answered.

The woman had beamed and Alyse had moved on, but she'd caught a glimpse of Leo out of the corner of her eye and uneasily noted his stony expression.

They didn't talk until they were in the royal jet, flying to London. Leo had snapped open his newspaper and, scanning the headlines, had remarked, 'More than you'd ever hoped, eh?'

Alyse had blushed. 'Well...'

'Somehow I think you hope for a bit more,' he'd said

softly, and her blush had intensified. She was trying so
hard to be patient and accepting, but everything in her
yearned for more. For love. Leo had glanced away. 'I don't
know why,' he said, 'but the pretending feels harder now.
More like a lie.'

Alyse understood what he meant. The deception cut
deeper, now that there was actually something between
them. Pretending you were in love when you felt nothing,
as Leo had, was easier than when you felt just a little. She
had a feeling their pretence was making Leo realise how
little he still felt, and that wasn't a revelation she felt like
discussing.

Sighing now, she turned away from the mirror. *Patience.*

A knock sounded on the door of her bedroom. Despite
their honeymoon status, she and Leo had been given a
royal suite with two bedrooms in the hotel where they were
staying, and their luggage had been delivered to separate
rooms. They'd dressed for the reception separately, Alyse
with her small army of stylists hired by Queen Sophia and
flown in from Paris.

'Are you ready?' Leo called from behind the door. 'The
car is here.'

'Yes, I'm coming.' She opened the door, her breath
catching at the sight of Leo at his most debonair and digni-
fied in a white tie and tails. Then she saw the lines of tension bracketed from nose to mouth and fanning from his
eyes. She couldn't ignore the stiltedness that had developed
between them since they'd stepped back into the spotlight,
and she didn't know how to overcome it. Everything between them felt too new and fragile to be tested like this.

Leo nodded in the direction of her fitted gown of silver
satin; from a diamanté-encrusted halter-top it skimmed
her breasts and hips and then flared out around her knees

to fall in sparkly swirls to the floor. 'That's quite a gown. The stylists chose well.'

'I suppose they felt I needed to make a splash, since this is our first public appearance as husband and wife.'

'Yes, I have a feeling tonight will have us both firmly in the spotlight.' Leo's mouth tightened and Alyse tried to smile.

'We did get a whole week away from it,' she said. 'And it's only one evening, after all.'

'One of many.' Leo slid his arm through hers. 'We should go. There are reporters outside.'

Once again flashbulbs went off in front of her as they stepped out of the hotel. Their car was waiting with several security guards to shepherd them from one door to another, but they paused on the threshold to smile and wave at the blurred faces in front of them. Leo's arm felt like a steel band under hers, his muscles corded with tension.

As they slid into the darkened sanctuary of the car, she felt him relax marginally, his breath coming out in a tiny sigh of relief.

'How have you stood it for so long?' she asked as she adjusted the folds of her dress around her. They were slippery to hold, and glittered even in the dim light of the car's interior.

'Stood what?'

'Being on display.'

He shrugged. 'It's all I've ever known.'

'But you don't like it.'

'I suppose I'm getting tired of it,' he allowed. 'It's been going on for a long time.'

'Since you were a child?'

'More or less.' He turned away from her then, so she could only see the shadowy profile of his cheek and jaw as he stared out of the window.

She couldn't imagine living like that for so long. The

last six years had been challenging enough, with her in-
termittent public appearances, and she at least had had the
escape of university and a relatively normal life. Leo never
had, had never experienced anything really normal—or
perhaps even real.

'We're here.'

The car had pulled up in front of one of London's exclusive clubs on Pall Mall, and another contingent of photographers and journalists waited by the doors.

They didn't pose for photographs or answer questions
as the security hustled them from the car to the door, and
then inside to the hushed foyer of the club. Yet even inside that hallowed place Alyse was conscious of a different kind of scrutiny: the hundred or so privileged guests
who mingled in the club's ballroom were eyeing them
with discreet but still noticeable curiosity. The Prince and
his Cinderella bride; of course people were curious. Even
alone in Durham she'd received those kinds of looks, had
seen herself on the covers of magazines. She'd tried not
to let it bother her, had made herself shrug it off and focus
on the positives, on engaging with the public in as real a
way as she could.

Yet she felt different now, and it wasn't because of the
looks or the photos or the endless attention and publicity.
It was because of Leo. She watched him out of the corner
of her eye as he fetched them both champagne, talking
and nodding with some important person, a stuffy-looking
man with greying hair and a paunch. Alyse thought he
looked vaguely familiar, but she didn't know his name.

And Leo… Leo looked remarkably at ease, the tension
he'd shown earlier firmly masked and hidden away. He
put his arm around her waist, and even as she thrilled to
his touch, as always, Alyse felt a chill creep into her soul
because how on earth could she actually tell when her
husband was being real?

Perhaps the last week had been as much about pretending as tonight. Perhaps Leo didn't even know *how* to be real.

'You need to smile,' Leo murmured, his own face set into easy, relaxed lines. 'You're looking tense.'

'Sorry.' Alyse tried to smile. This was so hard now, so much harder than it had ever been before. She was sick to death of pretending, sick of all this fear and uncertainty. Sick of wondering just what Leo felt for her, if anything.

'Now you look terrified,' Leo remarked in a low voice and she felt his arm tense around her waist. 'What's wrong? We've done this before.'

'It feels different now,' Alyse whispered. *She* felt different. But she had no idea if Leo did.

'It shouldn't,' he answered shortly, and steered her towards a crowd of speculative socialites. She forced herself to widen her wobbly smile, feeling more heartsick and uncertain than ever.

Leo fought the urge to tear off his white tie and stride from the club without a backward glance. Every second of this evening had been interminable, and the falseness of his and Alyse's behavior rubbed him horribly raw. He'd never minded before or, if he had, he'd shrugged it off. He'd had to. He'd *always* had to.

Yet now… Now the pretence irritated and even sickened him. The last week had been difficult at times, uncomfortable at others, but it had been real—or at least as real as he knew anything to be. The days and nights he'd spent with Alyse had fed something in him, a hunger he'd never known he had. He wanted more even as he doubted whether he should—or could.

He glanced again at Alyse, her eyes troubled even as she smiled at someone, and he desired nothing more in this moment than to take her in his arms and strip that shimmery gown from her body, let it slide into a silver puddle at her feet...

Her smile, he thought, looked decidedly wooden. Why was it so hard to pretend to be in love, when they'd been getting along better than ever? It should have been easier, but it wasn't. Friendship *had* complicated things, he thought darkly, just as he'd predicted. The parody of head-over-heels emotion they were enacting now only made their real relationship—whatever that was—seem paltry in comparison...and he had a feeling Alyse knew it.

I don't know how much I have to give. The words had come from him with sudden, startling honesty, because in that moment after they'd first made love he hadn't known what he was going to say, only that everything had changed.

But perhaps it hadn't changed. Perhaps even that had been nothing more than a mirage, a fantasy, just as tonight was. Everything in his life—every emotion, every caress, kiss or loving touch—had been faked. How on earth could he expect this to be real?

He didn't even know what real was.

Two hours later they were back in the car, speeding towards their hotel in Mayfair. All around them the lights of the city glittered under a midsummer drizzle, the pavement slick and gleaming with rain. Alyse hadn't spoken since they'd got into the car and Leo eyed her now, her face averted from him so he could only see the soft, sweet curve of her cheek, the surprising strength of her jaw. He longed to touch her.

He didn't.

This was their life now, he reminded himself. This pretending. No matter what might be developing between them, neither of them could escape the grim reality that every time they stepped outside of the palace they would be pretending to feel something else.

A simple, emotionless business arrangement would really be easier.

Yet, even as he told himself that, he couldn't keep from reaching for her as soon as they were back in their suite. She came willingly, her dress whispering against his legs, but he saw shadows in her eyes and her lip trembled before she bit it. He wanted to banish it all: the party, the pretence, the doubt and fear he felt in her now—and in himself. He wanted to make her smile, and the only way he knew of doing that was to kiss her, so he did.

Gently at first, but then he felt the softness of her mouth, the surrender of her sigh, and he drove his fingers into her hair, scattering all the diamond-tipped pins, as he pressed her against the wall of the foyer and devoured her with his kiss.

Alyse responded in kind and he felt a raw desperation in both of their need, a hunger to forget all the play-acting tonight and simply lose themselves in this—perhaps the only real thing they shared.

And lose himself he did, sliding his hands under the slippery satin of her gown, bunching it heedlessly about her hips as she wrapped her legs around his waist and he drove into her, lost himself inside her, his face buried in the warm curve of her neck as her body shook with pleasure.

They didn't speak afterwards and silently Leo led her from the foyer, leaving the hair pins and her shoes scattered on the floor. He peeled the dress from her body and shrugged off his own clothes before he drew her to the bed, wrapped his body around her and tried to shut out the world.

He woke several hours later, the room still swathed in darkness, and a glance at the clock told him it was an hour or so before dawn. He felt relentlessly awake and silently he slipped from Alyse's embrace, leaving her sleeping in his bed.

In the sitting room he powered up his laptop, determined to do a few hours' work before Alyse woke. They had engagements planned all day today, and they flew to Paris tonight for yet another reception, another full day tomorrow, yet another day of pretending. He pushed the thought away.

He would focus on work, the one thing that gave him satisfaction, a sense of purpose. He still needed to work on the wording of the bill for parliament regarding improvements to Maldinia's technological infrastructure, something his father had never remotely cared about.

He opened an Internet browser on his laptop to check his email and stopped dead when he saw that morning's news headline blaring across the screen:

Cinderella's Secret Lover Tells All.

Slowly he clicked on the article and scanned the first paragraph.

Prince Leo and his bride have always been the stuff of a fairy tale, and perhaps that's all it has been—for Matthew Cray, a student with the new princess at Durham University, has confessed to having a secret love affair with Alyse...

The game was up, Leo thought numbly. Everyone would know their relationship was fake, just as every relationship he'd ever had was fake. Sickened, he sat back in his chair. His mind spun with the implications of the article, the damage control that would need to be done—and quickly. But underneath the practicalities he felt something he hated to feel, didn't want to acknowledge now—the pain of hurt, the agonising ache of betrayal. He knew it wasn't fair; he'd forgiven Alyse, and it had been a long time ago anyway.

But seeing it all there on the page, knowing she'd convinced herself she loved him when she really hadn't…why should now be any different?

There's no such thing as love, he reminded himself brutally. *You've been playing at it this last week, but it's not real. It can't be.* And, swearing under his breath, he clicked on another glaring headline and began to read.

CHAPTER ELEVEN

'Leo?'

Alyse stood in the doorway of the bedroom, her gaze fastened on her husband and the stricken look on his face. He was staring blankly at the screen of his laptop, but as he heard her call his name he turned to her, his expression ironing out.

'What are you doing awake?'

'What are you?' She bit her lip. 'I woke up and wondered where you were.'

He gestured to his computer. 'Just getting a little work done. I couldn't sleep.'

Alyse took a step closer. Although Leo's face was implacable and bland now, she sensed the disquiet underneath. Something was wrong. 'What's happened?' she asked quietly.

'Nothing.'

'What were you looking at on the computer?'

'Just work—' He stopped, raking a hand through his hair. 'I suppose I'll have to tell you,' he said after a moment. 'We'll both have to deal with the damage control.'

Her stomach plunged icily. 'Damage control?'

Sighing, he clicked on the mouse and pointed to the screen. Alyse read the headline, everything in her freezing.

Cinderella's Secret Lover Tells All.

'Oh no,' she whispered. 'Oh no. How could he?'

'I imagine he was offered a great deal of money.'

'But it was years ago.' She stopped, swallowing hard, nausea rising in a roiling tide within her. She could just glimpse snatches of the awful article, phrases like 'drunken passion' and—heaven forbid—'marriage masquerade'.

She leaned forward, her eyes darting over the damning words.

According to Cray, Alyse and Prince Leonardo of Maldinia have simply been pretending to be in love to satisfy the public.

They knew. The whole world knew the truth about her and Leo. She stumbled back, one fist pressed to her lips, and Leo closed the laptop.

'I'm sorry,' she whispered and he shrugged.

'It was years ago. You have nothing to feel sorry for now.'

'But if I hadn't—'

'We'll deal with it,' he cut her off flatly. 'You should get dressed. I imagine we'll have to go back to Maldinia this morning to talk to the press office. We want a united front about how to handle this.'

He turned away and Alyse felt her insides twist with anxious misery. This was all her fault. And, while she accepted that Leo had forgiven her for her indiscretion from so many years ago, she feared their fragile relationship would not survive this ordeal.

With an icy pang of dread she remembered Queen Sophia's words: no use to Leo.

The worst had happened. She was a liability—to the monarchy and to Leo. And, if he didn't really feel anything for her, did he even want to stay married to her? What would be the point?

Miserably she went to shower and dress, her heart like lead inside her, weighing her down. The media frenzy would be excruciating, she knew. Who else would come forward to pick apart her university years? She might only have had that one lamentable experience, but she knew how the media worked, how people were tempted. Other stories would be made up; she could be depicted as a heartless, conniving slut.

And what about Leo? Her heart ached then not for herself, but for him. He'd have to deal with the shame and humiliation of being seen as the betrayed lover, the duped prince. She closed her eyes, forced the tears back. Recriminations would not serve either of them now.

Several grim-faced stylists were waiting when she emerged from the shower and they launched into a description of their strategy before she'd even taken the towel from her hair.

'You want to look muted and modest today, but not ashamed. Not like you have something to hide.'

'I don't have anything to hide,' Alyse answered before she could stop herself. 'Not any more.'

The stylists exchanged glances and ignored what she said. 'Subtle make-up, hair in a loose knot—earrings?'

'Pearl studs,' the other one answered firmly, and numbly Alyse let them go to work.

Forty-five minutes later she emerged into the sitting room where Leo was dressed in a charcoal-grey suit and talking on his mobile, his voice terse. Nervously Alyse fiddled with her earrings, her heart seeming to continually lurch up into her throat. She'd always managed to handle the press before, but then they'd always been on her side. How hard was it, really, to smile and wave for people who seemed to adore you?

Today would be different. She'd turned on the television while the stylists were organising her outfit and had seen that Matt's interview was breaking news even on the major networks. Ridiculous, perhaps, but still true. They'd managed to dig up a photo of her walking to lectures with him and, innocent as it had been then, it looked damning. She had her hand on his arm and her head was tilted back as she laughed. She didn't even remember the moment; she'd only walked with him a couple of times. They hadn't even been that good friends, she thought miserably, but who would believe that now? The media was implying she'd indulged in a long, sordid affair.

'No need for that,' one stylist, Aimee, had said crisply, and turned off the TV. 'Let's get you dressed.'

Now as she waited for Leo to finish his call—he was speaking in rapid Italian too fast for her to understand—Alyse smoothed the muted blue silk of her modest, high-collared dress, a satin band of deeper blue nipping in her waist. 'Virgin blue', the colour was apparently called. How unfitting.

Finally Leo disconnected the call and turned to her, his brows snapping together. 'A good choice,' he said, nodding towards her dress. 'The jet is waiting.'

'The jet? Where are we going? What's—what's going to happen?'

'We're heading back to Maldinia. I considered keeping our heads high and honouring the rest of our engagements in Paris and Rome, but I don't think that's the best course of action now.'

'You don't?'

Leo shook his head, the movement brisk and decisive. 'No. I think the best thing is to come clean. Admit what happened and that I've forgiven you. Keep it firmly in the past.'

'And how...?'

'I've arranged for us to do a television interview.'

'A television interview?' Alyse repeated sickly. She might have been on the cover of dozens of magazines, but she'd never actually been on TV. The thought of being on it now, a public confessional, made her head spin and her nerves strain to breaking. 'But—'

'I'll explain it all on the plane,' Leo said. 'We need to get going.'

The outside of the hotel was mobbed with paparazzi and the security guards had to fight their way through to get to them as they waited at the door.

Alyse ducked her head as she came out, Leo's arm around her, flashbulbs exploding in her face, questions hammering her heart.

'Did you ever love Leo, Alyse?'

'How long were you seeing Matthew Cray?'

'Have there been others?'

'Was it for money or fame, this marriage masquerade?'

'Do you have any conscience at all?'

She closed her eyes, her heart like a stone inside her as Leo and the security guard guided her into the waiting limo. As soon as the doors had closed she let out a shaky sigh of relief, halfway to a sob.

'That was awful.'

Leo turned away from the window, his face expressionless. 'It will get worse.'

'I know.' She took a deep breath, let it fill her lungs before releasing it slowly. She still felt shaky from her first encounter with a malevolent press—one of many, she had no doubt. 'Leo, I'm so sorry this has happened. I know it's my fault.'

'As far as I can tell, it's Matthew Cray's fault.'

'But if I hadn't—'

'Alyse, you can beat yourself up all you like about what

happened years ago, but it doesn't change things now, so really there's no point.' His expression didn't soften as he added, 'And I don't want you to. I know you're sorry. I understand you regret it.'

'But—but do you forgive me?'

'There's nothing to forgive.'

She should have been comforted by his words, but she wasn't. He spoke them so emotionlessly, his face so terribly bland; any intimacy they'd once shared seemed utterly lost in that moment. Cold, stern, unyielding Leo was back, and she had no idea how to find the man she'd begun to fall in love with. Perhaps he didn't exist any more; perhaps he'd never existed.

Weary and heartsick, Alyse leaned her head back against the seat and closed her eyes.

Leo gazed at Alyse, her face pale, her eyes closed, and felt a needling of guilt mixed with an unexpected pang of sympathy. After being adored by the press for six years, it had to be hard to be cast as the villain.

Not that *he'd* ever cared what the media thought of him one way or the other. Perhaps Alyse didn't care either. Perhaps it was simply guilt that made her look so tired and wretched.

Leo knew he should have tried harder to comfort her. He probably should have held her and told her not to worry, that they'd get through this together. That none of it mattered. He hadn't done any of that; he hadn't thought of doing it until now, when it felt too late. He simply didn't have it in him.

I don't know how much I have to give. No, he sure as hell didn't. Ever since the news of Alyse's indiscretion had broken he'd felt his fragile emotions shutting down, the familiar retreat into cold silence. It was safer, easier, and it was what he knew. And he also knew it was hurting Alyse. He supposed that was a step in the right direction; at least he was aware he was hurting her.

But he still didn't have the ability, or perhaps just the strength, to stop it.

Alyse opened her eyes, her gaze arrowing in on him. 'Tell me about this television interview,' she said and Leo nodded, glad to escape his thoughts.

'It's with Larissa Pozzi,' he said and Alyse blanched.

'But she's—'

'Broadcast on all the major networks. We need the publicity.' Alyse just shook her head, and Leo knew what she wasn't saying. Larissa relished scandal and melodrama, was always handing her guests tissues with her overly made-up face in a moue of false sympathy. Being interviewed by her was a necessary evil; he had chosen it because it would get their message across to the most people most quickly.

'And what are we meant to say?' Alyse asked.

'That we'd had a fight and you were foolish. You've regretted it deeply ever since and I've known all along and forgave you ages ago.' He spoke tonelessly, hating every lie that he'd come up with with the approval of the royal press office. Hating that, even in telling a bit of the truth, they were still perpetuating a lie. And he was sick to the death of pretending. Of lies.

He could not imagine saying them on live television. Every word would stick in his throat like a jagged glass shard. He wanted to be done with deception, with pretence, for ever, even as he recognised how impossible it was.

Alyse's face had gone chalk-white and she glanced away. 'I see,' she murmured, and he knew she did: more lies. More pretending. They would never be done with them, never have the opportunity to be real.

So how on earth could they have any kind of real relationship in that toxic environment, never mind love?

Not that he loved her. He didn't even know what love was.

Did he?

The question reverberated through him. The last week had been one of the sweetest of his life, he had to admit. The memory of Alyse's smile, the sweet slide of her lips against his, how he'd felt when he'd been buried inside her...

If that wasn't love, it was something he'd never experienced before. It was intense and overwhelming, addictive and, hell, frightening.

But was it love?

Did it even matter?

'Why don't you get some rest?' Leo said brusquely. 'You look completely washed out, and we'll be there in another hour.'

And, putting those troubling questions firmly to the back of his mind, he reached for his attaché and some paperwork that needed his attention.

Alyse's stomach clenched as they stepped off the royal jet and were ushered quickly into the waiting limo with its accompanying motorcade of security. They were to go directly to the palace for a press briefing, and then the television interview that would take place in one of the palace's private apartments. Alyse dreaded both events. She dreaded the condemnation she'd see on everyone's faces, from King Alessandro to Queen Sophia to the cloying Larissa Pozzi...to Leo.

He'd said there was nothing to forgive, but his stony face told otherwise. She had no idea what he was really thinking or feeling, and she was desperately afraid to ask. That was how fragile and untried their feelings for each other were, she acknowledged with a wry despair. It couldn't face up to a moment's honesty, never mind any hardship or scrutiny.

The press secretary, along with the Queen, were waiting for them as soon as they stepped into the palace. Alyse's stomach plunged straight to her toes as they entered one of the smaller receiving rooms. Queen Sophia stood at one end in all of her icy, regal splendour.

'Mother.' Leo's voice was toneless as he went forward to kiss his mother's cheek. She didn't offer any affection back or even move, and despite the nerves jangling inside her Alyse felt a kind of sorrowful curiosity at the dynamic between mother and son.

Queen Sophia swung her cold blue gaze to Alyse. 'This is a disaster,' she said, 'as I'm sure you're aware. A complete disaster.'

'It's under control—' Leo began tightly, but his mother cut across him.

'Do you really think so, Leo?' Her voice rang out scornfully but Leo didn't react. 'People will believe what they want to believe.'

'They've always wanted to believe in Alyse,' he answered quietly. 'They've always loved her.'

'And they'll be just as quick to hate her,' Sophia snapped. 'That's the nature of it, of publicity.'

'Then I have to wonder why we've always been so quick to court it,' Leo responded coolly. 'Oh, I remember now—because you needed the positive press. You've needed Alyse, to make up for all the selfish choices you and Father have made over the years.'

'How dare you?' Sophia breathed.

'I dare,' Leo answered, 'because you've been using me and then Alyse—using everyone you can—to make up for your own deficiencies. I won't have you blaming us for them now. We'll handle this, Mother, and you need not concern yourself at all.'

Sophia's eyes glinted malice. 'And what happens when they hate her, Leo? What happens when it all falls apart?'

Ice slid down Alyse's spine. *When they had no use for her.*

'We'll deal with that possibility when and if it happens,' Leo answered, and turned away.

Sophia whirled away from them both. 'I'll send Paula in,' she said tightly, and with a slam of the doors she was gone.

'Thank you,' Alyse said quietly, 'for defending me. Even if I don't deserve it.'

'You do deserve it. Enough with the *mea culpa* bit, Alyse.'

'I'm sorry.'

'You're still doing it.'

She smiled wanly. 'Habit, I guess.'

'I'm not angry,' Leo said after a moment. 'At least, not at you. I might be harbouring a little rage for the paparazzi, but I can't really blame them either. They're just doing their job and we've been feeding their frenzy for years now.'

'And you're sick of it.'

'Yes.' He lapsed into silence, his forehead furrowed into a frown as he gazed out of the palace windows at acres of manicured lawn. Alyse watched him warily, for she sensed some conflict in him, something he wanted to say—but did she want to hear it?

'Alyse…' he began, but before he could say any more Paula bustled in with a sheaf of papers in one manicured hand.

'Now, we need to go over just what you'll say.'

'It's under control,' Leo said shortly. 'I know what I'm going to say.'

Paula looked surprised, a little insulted. 'But I'm meant to brief—'

'Consider us briefed,' Leo answered. 'We're ready.'

Alyse fought down nausea. She didn't feel remotely ready, and frankly she could use a little help from Paula. 'What are we going to say?' she whispered as they headed towards the suite where the interview would take place. 'I could use—'

'Leave it to me.'

'But—'

'Let's go in,' he said, and ushered her into the reception room with its cameras and lights already set up. 'They're waiting.'

The interview, at least at first, was a blur to Alyse. She shook Larissa Pozzi's hand and the woman, all glossy nails and too-white teeth, gushed over the two of them.

'Really, we're doing this for you,' she said, laying a hand on Alyse's arm, her long, curved nails digging into her skin. 'The world wants to hear your side of the story.'

'My side,' Alyse repeated numbly. It didn't sound good—that there were already sides, battle lines clearly drawn.

Assistants prepped them both for make-up and hair as they sat on a sofa facing Larissa and the cameras. Alyse could feel the tension coming off Leo in waves and, though he managed to convey an air of relaxation, chatting easily with Larissa, she knew he was beyond tense.

She *knew* him. She knew him now more than ever before, and that was both comforting and thrilling—that this man was no longer a stranger but someone she knew and—*loved*?

Did she love him? Had she fallen in love that quickly, that easily? And yet nothing about the last week or so had been easy. It had been wonderful, yes, but also painful, emotional, tense and fraught. And still the best time of her life.

She just prayed it wasn't over, that this wasn't the beginning of the end. Glancing at Leo's profile, his jaw taut even as he smiled, she had no idea if that was the case.

'We're just about ready,' Larissa told them both as she positioned herself in her chair, and if anything Alyse felt Leo become even tenser, although his position didn't change.

Three, two, one…

'So, Prince Leo, we're so thrilled to have you on the show,' Larissa began in her gushing voice. Alyse felt her smile already become a rictus, her hands clenched tightly together in her lap and a bead of sweat formed at her hairline under the glare of the lights and cameras. 'And of course everyone is dying to hear your side of the story…as well as your bride's.' The talk show hostess's gaze moved speculatively to Alyse, and she didn't think she was imagining the glint of malice in those over-wide eyes. No matter how Larissa gushed to Leo, Alyse knew she'd still be cast as the scarlet woman. It made for a juicy story.

'Well, it's really rather simple, Larissa,' Leo began in a calm, even voice. He had one arm stretched along the back of the sofa, his fingers grazing Alyse's shoulder. 'When that photograph was taken all those years ago—and you know the photo I mean, of course.'

'Of *course*.'

'Alyse and I barely knew each other. We'd only just met that very evening, actually.'

'But you looked so in love,' Larissa said, eyes widening even more. She glanced rather accusingly at Alyse, who only just managed to keep her smile in place. Nothing about that photo, she thought, had been deliberately faked. It was, perhaps, the one honest moment the press had actually captured between her and Leo.

Leo lifted a shoulder in a 'what can I say?' shrug and Larissa let out a breathy sigh. 'But it was love at first sight, Prince Leo, wasn't it? You haven't actually been faking your engagement all these years, as people are so cruelly suggesting?'

Smiling, he held up one hand, his wedding ring glinting on his finger. 'Does that look fake to you?'

'But your *feelings*…'

'Alyse's and my marriage was always one of convenience,' Leo said and Alyse stiffened in shock. She had a feeling this would not have been part of Paula's brief.

Larissa drew back in exaggerated shock. 'Convenience? No! Not the prince and his Cinderella bride?'

Leo just smiled and shrugged. 'Royal marriages often are.'

'But you've been portrayed as being so in love, an inspiration to couples—as well as singles—everywhere.'

'And we are in love,' Leo replied steadily. 'Now.' A moment of silence spun out as Larissa stared at him; Alyse stared at him. *What was he saying?*

'It took a long time for those feelings to come, especially on my part,' he continued in that same steady voice. 'But they have come, and that's really the important thing, don't you think? Not what happened—or didn't happen—before.' He let this sink in for a moment before continuing. 'The main thing—the beautiful thing—is that I love Alyse now. I've fallen in love with my wife.'

And then he turned to her, while Alyse tried not to gape like a fish, and gave her a smile that felt both private and tender, and was being broadcast to a billion people around the world.

A smile that was surely a lie…wasn't it? Wasn't he just pretending, as always?

'Alyse, you look surprised,' Larissa said and, blinking, Alyse tried to focus on the talk-show hostess rather than her husband.

'Not surprised so much as thrilled,' she managed, barely aware of what she was saying. 'And so happy. I admit, it's been a rocky road to get to where we are. Leo and I have always been committed to marriage, but love isn't something you can force.'

Larissa pursed her lips. 'Let's talk about Matthew Cray.'

'Let's not,' Leo interjected swiftly. 'Whatever happened was a single moment many years ago, and not worth our time or discussion. As I've said before, what matters is now—and our future.' Again he smiled at Alyse, but this time she looked into his eyes. They looked dark and hard and her heart quailed within her. He didn't look like a man in love. She could feel the tension thrumming through him and her insides roiled. He was faking; of course he was. This was just another part of the pretence, and she was a fool for thinking otherwise even for a second.

She didn't remember the rest of the interview; her mind was spinning too much and Leo did most of the talking.

After an interminable half-hour they were done and Larissa and her crew were packing up. Leo ushered her from the filming area, one hand firmly on her elbow.

'Hopefully that did the trick,' he said, and that last frail hope died.

'A very clever way to spin it,' she managed and Leo gave her a sudden, penetrating look.

'Is that how you saw it?'

She stared at him, longing to ask him what he meant, but so afraid to. Afraid to trust his feelings, or even hers. *What was real?* 'I…I don't know.'

'Prince Leo… Your Highness.' Leo turned and Alyse saw one of his father's aides hurrying towards him.

'Yes?'

'Your father requests your presence in his private study immediately.'

Leo frowned. 'Is something wrong?'

The aide looked uncomfortable as he answered, 'Prince Alessandro has arrived at the palace.'

Leo went completely still, his face draining of colour, and Alyse felt shock blaze through him. Prince Alessandro…Leo's brother. He'd returned.

Leo swallowed and then his expression ironed out. 'I'm coming,' he said shortly, and walked away from Alyse.

CHAPTER TWELVE

SANDRO WAS HERE. Leo blinked, still finding it hard to believe his brother was here, just a room away. He'd come home. After fifteen years away—a decade and a half of complete silence—he'd returned, the prodigal son. Leo could not untangle the knot of emotions that had lodged inside him, rose in his throat. Fear, anger, confusion, disbelief…and, yes, love and joy.

Too much.

He was tired of feeling so damn much. After years of schooling himself not to feel anything, not to care or want or allow himself to be hurt, it was all coming out—just like it had during that interview.

I've fallen in love with my wife.

What on earth had made him say such a thing? Made him confess it—if it were even true? The words had spilled out of him, needing to be said, burning within him. Now he fought against such an admission, attempting, quite desperately, to claw back some self-protection. Some armour.

And now Sandro.

'Leo…' Alyse hurried after him. 'Why is Sandro here?'

He turned to stare at her. 'You know about Sandro?'

'Your mother told me a few days ago.'

He shook his head, unable to untangle his emotions enough to know how he felt about Alyse knowing and not saying a word. This was intimacy? Honesty?

'Let's not talk about this here,' he said. 'My father is expecting me.' She followed him to his father's study but he barred her at the door. 'This meeting is private, Alyse. I'll talk to you after.' He knew he sounded cold and remote, but he couldn't help it. That was who he was. Everything else had been an aberration. A mistake.

A mistake he would miss.

'I'll see you later.'

She bit her lip, her eyes wide with fear and uncertainty, but then she slowly nodded. 'Okay,' she whispered, and slowly walked down the hall.

Leo knocked once and then opened the door to his father's most sacred room, his private study, and stared directly into the face of his older brother.

Alessandro. Sandro. The only person he'd ever felt was a true friend, who understood him, accepted him. Loved him. He looked the same, and yet of course so much older. His unruly dark hair had a few silver threads, the strands catching the light and matching the grey glint of his eyes. He was taller and leaner than Leo, possessing a sinewy, charismatic grace, just as he had at twenty-one when Leo had last seen him.

Don't go, Sandro. Don't leave me alone. Please.

He'd begged and Sandro had gone.

'Leo.' Sandro nodded once, his expression veiled, and Leo nodded back. Quite the emotional reunion, then.

'I've summoned Alessandro back to Maldinia,' King Alessandro said with the air of someone who trusted his innate authority.

'So I see.' Leo cleared his throat. 'It's been a long time, Sandro.'

'Fifteen years,' his brother agreed. His silver gaze swept over him, telling him nothing. 'You look well.'

'As do you.' And then they lapsed into silence, these brothers who had once, despite the six years' difference in

their ages, been nearly inseparable—compatriots as children, banding together as they had determinedly tried to
ignore their parents' vicious fights and sudden, insensible
moments of staged affection.

Later they'd gone to the same boys' boarding school
and Sandro had become Leo's champion, his hero, a sixth
former to his first year, cricket star and straight-A pupil.
Yet always with the time, patience and affection for his
quieter, shyer younger brother. Until he'd decided to leave
all of it—and him—behind.

Childish memories, Leo told himself now. Infantile
thoughts. Whatever hero worship he'd had for his brother,
he'd long since lost it. He didn't care any more, hadn't for
years. The damnable lump in his throat was simply annoying.

'Alessandro has agreed to return to his rightful place,'
his father said and Leo's gaze swung slowly to the King.

'His rightful place,' he repeated. 'You mean…?'

'When I am gone, he will be King.'

Leo didn't react. He made sure not to. He kept completely still, not even blinking, even as inside he felt as if
he'd staggered back from a near-fatal blow. In one swoop
his father had taken his inheritance, his *reason*, away from
him. For fifteen years he'd worked hard to prove he was
worthy, that he would be a good king. He'd sacrificed desire for duty, had shaped his life to become the next mon-
arch of Maldinia.

And just like that, on his father's whim, he wouldn't
be. He turned to Sandro, saw his brother's lips twist in a
grimace of a smile.

'So you're off the hook, Leo.'

'Indeed.' Of course his brother would see it that way.
His brother had never wanted to be king, had walked away
from it all, hating both the artifice and the pretension of
royal life. He'd forged his own path in California; had

started a highly successful IT firm, or so Leo's Internet searches had told him. And now he was leaving that all behind to return, to take Leo's place?

And leave Leo with…nothing?

Not even a wife. There was, he realised hollowly, no reason at all for him and Alyse to be married. To stay married. A week or so of fragile feeling surely didn't justify a life sentence. She would want to be free and so would he.

He *did*. He would.

He turned back to his father, unable to miss the cold glitter of triumph in the King's eyes. 'So how did this come to pass?' he asked in as neutral a tone as he could manage.

'I've always wanted Alessandro to be King,' his father answered shortly. 'It is his birthright, his destiny. You've known that.'

Of course he had, just as he'd known he was a poor second choice. He'd simply thought he'd proved himself enough in the last fifteen years to make up for the deficiency of being born second.

'And after this latest debacle…' King Alessandro continued, his lips twisting in contempt. 'All the work we've done has been destroyed in one careless moment, Leo.' *The work* we've *done?* Leo wanted to answer. *To shout.*

His father had done nothing, *nothing* to restore the damn monarchy. He'd let his son—his second son—do all the work, shoulder all the responsibility. He said nothing. He knew there was no point.

The King drew himself up. 'Bringing Alessandro back will restore the monarchy and its reputation, its place at the head of society. New blood, Leo, fresh air. And we can forget about what happened with you and Alyse.'

Forget them both, tidy them away just as his father had done with Alessandro all those years ago. Move onto the next chapter in this damnable book.

But he didn't want to move on. He wouldn't have his life—his love—treated as no more than an unfortunate mistake. He didn't care so much about being king, Leo realised with shock, as being Alyse's husband. *I've fallen in love with my wife.* And it didn't matter any more.

Alyse didn't love him, not really. She might have convinced herself once, and she'd probably do so again, but it wasn't real. It wouldn't last, just as nothing had been real or lasting in his life.

Why should he trust this? Her? Or even himself, his own feelings that might vanish tomorrow?

'The matter is finished,' King Alessandro stated. 'Alessandro has accepted his birthright. He will return to live in Maldinia and take up his royal duties.'

Without waiting for a reply, the King left the room, left the two brothers alone as a silence stretched on between them.

'He's still the same,' Sandro said after a moment, his voice flat and almost uninterested. 'Nothing's really changed.'

Everything's changed. Everything has just changed for me. Leo swallowed the words, the anger. He didn't want to feel it; there was no point. He wouldn't be king; he had no wife. 'I suppose,' he said.

'I'll need you, if you're willing,' Sandro said. 'You can pick whatever post you want. Cabinet minister?' He smiled, and for the first time Leo saw warmth in his brother's face, lighting his eyes. 'I've missed you, Leo.'

Not enough to visit, or even write. But then, he hadn't either. First he'd been forbidden, and then later he'd told himself he didn't care.

Now grief for all he'd lost rushed through him and he turned his face away, afraid Sandro would see all he felt in his eyes. 'Welcome back, Sandro,' he said when he trusted himself to speak and then he left the room.

* * *

Alyse paced the sitting room of the apartment they'd been given in one wing of the palace, her hands clenched, her stomach clenched, everything inside her taut with nerves. Her worries and uncertainties about the TV interview, and what Leo had said, had been replaced with the fear of what Sandro's return would mean for Leo—and her.

For she'd had a terrible certainty, as she'd watched Leo head for his father's study like a man on his way to the gallows, that everything had changed.

The door opened and she whirled around.

'Leo.'

His mouth twisted in what Alyse suspected was meant to be a smile but didn't remotely come close. 'It seems,' he said, striding towards the window, 'that we're both off the hook.'

'Off the *hook*? What do you mean? What's happened, Leo? Why has Sandro come back?'

'My father summoned him.'

Alyse stared at him, saw the terrible coldness, almost indifference, on his face. 'Why did he leave in the first place?'

Leo shrugged and turned away. 'He hated royal life. Hated the way we always pretended and hated the burden of becoming king. He went to university, and when he received his diploma he decided to trade it all in for a life of freedom in the States.'

There was something that Leo wasn't saying, Alyse knew. Many things. He spoke tonelessly, but she felt his bitterness, his rage and even his hurt. She took a step closer to him. 'And why were you never in touch?'

'My parents forbade it. You don't walk away from royalty, especially not when you've been groomed to be king for your entire life.'

Shock blazed coldly through her as she realised what he was saying. 'So when he walked away, you were the heir.'

'Were,' Leo repeated. 'Yes.'

His voice was toneless, yet to Alyse he still sounded so bleak. She knew this man, knew when he was angry or happy or hurt. And right now she wanted to help him... if only she knew how. 'Leo, talk to me. Turn around and look at me, please. What's happened? Why are you so...?'

'I'm not anything,' he answered, and he turned around to look at her, his face as blank as his voice. 'I told you, Alyse, we're both off the hook.'

'I don't understand why you're saying that. What it means.'

'I'm off the hook for becoming king,' Leo explained slowly, as if she were a dim-witted child. 'And you're off the hook for being married to me.'

As if her wits were truly affected, it took her a few seconds to realise what he meant. 'What does your brother have to do with our marriage?' she whispered.

'Everything and nothing. Admittedly, I doubt he even knew I was married, but since he's accepted his birthright once more I'm no longer heir to the throne. Our marriage was a royal alliance, admittedly a forced one due to all the media attention. But there are no more reasons, Alyse.' He spread his hands wide, eyebrows raised in expectation. 'The media has sussed us out, and I'm not even going to be king in the first place. So it doesn't matter what either of us do.'

'And just what is it,' Alyse asked, her voice shaking, 'that you *want* to do?'

He lowered his brows, his expression flattening out. 'I see no reason for either of us to stay in a sham of a marriage.'

A sham of a marriage. She thought of what he'd said on air, how it had filled her for a few moments with a wary hope. A hope she hadn't quite been able to let go of, even now. *I've fallen in love with my wife.* Obviously he'd been spinning more lies to Larissa Pozzi, just as everything had been lies, perhaps even this last week or so.

'So you're suggesting a divorce,' she said flatly and for a moment Leo didn't respond.

'It seems sensible,' he finally said and a sudden, choking rage filled her, made her unable to speak.

'You bastard,' she finally managed, her voice thick with tears. 'Have you meant *anything* you've ever said? Do you even know how to be real or honest or *anything*?'

'Probably not.'

Alyse pressed her fists to her eyes and drew a shuddering breath. Now was not the time for tears. She'd have plenty of time, endless amounts, later to weep, to mourn. 'Leo.' She dropped her hands and forced herself to meet his cold, blank gaze. 'What about these last few weeks? What about how things changed between us, about how you said—'

'How I didn't know how much I had to give?' he filled in, a mocking edge to his voice. 'Well, now I do, and it turns out it's not all that much.'

'Why are you doing this?' she whispered. 'When just last night—'

'That was last night.' He swung around sharply, his hands jammed in his pockets as he stared out the window once more.

'And the fact that you won't be king changes your feelings towards me?' Alyse asked helplessly. 'I don't understand how that happens—'

'It was a *week*, Alyse. Ten days at most.' His voice echoed through the room with the sharp report of a rifle as he turned back to face her. 'A single bloody week. And yes, there were very nice parts, and the intensity made both of us think it could turn into more, which is understandable. We were looking at a marriage, after all, and trying to find a way to make it work.'

'We're still looking at a marriage—'

'No,' he answered flatly, 'we're not.'

It was like hammering on an iron door, she thought hopelessly, battering her fists and her heart against a stone wall. There was simply no way inside him, no way to understand what was going on behind that cold mask.

'Don't do this, Leo,' she whispered, her voice breaking. 'Please.' He gave no answer, not even a flicker of emotion in his eyes or a grimacing twist of his mouth. 'So what is meant to happen now?' she asked, her voice turning to raw demand. 'Am I just meant to…leave? Are you kicking me out?'

'Of course not. You may stay in the palace as long as you like. I'll leave.'

'Where will you—'

'It hardly signifies. I'll send you the paperwork.'

Alyse stared at him, those stern, hard features she'd come to know so well. Those mobile lips she'd kissed, the body she'd touched…*the heart she loved.*

She loved him, she knew that now, felt it inside her like a shining gold light, and Leo was doing his damnedest to extinguish it. They'd been married for ten days.

'Please,' she said one last time, and he didn't reply. Didn't move, didn't even blink. Taking a deep, shuddering breath, Alyse slowly turned and walked out of the room.

She walked down the corridor with its crystal chandeliers and sumptuous carpet, barely aware of her surroundings, or the liveried footmen standing to attention as she came to the top of the double staircase that led down into the palace's entrance hall. Her mind was spinning and she tasted acid in her mouth. Swallowing hard, she sank onto a spindly little gilt bench, her head in her hands.

'Your Highness—' One of the footmen started forward in concern.

'Just leave me,' she whispered, her head still in her hands. 'Please.' The footman stepped back. Alyse tried to marshal her thoughts. What would she do now? Where would she go? Her entire life, since she was eighteen years old and little more than a naïve child, had been oriented towards being Leo's wife, Maldinia's queen, and now that was taken away from her she was left spinning in a void of uncertainty.

Why was he doing this? Why didn't he believe their marriage was worth saving, that she loved him?

Just like you loved him when you were eighteen? When you told him you loved him, and then took it back? And haven't told him since, haven't trusted that any of this is real?

Could she really blame Leo for doubting not just his feelings, but her own? *She'd* doubted them. She'd insisted she was in love with him once, only for him to prove her disastrously wrong. Was it any wonder he doubted? His whole life people had been telling him they loved him— his parents, his brother, and they'd all, in their own way, been liars.

Why should he think she was any different?

She straightened, her gaze unseeing as thoughts tumbled through her mind. Did she love him now, a real, strong love, not the girlish fancy of before? She felt the answer in her heart, beating with strong, sure certainty.

Yes.

And she'd never told him. She'd begged him to change his mind, had acted as if it was all up to him, when she was the one who needed to take control. Who could be strong.

Her legs felt shaky as she stood up and walked slowly back to the apartment where she knew Leo waited. Where her heart, her whole life, waited.

Taking a deep breath, letting the air buoy her lungs, she opened the door and stepped into the room.

Leo sat on the bed, his elbows braced on his knees, his head lowered. Alyse's heart ached at the sight of his wretchedness even as new hope flickered to life within her heart. This wasn't a man unaffected by what just happened, the man who had coldly stared her down and almost—almost—won.

'Leo.'

He looked up, blinking as if she were an apparition. Alyse saw grief etched in the lines of his face before he deliberately blanked his expression. She knew how he did that now. She was starting to understand why. 'What are you doing here?'

'I want to finish our conversation.'

'I think our conversation is quite finished, Alyse. There's nothing more to say.'

'I have something more to say.'

'Oh?' He arched one eyebrow, coldly skeptical, but Alyse knew it was only a mask. At least, she hoped it was only a mask, that underneath the stern coldness beat the heart of the warm, generous man she'd come to know—and love. Yet even now fear and doubt skittered along her spine, crept into her mind. She forced them back.

'You told me once you wanted there to be no lies or pretence between us.' He jerked his head in a tiny nod, and Alyse made herself continue despite the fear coursing through her veins. 'And I don't want there to be either. So if you're going to dissolve our marriage, ask for a divorce, then you need to give me the real reason.'

'I did give you the real reason.'

'I don't think you did.'

His mouth tightened. 'That's not my problem, Alyse.'

'No, it's mine. Because I haven't been honest either. I've been so afraid—afraid of losing you by pushing too

hard or asking for too much. And afraid of my own feelings, if I could trust them.' He didn't respond, but she saw
a wary alertness in his eyes and knew he was listening.
Emboldened, she took a step forward. 'I really did believe
I loved you all those years ago, you know,' she said softly.
'And then when I started to get to know you properly, I
began to doubt the feelings I'd had…just as you doubted
them.' She hesitated, wanting to be honest yet needing to
search for the words. 'It was a terrible feeling, to realise
I'd fooled myself for so long. It made me wonder if I could
ever trust my feelings—my own heart—again. Or if anyone else could. Like you.'

Still nothing from him, but Alyse kept on. She sat next
to him on the bed, her thigh nudging his, needing his
touch, his warmth. 'I've come to understand just a little
how you must have endured the same thing. Your parents
telling you they love you, but only for the cameras. Not
really meaning it.' She waited, but he didn't answer. 'And
your brother too—leaving you like that. You were close,
weren't you?'

His throat worked and he glanced away. 'Yes,' he said,
and his voice choked.

She laid a hand on his arm. 'For your whole life people
have been letting you down, Leo, pretending they love you
and then doing something else. Is it any wonder you're
afraid of relationships, of love, now? I'm afraid and I didn't
have that experience.'

'I'm not afraid—'

'Don't lie to me. Love is scary, even when you don't
have the kind of emotional baggage you do. Or I do, for
that matter. Pretending we're in love for six years didn't
do either of us any favours.'

'That's why I want this marriage to end. No more pretending. No more lies.'

Alyse drew a deep breath. 'So you'd be telling the truth

if you said you didn't feel anything for me?' No answer, but at least a vigorous *yes* hadn't sprung to his lips. 'Because I wouldn't. I do feel something for you, Leo. Something I didn't trust at first because of everything that had gone before. And maybe I'm still not exactly sure what love is, what it feels like, but with every moment I'm with you I believe I feel it for you.' She took another breath and let it out slowly. 'I love you, Leo.'

He let out a short, hard laugh. 'I've heard that before.'

'I know, which is why I've been so afraid of saying it again. What I felt for you before was a schoolgirl crush, a childish fancy. I was overwhelmed by how everything had moved so quickly, by the attention of the press, and the way my parents were thrilled—the whole world was thrilled. I wanted the fairy tale, and so I bought into it.' She reached for his hand, laced her fingers through his. He didn't, at least, pull away or even resist. 'But this last week has shown me that love isn't a fairy tale, Leo. It's hard and painful and messy. It hurts. And yet it's also wonderful, because when I'm with you there's nowhere else I'd rather be.' Still no words from him, but she felt him squeeze her fingers slightly, and hope began to unfurl inside her. 'I love seeing you smile, hearing you laugh, feeling you inside me. And I love the fact that I've come to know you, that I can tell when you're amused or annoyed or angry or hurt. That I recognise the way you try to veil your expression and hide your pain. That I know when you're reading something that bores you in the newspaper but you keep reading anyway because you just *have* to finish the page.'

Leo's lips twitched in an almost-smile and Alyse laughed softly, no more than a breath of sound. 'Loving someone is knowing them,' she continued quietly. 'I didn't understand that at first. I thought it was a lightning bolt, or an undeniable rush of feeling. But it's more than that. It's *understanding* a person inside and out. I can't pretend

I understand you completely, but I think I'm beginning to. I'm starting to see how a childhood of pretending—a lifetime of pretending—has made you not just doubt other people's feelings, but your own. You told me you loved me when we were on television, and I was afraid to believe you. I think you were afraid to believe yourself. That's why you tried to deny it afterwards. It's why I didn't press the matter. All out of fear.'

He gazed down at their intertwined hands, his thumb sliding over her fingers. 'You did say love was scary,' he said in a low voice.

'Absolutely. It's terrifying. But I also think it's worth it—it's worth the risk of being hurt. Loneliness might be easier, but it's bleak too.' She squeezed his fingers, imbuing him with her strength. Her hope. 'I don't expect you to love me yet. I know we both need time to learn to trust each other. To know each other. But I'm asking you, Leo—I'm begging you, give us that chance. Don't turn away from our marriage just because you're not going to be king. I never cared about you being king. I was scared of being queen. I just want to be with you.'

'That's not why I turned away.'

She stilled, her fingers frozen in his. 'No?'

He took a deep breath. 'I turned away because I was afraid. Because I've learned it's easier to be the first one to pull away, before you're pushed.'

'And you thought I'd...I'd push you? Because you weren't king?'

'I don't know what I thought, to be honest.' He glanced up, his gaze hooded, his eyes dark with pain. 'I was acting on instinct, shutting down, closing up. It's what I've always done, and I knew I had to do it with you. You've had more power to hurt me than anyone else, Alyse. Do you know how utterly terrifying that is?'

She managed a shaky smile, felt the sting of tears

behind her lids. 'Yes,' she answered. 'As a matter of fact, I do.'

'You're wrong, you know. I don't need time to learn to love you, or know you. I already do. I didn't mean to say that on television—the words just spilled out. It was as if I couldn't *keep* from saying them. I had to be honest about how I felt, not just to you, but to the whole world.'

Alyse felt her mouth curve in an understanding smile. 'And then as soon as you were, you wanted to take it all back.'

'Self-protection, just a little too late.'

'This is hard, no question.'

'As soon as you left the room I wanted to run after you. Take it all back. Beg—just like I used to beg my mother to spend time with me, to *love* me, or my brother not to leave.' He was quiet for a moment, his gaze still on their twined hands. 'He was a hero to me, you know. I adored him. He always looked out for me at school, he felt like the only person who really knew me—'

'And he left,' Alyse finished softly. 'He left you.'

'I can't really blame him. The atmosphere in the palace has always been toxic, and he had it worse than I did, buried under my parents' expectations.' Leo sighed and shook his head. 'But yes, he left, and it hurt. A lot. I told myself I'd never be like that again, needing someone so much, begging them to stay.'

Her heart ached and she blinked back tears. 'I'm sorry.'

'I don't know what kind of relationship we can have, now that he's back.'

'You'll find a way. Love endures, Leo. And you still love him.'

He nodded slowly. 'Yes, I suppose I do.'

It was, she knew, a big admission for him to make. And yet she needed more; *they* needed more. 'And what about

us, Leo?' Alyse touched his cheek, forced him to meet
her soft gaze. 'What kind of relationship can we have?'

His navy gaze bored into hers, searching for answers,
and then his mouth softened in a slight smile. 'A good one,
I hope. A marriage…a real marriage. If you'll have me.'

'You know I will.'

He turned his head so his lips brushed her fingers.
'I'm not saying I won't make mistakes. I will, I'm sure of
it. This still terrifies me, now more than ever. I've never
loved anyone before, not like this.'

'Me neither,' Alyse whispered.

'I don't want to hurt you,' he continued, his voice turning ragged. 'I love you, Alyse, so much, but I'm afraid—
afraid that I will—'

'That's part of loving someone,' she answered, her voice
clogged with tears, tears of happiness, of hope and relief
and pure emotion, rather than sorrow. 'The joy and the
pain. I'll take both, Leo, with you.'

Yet as his arms came around her and his lips found hers
in a soft and unending promise, Alyse knew only joy. The
joy, the wondrous joy, of being known and loved.

* * * * *

DOCTOR'S GUIDE TO DATING IN THE JUNGLE

TINA BECKETT

To my amazing husband who believed I could
succeed at anything I put my hand to.

With special thanks to my fabulous critique
partners at Write Romance. I owe you ladies
so much!

And to the amazing bunch of writers who hang
out in Subcare over at eharlequin.com.
The hand holding and support found there is
beyond compare.

CHAPTER ONE

'ALL we're doing is pasting a bandage over a gaping wound.'

Dr. Matt Palermo, in the middle of resectioning a femoral artery, ignored the exasperated mutter from the doctor beside him, knowing his colleague wasn't speaking literally. The neighboring gurney housed an injury just as frightening as the one Matt was working on. Except the patient's foot was long gone, lost somewhere in the depths of the rainforest.

The quick shrug of his shoulders had nothing to do with indifference and everything to do with dabbing a stray bead of perspiration that threatened to contaminate his surgical site. That was, if the sticky heat and buzzing flies hadn't already coated all the equipment with noxious bacteria.

He fought the frustration that rose in his throat. He knew exactly what the doctor to his left was going through. Hadn't he experienced the same overwhelming sense of hopelessness when he'd first come to this part of the Amazon? He still felt it at times. But that had had nothing to do with Brazil and everything to do with burying a large chunk of his heart in Tennessee. Even his bout with break-bone fever a couple of years ago couldn't compare to the agonizing phrase that had changed his life for ever: *I'm sorry; we did everything we could.*

He shook off the memory and eyed the newly closed artery, checking it manually for leaks. Satisfied with the job, he prepared to close.

'You need any help?' he asked, risking a quick glance at the other doctor, who now sat slumped in a chair while his patient slept on, unaware that life as he knew it was over.

Just like Matt's had been.

'I'm done.' Averted eyes and fingers scraping through hair that was stiff with a mixture of sweat and hair gel told Matt those two words would prove prophetic. After the city guy's two-week stint down the Amazon on the medical boat was over, he'd catch the first flight home to Chicago. He'd go back to his urban medical practice. Back to his pristine surgical suite and soft piped-in music. He wouldn't be coming back to Brazil.

Ever.

And Matt would again be left to fight the losing battle of man against nature.

Alone.

The blast of heat punched hard and fast as Stevie Wilson stepped from the cocooning shelter of the plane. She had to lock her knees and force herself to remain upright, or she'd end up melting onto the shiny black tarmac that danced and shimmered around her.

Wow. Coari was even hotter than she'd expected.

A quick tap of her hand sent her sunglasses toppling from their perch on her head to the bridge of her nose, where they cut the glare of the sun by half. She gave a sigh of relief and headed toward the worker who was busy tossing suitcases and foot lockers from the underbelly of the ancient aircraft.

'Oi, Senhor! Cuidado com a mala vermelha, por favor.'

The man smiled and gave her a thumbs-up signal, and then, despite her request to the contrary, dropped her medical bag with a *thunk* onto the growing mound of luggage.

She winced. 'Things can only get better from here, right, Stevie?'

Moving a few yards toward the vacant exterior of the airport terminal, she prayed someone was inside to meet her. She'd only dealt with the director of *Projeto Vida*, and though the woman had been cordial, she'd given a noncommittal 'Have the applicant e-mail his full résumé, including qualifications and a copy of his medical license. We'll get back to him.' She'd rung off before Stevie had a chance to admit the 'friend' she'd been calling for was actually herself.

Much to her shock, after sending in the requested information, she'd received an affirmative response, along with a list of necessary vaccinations and visa requirements. A month later, here she was.

Free and clear.

Free from her lying fiancé-cum-hospital-director and the political maelstrom that had arisen in the wake of their broken engagement. Free from the subtly averted eyes of the nursing staff that had torn at her heart and shredded her confidence.

She was free to do what she'd gone into medicine to do: treat those in need. And if traveling down the Amazon on a floating hospital ship was the only way she could meet that goal, so be it.

She tugged her sticky cotton shirt away from her body and fanned it against her ribcage, hoping her deodorant proved to be as Kevlar-strong as the ads claimed. A flatbed cart raced by, heading toward the growing mountain of luggage. Well, at least she didn't have to worry about unearthing the rest of her bags from that stack. Except that if her medical bag was now on top of the heap, it would soon be…

Turning, she took off at a sprint towards the pile and waved frantically at the two men. They stopped what they were doing, obviously wondering what the crazed foreigner was so upset about this time. She skidded to a stop and motioned to her bag, telling them what she wanted in Portuguese. Well, *continental* Portuguese, which she'd been told was different than the Brazilian version of the language, but it was all she had.

They evidently understood because the thumbs-up signs were again flashed in her direction before her bag was plucked from the stack and handed down—rather than tossed, this time.

'*Obrigada.*' She pulled a couple of small bills from her wallet and handed them to the men, directing them to her bags and asking if they'd bring them to the terminal for her. They nodded as she righted her case and set it on its wheels so she could tow it behind her.

A minute later, she was inside the main building, where the lack of air-conditioning—or even a fan—made the closed space seem more oppressive than the air outside. A rivulet of sweat ran down her back, lodging in the waistband of her low-rider jeans. Glancing around, she saw no one, other than employees and the fellow passengers who'd boarded the air taxi with her in Manaus. Stevie wondered for the first time if she'd made the right decision in coming. She'd expected—if not a giddy cheer by a pack of overworked doctors—at least one person to meet her at the airport and help her get to the boat.

Making her way to the desk, she asked if anyone had mentioned meeting a doctor here today.

'Ninguém, Senhora, desculpa.'

Not the answer she'd hoped to hear. She moved away from the counter and stood in the center of the room just as a wave of panic broke over the top of her. Despite her sensible flat sandals, her legs wobbled threateningly. Ignoring the scolding she'd just given the baggage handler over her medical bag, she shoved the telescoping handle into place and plunked herself down on the hard plastic casing. She dropped her handbag onto the cracked concrete floor beside her, wondering if she needed to put her head between her knees. No, then she might miss whoever was coming to pick her up. She settled for propping her elbows on her thighs and sinking her chin into her cupped palms.

Slow, deep breaths. That's it.

Surely she wasn't going to be abandoned.

A door on the other side of the building swung open and a man appeared, his gaze sweeping across the interior of the terminal as he strode toward the ticket counter. His height and close-fitting khaki slacks—as opposed to the uber-casual clothing worn by the male workers—marked him as an outsider. She couldn't quite see his eyes, but Stevie sat up straighter anyway and attempted a smile, praying this was her ride. But his glance merely clipped hers as he went by, a frown now marring the tanned flesh between thick, dark brows. He continued on to the desk and spoke in hushed tones, his black polo shirt pulling taut across powerful shoulders as he leaned over the counter. When the woman's hand swept in Stevie's direction, her heart leaped and she waved, stopping in midstream when he looked right past her.

As if she were invisible!

The flicker of hope went out, and she cringed at how desperate her madly waving arm must have appeared.

Desperate with a capital D.

She forced back her thoughts before they took a more destructive path. The man wasn't rejecting her personally, he was simply here to meet someone else.

'*Onde?*' he asked the woman at the counter, his voice loud enough for Stevie to hear this time.

'*A loira sentada na mala, senhor.*'

The blonde sitting on the suitcase? She glanced behind her just to be sure. There was no one sitting on a suitcase, except for...

The words slowly sank in. Oh, no. Surely not.

If her expression was horrified, the man's was doubly so. Triply so, if the brackets now etching the sides of his mouth were anything to go by.

He stalked toward her, every step appearing a battle of wills, one that he seemed determined to win. Stopping in front of her, he paused. 'Is this some kind of joke?'

'Excuse me?' Her neck had to crane back to look up at him, and her sunglasses slid off her head in the process, crashing to the floor. She ignored them, forcing herself to keep meeting those icy blue eyes.

'I'm here to meet Dr. Stefan Wilson,' he said, mangling her first name.

Stevie bit her lip, realizing just how tall he actually was, especially from her perch on the suitcase. If she weren't so worried about the still-shaky condition of her legs, she'd stand up. 'It's Stefani, not Stefan. 'Dr. *Stefani* Wilson. Most people call me Stevie, though.'

He shoved a hand through his hair and swore, before pulling a folded group of papers from one of his back trouser pockets. He took his time opening them and going over the documents. 'It says Stefan on the application. I was expecting a man.'

She gulped. Maybe he really was rejecting her.

Taking the papers he handed her, Stevie perused them, frowning over the missing 'i' on the application. So that's why he'd brushed her off earlier. 'I don't understand. I filled this out online and sent it to the director of *Projeto Vida* myself.'

She flipped the pages until she found her license. 'Here. See? It says Stefani, right here on my medical license. I also included a copy of my passport photo...hmm, which doesn't seem to be here either.'

'Great.' He took the papers and jammed them back into his pocket then looked off into the distance. 'Looks like the joke's on me.'

A woman.

Matt couldn't believe Tracy would have the nerve, when he'd specifically asked for a *male* doctor. She knew what this job was like. So far, no one—not even the last three men who'd signed up for the position—had been able to endure the tough working conditions. And Tracy thought this little scrap of a person could? That she'd be able to hack off a putrid, rotting leg, if the situation called for it?

He took in her white blouse, which clung to her curves wherever perspiration had gathered, becoming almost sheer in spots. At least it was thin and cool, which was so... *Practical* was the only word he allowed himself.

Even as the unlikely description bounced around his skull, he noticed a heavy droplet of moisture beside the coil of wheat-colored hair. As he watched, it slid down the side of her neck, gathering speed until it dipped into her collarbone. It hesitated as if unsure where to go next, then found the right path and headed down. Straight down. He swallowed and tore his eyes from the sight.

'Forget it. You're not staying.' He sent her a glare that he hoped would send her fleeing back to whatever cushy hospital job she'd left behind. If she was looking for adventure, she'd come to the wrong place. And he sure didn't need his mind wandering into areas it didn't belong.

'Forget it? You've got to be kidding me! I've just traveled four thousand miles to get here.' Her eyes flashed a warning. 'I'll have you know I'm a well-qualified vascular surgeon—'

'For which there's little use in the jungle.' He ignored the silent voice that reminded him he could have used her skills on the leg wound he'd treated a month and a half earlier.

'I've also done a year's residency in the emergency room, which means I'm well versed in the art of triage.'

'The *art* of triage?' He gave a hard laugh. 'It may be an art form where you come from, but battlefield triage is something completely different.'

Her head came up, and a vein in the damp skin just below her jaw pulsed with what could be either anger or fear. He'd bet fear. Good. That meant she'd soon be running back home, like Craig had done before her. And Mark before that.

And he'd bet his life he'd never *once* stared at a pulse point in either man's neck.

A baggage carrier came up behind them and set three giant red bags beside her, color-coordinated matches of the one she was currently sitting on. They were all spotless, evidently purchased just for this trip.

It figured.

He was surprised there weren't white roses embroidered across the fronts of them, or little save-the-rainforest slogans like the ones Craig had had on several of his T-shirts.

The carrier held up three fingers as if asking if these were all of her bags.

The woman in front of him gave the ubiquitous thumbs-up signal. The carrier nodded and hurried away without even waiting for a tip. Probably knew it was a lost cause.

Matt rolled his eyes. She knew nothing about this culture. 'I bet you don't even speak Portuguese.'

'Well, that's a bet you'd surely lose. And as far as 'battlefield triage' goes, the last time I checked my history books, Brazil was a pacifistic nation.' She scooped up the sunglasses, which lay broken on the floor, and dumped the remains into the open handbag that sat beside her. Picking up her purse, she stood to her feet, the top of her head barely reaching his chin.

'You can't learn everything about a country from a history book.'

'Ri-ght.'

The sing-song intonation she gave the word only served to tick him off further. *Women.* When he got hold of Tracy, he was going to give her hell.

But Tracy wasn't here at the moment, and Dr. Stefani Wilson was. 'I don't think you and this job are going to mesh.'

She hitched her handbag higher onto her shoulder, but there was now a hint of wariness in her gaze that made him frown. 'Is that right? You know…I don't believe I caught your name.'

'Matt. Matt Palermo.'

'Well, Mr. Palermo. Why don't you let me worry about whether the job and I are going to suit each other? If you'll just take me to Tracy Hinton—who evidently felt I was adequately qualified for this position—I'll soon be out of your hair.'

'Not bloody likely.'

'Meaning?'

'Two things. One, if you take this job you won't be "out of my hair" for a very long time. And, two, Tracy obviously didn't inform you of the living arrangements.'

'She spelled it out quite nicely. She and I will be living on a hospital boat, traveling from village to village. We'll be out for weeks at a time.'

'You…and Tracy.' He nodded, a small smile coming to his face when he realized she had no idea who he was. And he wondered if that was a simple mistake, or if Tracy had her hand in that as well.

'Yes. Why? Don't you think two women can handle the job?'

'What I think has no bearing on anything, or Tracy never would have hired you.'

'What an awful thing to say.'

'Not really. And Tracy won't be the one living with you.'

She blinked once, then again, his response evidently surprising her. 'Okay, so it'll be another doctor. It doesn't really matter who it is.'

'Doesn't it?'

A hand went to her stomach and she plucked at the hem of her shirt. 'Not at all.'

'So it wouldn't bother you to discover that we—you and I—will be living together, if you take this job.' He caught sight of a pale sliver of skin beneath her blouse as she fiddled with it. He forced the rest of the words from his suddenly dry mouth. 'We'll be under the same roof. For weeks at a time. Possibly months.'

She sucked down an audible breath and held it for a second or two before the muscles of her throat relaxed. 'I can handle it, if you can. Besides, there'll be another doctor on board to play chaperone, if you're worried about me throwing myself at you.' Her brows arched. 'Are you the ship's captain or something? The cook?'

He laughed. 'Unfortunately for you, it's neither of the above. And if you get on that boat, you'll have to put up with me 24-7.'

'Because?' Her teeth came down on her lower lip as if she realized something terrible was heading her way.

'Because *I'll* be your traveling companion, not Tracy. And I happen to be the only critical-care doctor within a hundred-mile radius.'

CHAPTER TWO

STEVIE perched on the seat of the Land Rover, keeping her body braced against the passenger side door as they navigated around the worst of the potholes. The ones they couldn't avoid, they plowed straight through.

With her teeth clicking together like castanets, she tried to gather her wits. Okay, so the introduction to her new job wasn't going quite like she'd expected. No cheering, no gratitude. Just a doctor who acted like he'd rather she drop off the face of the earth.

So what? She wasn't here to bask in anyone's praise. She'd come to help people.

The memory of Michael's laughter when she'd shown him the article on *Projeto Vida* swept through her mind. 'Seriously?' he'd said. 'What kind of person practices medicine in the jungle?'

Too embarrassed to admit she found the idea fascinating, she'd laughed along with him and had quickly blanked out the computer screen. The truth was, she'd toyed with the idea for the past year. She used to think Michael felt the same way, that he wanted to give back to those in need. Why else would he be at the helm of a public hospital?

Certainly not just to commandeer a private room for his little no-tell rendezvous, like the one she'd caught him having with a female doctor. On her birthday, of all things.

Humiliation and pain washed through her, bringing with it an inner scream of frustration. Why couldn't she get past this?

She must have made some sound because her new colleague's

head swiveled toward her. She squirmed in her seat before tilting her chin a bit higher.

Just because the good doctor wasn't thrilled about having her on board it didn't mean she should tuck her tail and go scurrying back to New York—no matter how much she wanted to right now. She'd agreed to stay for two years, and she intended to see them through, down to the very last day.

'So, why leave New York and come to our little neck of the rainforest?'

She gave a guilty start. He couldn't possibly know what she'd been thinking. 'Why do people normally do these types of things?'

His eyes searched hers before turning back to the road. 'Sometimes they don't think through the realities like they should.'

'And sometimes they just want to help.'

'Right. The last two doctors who "wanted to help," ended up leaving before they'd been here a month. It would have been better if they'd just mailed *Projeto Vida* a check.'

'Money can take the place of qualified doctors these days?'

His hands tightened on the wheel. 'No, but it doesn't help our cause when the faces change each time the boat pulls into a village.'

Interesting.

'You're talking about earning people's trust.'

'Yep. And it's mighty hard to come by these days.'

No kidding. She knew that for a fact.

She turned in her seat, her attitude softening a bit as she watched him shove a dark lock of hair off his forehead with an attitude of resignation. 'Every time someone leaves, you're the one who has to break the news to the villagers, aren't you? How long have you been with *Projeto Vida*?'

'Long enough.'

'Maybe it's time you started thinking about packing it in yourself, Dr. Palermo.'

'No.' He glanced back at her. 'And if you're going to take a trial run down the river with me, you'll need to call me Matt.

We try to be as informal as possible. The villagers will use your first name as well.'

She ignored the last part of his speech and concentrated on the first. 'Trial run? I signed up for two years.'

He grunted. 'So did the others.'

'Maybe I'm tougher than they were.' She smiled at him. 'Maybe I'm even as tough as you.'

Dark brows winged upward. 'Doubtful.'

'That sounds suspiciously like a challenge.'

'Does it?'

Stevie could swear his lips twitched as he said it and that the grooves where his frown lines sat became a little less pronounced. 'It does. And you might be sorry later, because I rarely back down from a challenge.'

Unless it came from her cheating ex as she'd hightailed it for the nearest exit. *If you leave now, you'll have a black mark on your record!* His shouted warning had cemented her decision to leave the hospital. To leave him.

'We'll soon see, won't we?' said Matt.

One of his tanned hands dropped from the wheel to the seat between them. There was a fresh cut across the knuckle of his middle finger that looked deep, and several old scars marring the back of his hand. Something about those hurts, old and new, made her stomach twist. This was a man who didn't play it safe. Who put his all into everything he did. That was something Stevie could relate to. She'd gained a few new scars of her own over the last month or so.

'You use protection, don't you?'

He glanced over, eyebrows high. 'Excuse me?'

Oops. That hadn't come out right.

'Surgical gloves,' she clarified, touching a spot just beneath his cut, not sure where the urge came from. 'Especially when you have injuries.'

He curled his fingers into a fist, the muscles in his forearm bunching. 'Of course.'

'Good.' She gave a brisk nod as if the heat from his skin hadn't just singed her. As if she wasn't scrubbing her fingertips across her thigh in a vain attempt to remove the sensation.

He frowned, and Stevie realized he'd seen her reaction. Heat prickled along her scalp, and she turned her head to look out at the scenery. 'How long until we get to the boat?'

'About a half-hour.' They hit another pothole, and she scrabbled for a handhold to avoid careening off the seat and onto the floorboards.

'Sorry,' he said. 'I keep forgetting you're not used to roads like this.'

'It's okay. At least it's not one big construction zone, like in New York.'

'Which is why the roads there don't swallow small children.'

She blinked. Wow, did the man actually have a sense of humor? Her mouth opened to respond when his cellphone went off.

He braked, fumbling to pull the phone from the holder on his belt. Stevie glanced back to make sure there were no cars heading their way, but the road was deserted, which made it odd that he'd stopped at all. Maybe he was a little more cautious than she'd thought.

''Ello?' He listened for a few seconds looking straight ahead. 'Yep, she's here. Listen, I told you what I wanted. Surely there were other appli—'

He sighed. 'Just keep looking, will you?'

Her brows went up. So much for his 'changing faces isn't good for the cause' spiel. It didn't stop him from trying to swap her face for someone else's post haste. Which meant she'd be out of a job, unless she went crawling back to Michael.

Fat chance of that happening.

'I don't know. She had quite a pile of suitcases, but she didn't say anything about... Hold on.' Matt pulled the phone away from his ear, glancing her way. 'Mosquito nets?'

She nodded. 'A hundred and fifty of them, just like Tracy asked for. I also brought a case of repellent wipes for use on board the boat.' She frowned. 'Don't tell me you actually thought I had clothes in all those suitcases?'

* * *

Matt suddenly found himself unable to meet her eyes. Okay, so he'd misjudged her on one count. 'Yeah, she brought them,' he said into the phone.

'Good,' said Tracy. A few seconds of silence crawled by. 'Listen, give her a chance, will you? You and I both know you need another doctor on that boat. So don't say anything stupid.' A laugh rose in his throat, which he quickly suppressed. Too late. He'd already said several stupid things. And for the past few minutes he'd suddenly realized how lonely his job was. The simple touch of Stefani's fingers and the concern in her voice when she'd noticed the scratch on his hand had hit him in a dark corner of his mind.

He sent her a quick glance to find her staring out the side window in an obvious attempt not to eavesdrop. A long strand of hair had come loose from her bun and now trailed down her cheek, the tip curling just above her shoulder.

A strange sense of longing swept over him. What had Tracy been thinking, sending a woman? Didn't she realize how flammable this situation could become? He tried to snuff out the image of Stefani's long nimble fingers sliding across his skin, her surgeon's brain dissecting and memorizing his every reaction. Or her long dark lashes fluttering shut as he...

He shook his head, realizing Tracy was waiting for his response. 'Right. "Don't say anything stupid." I'll do my best.'

She laughed. 'Don't make me come down there.'

As much as he wanted Tracy to witness her folly firsthand, he knew he couldn't afford to hang around the port and do nothing. Waiting for Stefani's arrival had already put him two days behind schedule, and he had people counting on him. As soon as they got to the boat, they needed to be on their way.

'Your concern is duly noted, but I'm a big boy, in case you haven't noticed.'

'Oh, I have. And I'm counting on you to act like one.'

Paint—long peeling ribbons of white—clung to portions of the boat. Other sections were laid bare, like bones stripped of their flesh. Stevie could have been looking in a mirror at her own reflection.

She was pretty sure this wasn't what Matt had in mind when he'd mentioned battlefield triage, but the vessel certainly looked like it had been through a warzone.

And come out on the losing end.

This couldn't be the medical boat. She tugged the doorhandle on the Land Rover and stepped out of the car, while Matt went around and hauled her luggage from the back of the vehicle.

The wall-to-wall grins on the faces of two men who'd disembarked from the ship and now hurried toward them said her premonition was correct. This vessel was indeed going to be her home for the next two weeks. Who was she kidding? Try two years. She shut her eyes and sent up a quick prayer. She'd put her name on a contract, effectively signing away her life. She'd see the far side of thirty before she left Brazil.

Matt smiled at the new arrivals and clapped each of them on the back before introducing them to her. 'Nilson and Tiago, this is Stefani Wilson, the newest member of our team.'

Everything was said in Portuguese, so she should have understood it easily, but Stevie found herself having to concentrate to make out the words through their thick accents. But they were friendly and welcoming, more than she could say for Matt. The two crew members gathered up her luggage as if it weighed no more than a couple of sacks of groceries and took off toward the ship.

She bit her lip, her hopes of being mistaken fading. Even if the men weren't already scampering up the gangplank, the raggedy lettering on the back of the boat spelled her fate out in no uncertain terms: *Projeto Vida*. This was the medical ship, for better or worse.

'Home, sweet home.' Low graveled tones slid across her senses like calloused hands moving over soft skin.

Palpable. Dangerous.

Shivering, she glanced up to find his attention fastened on the boat and not on her. Anything that could wring that kind of reaction out of the man couldn't be all bad. Right?

Maybe she should try to see the ship from his perspective. 'So this is it, then?'

He nodded, the warm affection in his eyes cooling as he studied her face. 'Ready to run away yet?'

'I don't run.'

'No?'

The way he said it made her wonder if he knew more about her situation than he was letting on. But so what if he did? She had nothing to hide.

Except for the tattered remnants of her heart. And the disciplinary note in her file.

Her lips tightened. She wasn't hiding those either. She'd told Tracy that her 'friend' had had a run-in with his hospital, but that he'd done nothing wrong. Why, then, had she hidden her identity at first? Though, after receiving her résumé, Tracy had to have realized Stevie had been talking about herself on the phone that day.

'No, I'm not going to run.' Not this time. Not even if the boat had the name 'Typhoid Mary' inscribed on its side.

She slapped at a mosquito on her arm and immediately wondered if it was a carrier of some deadly ailment. Running didn't seem like such a bad option all of a sudden.

'You'll need to wear repellent. They seem to attack newcomers more than residents. Must have sweeter blood or something.'

'I bet they don't attack you at all,' she said, then realized how childish the words sounded.

A muscle worked in his jaw and one hand went to the back of his neck and rubbed as if trying to ease a knot from the firm muscles. 'Ready to get to work?'

'That's why I'm here.' The sharp tone made her cringe. 'Ugh, sorry. Chalk up my bad manners to jet lag, okay?'

'No problem.' He lowered his hand and rotated his neck half a turn. Stevie heard several soft pops as the vertebrae along it cracked. He gave a low groan of relief.

'Do you have back problems?' No way would she admit she'd begun her education in chiropractic before switching to traditional medicine.

'Nothing serious. Just getting old.' But even as he said it, she noticed he slightly twisted his upper body—instead of just his neck—when looking down at her, a classic sign of pain. He'd been fine in the car when glancing over at her, so it was limited to one side. Her brain worked through possible diagnoses before she stopped herself.

It's none of your business, Stevie. Just leave it be.

'Shall we go aboard?' she asked.

'If you're sure you're up for it.'

Something about the way he said it made prickles rise along the nape of her neck. Surely the inside of the boat couldn't be in worse condition than the outside. She could understand being busy, but lack of hygiene and sterility were things she wouldn't stand for.

Once she stepped from the rickety dock onto the boat, her heart sank. More peeling paint and the deck's wooden surface was gouged and pitted. 'You see patients onboard?'

'Yes, in the exam-room-slash-surgical-suite.'

Surgical suite. Wow. And maybe they still bored holes in skulls, too. She forced her tongue to the roof of her mouth and held it there, where it couldn't flap around and say things she would later regret.

Their next stop was the galley. Stevie was relieved to find the food preparation area neat and tidy. 'Where do you get your drinking water?'

'The river. The filtration unit on the counter was donated by a relief agency. It's a three-stage system that filters out particles and then zaps the water with UV rays to kill most bacteria. We can send it through an additional stage that injects a chlorine solution in areas where cholera is endemic.' A lean finger hooked around the handle of an empty plastic bottle and lifted it. 'Before the filter, we had to carry clean water aboard in these, which made scrubbing for surgery a complicated affair.'

'I can imagine.' She wandered over to the rectangular unit. The metal casing was spotlessly clean. She relaxed a bit. Maybe things wouldn't be as bad as she'd feared. 'I knew filters like this existed, but wow. It looks like something NASA would have.'

'I hear the system used on the space station is similar.'

Matt lounged against a nearby doorframe, one shoulder propped against the wooden surface, observing her. Although lean, his body filled the opening, his dark silky hair brushing the top of the frame. She swallowed, feeling trapped all of a sudden and not sure why. He wasn't threatening in a scary kind of way.

She rephrased that thought. He was scary, but only because he made her blood rush through her veins simply by looking at her. And that made the man doubly dangerous, since she could no longer trust herself to make wise choices when it came to the opposite sex. Meeting problems head on might work for some people, but for Stevie, avoidance was now the name of the game. And that included avoiding the six-foot-two-inch problem who stood right in front of her.

'*Com licença, Mateus.*' The voice came from behind him, and Matt moved into the room to let the crew members pass.

Mateus, the Portuguese equivalent of Matthew.

So they *did* go by first names, just like Matt had said. She liked that. Michael would have insisted on formality at all costs. He'd said that to get respect, you had to demand respect. She used to agree, but now she wondered. That kind of respect could be lost in the blink of an eye—or behind the closed doors of an examination room. Besides, she sensed an admiration from these men that wasn't a result of social standing or titles, but something earned through time and trust.

Would she ever be included in their little circle? Probably not.

'We've put the new doctor's bags in your room.'

Dull color crept into Matt's face, and Stevie sensed her scalp heating as well. They'd put her bags in *his* room? She hovered between saying 'Thank you' and squeaking out the protest that scrabbled up her throat, seeking the nearest exit. Before she could do either, Matt wrapped a hand around her upper arm. 'I'll show you where your things are.'

As soon as they were through the door, she planted her heels to stop their forward motion, ignoring the way the warmth from his fingers burrowed beneath her skin. Uh-oh. There went that blood-rushing-through-the-veins sensation again.

She tugged free of his hold, furious with herself for having any kind of reaction at all.

'Why did they put my suitcases in your room? I don't know what's going on, but—'

'Not here. Let's get out of earshot, okay? They've already got enough to gossip about for the next two weeks. We all thought the new doctor was going to be…well, a man. Now you see why it's so complicated.'

She didn't. Not at all. 'Just have them move my bags to another room.'

His brows went up. 'You'd rather sleep with Nilson and Tiago in the crew's quarters, then?'

'What? No, of course not. There must be somewhere else.'

He walked down the narrow aisle, forcing her to follow him. She noted he had to hunch his shoulders to accommodate the low ceiling. 'There's not. The space is cramped as it is, there are no extra rooms.'

No wonder he'd flipped out when he'd realized 'Stefan' was a woman. Kind of hard to avoid someone when you had to share a bedroom with him. What was she going to do? Lordy, what if he only had one bed in that room?

She'd camp on deck if she had to.

And risk being devoured by mosquitoes?

Maybe.

They came to a doorway, and her heart raced as Matt pushed it open, motioning her through. She squeezed by him, careful not to touch, but all the precautions in the world couldn't prepare her for the clean masculine scent that followed her into the room. It permeated the space, branding everything in it as his. If she stayed here, would it mark her as well?

She swallowed and forced herself to take shallow breaths as she examined the room. Even with her suitcases piled one on top of the other in the corner, there was barely enough room for two people to stand, much less move about.

She went slack with relief, however, when she spotted two beds, rather than one. Thick woven hammocks, actually, one above the other. A shared mosquito net hung suspended from a hook, tied to the side with a worn bungee cord at the moment. But at night it would be set free, encasing both hammocks in a tight intimate circle. As if they were in their own little world.

Her hard-won composure finally cracked, allowing panic to ooze between the gaps as she stared at the folded blanket and pillow resting on the bottom hammock. A worn paperback—Tom Clancy's *The Sum of All Fears*—lay on top of the bedding. How apropos that title was.

Matt had mentioned seeing how tough she really was. They were about to find out.

Her laugh, when it came, was one cackle short of hysterical. 'Well, I guess this means you want me on top.'

CHAPTER THREE

Her on top? Matt pinched the bridge of his nose, trying to eradicate the image that sprang to mind.

'Don't worry, I'll bunk with the crew,' he said, his voice coming out as a croak.

She swung around, her green eyes shining with relief. 'But if their room is as small as this one…'

'We'll make do. I'll hang a third set of hooks above theirs for my hammock.'

She eyed the beds. 'That will put you almost flush against the ceiling. You'll have no room to move.'

Yeah, almost like being inside a fabric coffin. His fingers massaged his neck muscles, trying to get rid of the ache that just wouldn't quit. 'Whatever it takes.'

'You are aware that hot air rises, right? I'm already dripping with sweat, and I'm on the floor.' Her eyes went to the ceiling. 'It'll be like being in a slow roaster up there.'

Exasperation washed over him, and he dropped his hand, allowing it to slap against his thigh. 'Thanks for pointing out all the positive aspects of our situation.'

'No problem.' She licked her lips and paused. 'Listen, we're both adults, and it's not like you'll be able to see…anything once I'm in bed. I can wear gym shorts and a T-shirt rather than my PJs. If we leave the door open at night and restrict our dressing and undressing to the bathroom, we should be fine.'

Good suggestion—except that Matt didn't normally wear *anything* to bed. And he wasn't sure how he felt about looking up at night, knowing those sweet curves were lying just over his head, close enough so that all he had to do was reach up and…

'Give me a couple hours to think it over.' He backed out of the room and into the hallway.

She shrugged as if he were the one with the problem, not her. 'Suit yourself. Don't say I didn't offer.'

It would almost be better if she'd wiggled her hips and implied that the offer went beyond mere sleeping arrangements. Then he could ship her butt back to Manaus with a clean conscience. The last thing anyone needed was a messy two-week fling. And a long-term relationship was out of the question. Vickie had been it for him. Now that she was gone…

He had no doubt Stefani would be going home at the end of those two weeks, if not before. Even if she didn't turn tail and run, he'd already asked Tracy to keep looking for a replacement. Surely Stefani could understand his concerns now that she'd seen the conditions. It wasn't just him, he had the crew to think about—and some of the tribes were bound to have a problem with him bringing in an unattached female. If the vessel were bigger, having team members of the opposite sex might be more feasible. Or if he and Stephani were married…

Who was he kidding? Even the thought of marriage made his stomach tighten with dread.

'How about showing me the rest of the facilities?' she said, forcing his mind back to the situation at hand.

'Sure. Let me tell the men to get under way first.' He paused. 'Unless you'd like to go back to the airport now that you've seen the boat?'

Her shoulders straightened. 'I knew what I was signing on for.'

'That would normally be my cue to argue and give you one more chance to change your mind, but we're already behind schedule. And, as Tracy continually reminds me, I really could use the help. I'll be right back.'

Once he asked Nilson to cast off, he gave Stefani the tour, stopping by the restrooms first. He suppressed a smile when her nose wrinkled at the mention of river water being pumped in for showers. 'We do run it through a filter, so you won't find anything crawling through your hair when you're done.'

'Ugh. It's better *not* to put images like that in my head.'

When they arrived at the examination room, her eyes widened. 'This is amazing.' She glanced up at him. 'I have to admit, you had me worried for a while.'

He peered at the room, trying to see the space through her eyes. 'How so?'

'When I saw the outside of the boat and the…er, restroom… Let's just say I wondered what I might find in here. But it's spotless.' She touched the gleaming chrome handle of the scrub sink. 'Does this water come from the river as well?'

'Yes, but it goes through a steam process, then stored in a sterile tank prior to use.'

'It seems you've thought of everything. How are the instruments sterilized?'

'Same method. Afterwards, they're shrink-wrapped into kits. It's time-consuming, but we don't do many surgeries.'

She tucked a stray wisp of hair behind her ear, drawing his attention to her high cheekbones and long dark lashes. There was a china-doll delicacy to her that made him wonder what crazy impulse had led her to sign up for a tour down the Amazon. Was she trying to prove something to herself? To someone else?

Wandering to the center of the room, she paused between the twin stainless-steel exam tables. 'These are top of the line. This set up must have cost a small fortune.'

'Yes. Which is why the rest of the boat looks a little worse for wear.' It was a half-truth, and he wasn't sure why he felt the need to defend the ship's condition, but now that the words were out, he stubbornly expanded on them. 'We put as much money as possible into caring for our patients. As long as the ship is solid and in good mechanical order, I figure the doctors and crew can afford to scrimp on the little things.'

She laughed. 'Like real beds.'

'Actually, no. Hammocks are more practical. No risk of bedbug infestations or other creepy crawlies that can hide inside a mattress. And they're cooler than traditional beds. I think you'll be surprised at how comfortable they are.'

He omitted the fact that the beds swung gently with every movement, whether that movement came from the boat or from other, more sensual, activities.

She tilted her head and looked up at him as if she could read his thoughts. 'I'll have to re-evaluate some of my opinions.'

Time to put some space between them and the subject of beds. 'Anyway, as far as this particular room goes, we need to keep the risk of contamination to a minimum. Which means access is limited to doctors and patients.'

'Understood. Do you ever keep patients overnight?'

'On occasion. If we've had to operate, for example. Or if...' he forced air into his lungs '...one of the team becomes ill and we have to transport them to a major city.'

She paused, her eyes sliding across his face. Her pupils dilated, and compassion flared within their depths. 'You've had to do that, haven't you? Transport a team member.'

He couldn't go down this road. Not today. Trying to head off any further questions, he checked his watch, relieved to find it was almost noon. 'Let's go see what Tiago has come up with for lunch.'

Lunch turned out to be a one-pot meal called *caruru do Pará,* featuring dried shrimp and okra. It was unlike anything she'd ever tasted, but delicious just the same.

'Do you like it?' Matt asked, forking a piece of shrimp into his mouth.

'It's wonderful. I've never had okra in anything but jambalaya.'

Tiago, who she'd found out was the team's cook, nodded. 'Good, yes?'

Reverting to Portuguese, she asked what other kinds of dishes were popular in the region. Smiling, he rattled off several names, but the words were unfamiliar. It was amazing how two languages could be the same and yet so very different.

Matt must have noticed her confusion as well. Keeping the

conversation going in Portuguese, he asked, 'Your accent is different. Where did you learn the language?'

'I lived in Portugal for seven years as a child. My father worked at the American Embassy.'

'That explains it.'

His furrowed brow made her sit a bit taller. 'Is there something wrong with the way I speak?'

'Not at all. But you'll find sentence construction is a little different here.'

'I've noticed.'

Tiago spoke up. 'I think your accent is very nice, Miss Stefani.'

She smiled her thanks. 'Stefani is my formal name, but all my friends call me Stevie. Won't you do the same?'

'Sh-tée-vee?' He struggled to get the name out, and she noticed Nilson—busy manning the helm, his plate balanced on the control panel—mouthed the word as well.

'Perfect,' she said.

Matt just shook his head. 'From Stefan, to Stefani, to Stevie. No wonder I was confused about your gender.'

'And now? Are you still confused?'

'Confused?' His lips tilted in a sardonic smile. 'More than ever.'

With that cryptic statement he stood and walked to the sink, carrying his plate. Since Tiago and Nilson followed his lead, she shoveled one last mouthful of the delicious meal into her mouth and stood as well. 'Thank you so much for lunch. It was wonderful.'

'I'm glad you liked it.' After Matt ducked through the door, Tiago leaned in a bit closer and whispered, 'I think you will be good for Mateus. He misses his wife very much.'

Wife? Matt was married? Oh, Lordy, and she'd practically insisted on playing share-sies with his bedroom. What was she thinking?

'Where is she? His wife, I mean.' The words were out before she could stop them. But she wanted to know. Because other arrangements definitely had to be made. No wonder he'd offered to sleep with the crew. Her face flamed. She'd told him not to worry about her throwing herself at him and yet she'd offered to sleep right above the man's head. Surely he didn't think—

'His wife is…she's…' Tiago bowed his head and pointed skyward.

'What? I don't understand.' Her eyes widened as she realized what he was trying to say. 'Oh. I'm so sorry.'

He waved his hands in front of him. 'Please don't speak of it with him. He might not like that I told you.'

'Of course not.' She glanced at the empty doorway, hoping Matt wasn't lurking outside. She wanted to ask some additional questions, like when and how his wife had died, but she didn't want to get Tiago in trouble. She also didn't feel right indulging in gossip behind Matt's back. If he wanted her to know, he'd tell her.

Although why would he? He'd made it pretty obvious he didn't want her here, and he certainly didn't expect her to last very long.

She hurried to catch up with him and found him on deck staring out at the dark waters of the *Rio Preto*. 'When do we reach our first stop?'

'Some time tomorrow afternoon.' He turned toward her, propping a hip against the rail and crossing his arms over his chest. 'Do you mind if I ask you something?'

Thinking of the personal information she'd just learned about his wife, she hesitated, wondering if he was going to ask about her last job—or whether she was involved with someone. 'I suppose not.'

'Why did you choose Brazil?'

Relief washed over her. That was easy. 'I knew the language.' She crinkled her nose. 'Well, kind of.'

His lips curved, and she caught a quick flash of teeth. 'There is that. But that's not exactly what I mean. As a vascular surgeon you could have gone to any hospital in the world. But this…' his hand swept to the side, indicating the river '…is a little outside your specialty, don't you think?'

She shrugged, forcing herself to smile back. 'Maybe I wanted to expand my horizons.'

'Surely there were other ways you could have done that.'

Her options had been rather limited when she'd called Tracy and inquired about the position, but she was loath to tell him that. At least at the moment. 'Possibly. Why does it matter?'

His eyes slid over her face, pausing at her lips before coming back up to meet her gaze. 'Just curious.'

'What about you? Why did you come here?' If he could pose the question, then it seemed only fair she should get a chance to do the same. Besides, it would move him away from this particular subject. And a part of her hoped he'd tell her about his wife, and get it out in the open.

'It was something I've wanted to do ever since med school.'

She nodded. 'Did you specialize?'

'Nope. Although, looking back, maybe I should have.'

'I imagine you've learned more here than some doctors learn in a lifetime.'

A muscle worked in his jaw. 'Maybe more than I wanted to.'

Something about those words made her heart clench. Was he talking about his wife's death? Now was probably not the time to ask.

'So we reach our first stop tomorrow.'

'Yep. We'll need to figure out how to introduce you to the villagers, if there are any questions about your presence.'

'What do you mean?'

He shrugged. 'Let's just say some of the tribes are more conservative than others.'

'They don't think women should be doctors?'

'Some of the chiefs might have trouble with us traveling together.' He studied her. 'You don't happen to have a husband stowed in your luggage, do you?'

A shaft of pain went through her, and it took her a second or two to respond. 'Nope, sorry. You've never brought a woman with you?'

'Not a female doctor, no.' He uncrossed his arms and straightened. 'But we can talk more about it later. You must be tired.'

'A little, but I'm okay. Is there something you want me to do?'

'Not at the moment. Tiago and Nilson are pretty proprietary

about the day-to-day boat chores. If you try to pitch in, they'll be offended. Let me think…'

He smiled suddenly, his eyes crinkling as he motioned toward one of her bare arms. 'You could always lie on deck and work on your tan. Try to blend in a little more.'

She laughed, the tension between them defusing. 'Nice try, Tarzan. With three guys roaming the place? Hardly. Besides, as you can tell by my vampire-like skin tones, the sun and I are sworn enemies. Even if I *could* tan, baking in this heat doesn't really appeal to me.'

'There's a wall-mounted fan in our…in the bedroom. You can read, then, or relax. Unpack.'

'What are you going to do?'

'Go over the navigational charts with Nilson.' He tugged at a chain around his neck and retrieved two keys from beneath his shirt. Unhooking one of them, he held it out. 'This is to the exam room. You'll need to put it somewhere safe. The door and medicine cabinets are keyed alike, so it works on both. The crew members can be trusted but, because of the drugs we keep on hand, it's better not to put temptation in anyone's way. So you and I will have the only copies.'

Her fingers brushed over his palm as she took the key from him, shivering as she noted the metal was still warm from resting against his skin. When he allowed his own key to slide back beneath his polo shirt, the image of steel pressed against a hard wall of flesh caused her to take a quick step back.

'Do you have a chain to hang it from?' Matt's gaze slid to her chest, and then jerked back to her face.

Had he just pictured the key nestled between her breasts? That would actually be a relief considering her response a few seconds ago. How humiliating would it be for her to nearly swoon over the stupid heat of a key and not have him notice her at all?

She glanced at his face, looking for confirmation.

Nothing. There wasn't a hint of interest behind those cool blue eyes.

The pendulum swung back toward humiliation. What kind of woman broke off her engagement and immediately started checking out every guy in town? Well, technically she was only checking out one guy in this particular area, but still.

She curled her fingers into her palms, allowing her nails to dig into her skin. 'I have something in one of my bags. I'll use that.'

'I'll leave you to it, then,' he said.

At her nod, he turned and walked away, and she couldn't help but notice the loose-limbed gait, which spoke of easy confidence, or the way his muscles flexed as he gripped the top of the door-jamb and ducked beneath as he headed down the hall.

As soon as the dark recesses of the boat swallowed him completely, she sagged against the railing and held the key to her chest.

What on earth was wrong with her?

Once they reached the first village, she'd be far too busy to think of anything but her patients. At least she hoped so.

Her mouth twisted. She'd forgotten to ask where Matt and the crew lived between trips down the Amazon. Surely they didn't stay on the ship year round.

And if they did? Could she live aboard this boat…in the same room with Matt…for the next two years?

Oh, boy. She didn't think so.

Because if she thought he was attractive now, when her instincts were on high alert, what would happen if she let her guard down even a little?

I don't run.

The words she'd thrown at him swirled around her, calling her a liar. Because if she couldn't get her silly libido under control, that's exactly what she was going to do.

Run.

CHAPTER FOUR

MATT awoke to something nudging his side. He opened one eye and squinted sideways, encountering a worn pair of flip-flops.

Tanned skin, calloused feet.

Not the creamy white toes sporting pale pink polish that had driven him from his hammock in the middle of the night. He'd decided it was safer to remain on deck.

'Why are you sleeping here, Mateus?'

Ah, yes, the question of the century, and one he'd prefer not to answer at the moment.

He shoved back the mosquito netting that was now tangled around him like a shroud and found Tiago, who stood with one hand scrubbing the top of his head, obviously still half-asleep.

'It's cooler,' Matt muttered.

The young man snorted. 'Really? On the Amazon, it is not cool anywhere.'

He had a point, but Matt chose to ignore it. 'It's still dark. Why are you up so early?'

'I heard a noise on deck and wanted to make sure everything was secure.'

Hmm…that would have been a better answer than his own response. 'Everything's fine.'

'Why do you not just stay in my quarters?'

Because Matt hadn't been able to resist answering Stevie's subtle challenge. *She* was adult enough to stay in a room with someone of the opposite sex, therefore he was determined to do the same. Only it hadn't worked out quite like he'd hoped.

He sat up and rubbed his hand over his face, trying to erase the image of that smooth white calf and ankle that had appeared over the side of Stevie's hammock and dangled close enough to give him nightmares of a different sort. And that damned sparkly polish on her toes hadn't helped. He'd nearly fallen out of bed in his rush to put some distance between them.

He sighed, trying to disguise the sound. 'Your quarters are cramped enough as it is.'

'What about the infirmary?'

'I'm fine.'

Tiago frowned. 'I know you want to keep the germs out, but you can't sleep on the hard deck for two weeks. What about your back? I can see it still bothers you.'

That was something Matt didn't want to talk about either. 'I'll survive.'

'But if you hurt it again, you might have to—'

'Go back to bed. We'll figure something else out in the morning.'

The other man tsked, but nodded. 'I'll at least hang the netting, so it does not strangle you in the night. Besides, the mosquitoes can feed right through it.'

The thing was so tangled, it probably provided a pretty good barrier, but he got up and helped Tiago suspend the midpoint from some fishing line and tack it to the wooden railing next to his makeshift pallet. Tiago was right, the netting was better this way.

Saying goodnight, Matt watched as the other man trudged back down the dark passageway to his own comfortable hammock, passing the quarters where Stevie was currently sleeping. Was her leg still on decadent display?

Forget it. He scooted beneath the netting and flopped down onto his blanket. That was another thing. He was used to sleeping in the buff and without the benefit of blankets. The additional coverings made him feel claustrophobic and hot. What had Tracy been thinking?

She hadn't been. That much was obvious.

But would it have bothered him as much if Tracy herself had come and stayed on the boat? If they'd shared a room?

No, because not only was she Vickie's sister, she was also a good friend. There was no attraction getting in the way of their work. Unlike with Stevie.

He snorted. Who said Stevie was attracted to him? Maybe it was purely a one-way street.

That wasn't the only thing bothering him. He still had to figure out what they were going to tell the tribes when they went ashore tomorrow.

Maybe no one would even ask about Stevie. And if they did? What then?

He'd only been half joking when he asked Stevie if she was hiding a husband inside one of her suitcases. Because it would make it so much easier if there was one.

Or if Matt could simply say he'd gotten married again.

He blinked. Maybe he had. Or he could pretend he had.

No one had to know that he wasn't bringing his new bride— who also happened to be a doctor—with him. Vickie had been a nurse, and they'd traveled together. No one thought a thing of it.

Would Stevie even agree to the ruse? He could tell her it was either that or she could go home. It was the truth, because he sure as hell couldn't think of another story that would take care of any questions with one fell swoop.

And what about him? Would he be able to pretend to be Stevie's husband, knowing he'd have to learn more about her to make their tale believable?

Putting his hands behind his head, he tried to go back to sleep and ignore what that would entail.

Matt Palermo, permanently grieving widower, might have to break his one iron-clad rule about women.

Don't get too close—ever.

Her dad spun her around and around, holding her suspended by one arm and leg, while her other limbs dangled in space. She half giggled, half screamed and then thrashed around when she realized the swaying hadn't been solely in her dreams. And her wiggling had just caused her to overbalance…

Scrambling, she clawed at the hammock with her hands, succeeding in grabbing the open woven fabric just as the whole contraption inverted itself. She found herself hanging upside down, her legs automatically wrapping around the center of the hammock and locking together at the ankles. She tightened her fingers to avoid dropping onto the hammock below hers.

Oh, no!

She blinked hard and twisted her head to stare at the bottom hammock before shuddering with relief. Abandoned. Matt was evidently already up and dressed.

Thank heavens. At least he hadn't witnessed her utter and complete humiliation. Now, if she could just…

'I didn't realize you were part bat. Although you did mention having an aversion to the sun yesterday.'

Stevie froze. The words, murmured in a low voice that flowed through her like dark fragrant honey, could only come from one man.

She slowly tilted her head further back and, through the veil of her mosquito net, saw Matt. Upside down, but showered and fresh, while she was…well…

'I had a slight accident.'

One side of his mouth quirked up. Or was it down? She couldn't tell any more. 'Yes, I can see that.'

'Instead of standing there, staring, maybe you could help me figure out how to get down?'

'I kind of like you the way you are.'

'Hey!' Her hair swung below her like a tangled skein of yarn, the lank strands almost brushing the lower hammock. 'Stop fooling around and get over here. I'm starting to get dizzy. I don't think you want a puddle of whatever's left in my stomach all over your bed.'

That did it. In a flash, he'd ducked beneath the netting and was at her side. Two strong arms came out and settled under her shoulders and buttocks. 'Okay, I've got you. Let go.'

'Are you sure?'

He laughed. 'Do you want to do this by yourself?'

The hard floor stared at her from a quite a distance away. Nope, she didn't. She unhooked her legs first and felt the bulge of Matt's biceps as he took the weight of her lower half. When she was certain he wouldn't send her careening to the ground, she unfisted her hands.

And wound up right side up, in his arms. With her face way too close to his neck for comfort.

And the scent she'd caught yesterday as she'd passed him in the hallway?

Heavens, it was still there, headier than ever. Against her better judgement, she closed her eyes and leaned just a bit closer, allowing the air around him to fill her senses. Breathe, exhale, repeat…just like the shampoo commercials advised.

'Better?'

She froze, her lungs ceasing all covert activity. Had she really been sniffing a strange man's neck?

'W-what?'

'Your dizziness. I don't want to set you down if you're going to collapse on me.'

'Oh. Um, no. I think I'm okay.' Her voice came out shakier than she'd hoped, and she wondered if she might fall in a heap after all.

Seemingly oblivious to her confusion, he craned his head to the side and looked at her, making no move to put her down. 'I see we should've reviewed the hammock safety video. If I had actually been in that bed and you'd dropped on top of me, things could have gotten rather ugly.'

No kidding. Especially since her T-shirt had been hiked to kingdom come as she'd dangled there. She glanced down, horrified to find a huge swath of her belly still exposed.

Keep talking, and he won't notice. 'No one mentioned that particular hazard when I applied for the job.'

A muscle twitched in his jaw for a moment or two and she realized how her words must have sounded. Especially when he pivoted away from the pair of hammocks and set her on her feet.

She yanked her Mets T-shirt down over her jogging shorts.

'Not that I'm saying landing on top of you would be hazardous or anything…'

Oh, yes, it would be. Even saying it out loud did wonky things to her breathing which, in turn, had nothing to do with nearly falling out of her hammock.

Thankfully, Tiago appeared behind her, saving her from having to explain her meaning.

'Nilson has breakfast ready, if you're hungry,' he said in Portuguese.

The man shifted from foot to foot as if embarrassed about something. Stevie wondered if he'd seen Matt holding her. Or if he understood enough English to know what they'd been saying.

'*Obrigada*,' Matt said, taking a step back.

'Where do you want me to put your blanket and netting from last night?' Tiago added.

Stevie glanced at the thin barrier surrounding the two hammocks. She would have thought they stayed in place at all times. What if someone wanted to nap? 'Do you normally store this during the day?' She moved the netting to the side and secured it with the bungee cord the way she'd seen it yesterday.

'No.' Color stained Matt's neck, and the word came out half-strangled.

Had she done something worse than hanging upside down from her hammock last night?

Tiago shook his head. 'No, not this net, the one from the deck, where he slept.'

'You…' Stevie's mind tried to work through what the man was saying. 'You didn't sleep here last night?'

'Mateus said it was too hot.'

The fiery color moved from Matt's neck to the tips of his ears. 'What I said was it was cooler out there.' He jabbed a thumb in the direction of the deck before turning away. 'Let's get that breakfast you mentioned.'

As he moved out of the room, Stevie wondered why he'd let her believe that he'd slept below her the whole night when obviously he hadn't. He'd even talked about what a disaster it would have been if she'd fallen on top of him, all the while knowing it hadn't been a remote possibility.

Had it all been an act? Or had he simply woken up to a stuffy room and moved his bed onto the deck?

Except Tiago's shifting seemed to indicate what he'd done wasn't an everyday occurrence. Which implied he normally stayed in his room.

All night.

Stevie stopped off at the restroom to dress and wash her hands and face the best she could. When she finally made it to the dining area, she'd halfway composed herself.

She filled the plate Nilson gave her and found Matt already sitting at the picnic-style table. Dropping onto the bench across from him, she set the food in front of her. 'You know, I can sleep on deck if you're uncomfortable sharing the room with me.'

'I told you why I moved. Besides, it's not good for Tiago and Nilson to have to worry about tiptoeing around during the night.' He glanced down at his plate. 'Or finding a half-dressed woman on deck. I'd prefer you sleep in the bedroom.'

He had a point. But it didn't seem fair to have kicked him out of his own bed. She glanced at the small eating space. 'How about this, then? We can string your hammock up in here before you go to bed and then stow it in the mornings.'

Tiago, who'd evidently been listening in on their conversation—putting paid to her hope that he didn't understand English—chimed in, 'This is a good idea, Mateus. I will install some strong hooks in the wall and center beam...and one in the ceiling for the mosquito net you insist on everyone using.' He paused, fiddling with his fingers. 'Although I understand now why it is so important.'

Matt nodded, a shadow passing through his eyes before he switched over to Portuguese. 'Thank you, my friend.'

Turning his attention to Nilson, he asked, 'How long before we reach the village?'

'We should arrive sometime before dinner.'

'Good. I'd like to go over the charts with you and decide our schedule for the next couple of weeks.' He glanced at Stevie.

'Can you fend for yourself for a little while? We'll still need to discuss our…story before we reach the village, though.'

She tensed. Their story. How could she have forgotten about that? She forced a smile to her lips, wondering what he had in mind. 'Don't worry about me, I'll be fine. Shall we meet back here in, say, three hours?'

'That sounds good.'

Three hours. Just enough time to focus some of her nervous energy on something other than the situation at hand.

Stevie ran a forearm over her damp brow, the piece of fine-gauge steel wool gripped between her fingertips.

Okay, boat varnish was a whole lot tougher than the glossy finish on the floors in her apartment in New York.

Which she guessed was a good thing, since the stuff was holding up nicely, despite being pitted and dark with grime. She'd hoped her scrubbing would take off the dirt and leave the finish intact. And that's exactly what was happening.

And that nervous energy she'd been worried about?

Gone. Washed away by rivers of sweat.

Kneeling on a towel to protect her legs from the scorching surface of the deck, Stevie leaned closer to her work area and rubbed at the one-foot section of planking. She paused to adjust her bikini top, admiring the area she'd just cleaned. It might take for ever, but hidden beneath layers of dirt the wood was a rich, glossy mahogany.

Just like the dark sun-kissed hair of the man she'd be working with. So different than Michael's blond hair and fair skin. The only thing they had in common were their blue eyes. But while Michael's were darker and sparkling with intelligence and determination, she hadn't noticed the flecks of cruelty that lay just below the surface until it had been too late. In one careless blow, he'd destroyed their future together, and then, when she'd dared to call him on it, reached out in a rage and crushed her dreams as well. It had only taken one phone call to a few key board members, and she'd been as good as finished.

She shuddered. Michael's eyes were definitely not her favorite feature. Not any more.

Matt's, on the other hand, seemed… She searched for the right word.

Haunted.

She scrubbed harder, forcing her fingers to the task. Why was she even comparing the two men?

A bead of moisture dripped into her eye, and she shook her head, as much to rid herself of any stray thought as to relieve the burning. She settled for blotting it on her bare shoulder, wishing she'd scrounged up a second towel to wipe her face. At this rate, her huge bottle of sunblock wouldn't even last a full day. She peered at the large area of deck behind her.

Three feet down. Thirty or so more to go.

She groaned aloud and pulled the brim of her baseball cap further down her forehead, thankful for the slight shade it provided, and went back to work. It couldn't be easy, keeping up a boat while tending to patients—and she had a feeling money was tight on the hospital ship. But surely someone could have tried to do something for the poor thing. It seemed weary of life in general.

It's not a living thing, Stevie. It's just a boat.

Maybe Michael was right when he'd poked fun of the *Projeto Vida* article. Maybe coming here had been crazy on more than one count, but she hadn't been able to just stay in New York and watch him run her reputation into the—

'You don't have to do that.'

The steel wool went spinning out of her hand, and she scrabbled for it, almost doing a face plant onto the deck. Glancing over her shoulder, she caught Matt standing just behind her, a pair of khaki shorts and grey shirt covering his powerful frame. Tanned feet, the lightest smattering of dark hair visible on top, were shoved into a pair of beige flip-flops.

She sat up in a rush, praying her top was still glued to the right spots. 'I thought we're agreed to meet in three hours.'

'Someone tattled on you, and I had to come see for myself.'

His brows went up, his glance trailing over her. 'So this is what a vascular surgeon looks like when swabbing the decks.'

She stood, all too aware of how grubby she must look in comparison to Matt's neatly groomed appearance. 'It takes quite a bit of talent, evidently, since no one here seems to have mastered the technique.'

He laughed and wagged a finger. 'Not nice.' Holding up a glass of water, the ice tinkled against the sides before he tilted it and took a long swig of the contents. 'Too bad, because I was just bringing you something cool to drink.'

She licked her lips, all thoughts of Michael sliding away as she stared at the condensation collecting on the icy surface of the glass. 'That's just mean.'

'And you're turning pink. I thought vampires hated the sun.' He blinked, his eyes zeroing in on her midriff region, then a frown appeared.

For once, she prayed her color really was due to the heat and not from standing in front of him half-dressed. But she'd expected to be able to run back to the room and change long before she was due to meet him. At least she'd opted for white shorts rather than her bikini bottoms.

'I do...I mean, they do. I've slathered on a ton of sunscreen.'

Handing her the glass, he picked up the bottle of sunblock propped on one of the redwood deck chairs and examined the label. 'You'll need something stronger than this. We're close to the equator.'

She gulped down a couple swallows of water, almost moaning as the icy liquid hit her parched throat. She couldn't resist holding the cold glass to her cheek. 'It's the same stuff I always use, but I guess you're right. It never dawned on me that it would be so hot here.'

'Like I said earlier, you can't learn everything about a place from books.' He glanced at her middle one more time before his eyes came back up and met hers. 'Why don't you go shower the dust off and change before we talk about what needs to happen once we reach the village? Tiago has an aloe plant in the back section of the boat that he keeps on hand for burns. I'll have him cut a piece for you.'

She took another drink. 'Thanks.'

Matt walked over to the area she'd cleaned, and his expression softened. 'I'd forgotten how nice the woodwork is on the boat. It's been a long time since anyone's…' His jaw firmed. 'But I don't expect you to do manual labor while you're here.'

'I want to pull my weight.'

'Don't worry, you'll be pulling your weight and a whole lot more, once we reach shore.'

CHAPTER FIVE

'OKAY. That sounds reasonable.'

Reasonable? That's all she had to say about his crazy idea?

Matt narrowed his eyes and leaned forward in the deck chair. He'd exhausted every other possibility before finally resigning himself to the inevitable: they had to pretend to be husband and wife.

But only if someone asked. And only until he could find a replacement for her.

He'd blurted the words as soon as she'd returned from changing her clothes, half expecting her to demand to be returned to the airport. 'Are you sure you're okay with this?'

'Is there another option?' Dressed in narrow khaki capris and an orange T-shirt, she sipped at a glass of water, seemingly more at ease with the situation than he was…and it was *his* damn idea.

'I haven't been able to come up with anything else.'

'What if I told people I was married—to someone else?'

'It would still raise eyebrows with some. They'd wonder what you were doing here in Brazil without your husband.'

Her lips tightened. 'They'd assume I was messing around behind his back, in other words.'

'Yes.'

'That's irony for you.'

'Excuse me?'

'Nothing. It's not like we're going to send out wedding announcements to all the villages or anything.' She sighed. 'You said we'd give as few details as possible and only if someone challenges the story.'

'Well, yes, but—'

'Listen, I know having a woman as part of your team wasn't what you wanted. You've made that abundantly clear. And now you're stuck with me. I get it.' She shut her eyes for a minute before reopening them and looking out over the deck. 'Let's just get through this one village at a time. Maybe the subject will never come up. If it does, just tell them whatever you want, and I'll follow your lead.'

Well, that was one way to make him feel like a royal ass.

He took a deep breath and touched her shoulder to bring her attention back to him. 'None of this is your fault. You thought you'd be traveling with Tracy, and I thought I'd be traveling down the river with a man. And you know what? Most of the male doctors I've worked with have bailed before the end of their first two-week run.' He smiled and searched for something nice to say. 'Be the one who makes it all the way, okay?'

Stevie's eyes moistened, and she nodded with a solemnity that made his chest tighten. 'I'm not going anywhere.'

The first village was nothing like she expected.

Kicking off her flip-flops, she took Matt's hand and stepped out of the dinghy they'd used to reach shore, her feet sinking into the silt just below water's surface. The slow current swirled around her toes and ankles, feeling deliciously cool after a morning spent working on the hot deck.

Matt squeezed her hand and released it. 'You ready for this?'

Not really, but, then, she hadn't been ready for anything that had happened recently. 'We'll soon find out, won't we?'

'Why don't you wait on shore while I gather a few things?' As if he sensed her sudden case of nerves, he smiled. 'I'll be right behind you.'

Wading just beyond the reach of the water, she shoved her feet back into her thong sandals and unrolled her pants legs while surveying her surroundings.

Wow.

Instead of a haphazard scattering of huts, the mud-bricked structures that lay a short distance ahead were arranged in a neat circle, each door facing a central clearing. A thin layer of smoke rose from a single fire pit. She didn't see anyone at the moment, but the sandy dirt around each dwelling could have come straight from a movie set, with pristine, parallel tracks—like those made from a rake—carving shallow furrows in the soil. Curving to and fro, the grooves flowed around whatever object they encountered, much like the river had drifted around her feet moments earlier.

Stevie breathed deeply, the musty scent of the river mixing with that of ancient vegetation.

It was so quiet here. Peaceful. So different from the turmoil that had ruled her life for the past month.

Even the fierce heat seemed to dissipate, wicked up and away by a canopy of towering trees. She smiled, suddenly glad she'd come.

She turned to see if Matt was as affected as she was, only to jump a mile in the air when a scream pierced the serenity around them. Wheeling toward the sound, expecting to see blood—and lots of it—she saw, instead, a toddler hurrying toward them as fast as her tiny legs would carry her.

That single high-pitched sound soon set off a chain reaction, and answering shrieks went up from every corner of the village. A few seconds later, about fifteen children of all sizes came at them in a mob, their feet obliterating some of the lines in the carefully groomed dirt. Stevie braced herself for impact, only to have them ignore her completely as they encircled Matt, who'd finally reached her side.

What in the world…?

He set his medical bag on the ground beside him and retrieved a large backpack he'd slung over his shoulder. Throwing the children a sly smile, he rooted around inside the bag for a minute or two before pulling out a handful of brightly colored…worms.

Gummy worms.

The things spilled between his fingers, the long strands seeming to take on a life of their own. Several kids screamed in horrified delight, while Stevie stared, hardly believing this was the same man who'd met her with a scowl at the airport a day ago and basically told her to go home. By now, several adults were headed their way, apparently unconcerned with the chaos Matt and Stevie's presence had caused.

'Here, hold these for a minute.' He held the tangled knot of worms toward her, and she crinkled her nose in disgust but allowed him to dump the jellied creatures into her cupped palms.

She swallowed. *They're not real worms. Not real.*

Even as she forced the thought to sweep through her mind, she swore she could feel one or two of them slither along her skin, trying to escape. It was everything she could do not to drop the entire bunch on the ground.

Lifting a brow as if he knew exactly what she was thinking, he gave her a quick grin. 'So, you never back down from a challenge, eh? Let's see if you can handle this one.'

He plucked a green worm from the bunch and held it up by the tail, making it dance a time or two before tilting his head back and opening his mouth. Without a word he dropped the creature inside—whole—then swallowed it. He rubbed his stomach, making fake groaning sounds of pleasure, while she could feel herself turning as green as the worm had once been. The children had evidently been through this routine before and knew it was all a game, because they laughed and began pushing to get a little bit closer.

Matt held up a finger. *'Espera aí. A doutora vai comer a próxima minhoca, não é?'*

No. Absolutely not. She was not going to eat a worm—candied or not.

But when a couple of children began to stomp out a rhythm with their feet—*left-left-right...left-left-right*—and one by one the rest joined in, huge smiles wreathing their faces, she knew she was stuck.

But, oh, she was going to make the man pay. Somehow.

She handed the worms back to Matt and selected the smallest one she could find—which still appeared huge. Closing her eyes, she bit down on its midsection, but the thing was tougher than she expected. Her teeth didn't sever it. She ended up having to slurp it up like a piece of overcooked spaghetti. Her groan, unlike Matt's, wasn't fake—or filled with pleasure—but at least the tart flavor allowed her to pretend the candy was the benign bear-shaped gummies she'd loved as a child.

When she chanced a look at him, a gloating comment on the tip of her tongue, the words died. His attention was focused on her mouth and not on the kids' reaction.

What? Did she have sugar stuck there?

She scrubbed her tongue across her lower lip, a sticky spot of sweetness attesting to the fact that's exactly what had happened.

Clearing his throat, and turning away, he addressed the children. 'So…who's next?'

Hands shot into the air. That was everyone…except for one little girl off to the side. Her hands were hidden behind her back, and she stared at the ground. Stevie elbowed Matt to get his attention, leaning her head in the girl's direction in silent question.

'She lost her mother a month ago to malaria.' Matt's low words were for her ears only.

Shock washed over her. 'Who's taking care of her, then?'

'Everyone, probably. They share responsibility, since most people in the tribe are related in some way or other.' The rest of the children pressed even closer. 'Want to help me divvy these up?'

'You start, I'll help in a minute.' She took one of the worms from his hand—the only pink one she could find—and went over to the girl. Kneeling in front of her, she prayed she could make herself understood despite her accent. 'Look, I chose the prettiest one for you. Would you like to try it?'

Large brown eyes met hers. 'But you didn't like it.'

'Of course I did. I just don't like to eat real *minhocas*.' She gave a mock shudder.

A small smile came to the child's lips. 'You ate a real worm before?'

'Well, no…but I'm pretty sure I wouldn't like it if I did.'

'Me neither.'

'Ma—er, Mr. Matt hasn't brought these little guys here before?' She touched the worm with her finger, glad she'd washed her hands before coming ashore. Then she rolled her eyes at the automatic need to clean everything in sight. Being a doctor, she knew it came with the territory. But she was in a different world now. With a completely different set of rules. She needed to watch Matt and follow his lead. The girl shook her head. 'He brought little bears the last time he came.'

Stevie laughed. 'The bears are my favorites! These taste just like them, though. Even if they do look a little less appetizing.' She held the worm closer. 'Wanna try?'

The shrug that followed appeared disinterested, but Stevie could swear a glimmer of curiosity lurked behind her eyes.

'My name's Stevie. What's yours?'

'Madelena.'

'That's a very nice name.' She glanced at Matt, who was still distributing the candy. Surprise again washed over her when his deep chuckle rose above the noise.

He truly loved what he did. It showed in the sparkle of his eyes, the ready smile that appeared whenever he addressed the kids, and most of all in that delicious laugh.

She turned back to the girl. 'How about if I sneak another worm and eat one with you? Would that be all right?'

A quick nod. 'You're not afraid?'

Something behind the words made her insides clench. This child had probably faced fears she herself could not even imagine. Not the least of which was losing someone she loved.

'No. Not of a candy worm.' She brushed a piece of the girl's straight dark hair away from her face. 'But I'm scared of plenty of other things. Let me get a worm, and I'll be right back.'

She stood on the fringe of the children surrounding Matt and waved at him. 'Can you spare another worm?'

At first she thought her words had been swallowed by the ruckus around him, but he made his way over and held out his hand, letting her choose.

'Thank you,' he said.

She picked up one of the worms and tried to ignore the way her fingertips sizzled when they connected with his skin. 'For what?'

'Caring.'

And with that single word, he returned to the other children, leaving Stevie to stare after him.

She shook herself and went back to Madelena. Handing the little girl the pink candy, she took the sickly yellow-green one for herself. 'Ready?'

'Ready.' Madelena cocked her head, another smile coming to her face at the way the candy quivered as she held it in the air.

They both downed their worms, their eyes meeting. Then they burst out laughing.

'Good?'

'Yes.' The child looked longingly at Matt.

Stevie stood. 'Go ahead. I'm sure he'll give you another one.'

The girl darted away and joined the other kids. Matt immediately noticed and drew her close to his side, sneaking another piece of candy into her hands. He glanced in Stevie's direction for a second and something like warm satisfaction flitted across his face before he went back to dealing with the children.

With all the worms devoured and the kids off doing other things, she helped Matt lug ashore a wooden fruit crate filled with health packets he'd brought for the adults, most of whom still lingered nearby as if knowing the drill.

She picked up one of the small sealed packages and looked at it curiously. 'What're in these?'

'Basic first-aid items, along with water purification tablets and condoms.'

'Condoms. Really? Do they use them?'

He shrugged. 'Who knows? We try to educate them in the hows and whys, but the rest is up to them. Along with the normal STDs, there've been several outbreaks of Lábrea fever in the neighboring villages. Condom use is one avenue of prevention.'

'I've never heard of Lábrea fever.'

'It's basically a co-infection of Hepatitis B and D. Very lethal.

We try to vaccinate newborns against Hep B, but since we're not present for most live births, it can be hit and miss.' He smiled at the adults and motioned them over. 'By bundling the condoms with the rest of the first-aid items, it removes any stigma or embarrassment and presents contraception as a normal part of staying healthy.'.

Matt took his time passing out the packets, speaking to each person in line about their family and health. A spark of admiration lit inside her. How on earth did he remember all these names and faces, much less each medical history?

A young lady took a packet, then hesitated. Matt asked her a few questions and then knelt down to examine a couple of swollen bites on her foot.

He pulled on a pair of surgical gloves, glancing at Stevie as he did. 'Can you finish distributing the kits while I deal with this?'

'Sure. What's wrong with her?'

'She has botfly larvae.'

Stevie crinkled her nose. 'Oh.'

'Not afraid of a couple of worms, are you?'

'The gummy variety are looking better and better.'

By the time the line of people had dwindled to nothing, most of the packets were gone. She gathered the few remaining kits and went over to where Matt and the woman sat on some stools, chatting like old friends.

Matt looked up and nodded at the packets in her arms. 'How many are left?'

'About ten.'

His brows rose. 'Good. Every trip the response gets better. We may run out of supplies before we reach the last village but, if so, we can cut our trip short and go back to Coari for more.'

'Sounds good.' Stevie sat on a third stool and smiled at their patient. '*Tudo bem?* How's your foot?'

'It will soon be well.'

Peering down at the three red welts on the upper portion of the woman's instep, she noticed a thick layer of goop covering each spot. 'What did you put on them?'

'Vaseline. It cuts off the larvae's air supply and will hopefully suffocate the little buggers. If we're lucky, they'll poke their heads out to try to breathe, and we can pull them out with tweezers. If that doesn't work, we'll wait until morning and hope they're dead.'

'Why not just numb the area and cut them out? It would be quicker and more efficient.'

He laughed. 'Spoken like a surgeon. Quicker is not better in this case. She'd be left with three incisions and stitches. If the site's not cared for, you risk infection. Besides, we may not be back in a week to remove the sutures.'

Okay, he had her there. 'So we wait.'

'Yup. I'm sure we'll have other patients in the meantime.'

He was right. By nightfall, they'd seen at least twenty people with a variety of minor ailments, while the woman with the botfly larvae waited for the Vaseline to work its magic.

Exhaustion rolled over her.

How had Matt handled this kind of caseload alone?

Tracy was right. He needed another doctor on the team…and Stevie intended to make sure she was a help, not a hindrance.

Matt switched on a large battery-powered lantern once dusk hit, and its strong glow chased away the darkness. Combined with the light from several cooking fires behind them, she could almost believe it was still day, if not for the dark sky stretching out above them—and the accompanying heaviness of her eyelids.

'Do you want to go back to the boat?' he asked. 'I'm going to take one more shot at removing our little friends.'

'I'll help. Just tell me what to do.'

'You sure? You look a little worse for wear.'

'Gee, thanks.'

He shook his head. 'I didn't mean it that way. It's late. You must be tired.'

'No more than you. I'm here to help, remember?'

'Okay.' He removed a pair of tweezers from their protective packaging and propped the woman's foot on his knee, giving her shoulder a comforting pat. 'Are you ready?' he asked her.

The woman nodded, stifling a yawn.

He glanced at Stevie. 'Here's what we're going to do. You squeeze each site with steady pressure, while I try to get a hold of the larva and pull it out. Some doctors are using venom extractors nowadays, but I've found the old-fashioned way works best.'

Stevie took a deep breath. 'I'm ready whenever you are.'

The removals went without a hitch, although Stevie's stomach twisted a little at times. Their patient, on the other hand, seemed to take everything in her stride, watching the process with interest.

Matt grinned. 'Well, that was easy.'

Easy? *Easy?*

He chuckled and went about wiping the bites with an alcohol-soaked pad, telling their patient to keep the site clean until it healed.

Before leaving, the woman took both of Stevie's hands in hers and gave her a light kiss on the cheek.

'Thank you for today,' she said. 'Madelena is my sister's child, and she is still very sad. I saw what you did for her. Her smile lit up my heart.'

Stevie nodded and tried to respond, but the words wouldn't make it past the lump in her throat. So she squeezed the woman's hands, then stared after her as she walked toward the circle of huts.

'I think we'll call it a night.' Matt's quiet voice brought her attention back to him.

Clearing her voice, she said, 'I agree. It's been a long day.'

She held out her hand, offering to help him up from the stool. He hesitated, then allowed her to haul him to his feet. Instead of releasing her immediately, his fingers curled around hers, the palm-to-palm contact sending shockwaves rippling across her skin.

'You did good today,' he said.

'Sorry about looking queasy the way I did. I just didn't expect the things to look quite so disgusting.'

'I'm not talking about the botflies.'

'Then what? I—I didn't do much of anything.'

'You did. You let them touch you.'

Puzzled, she shook her head. 'So did you.'

'No, I don't mean they touched you like this.' His thumb strummed across her knuckles, the friction from the calloused pad sending a shiver over her. He released her and put his hand to his chest. 'You let them touch you here.'

She'd touched more than just the villagers.

And over the next two days Matt took pains to avoid any physical contact with Stevie, even by accident. Because while he'd complimented her for opening her heart to the people they worked with, holding her hand had almost caused him to open a part of himself as well.

And that couldn't happen.

She seemed to be adjusting remarkably well, but he had to remember she was still in the 'tourist' phase of her visit. The honeymoon period when everything about Brazil was new and fascinating. That would wear off soon enough. Then culture shock would set in. Fascination would turn to irritation, and irritation would change to something far worse.

The day-to-day drudgery had worn every other doctor down. Each had walked up the gangway full of hope and good will. They'd left, simmering with frustration and resentment. For all he knew, Stevie would follow suit. She'd scoot out of the Amazon just as fast as she could.

If she did, the next time Tracy hired someone, Matt would make sure she stuck to their bargain.

Men only.

Seeing Stevie in that white bikini top the other day had reaffirmed that policy. It had also caused him to lie awake in his hammock for hours every night. When he did manage to sleep, the dreams…

It was no wonder he was exhausted.

He closed his eyes, trying *not* to see her swivel towards him in slow motion as she rose from the deck, her sleek blonde ponytail swinging from the back of the baseball cap, a dusty handprint stamped across the pale bare skin of her stomach. It didn't work. Every freckle on her shoulders, every luscious curve of her body was forever tattooed onto his brain. He'd wanted to take the steel wool from her hands and…

'Oh, my!' Stevie's voice came from behind him, throwing a bucket of cold water over his thoughts, dashing them away and hopefully taking care of the growing problem behind his zipper.

She continued to speak, having no idea she'd just been the object of some pretty explicit inner commentary. 'I can't believe what you've done.'

He glanced at the newly scrubbed deck, praying to God that's what she was talking about. 'Nilson did most of it, I just finished it off.'

'When? It wasn't like this when I went to bed last night.'

No, and he couldn't very well tell her *she* was the cause of his working late into the night. Again.

'Tiago and Nilson wanted to surprise you.'

She smiled. 'Well, it worked. It's gorgeous.'

She was right. The neglected woodwork gleamed from their efforts. A sense of shame swept through Matt. It was almost like he'd been punishing the boat for what had happened to Vickie. Or, maybe, like his life…he simply hadn't cared enough to make the effort once she'd died.

So why now?

Guilt for Stevie taking on the job herself?

Or was it more than that?

Squatting down, Stevie ran her fingers across the rich wood. 'Where did you get the varnish? I couldn't find any when I looked in the storage room.'

'It's boiled linseed oil. The stuff has been around for ages. I wasn't sure it was still good, but Nilson tried it on a small area and it came out great.'

'I'll say. I honestly thought it was some kind of commercial finish. It's just so…' She glanced up at him, her teeth worrying the lower left corner of her lip. 'It really means a lot to me that you did this. I'll have to thank the guys.'

She stood. 'Oh, I found some lemons in the fruit bin and made some lemonade, I hope you don't mind. I brought you a glass.'

'Of course I don't mind. The supplies belong to all of us.' He spied the bamboo tray on the table between the two lounge chairs, a wedge of lemon jammed onto the side of each glass.

Why hadn't he heard her come up?

Easy, he'd been too busy trying not to mentally undress her. He glanced at her clothes. At least she was fully covered in a lime green T-shirt and pants that came to mid-calf. Her hair, wet from a recent shower, was scraped back in a high ponytail. She looked clean scrubbed and cool.

And totally kissable.

He was insane. That had to be it. River fever.

He followed her to the seating area and before dropping into the nearest chair he swabbed the sweat from his face and neck the best he could with a nearby rag, the perspiration having little to do with work and everything to do with the woman standing in front of him.

'Smart.' She nodded at the piece of cloth. 'I ended up wiping the sweat with my hands and found filthy handprints all over myself later.'

Yes. He remembered. And he'd been tempted to add a few dirty handprints of his own.

She sat in the other chair and handed him a glass. 'Drink it while it's cold.'

Careful not to touch her fingers, he took the glass, then downed a third of the drink in one gulp. The tart liquid did the trick, cooling him in an instant. Sighing, he stretched his legs out in front of him. 'I can't remember the last time I had lemonade.'

It had probably been with Vickie, but that seemed ages ago now. He tried to dredge up the memory of them sitting on the deck like this. A sliver of panic went through him when he couldn't remember what they'd talked about the last time life had been normal.

And he preferred not to think of the hours they'd spent rushing back to the nearest city, trying to reach a hospital in time.

Cool fingers slid across his wrist. 'Are you okay?'

He moved his hand, but not before the touch he'd frantically been avoiding did some lasting damage. To cover his brusque withdrawal, he dragged his fingers through his hair, hoping the light wind blowing across the bow had ruffled it enough to give him a valid excuse. 'I'm fine. Just enjoying the quiet.'

Agonizing in the quiet was more like it.

Only when she picked up her glass of lemonade, her knuckles white as she carefully sipped from it, staring out at the river, did he realize how his words might have come across. 'Listen, I didn't mean you were talking too much. You're not. I just have a lot on my mind right now.'

That was the understatement of the century.

'It's fine. I actually just came up to bring you some lemonade and to ask how long until we reach the next village.' She stood, her half-empty glass still in her hand. 'I'll get out of your hair.'

Something in her face—*hurt, maybe?*—made him reach out and do exactly what he'd sworn not to do: touch her…his fingers connecting with hers for a second. 'Don't go. We've still got a couple of hours before we reach our next stop.' His jaw clenched for a second, wishing he could swallow the request. He settled for qualifying it. 'If you've got something else to do, though…'

She studied him for a minute, then the tense lines around her mouth relaxed into a smile that cut right through the defenses he'd erected over the last couple of days. 'Are you sure you don't mind?'

'I'm sure. It's nice having someone to enjoy the view with.' He lifted his lemonade. 'And thanks for this.'

'You're welcome.' She lowered herself back in the chair and looked at the water. 'It is beautiful here.'

'It can be.' He took in the trees hanging over the river bank, heard the ordinary sounds of the jungle. On the surface, he supposed she was right. But underneath… 'The Amazon can also be cruel. Unforgiving.'

'I imagine it can be.' Stevie propped her chin on the backs of her laced fingers, silent for a moment, then turned toward him.

'I really do want to help. Give me some time to prove I'm up to the task, okay?'

'And if you're not?' Matt knew he was the one with the problem. But what could he do? He'd mentioned enjoying the scenery a minute or so ago. Unfortunately, the scenery included a whole lot more than the river beneath the boat. And right now Stevie was high on that list of local attractions.

She shrugged. 'If I'm not, I'll be the first one to admit it.'

'Will you?'

'Yes.' Her green eyes held his for several long seconds. Matt's chest tightened as he met her steady gaze. He struggled to keep his attention centered, but the quick moistening of her lips tossed his good intentions right over the side of the boat, where he swore they hit the water with an audible *splash*.

His body went on full alert, and he realized a few seconds too late that when she'd shifted to the right, he'd mirrored her movement and wound up way too close. If not separated by the small table, their shoulders would have bumped.

Lean back toward center. Now.

Despite the command, his body stayed right where it was.

'Matt…I need to tell you something.'

The words were so quiet he gave up trying to move, angling his head to hear her. As he did, the scent of the lemons she'd squeezed—and something uniquely feminine—rose to tease his nostrils.

'Okay.'

Why the hell was he whispering all of a sudden?

He cleared his throat. 'What is it?'

Her tongue skidded across her lips again and disappeared. 'I wanted to tell you that I know about—'

Tiago appeared in the doorway, the worried grooves on either side of his mouth slicing through the cozy atmosphere like a guillotine.

Matt stood. 'What's wrong?'

The other man twisted his hands in front of him, his mouth opening then snapping shut. He took a deep breath and tried again. 'Miss Tracy's on the radio. There's an outbreak in one of the villages.'

Tiago paused for several long seconds, and Matt saw the truth written on the other man's face even before his next words registered. 'Mateus, it's dengue fever.'

CHAPTER SIX

'WHICH village?' Matt held the microphone to his mouth, his other hand gripping the wheel. He wasn't steering the boat since Nilson had cut the engine the moment Matt had entered the room, but he'd needed something solid to hold onto.

His crewmembers stared at him from across the bridge, their faces twin masks of dismay. Tiago had even crossed himself the second Matt had reached for the radio.

'Tupari.' Tracy's voice came across the airwaves, the crackle of static making it hard to understand what she said.

Matt swore softly. 'It'll take me a day and a half to get there.'

'How serious is it?' The question came from Stevie, who stood to his right.

He held up a finger, signaling her to wait.

Tracy's garbled answer came back. 'I know. And unfortunately, by the...you arrive the rest...village will have been exposed.'

'I realize that.' His eyes closed for a minute, tension grabbing him by the throat and threatening to slowly squeeze the life from him. He knew he'd eventually have to face a dengue epidemic again, knew that it had been far too long since the last outbreak. But recognizing his fears and confronting them were two different things.

'Do you...me to come down for this one?'

His glance clipped Stevie's before looking away. Her presence made an already difficult situation unbearable. 'No, even if you could get a direct flight out of São Paulo, we don't have time to go back to Coari and pick you up.' He paused. 'Did you have a chance to do any more looking?'

'I'm having trouble hearing…say again…chance to…?'

He sighed. 'Never mind.'

'Matt, douse yourselves…repellent before you get anywhere near that place. You'll…no use to anyone if you contract dengue again.'

Despite the interference on the line, he understood exactly what she was getting at. Once you'd acquired one strain of dengue, you were immune to it, but there were still three other types waiting in the wings. And, worse, the sufferer's antibodies tended to play a nasty trick with the next infection, unwittingly helping it gain a foothold. If that happened, the virus could escalate into the deadly hemorrhagic form.

He swallowed. She hadn't mentioned what had happened to Vickie. There was no need. He and his wife had both been young, naïve and stupidly certain of their own immortality. How wrong they'd been.

'I'll be careful.'

'Do. And, Matt…sure to check in when you get there.'

'Will do. Over.' He ended the transmission and slid the mouthpiece back into its holder, fiddling with it for a second or two. Anything to give himself time to wrench his mind away from the horrors of the past. Of racing to the nearest hospital, which was a day away, only to be told it was too late. His wife's organs were shutting down, bleeding from countless spots inside her. And their baby…

'What's going on?' Stevie's voice did what he couldn't do on his own: pulled him back to the present.

'There's an outbreak of dengue fever in one of the villages.'

'I heard that part.'

'It's mosquito borne, which means we'll need those nets you brought.'

She nodded. 'Will a hundred and fifty be enough?'

'They'll have to be.' He glanced to the side, realizing Nilson and Tiago were hanging on his every word, even though he'd been speaking in English. He turned back to Stevie. It was too late to take her back now. Besides, she'd fight him tooth and nail if he even tried. The best he could hope to do was protect her from exposure. He swallowed. 'You wanted a chance to prove you could do the job? You've got it.'

Her chin went up. 'I'm ready.'

'Good, but I won't tolerate anyone taking unnecessary risks.'

'Understood. Listen…I, uh, studied dengue briefly in medical school, but it's been a while. You've seen cases firsthand. Can you fill me in?'

Perfect.

Even as his teeth ground together in useless frustration, he knew she wasn't to blame. A vascular surgeon wouldn't have much cause to keep up with the changing face of tropical medicine. 'I have a desk reference with a whole section on dengue. You'll need to read it and bring yourself up to speed.'

'Is it Manson's reference?'

He nodded. 'You're familiar with it?'

'I have a copy at home that I started reading, but with all the extra luggage I brought, I didn't dare add any more weight. I hadn't reached the section on dengue yet.'

'Like you heard me tell Tracy, it'll take us over a day to reach the village, so you can catch up while we travel. I also have some case files you can read through.'

'Any casualties from this particular outbreak?'

'One child so far. Several others are ill.'

Her arms wrapped around her waist. 'How awful.'

'Remember what I said at the airport about battlefield triage?'

She nodded.

'You're about to experience it firsthand.'

Stevie reached the exam room and pulled the silver chain holding the key from beneath her T-shirt. Fumbling with her mother's wedding ring, which was housed on the same necklace, she tried to separate it from the key. She ended up having to pull the whole thing over her head. Instead of pushing the ring aside, she stared at it for a second before closing her fingers around it and holding it to her mouth.

More precious than the gold it was made from, she kept the simple piece of jewelry next to her heart, like her own personal set of dog tags—the symbol of who she was and where she'd come from. Sighing, she unlocked the door and dropped the chain back over her head.

The light switch should be right… *Click*. Yep, there it was. A low-hanging ceiling fan came on in conjunction with the bulb, the low *whump, whump* of the rotating blades a soothing cadence that helped calm her jangled nerves.

Why was she so edgy, anyway? Was it because of the outbreak?

No, it had more to do with Matt's reaction to it. And the fact that he'd asked Tracy, 'Are you still looking?'

She could only take that to mean he still wanted to replace her. A lump of hurt that never seemed go away rose in her throat. Michael had certainly had no trouble replacing her with another woman, so why would Matt be any different? He seemed anxious to find another doctor and send her on her way. The faster, the better. The hurt grew until she struggled to breathe past it. Maybe this was how the botflies felt as they slowly suffocated beneath the weight of the Vaseline.

Why didn't Matt want her here? Because of the marriage issue? But they'd resolved that. Or so she'd thought. She could have sworn he'd been softening toward her back at the last village, and then a few minutes ago on deck. But evidently she'd imagined it. All of it.

Her mouth twisted. She wanted to stay, no matter what he thought of her. Her initial reasons for traveling to the Amazon might not have been purely philanthropic, but she'd toyed with the idea of doing this very thing some time in the future—only that future had appeared out of nowhere, landing on her head like a block of granite.

Besides, what was the alternative? Go back to New York? Beg Michael to intercede on her behalf with the hospital's board of directors after what he'd done?

Right.

He was the one who'd written her up in the first place. And

her tentative overtures to a few of the other local hospitals had been met with polite smiles that had ended in silence. No one liked a doctor who refused to play by the rules.

Realizing she'd been staring off into space, she quickly scanned the bookcase until she found *Manson's Tropical Diseases*, its green cover identical to the one she'd left at home. She tugged it from its spot, and found a chair beneath a low Formica desk at the far end of the counter. The enlarged image of an *Aedes Aegypti* mosquito on the cover caught her eye as she sat down. Taking a moment, she studied it. Perched on a vibrant green leaf, the creature's white striped legs and graceful curves gave it a delicate appearance. It was quite beautiful, actually.

Until you looked closer and realized the red abdomen was full of blood from a recent feed.

She shuddered. Looks were deceiving. What seemed harmless on the outside could cause a wealth of misery if you allowed it to venture too close. Because once it achieved contact, it anesthetized you. You wouldn't even know what hit you, until it was too late.

Just like with Michael.

Thumbing through the index, she found dengue…already circled by someone. Her brows went up. Matt had evidently encountered this disease more than once, which made sense, given his reaction to Tracy's call. The nets she'd brought would help, but they were a drop in the bucket compared to the number of people who made their homes along the Amazon River. Unless people were educated in mosquito eradication, they would remain vulnerable.

She started to flip back through the book, but it fell open to the very page she was searching for.

Weird.

Even stranger were the handwritten notes crammed into every available space along the margins. The words caught and held her attention, and she turned the book sideways in an attempt to decipher them.

She couldn't picture Matt having this kind of writing. The small, neat letters were formed with a flowing hand…feminine.

Her teeth came down on her lip.

Matt hadn't scrawled these notes at all. A woman had. And they told a story that made her heart cramp within her chest. As she read further, the notations changed from concise observations to rambling, emotional editorials bulleted with dates. Matt's name appeared periodically along with another name she didn't recognize. The handwriting grew shaky as the days rolled by. A rusty, smudged fingerprint at the top of the next page looked strangely like…

Everything came together in an instant, and tears sprang to her eyes as she stared blindly at the wall.

These notes had been penned by Matt's wife. And they recounted a struggle to the death.

Her death.

From the very disease they were on their way to fight.

CHAPTER SEVEN

'DID you find the information on dengue?' Matt never took his eyes off the river, his hip propped against the deck's railing.

'I finished the chapter.' Should she tell him what she'd found in the process? He must have forgotten the writing in the book's margins, or surely he wouldn't have suggested she read it.

Or had he meant it as a warning, trying to scare her off?

'Good.' His fingers went to the back of his neck and massaged before tilting his head to pop the joints. Something he'd done regularly for the last four days.

The need to relieve the suffering of another—no matter what the personal or professional cost to herself—quickly overcame her feeble argument that this man could hurt her if she got too close.

'Turn around,' she said.

'What?' He twisted to look at her, wincing slightly when his cervical spine rotated past the thirty-degree mark.

'Your neck is bothering you. I studied chiropractic medicine for a while. Did someone diagnose the problem?'

He shrugged. 'I fell off a ladder a while back. Muscles are still a little stiff. It's nothing.'

'If it's nothing, then you won't mind my taking a look, will you?'

She'd been tempted to offer to work on his neck the first time she noticed him in pain, but he'd been unapproachable, and her courage had failed her. And since then even their accidental touches had sent her hormones on a rampage, which made her wary of anything more than momentary contact.

Yet here she was, *asking* to lay her hands on him?

Before she could retract her offer, he turned around and faced the water without a word.

Okay, that was as close to an invitation as she was likely to get.

She moved in a step or two, her head tilting as she tried to figure out where to begin. With the difference in their heights, there was no way she'd be able to do this with him standing up. She glanced around, noting one of the redwood chairs off to the side. The back was low enough to let her access his neck and high enough so she wouldn't have to hunch over while she worked.

Hefting it, her breath hissed out in surprise at how heavy it was. She waddled a few feet, then set it down in the middle of the deck with a slight '*Oomph*'.

He turned at the sound, frowning at the chair. 'Stevie, I really don't think—'

'Then don't.'

'Don't what?'

'Think.' Because she evidently wasn't. 'You're too tall. I need you to sit down.'

Something in her face must have warned him not to argue further because, to her surprise, he did as she'd ordered.

She stood in front of him and raised her brows.

'What?' he asked.

'Shirt.'

'You've got to be kidding me.'

'I'm a doctor. I've seen it all before.' She laughed. 'You know, I've always wanted to say that, but my patients tend to be out cold by the time I get to them.'

'Lucky them.'

She chuckled again. 'Come on, don't be a spoilsport.'

'I'm glad you think this is funny.' Even so, he grabbed the hem of his shirt and yanked it over his head,

Her breath hitched when the firm, tanned skin of his chest

came into view, her stomach doing a couple little back flips in the process.

Okay, this might not have been one of her smartest ideas.

To cover her reaction, she took the shirt from his hands and laid it over the matching chair a few feet away before moving behind him. Unfortunately the view from the back was just as delicious as the front, and she couldn't help but mouth, '*Oh. My. God.*' Just to get the words out of her system.

You've seen it all before, remember?

She rolled her eyes, but went about opening and closed her fingers to limber up the joints and prepare them for the inevitable. There was nothing to do but go through with it now that she'd opened her big mouth.

The first contact with his flesh was every bit as bad as she'd feared, a running jolt of electricity leaping the gap between his skin and her fingertips and racing along her neural highway. Its destination? Well, it certainly wasn't her brain.

Ignore it. You can do this.

Palms flat, she curled her fingers around his nape and massaged with strong firm strokes. She allowed herself a brief rush of pleasure at the heat coming off him, before beating the feeling back and working out a strategy.

A professional one.

She took a deep breath. Okay, once she got his muscles loosened up, she could probe further into the structures of his neck.

Only they didn't loosen. If anything, the flesh beneath her hands tightened even more.

She stopped what she was doing to give his shoulders a quick jiggle. 'Don't tense up on me.'

'I'm not.' The stiff, tight growl belied his words.

'Ha!' She dug the pads of her thumbs into the rigid muscles of his shoulders. 'You think I can't feel that?'

When he winced but said nothing, she shook her head in exasperation. 'We're not leaving here until I see what I'm dealing with. Unless you'd prefer to do this on one of the exam tables.'

His spine turned to stone…her knees to jelly.

Oops.

'I mean, I can't do a whole lot of structural manipulation while you're sitting up. You know…like an adjustment.'

'Were you even licensed?'

She relaxed and grabbed the lifeline he'd unwittingly thrown out. 'Nope. But almost. One man's back did me in. Too much fur.'

Unlike Matt's back, which was warm and smooth, with a nice ripple of muscle just beneath the surface. Except for this one spot on the right-hand side where his neck met his shoulder. Her fingers danced toward it, located the insertion point of the muscle and dug in. Deep.

'*Ow!*'

Stevie laughed. 'Just sit back and enjoy the ride.'

'Enjoy?' His next groan skated the line between pain and pleasure. If she was judging the sound correctly, it tipped slightly toward the pleasure end of the spectrum.

Working the taut muscles for a few more minutes, she made sure she found the sore areas and smoothed them with long brushing strokes of her palms.

She leaned closer. 'Better?'

'No.'

Oh, yes, it was. Because that low word ended on a sigh. 'Give me fifteen minutes, and I'll have you singing a different tune.'

He grunted a negation, but his head tilted slightly to the left, allowing her more access. She kept one step ahead of her hands, not letting them know what was coming next. Because if her hands didn't know, Matt wouldn't. And he couldn't tense himself against the deeper strokes.

'I thought vascular surgeons were supposed to have a light touch.'

'Is that an insult?' She kneaded higher, moving to the spot where the muscles attached to his skull.

'No.' He rolled his shoulders forward and gave a deep sigh. 'Never.'

'Want me to stop?'

'Uh-uh. Not yet.'

'See? That's the way it always plays out in the end. First they cry…then they sigh.'

'Very funny. I thought you said you'd never treated chiropractic patients.'

'No, I said I stopped when I got the *wrong* patient.'

'I think you missed your calling.'

She grinned, still trying to ease the tightness in a particularly stubborn area. 'That's not what you said earlier.'

'I was an idiot earlier.'

'Ha! You need me, whether you want to admit it or not. I'll soon have you begging me to stay.'

Matt had no intention of begging her for anything, even though his flesh was now loose as a goose. Except for one vital part of him, which was quickly becoming an embarrassment.

'I think that's enough for now,' he muttered.

'Are you sure? There's this one spot that I can't quite get to co-operate.'

No kidding. She wasn't the only one. But that spot wasn't going to get any better until she stopped what she was doing. 'Yes. I'm sure.' He cleared his throat and cast around for another subject. 'Tell me about the chapter on dengue.'

Her hands went still, but the coolness of her skin against his made him very aware of the continued contact.

'What do you mean?'

'I mean, did you learn anything new?'

'Matt…I…'

Why was she hesitating?

Hell.

He remembered exactly what was in his Manson's reference. 'You saw the writing.'

She broke contact and came around to the front, squatting in front of him. Her eyes had darkened, the shimmer of tears hovering near the surface. 'Yes.'

Maybe it was for the best. The thought of taking her into the middle of that outbreak made his stomach churn, a sensation that would only get worse the closer they got to Tupari. 'Then you know what we're about to be faced with.'

'I do now.' She took his hand, wrapping both of hers around it. 'I'm sorry.'

He closed his eyes to shut out the compassion on her face, and focused, instead, on the steady grip of her fingers. 'Don't be sorry. Just be ready.'

The shore was crowded, the faces solemn testaments of what Matt knew they'd find.

'Oh, my God,' said Stevie.

He watched her slide her feet into a pair of white flip-flops as Nilson lowered the dinghy over the side of the boat and into the water. The pink polish glinted up at him as a reminder of her first night on the boat. It seemed like ages ago.

Her khaki cargo shorts and T-shirt suddenly took on new meaning. Too much exposed skin. All it would take was just one bite. 'Go put on repellent.'

'I already did, this morning.'

'Do it again. These mosquitoes feed during the day. And with the number of villagers infected, lying in the open…' He swallowed, knowing exactly what might happen. 'There could be a catastrophe. No one gets off this boat without protection.'

'What about you and the rest of the crew?'

'I've already put mine on, and Tiago and Nilson know the drill. You can unpack the nets you brought while you're at it. We're going to need them.'

Her green eyes scanned the shore. 'I brought some citronella candles as well.'

'Good. Bring a couple on deck, put each one in a pan of water, and light them. We'll need all the help we can get.'

She nodded and turned to walk away, but he reached out and wrapped a hand around her wrist, not sure why it was suddenly so important to spend one more minute with her before they went ashore. The soft skin beneath his fingers was already damp with humidity, but she felt warm and alive. Brimming with good health.

For now.

He swallowed. What had he been thinking, bringing her into a situation like this?

A glint of worry passed through her eyes as she peered up at him. 'What is it?'

'Remember what I said. Don't take any chances.'

'I'll try not to.'

When he spotted a canoe being launched into the water with the village chief himself onboard, Matt knew things were bad. Really bad.

He let go of Stevie's arm. 'Go.' He nudged her toward the passageway that led to their quarters. 'And don't come back on deck until you've sprayed yourself from head to toe.'

CHAPTER EIGHT

'SHE has it.'

Stevie already knew the answer, but hearing Matt confirm the diagnosis made her chest ache even more.

They'd been battling the outbreak for the last four days, and even though they'd worked in shifts, she was emotionally and physically exhausted.

'What about her baby?'

His eyes took on a hard edge. 'She's the patient. Concentrate on her.'

In the middle of swabbing the woman's feverish brow, Stevie's hand stopped in mid-stroke. 'How can you say that?'

Matt's attitude since they'd arrived had been unbelievable. No more jokes. No candy. Not even a reassuring word to his patients. He'd handled the ill tribe members with an icy efficiency that made her cringe. She understood why doctors needed to maintain a certain emotional distance, but his lack of compassion went beyond the pale.

He hadn't been like this at the previous village, so it must be a reaction to facing the illness that had taken his wife's life.

Even so, that didn't excuse his—

'If you treat her, you treat the fetus.'

His cool pronouncement interrupted her mental rant. But it didn't stop the metaphorical steam from shooting out her ears in angry waves.

The man standing to the side of the clearing watching them through the opening of the hut pulled her attention from Matt.

He was the same person who'd been in the first canoe after the *Projeto Vida* dropped anchor. His attitude seemed as detached as Matt's, but she sensed an undercurrent of worry running through him, despite the austere, emotionless cut of his face.

'Who's that?' She nodded in the man's direction.

Matt glanced up, taking his stethoscope from the woman's belly, where he'd been listening. 'The woman's father.'

'And her husband? Where is he?'

He shrugged. 'I have no idea. Probably meeting with the medicine man.'

The woman in question shuddered as the fever again racked her body, a moan passing through parched lips. Stevie was seeing firsthand why dengue had earned the nickname break-bone fever. She'd watched person after person shake with chills so violent their teeth rattled in their heads. There'd been one death since their arrival, bringing the total number of victims to two. But a few other patients were critical, including the one they now tended.

Matt's fingers palpated the woman's abdomen. His earlier words said he didn't care, but his actions belied that as he checked the baby's condition. Surely he wanted it to survive as much as she did.

'At least we haven't had any hemorrhagic cases,' she said.

'The village is lucky. This is their first outbreak in recent history. When it strikes again, they won't be so fortunate.' He glanced into her face. 'The baby's fine, by the way. I'll go update her father.'

Stevie sagged in relief as he climbed to his feet and went over to the man. The girl's father was taller than most of the other villagers she'd seen, but Matt still towered over him. Lithe and powerful, her fellow doctor projected authority—from his straight bearing to his hard carved features. The only weakness she'd seen in him had been his stiff neck, which seemed a little better since she'd worked on him. But with the stress he was under, those muscles were going to seize up again, if he wasn't careful.

Remembering the icy intensity of his eyes as he'd gripped her arm and told her to go below and spray herself with repellent sent a shiver over her. The reaction had nothing to do with the fear of illness and everything to do with the heat of his touch.

He leaned down and took something out of his pack before trying to hand it to the girl's father. The man waved it away with a dismissive gesture. What was he doing? Matt's voice rose enough for her to hear it.

'These people will follow your lead. If you won't protect your-self, neither will they, and more people could die.'

Repellent. Matt was trying to get him to take a bottle and use it.

The man glanced at his daughter who lay on the pallet, her head tossing from side to side in agony. Stevie could almost see the wheels turning in his brain. He felt like he'd be betraying his daughter if he did something to keep himself from getting sick while she lay there, both she and her baby in danger.

Stevie finished swabbing the girl's head and ducked beneath the mosquito netting that, while too late to protect the young woman, kept mosquitoes from getting to her and then biting her friends and relatives, thus spreading the illness. She walked over to the two men. Matt frowned a warning, but she chose to ignore it, addressing the man instead.

'You need to stay healthy for your daughter's sake. You don't want her to wake up and find you sick. She'd blame herself, and she needs to focus all her energy on getting better.' She didn't mention that his daughter was also one of the sickest in the vil-lage. No sense alarming him more than he already was.

The man didn't glance in her direction, not even once. 'Who is this woman you've brought with you? A new wife?'

Matt rubbed a hand over the back of his neck and twisted his head slightly to the right as if physically trying to relieve the pain. 'She's a doctor with *Projeto Vida*.'

'Your wife was also a doctor.'

'My wife was a nurse.'

Stevie hadn't known that. Matt had been very tense over the last week and a half, and it seemed to have more to do with her than with the dengue outbreak. She'd assumed it was because of their living conditions. But now she wondered if it was more than that. Surely he didn't have a problem with female doctors in general? She knew some cultures had a difficult time accepting women in a primary role, but hopefully Matt hadn't picked up that attitude while working here.

'She's not Brazilian,' the man continued, stating the obvious.

'No. She's American, like I am.'

'Her Portuguese is different than yours.' For the first time, the man looked at her, and she saw both intelligence and distrust in his dark eyes. Her heart sank. The last thing she wanted to do was make waves. Would the man try to keep her from helping his daughter?

'She hasn't been in Brazil as long as I have. She's a very good doctor.' Matt deftly sidestepped the question.

'You should pay her bride price and make her stay with you, then,' the man said. 'She will soon learn our ways.'

Stevie's brows went up. 'Bride price?'

Matt must have seen the shock on her face because he took her hand and gave it a warning squeeze. 'Bride prices are uncommon in my culture, so I gladly married her without one.'

Her heart flipped in her chest. He'd warned her they might have to pretend to be husband and wife, but the last village had been so accepting of her presence, she'd hoped Matt was mistaken. The warm flush of pleasure that rushed up her spine at his words had also surprised her.

He'd *gladly* married her.

'She must be worth much to you, then.' The man glanced over at the shrouded pallet a short distance away. 'My daughter is also worth much, in the eyes of her father. The village will pay any price, if you can save her.'

Matt frowned. 'We'll do our best. You don't need to pay us anything.'

'I need to go back over there to check on her,' Stevie said in English.

A few minutes later he squatted by her side beneath the mosquito netting. 'He used the repellent, thanks to you.'

'So did you both agree on his daughter's monetary value and which currency should be used?'

'I know it's hard to understand his line of reasoning, but suffice it to say this village isn't as progressive as some of the others.' Matt took hold of her chin and coaxed her to look at him. His fingers were dry and deliciously cool against her overheated skin. 'He's the village chief, Stevie. You took a big risk speaking to him without permission.'

His words stung and reminded her of the reason she was in Brazil in the first place.

Dr. Wilson doesn't follow hospital protocol.

But there hadn't been time. Her tiny patient had been fighting for his life, and his parents had been desperate. As desperate as the chief was to save his own daughter. Unfortunately, in the Western world there were rules to follow and miles of red tape to wade through for most medical procedures. There were lawsuits and malpractice insurance to consider. The tests she'd run had said the infant didn't have time for Stevie to make her case. So she'd bypassed the system in the same way she'd bypassed the baby's heart, giving him the surgery he needed. The saving of a life should have mattered—it should have meant something to those in charge. In the end, her ex had twisted things, making sure the only thing in evidence was her flouting of authority.

She shook her head to clear it. 'I'm sorry. I didn't know he was the chief.'

'I should have made it clearer. We can continue coming here only as long as the chief allows it, so I need you to keep a low profile until the worst of the crisis is over. There are rumblings that the medicine man wants us out of here.'

That surprised her. 'Even though it means people might die?'

'His hold over them weakens if people lose faith in him. I've been coming to this particular village for the last six years, and there's never been a problem until—'

'Until I showed up.'

'That's not what I was going to say.' He let go of her chin and brushed back a strand of hair the breeze had blown across her face. 'I'm not sure what will happen if the chief's daughter dies.'

'She won't. We won't let her.'

A shadow darkened his eyes. 'It's not always up to us.'

Stevie bit her lip. 'No, you're right. All we can do is our best.'

'And when that's not enough?'

'Then we pray.' The words were out before she could stop them.

Rather than scoff at her naivety, he murmured, 'Start praying, then.'

Matt's fingers, which had started out tucking her hair behind her ear, now lingered on her cheek, his thumb strumming across it with slow gentle strokes. He hadn't touched her since they'd arrived at the village four days ago, so the sensation was shocking…intoxicating. Her resolve to keep her distance crumbled, and she couldn't stop herself from leaning into his hand.

His glance fell to her mouth, and the breath whooshed from her lungs.

Lordy, was he going to kiss her?

The woman on the pallet stirred and cried out in her sleep, breaking whatever spell had fallen over them.

Matt stood so fast, a draft of air swept over her. 'I need to check on the other patients.'

Before she could say or do anything, he was gone. She stared down at her shaking hands as if they belonged to someone else. Taking a deep breath, she tried to help the chief's sick daughter find a more comfortable position, all the while convincing herself that Matt's touch hadn't affected her. It had to be nerves… and exhaustion. A good night's sleep, and she'd be as good as new.

Sure she would. As precious a commodity as sleep was these days, she had a feeling it wouldn't change a thing.

Her throat contracted, making it difficult to breathe. And she had no idea where to find an alternate solution, because she hadn't even begun to understand the problem.

Why had he stroked her cheek?

He'd known from the second she'd massaged his neck that touching her again would be a bad idea. Her soft, fragrant form had done awful things to his equilibrium as she'd stood behind him, her silky hair sliding over his shoulder from time to time as she'd worked. Not since his wife had died had he been hit with a lust so strong that it had kicked his feet from under him.

And that's *all* it was. Lust.

He sat on a log facing the river, a pile of mosquito nets to his left. Taking his time, he checked each one for holes or defects, having to repeatedly force his mind back to the task. The jungle around him hummed with activity, and a couple of tribesmen knelt in hand-crafted canoes, tossing fishing nets into the water.

People had to eat, even during an epidemic. Some of these men had ill family members, but they had to keep going—keep working.

Which was what Matt should be doing. But he'd needed to get away for a little while. Everywhere he went, Stevie was there, her long fingers deftly swabbing brows, her melodic voice murmuring to those in distress.

Her every action seemed to ignite his senses and send them spinning out of control.

She'd come to Brazil to help people—just like he had. Maybe that was part of what drew him to her. He'd known in medical school this was what he wanted to do. He'd married Vickie soon after finishing his internship and had talked her into giving it a try. They'd ended up staying.

And because of that decision, his wife was gone. If they'd stayed in a nice safe hospital inside the United States, she'd probably still be alive…their child would be growing. Thriving.

He balled his hand into a fist, the netting bunching around it, and tried not to think about the baby that had died inside his wife's womb. He stared across the water at the lush jungle on the other side of the river, wanting to push the memories away, but they came at him in waves. She'd only been four months along when she'd contracted dengue. And when she'd fallen ill, she'd been more worried about the baby than herself.

Seeing the chief's daughter writhing on that bed, her belly swollen with child, had brought it all back. And having Stevie fret over the baby's well-being…

He couldn't touch her again.

'Matt!' His name coming from somewhere behind him

brought him back to the present. He twisted on the log and saw Stevie hurrying toward him from across the clearing.

'What's wrong?'

'I've been trying to find you for the last half-hour.' She reached him, her breath coming in quick gusts. 'Nilson sent me.'

'And?' He avoided looking at her, busying himself with untangling the mosquito net that was still clenched between his fingers.

She knelt in front of him, stopping his hands with her own. 'The tribal healer is demanding to meet with you. Right now.'

CHAPTER NINE

'IF THE *chief's daughter lives, there will be a celebration in your honor. If she dies...'*

The medicine man's voice had trailed off, but Matt could read between the lines. *Projeto Vida* had official NGO status in Brazil, but if Matt and Stevie suddenly disappeared, no one would come looking for them, except maybe Tracy. Matt's one remaining brother hadn't seen him in so long it might be years before he realized Matt had gone missing.

They'd been given until sundown to make their decision. Either they stayed and fought for Belini's life or they were to leave and never come back. And in reality, while the chief was the symbolic head of the village, it was the medicine man who wielded the real power, and he flexed that muscle every chance he got.

Going against him wasn't an option.

The minutes ticked by, the only sound the low hum of *Projeto Vida's* generator as it powered the boat's refrigerator and other electrical components. Stevie stood off to the side, lobbing pebbles into the water. She'd been furious with him for even considering leaving. And if it were just his life hanging in the balance he wouldn't have hesitated, but it wasn't. He'd brought Stevie here, could he face risking both their lives on a situation whose outcome was far from certain?

Stevie headed toward him, her hips weaving a delicate rhythm against the ruby backdrop of the setting sun. Her eyes glittered up at him. 'I'm not leaving. You can do whatever you want, but I won't leave that woman to die.'

'It's not your decision to make.'

'Maybe not, but I'm making it anyway. You can't force me to go.'

Anger washed over him. 'I can and I will.'

Her gaze didn't flinch. 'Then I'll find a way to come back on my own. I'll...I'll hire someone to bring me back down the river.'

And probably get herself killed in the process. Or worse. She had no idea the kinds of men who worked this river. A few were honest. But some hired themselves out as guides and then robbed their unsuspecting clients, abandoning them to their fate along the banks of the Amazon.

'Damn it, woman. You're acting like a fool.'

'Then help me save Belini.' She twisted her hair into a rope and tossed it over her left shoulder. 'If I weren't here, you'd stay. You know you would.'

But she was here.

Hell, what was he going to do? He already had the guilt of one woman's death on his conscience. Did he really want to make it two?

And if he forced her to go back? He didn't for a second believe she'd stay in Coari. She'd do exactly as she threatened. Come back and try to finish the job.

What exactly was his choice, then?

'If we treat her, we do it on my terms. You follow my lead and trust me to know how the medicine man's mind works.'

Her eyes widened, and she took a step closer, until she stood a mere foot away. 'Does this mean we're staying?'

He had to force himself not to retreat. 'On two conditions. The first is that you listen to me. The second is that if things start to go south, and I decide we need to leave, you come with me, no questions asked.'

'Oh, Matt, thank you. You won't regret it.'

He already did, because she was now so close that her light feminine scent rose on the heated air to swirl around him in dizzying eddies. Her lips, soft and inviting, lay far too close for comfort.

Moist. Kissable. Doing crazy things to his head.

If she asked him to walk through hot coals, he'd agree. Without hesitation.

She laid a hand on his arm. 'I only wish I could—'

Before she had a chance to finish her sentence, the medicine man appeared with two other men from the village. Matt's hands unclenched, and he took a step back, a less pleasant kind of tension rising within him.

'You have decided to stay?'

Matt nodded. 'We have.'

'Then you both will stay at the village—separately—with two host families, as we agreed. Not on your boat.'

Stevie's eyes went wide before looking wildly in his direction. The fear he saw in their depths did him in.

He stepped in front of her. No way would he let anyone drag Stevie away from him. 'I didn't agree to separate quarters. We are married. We prefer to stay together.'

'It will be easier for you to honor our agreement if you don't have access to the woman.'

So much for his idea of them sneaking out of the village in secret if things didn't go the way he'd hoped. The medicine man must have realized this as well. 'I need her help with the patients.'

The shaman folded his arms over his chest. 'You shall have it. But you'll tend them separately. No contact until things with the chief's daughter are settled.'

Not good.

'Then I refuse to—'

Stevie gripped his hand. 'I'll be okay,' she said in English. 'I can do this.'

Her voice trembled, and he got the impression she was trying to convince herself more than him.

Dammit. He couldn't believe he'd dragged her into this mess. He'd been traveling among these villages for many years, but Stevie was a city girl. She had no experience dealing with tribal mentality. Of course she'd be terrified. He would too if he were in her shoes.

His fingers tightened around hers. 'I think we should stay together.'

'But his terms—'

'Yeah, well, I'm having second thoughts about agreeing to them.'

She gave him a shaky smile. 'Hopefully, they're taking your reluctance to let me go as a sign of affection. Very husband-like. Good job.'

It was anything but a job. And the thought of not seeing her for days, possibly longer, hit him harder than it should have.

'If you run into trouble, come to the boat. I'll tell Tiago and Nilson to be on the lookout for you. They'll come and find me.'

'I'll be fine. Don't worry. Let's just tend our patients and get through this.'

He couldn't resist touching the twist of sleek hair that still hung over her shoulder. 'You've worked hard today. Rest. I'll see to the patients tonight.'

'Are you sure?'

The annoyed rustling from the medicine man reminded him they were waiting to lead Stevie away to God knew where.

'I am,' he said. 'I'll try to talk some sense into the chief while I'm at it.'

She nodded, glancing toward the three men who'd moved a couple of steps forward. Matt forced his hand away from her hair and back to his side.

'I think they want me to go with them,' she said. 'I'll see you tomorr—soon, I hope.'

Soon.

As soon as they knew whether Belini was going to live…

Or die.

CHAPTER TEN

'Mmm, delicious! What's this called?' Stevie sat cross-legged on the ground and took another bite of the bread-like substance her hostess had prepared for breakfast.

'It's called *bejú*.'

She cocked her head, her eyes unconsciously scanning the still dark area hoping to catch a glimpse of her new 'husband'.

Husband.

Ha! Nothing like jumping from a fiancé you thought you knew but realized you didn't to a husband you literally didn't know at all.

Good going, Stevie, girl.

Returning her attention to the shy young woman who sprinkled what looked like dry white powder over a hot skillet, Stevie watched in amazement as the particles magically coalesced into a solid whole. '*Beijo*? You mean, like a kiss?'

The woman giggled, her brown eyes dancing as, with an expert flick of her wrist, she flipped the tortilla to the other side. 'No, not a kiss. *Bejúuuu*.' She drew out the last syllable, emphasizing it.

Tipping the skillet to slide the bread onto a plate, she then slathered it with butter and folded it in half. She offered the fresh hot bread to Stevie, who'd just polished off her other piece.

'You eat this one,' Stevie protested.

The woman ignored her request and pushed the bread onto Stevie's wooden plate.

Unable to resist, she picked it up and took a bite, groaning in ecstasy. 'I sure hope these aren't as fattening as pancakes.'

'Pan-cakes?'

Stevie laughed. 'I'll show you someday.' Her laughter caught in her throat as a dark familiar shape strolled from the direction of the river, heading toward the chief's daughter's sickbed. The morning sun was just peeking over the horizon and backlit the man's form, but she knew without a doubt it was Matt. His hands were stuffed in his pockets, a habit that seemed ingrained. What wasn't normal, however, was the slight stoop of his broad shoulders.

She started to wave to him, but remembered the medicine man's words and stopped herself. She didn't want to risk endangering their precarious situation, especially when the chief's daughter was reaching the critical stage of the illness. Instead, she turned her attention back to her hostess and tried to concentrate on what the woman was saying.

Their patients had been cleverly divvied up by the chief so there was no overlap, and no chance to talk to each other.

No longer hungry, she nevertheless forced down the last few bites, managing a smile that felt a bit more watery than usual.

She would not dwell on the fact that she should be back in New York, blissfully planning her wedding, the horror of finding her fiancé in bed with a colleague banished to the land of bad dreams.

As was the disciplinary note in her file.

At least the baby she'd operated on was safe in his mother's arms. That's all that mattered in the end. The board of directors could fire her. Roast her. Tear up her medical license. But nothing could take away the joy that poured into her when the baby had given his first strong cry as he'd come out from under the anesthesia. Or the excitement of seeing those once-blue lips flush a deep pink as his repaired heart pumped life-giving blood to the farthest reaches of his tiny body. She sighed. That moment had been worth it all.

She wanted to feel that same joy as she watched the chief's daughter recover. But there was no chance of that, as they'd assigned Stevie to the least ill of the villagers, giving Matt all the tough cases, including Belini's. He must be totally exhausted by now.

'Can I help wash the dishes before I start my rounds?' she said.

The woman shooed her away from the cooking area before she could touch a single dirty plate.

Deciding to go down to the river and dip her dusty feet before heading off to work, she wandered down to the water's edge. Her wet flip-flops would just attract more grime, but the water would at least cool her senses.

What was wrong with her? Surely seeing Matt for a few seconds shouldn't affect her like this?

She waded into the river, until it just barely covered her feet, leaving her shoes on in case of sharp stones. Closing her eyes, she sighed as the silken flow caressed her skin.

'Not worried about anacondas?'

The low voice came out of nowhere, and a shriek climbed the walls of her throat. A firm hand clapped over her mouth just in time, preventing the sound from exiting. 'Shh, we're not supposed to be together, remember?'

Matt. She'd recognize that low murmur anywhere. And as soon as he let her go, she was going to kill him for scaring her like that.

She swallowed. Except that the sensation of his bare feet against hers and the pressure of his thighs against her backside shoved the murderous thoughts aside, replacing them with something else altogether.

He edged her out of the water, hand still over her mouth, and then half carried her to the stand of trees growing along the bank. Once hidden within the thick growth, he released her.

Stevie whirled to face him, a sudden sense of panic welling in her chest as she realized something might be wrong. 'Is Belini okay?'

'She's fine for the moment. Keep your voice down,' he warned, glancing back toward the river.

'What are you doing here, then? The last time I saw you, you were headed in the opposite direction.'

'Trying to avoid me?'

At least it wasn't *her* who was flouting protocol this time. 'I'm trying to play by the rules.'

'So I see.' His gaze ran over her face before lingering on her throat for a minute. A frown appeared between his brows. Lifting his hand, he picked up her mother's gold band, which was normally tucked safely beneath her T-shirts. But her blouse today had a deep V neckline that exposed the ring's hiding place. He looked up. 'Is this what I think it is?'

'Yes, but it's not mine.' The words came out faster than she'd have liked, but she had no desire to relive the pain and humiliation of catching her fiancé with another woman. Of knowing that for whatever reason she hadn't been enough for him. Neither did she want to remember the devastating cost of his betrayal in both personal and professional terms. Maybe someday she'd be able to share those things with someone. But not now. Not when the emotions were still so raw and fresh.

She met his eyes. 'The ring was my mother's. She passed away two years ago. It seems silly, but it helps me keep her close.'

He toyed with the delicate chain that held the ring next to her heart. The sensation of his fingers sliding across her skin sent a ripple of need down her spine. She gritted her teeth and prayed he didn't notice her strange reaction.

'I'm sorry,' he said. 'It's none of my business. I shouldn't have asked.'

'It's okay.'

His glance left hers, going back to the ring. 'I don't know that much about you, other than what was on your job application. And some of that was suspect, thanks to Tracy.' The slight smile disappeared. 'With everything that's happened over the last several days… Well, the ring made me wonder if you had someone special waiting for you back home.'

'There's no one. Not any more.' She was shocked to realize her feelings for Michael had dried up as surely as a drop of water in the desert. When had that happened?

'But there was.' Something dark passed across his face.

'Yes. But it's over.'

The acknowledgement was easier than she'd expected. And maybe it was due to the fact that she knew less about the man in front of her than he apparently knew about her. She hadn't even had a short bio to go by, like he'd had. In fact, she only knew about his wife's death because she'd discovered the handwriting in his medical reference. But Matt himself had shared nothing about his life outside the ship. Not even in passing.

He was right. They knew nothing about each other. She suddenly wanted to change that.

'My mother committed suicide.' The words were out before she could hold them back.

A few seconds passed, and she wondered if he'd even heard her. Then his hand fisted around the ring, pulling the chain taut against the back of her neck and bringing her a step closer to him. 'Ah, hell, Stevie. I'm sorry.'

Stevie licked her lips, trying to keep her words steady. 'She was in a lot of emotional pain. No one realized how much...' she pulled in a deep breath '...until it was too late.'

'Your father?'

The man she'd worshipped as a child had turned out to be a bastard who'd driven her mother to the depths of despair. And possibly the reason Michael's final betrayal had marked her so deeply. 'My father...cheated. He's no longer a part of my life.'

'I'm sorry.' His eyes searched hers. 'What about the rest of your family? Do they know you're here with me?'

With me.

The intimacy of the words made her heart flip, until she realized he was simply asking if they knew she was in Brazil. Not specifically with him.

'My friends do.' And how pitiful did that sound? The girl with no family. With no one to care about her.

He let go of her necklace and traced a finger along her collarbone. 'You should wear long sleeves and a higher neckline.'

The breath she'd sucked in wheezed back out in a rush of sound. She was suddenly aware of their isolation—of the cool press of trees that screened their presence from casual passers-by. They could do anything back here, and no one would know. She swallowed. 'I—I used repellent.'

His mouth quirked. 'Too bad it doesn't work on bigger pests.'

She couldn't help herself and smiled back.

His eyes dropped to her lips and held, then he took a sudden step back, his hands returning to his sides. 'I checked on Belini this morning. She's better. We can tell the chief we think she'll fully recover. Then we can leave.'

'You think?' Stevie frowned. 'But she's pregnant. Are you willing to take that chance?'

'Yes.'

She didn't believe him. 'No, you're not. And even if you were, I'm not. Besides, you don't know that others won't be infected by the ones who are sick. The incubation period hasn't passed yet.'

His throat moved, his Adam's apple taking a quick dive. 'And you could get it, if we stick around too long. On the boat I can at least offer you some prot—' His voice trailed off.

'Protection?' Her chest contracted at the stark despair she heard in his voice. So that's what this was about. She moved forward, touching his arm. 'You're not God, Matt. You can't protect the whole world.'

Something unbearably sad passed through his eyes. 'It's a good thing, because the world would be in trouble if I were.'

'I don't believe that. You're doing a good thing here.' She forced a smile and put her hand to his cheek. 'Speaking of which, I should go and see to my own patients.'

'I've already checked on them.' His hand came up to cover hers, his palm warm against her skin.

'On all of them? But you were told to stay away from my assigned cases. The medicine man made a rule, remember?'

'I was also told to stay away from you, and yet here I am.' He gave a slow smile. 'I don't *always* follow the rules.'

'You don't?'

His gaze dropped again to her lips. 'Not all of them.'

The touch of his fingers sliding across her cheek and burrowing into her hair made her knees turn to water. 'Are you about to break one right now?' she whispered.

'Oh, yeah.' His head lowered until he was just a heartbeat away. 'Can you guess which one?'

CHAPTER ELEVEN

RULES. Who needed rules?

The second he touched his mouth to Stevie's he was lost. He'd fantasized about this kiss from the moment he'd seen her sitting on that suitcase looking so forlorn at the airport. Oh, he'd denied it, acting like some macho hulk who could take anything life dished out, but he couldn't pretend. Not any more.

He was proving that. Right here. Right now.

And when her fingers climbed his chest and clutched at his shoulders, he growled low in his throat. He'd been content to go about his work and leave thoughts about family and future in the past, figuring it was the sacrifice he had to make to help others.

But if Stevie had the same goals as he did…

He angled his mouth to deepen the kiss, even as other, more troubling thoughts began surfacing. It didn't matter what her goals were. He'd left certain things out of his life for a reason. He didn't want to be responsible for anyone other than himself and his patients. Emotional attachments meant he couldn't do his job properly, and when he allowed his feelings to interfere, people got hurt.

People died.

His heart sank. What he was doing was wrong on so many different levels.

The touch of Stevie's tongue against his jarred him fully back to reality. His fingers slid from her hair and went to her shoulders, using light pressure to break contact with her mouth.

She blinked up at him. 'W-what's wrong?'

His teeth clenched, once, twice, three times before he won the war over his body and relocated his voice. 'I'm sorry.' The hoarse quality of the words made him cringe.

'Sorry?'

'I shouldn't have done that.'

Hurt flashed through her eyes, and she took a step back, shoving a lock of hair out of her face. 'I see.'

She did? Because he had no idea what the hell was going on here. 'I guess I'm not a rule-breaker after all.'

Her lips tightened. 'Right. Well, maybe you've just never run across a situation that made those so-called rules seem unimportant.'

That's where she was wrong. He'd found it. But that didn't mean he had to follow his impulses and greedily satisfy his own wants. Because that's all it would be. That's all it could be. A few snatched hours of heaven in her arms. He wasn't willing to risk more than that. Not for anyone.

'Most rules are put in place for a reason.'

'Like the save-the-chief's-daughter-or-you'll-be-sorry rule given by the medicine man? I can really see the validity behind that one.' She snatched her hair into a ponytail and tossed it over her left shoulder.

'Like I said, she's getting better, so it's a moot point. We should still think about leaving.'

'There could be others who'll become ill. You have no way of knowing which ones will develop dengue shock syndrome or the hemorrhagic version, do you?' There was a big pause. 'Neither you nor your wife knew she'd become one of those statistics.'

As soon as the words were out of her mouth, she blanched, turning a pasty shade of white. 'Oh, Matt, I shouldn't have said that. It's just that she seemed to think she'd be up and around in a week or two, right?'

He swallowed, remembering his discovery of the heart-wrenching account of her illness. 'We both thought the worst was behind her. Until she got the first nose bleed.'

She touched his arm. 'Exactly. That's why we have to stay. What if the same thing happens to Belini, and we're not here to help?' She paused. 'How will you live with yourself knowing we might have done something to prevent it?'

He filled in the blanks: *the way he could have—should have—prevented his wife's death.*

His shoulders slumped. 'You're willing to see this through to the end?'

'Yes.'

'And if—'

The sound of his name being shouted up at the village interrupted what he'd been about to say.

Tiago. He'd never heard the man raise his voice. Ever.

'Something's wrong. I have to go.' He turned to leave, only to have her grab his arm.

'I'm coming with you, rules or no rules.'

He nodded, his heart racing as a hefty dose of adrenaline hit his system.

By the time they reached the village, a cluster of people had gathered outside Belini's hut.

On the periphery, Tiago waited, his eyes obviously searching for them. Matt strode over to him. 'What's going on?'

His crew member shook his head. 'I'm not sure. The medicine man's just gone inside.'

'Why?' The shaman had seemed okay with leaving Belini's care to them a day earlier.

'I think she's gotten worse. Her husband tried to find you a few minutes ago, and when he couldn't, he came back with the medicine man and the chief.'

A wave of guilt crashed over him. While he'd been dragging Stevie into the bushes—making out with her—all hell had broken loose. Belini had been his responsibility. No one else's.

'Matt said she was fine a half-hour ago,' Stevie said, as if to defend him.

When a sudden scream pierced the air around them. He didn't wait for permission, he went through the door flap of the mud dwelling, Stevie right on his heels.

What he found made his skin crawl. Belini was curled in a

fetal position, moaning, a small pool of blood on the mat beneath her. Her husband stood to one side, his hands clenched.

Could she have gone hemorrhagic despite how she'd appeared earlier?

'Let me examine her.'

The chief, who was next to the bed, moved aside, but the medicine man eyed him and stayed where he was, spreading a pack of herbs on the ground next to the girl while chanting in the native tongue. Matt let him do his work, while quickly squatting beside Belini. He tried to reassure her as he lifted her lids to examine her eyes, then glanced at the rest of her pale face. No blood coming from her nose or ears.

'Matt, I think she's going into labor.' Stevie's voice came from just over his left shoulder, speaking in English.

Not good. The girl wasn't due for several more weeks.

The stress of the fever could have triggered premature labor. His teeth ground together in frustration. And for her to try to deliver a baby in such a weakened state could prove disastrous.

Coaxing her from her side onto her back, he felt the truth the second his hand settled on her belly. His own gut tightened.

Stevie was right.

He could pray the rock-hard stomach was evidence of harmless Braxton-Hicks contractions rather than the beginning of actual labor, but, judging from the beads of sweat on the girl's upper lip, that prayer would probably be in vain. Still speaking in low English so as not to alarm anyone, he glanced at Stevie, who was kneeling next to him. 'I need my bag. It's by the main campfire.'

She nodded and hurried out of the hut without a word.

Matt went over to the chief. 'Can you ask everyone to leave the room?' He hesitated. 'Everyone…except the medicine man?'

Now was not the time to fight over who was in charge. Besides, he needed all the help he could get, and if the man's rituals could reach someone in the spirit world, he wasn't about to interfere.

'What is wrong with her?' The chief's voice was strong and sure, but Matt got the feeling it was for the benefit of the others in the hut. Underneath that fierce façade beat the heart of a father—one who was mentally tearing his hair out with each terrible moan his daughter made.

'I'm not sure yet. But it's possible she's going to have her baby.'

The chief stood straighter. 'Then I will call for one of the midwives to take your place. A man should not be here.'

Matt thought fast, remembering Stevie's comments about rules sometimes needing to be broken. 'Stevie will be here, but she might need my help.' He glanced at the medicine man, knowing he was taking in every word, even if he seemed lost in his own preparations. 'I lost my wife to dengue, remember? I won't let your daughter follow that path. Not if it's in my power to save her.'

The chief gave a visible swallow before nodding. 'Yes. I believe you.' He laid a hand on Belini's husband's shoulder. 'Do you wish this man to treat your wife?'

Belini's husband glanced down at her writhing form, then his anguished eyes met Matt's. A wealth of meaning passed between the two men. He nodded at the chief and glanced at the others in the room. 'Yes, I wish it. Do as he says.'

As Matt ushered them out of the hut, Stevie arrived with his bag. He knew he had to walk a fine line here. The medicine man, just as he'd expected, hadn't left with the others—he meant to watch their every move.

'You're going to take the lead,' he said to her, making sure to keep the conversation in Portuguese to prove his transparency. 'The chief is only letting me stay because I've had experience with dengue. Men aren't welcome at birthing ceremonies.'

Stevie's eyes widened. 'What? Surely the tribal elders can make an exception in this case.'

Losing his wife had been almost too terrible to bear, and he wouldn't wish that on Belini's husband or anyone else. But her death was allowing him access, where he'd normally have none. He meant to make the most of the opportunity.

'I told them you might need my help.' His glance went to the medicine man, hoping Stevie would follow his train of thought and not argue the point.

Thankfully, she nodded her understanding. 'How likely is she to hemorrhage during the birth?'

'She's spotting, but she's not bleeding anywhere else that I can see. Let's just take it one step at a time.'

As he prepared the instruments, Stevie moved in close to the woman's head and placed her palm gently on the girl's cheek to capture her attention. 'Hi, sweetheart. I know you're scared and that you don't feel well, but I think your baby wants to meet you.'

'Tired.' Belini groaned as another contraction hit. 'Hurts so badly.'

'I know, honey. But we're here. We're going to help you.' She didn't wait for the woman's answer, knowing she'd already turned inward to deal with the contraction. As soon as it let up, she held Belini's hands, giving them a quick squeeze. 'When you feel the pressure building again, I want you to take a deep breath and release it.'

Two hours of pushing and still no birth.

Stevie used the flats of her hands on the next contraction, hoping the steady downward pressure would coax the baby further into the birth canal. Speaking with low, calming murmurs, her own heart raced with fear as she watched Matt work.

With each push, the baby inched closer, only to be drawn back to its original position when the contraction was over. Exhaustion was taking hold. Soon there would be no choice but to take her aboard the boat and attempt an emergency Cesarean. But she knew Matt was afraid the anesthesia would be too much for the woman at this point—even if the chief allowed it.

He swore softly. 'The baby's still sunny side up. There's no way he'll fit like this—the pelvis is too narrow. I'm going to have to try turning its head again on the next contraction.'

Stevie cringed, knowing the agony Belini had experienced during the previous two attempts, but she forced herself to collect a deep breath and nod her understanding. Matt knew what he was doing. Still, the other two tries had ended with the baby stubbornly reverting to its original position, with the back of his head firmly pressing on his mother's spine. A much harder way to deliver. And for someone of Belini's petite size and debilitated condition…almost impossible.

'Here we go. Help her push.'

Stevie bore down, noting the stiff concentration on Matt's face, the muscle in his jaw contracting as he felt for the baby's head and attempted to rotate it manually. Belini's weak moans tore at her heart.

'Come on, sweetie,' she whispered to the baby. 'Stay where Uncle Matt puts you.'

'Tell her to keep pushing. If we can move him down the canal a little bit more, his body should turn in unison with the head.' There was a pause. 'Almost there. Keep going.'

'*Empurre.*' The soft command was as much for Stevie's benefit as it was for Belini's. She kept her hands firm on the girl's abdomen, her fingers sensing each and every inch of ground they gained.

'Wait! Wait! Don't push!' Matt's harsh shout stopped everyone in their tracks. Even the medicine man stopped his incessant chanting.

'What is it?' She held back the fear that gnawed at her throat.

'Head's out.' He looked up and although his hair was plastered to his head and sweat had worn tracks down his face, his shaky smile lit up the darkening room. 'The hard part's over. Now we just need to ease the shoulders out.'

Stevie's heart stopped then started beating again. She leaned close to Belini's ear. 'Your baby's about to be born.'

Within ten minutes an angry-sounding cry split the room, strong and sure, as if the baby—and not his mother—had won this particular round.

Belini's exhausted brown eyes met her own. 'He cries.'

A laugh came out unbidden. 'Yes, he does.'

'And a "he" it is. The baby's a boy,' said Matt, working to clear the baby's nose and throat. 'Small, but healthy and pink.'

'Thank God.' Stevie's knees went rubbery, and she dropped back onto her haunches. 'Any signs of dengue?'

Matt wrapped the baby in a clean blanket. 'Not a trace, but then again, it's…' There was a pause and Stevie could swear his voice caught for a second. When he continued, the sensation was gone. 'It's rare for the fetus to be affected.'

She looked at him, trying to gauge the change in his mood. He should be elated. He *had* been a couple of minutes ago. But now he seemed flat, as if all emotion had been sucked out of him.

He's exhausted.

That had to be it. She felt like a wet noodle herself.

Without a word, the medicine man folded up the small cloth that held his amulets and incense herbs and tucked it into a pouch that hung around his neck. He stood and went through the flap on the hut.

Matt put the baby into Belini's arms. The woman glanced at him as her fingers stroked one of the infant's hands. 'He's so tiny. I fear I will break him.'

When Matt didn't respond, Stevie scooted closer and smoothed damp strands of hair from the woman's forehead. 'You won't. He's tough. As tough as his mama.'

Belini nodded, lost in that special world in which only she and her baby existed.

Matt climbed to his feet, hands clenched by his side, and Stevie's heart ached at how alone he appeared. He'd worked so hard, she expected him to express relief that it was over, or to break into another of those rare smiles like the one he'd given her when the baby's head had crowned.

'Are you okay?' she asked, standing up and laying her hand on his arm.

His skin seemed icy, despite the heat inside the hut.

Something was definitely wrong.

His eyes shut for a moment, then he turned away to gather his equipment. 'I'm fine. Just tired.'

So was she. So was Belini.

This was different.

'Matt—'

'Just leave it alone, Stevie.' He turned to face her. 'Belini's fine. The baby's fine. *Everything's* fine.'

She blinked. Not everything. But like he said, now was not the time to push it. 'I'm glad it all worked out.'

'Yeah. Me, too.'

Before she knew what was happening, he'd shoved through the doorway, and the chief came in, along with Belini's husband. All of them started speaking at once. The chief's face was the softest she'd seen it since their arrival. He stared down at the pair reclining on the pallet.

'They are both well?' he asked.

She nodded, giving him a reassuring smile. 'Belini needs a lot of rest, she's still ill from the dengue, but the baby is healthy.'

'A boy?' Belini's husband glanced up at her.

'Yes.' She gritted her teeth, expecting the normal macho swagger to appear. Instead she was surprised when the young man knelt and brushed his fingers across Belini's cheek. 'A girl would have looked like you.'

Belini smiled, and the young couple's eyes caught and held. A prick of tears appeared behind Stevie's lids.

Okay, so her own reactions were a bit off kilter, too, so who was she to judge Matt's response? Adrenaline affected everyone differently.

'I'll leave you alone for a while,' she said. 'But make sure you let Belini rest, okay?'

The chief nodded. 'I'll send for some of the women to help with the baby.'

'Good idea.' She ducked out of the tent, intending to search for Matt, but she spotted him as soon as she emerged. He stood about fifty yards away with the medicine man. The two either didn't see her or they ignored her. Judging from the harsh set of Matt's cheeks, she guessed they were arguing.

As soon as she started toward them, though, Matt's eyes met hers. He gave his head a slight shake, telling her to stay put.

So he had seen her. She stood there and brushed the dust from her shirt, undecided whether she should ignore his unspoken warning and demand to know what was going on or simply go to the boat and shower. If she made the shaman angry, it could harm what Matt was trying to accomplish.

A shower it was, then.

Thankfully she found Tiago by the shore. 'How is she?' he asked.

She forced a smile to her face. 'She and the baby are fine.'

'That is good.' He nodded his head. 'Very good.'

'Could you row me to the boat?'

'Of course.' He glanced past her. 'Is Mateus not with you?'

'No. He's...tired.' Those had been his words, right?

And if he'd lied, tough. He could find his own way back to the medical ship. Or maybe he wouldn't bother, he'd just go to his host's hut and not bother to say goodnight.

She stepped into the dinghy and flopped down onto the nearest bench. Tiago took up the oars and started rowing, while Stevie stared morosely into the murky water of the Rio Preto.

Matt's mood was obviously catching. She gave a soft snort of disgust and muttered under her breath, 'Like the man said: Belini's fine. The baby's fine. *Everything's* fine.'

CHAPTER TWELVE

'THEY want to give us a wedding ceremony? Why?' Stevie's eyes flashed at him. 'They think we're already married.'

'Remember the celebration the medicine man promised to throw in our honor if Belini recovered? And how the chief was concerned about the lack of a bride price? Well, this is the village's way of thanking us.'

He didn't need this. Not today. Delivering that baby had taken what little was left of his soul and wrung it dry. All he could see was Vickie fighting for every breath, the fear etched across her face. Not for herself, but for the baby. If she died, their baby died, she'd whispered.

Don't let our baby die.

But he had. He'd let both of them die. And Stevie had almost witnessed the wave of grief that had crashed over him as he'd looked down at the new mother and her baby.

Alive.

Even now. God help him…even now, something inside him threatened to break loose.

'Matt?' Her voice brought him back to the question at hand.

He cleared his throat. 'I assumed the medicine man meant us to be honored guests at a normal tribal celebration. But he's insisting on doing it this way, and so is the chief. Especially now. The chief doesn't want to risk his grandson's well-being.'

Her brows shot up. 'He thinks the medicine man will put a curse on the baby or something?'

'It's a possibility.'

'Surely he doesn't believe—'

'He does.' There was a pause. 'This is their life. Their culture. Would you take that risk if it were your baby?'

A furrow appeared between Stevie's eyes. 'Probably not. What are we going to do?'

'We could always leave. Right now. They wouldn't notice for a couple of hours.'

'Would they come after us?'

'Doubtful.'

She nodded. 'Would we be allowed back in the future if we refused to participate? Or if we left without warning?'

Did he even care? At the moment, no. But later, when things returned to normal…when his emotions were no longer being dragged across a jagged set of rocks, he might. 'No, I probably wouldn't be welcomed back with open arms.'

'You mean "we".'

'Excuse me?'

'*We* wouldn't be welcomed back with open arms.'

Right. Not if he had anything to do with it. Stevie wasn't coming back here with him. Ever.

'Fine,' he lied. 'We.'

'Belini's better, but is she well enough to be left without medical care?'

He dragged a hand through his hair. The last thing he needed was to be reminded of Belini and her baby. 'Listen. I just came to relay the medicine man's wishes. You tell me what you want to do.'

'You *want* to leave, don't you? Even if it could be detrimental to Belini's health.'

'I'm not thrilled about having a tribal wedding, no. Pretending to be married was one thing, but this is something else entirely.'

Stevie sucked in a quick breath and pressed her hand to her stomach. Then her chin lifted. 'That doesn't answer my original question.'

Suddenly angry that she kept finding his weakest point and probing it again and again, he stepped closer. 'Yes. I want to leave. Right now.'

She flinched, but instead of backing away her fingers touched his hand. 'Is it because of the illness? Because of your wife?'

The wave of pain beat against the wall of his heart with such force he thought his knees would give out. The urge to grab Stevie and yank her close, to bury his face in her hair and hold her until the horror of the past receded, welled up and threatened to spill over into action. He stood there, hands clenched, waiting for the agony to cease. Waiting for his legs to steady.

Long moments passed as they stared at each other.

'Yes. It's because of my wife.' The husky words came out before he could stop them.

Stevie's hand, still touching his, curled around his fingers, gripping tight. 'It must have been hard last night, knowing—'

'She was pregnant.'

This time he knew exactly what he was saying. Stevie needed to know, in case he lost the war being waged inside him.

'Pregnant? Belini, you mean?'

'No, my wife.'

Her lips parted, eyes widening. 'Your wife was pregnant when she contracted dengue?'

He nodded.

The hand gripping his let go so suddenly, his fingers reflexively reached out to find hers again. Within a second or two, her palms settled on his shoulders.

'Oh, Matt, I had no idea. I'm so sorry.' Her eyes met his. 'And then to be faced with the very same situation last night.'

He shrugged. 'We all have to face things that make us… uncomfortable.'

'Uncomfortable. Don't you think this ranks a little higher than that?'

Yes. But that didn't mean he had to admit it. 'It was a long time ago.'

'It still hurts, though, even now.'

He took a step back dislodging her hands. 'It's over and done.'

'Is it?' Stevie's teeth came down on her lip. 'I think we need to go ahead with the celebration if that will help us see Belini's case through to the end. It might help with…things.'

His eyes narrowed. 'If you're referring to me, don't bother. I'm fine.'

'I'm serious, Matt. Let's just stay for a few more days. Take yourself out of the equation for a second. Maybe *I* need to make sure Belini completely recovers. We'll go through with the celebration.' This time she shrugged. 'It's not a legal wedding ceremony. It'll mean nothing to anyone outside this village, and certainly not to us.'

Well, that put him in his place, didn't it? 'You can't be serious.'

'Oh, but I am.' Her brows went up and she smiled. 'Let's get married.'

The bride didn't wear white.

But she did wear a shirt.

A concession for which Stevie was eternally grateful. And from the relief evident on her groom's face as his pale eyes swept over her, she wasn't the only one who was grateful that her assets remained safely under cover.

They'd placed him on a small stool in the center of a group of men. His dark hair, damp from a recent washing, lay slicked back from his forehead, and the black shirt he wore pulled tight across the taut muscles of his arms.

She swallowed—hard. Lordy, did he ever look good.

A tiny curl of smoke caught her attention and her eyes drifted down his chest until she came to a long wooden tube with a bowl at its end. He held the object tightly, his fingers curled around the stem.

A pipe of some kind.

While the giggling woman behind her urged her to move closer, Matt handed the pipe to another man, who took a couple of puffs then passed it on to the next one in line.

She stood over him, unsure what was expected of her but acutely aware of the large quantity of kohl the women had used in crafting and sculpting her eyes—she could have come straight out of a painting from ancient Egypt. Raccoons all across America would be green with envy.

A quick shiver went through her when Matt studied her, his warm fingers wrapping around hers and forcing her to bend towards him. She stooped until her ear was inches from his lips, praying the loosely draped fabric that crisscrossed key areas of her chest didn't gape and give everyone an eyeful. Not that they hadn't seen it all before, since none of the women present had anything on up top.

Matt whispered into her ear, and she closed her eyes as the silky smooth vibrations flowed across her senses and reached her innermost being. Her brain took extra care in reassembling the words until the meaning took hold. 'The pipe contains a hallucinogen. Don't breathe the smoke.'

Don't breathe the smoke.

She blinked. That couldn't be right. Then she glanced at his face and saw the truth.

He hadn't said, 'You look ravishing' or 'Are you okay?' He'd simply given the type of cold medical analysis she should have expected from him by now. A quick laugh erupted from her throat.

She straightened, noting the wide dilation of his pupils as she did. Had Mr. By-the-Book followed his own advice?

Surely the man wasn't high.

Her arched brows threw him a question, and his lips quirked in response.

'No. I didn't,' he murmured, in English. 'Although with the way you're dressed, I'm thinking maybe I should have indulged. More than once.'

Okay, maybe he hadn't told her she was beautiful, but he'd definitely noticed the large swaths of exposed skin. She smiled back, more pleased than she should have been. 'It could have been worse.'

He shifted on the stool. 'I doubt it.'

The medicine man cleared his throat behind them and waved his hand, indicating the ceremony was about to begin. Those too ill to attend had stayed in their huts, including Belini, but it looked like everyone else was anxious to witness the nuptials firsthand, including Tiago and Nilson, who stood on the periphery, grinning like loons.

Stevie resisted the impulse to roll her eyes. Surely they understood this was all a farce. If not, she'd set them straight at the first available opportunity. No need to make this trip more awkward than it already was.

Through all the dancing, feasting, and ceremonial pronouncements that followed—of which she understood nothing—she considered herself a pretty good sport. She even managed to sit next to Matt at the hand-carved banquet table and not give away how shaky she felt or how nervous his proximity made her. All in all, things had gone easier than she'd expected. The tribe hadn't even made her promise to love, honor, and obey Matt. Which was a good thing. Because she couldn't pledge to do any of it.

As the night shadows crept over the village, she breathed a sigh of relief. Until she spied a young girl carrying a banana leaf in both hands. Nestled inside lay a piece of cloth, a cork and a long, thin needle pre-threaded with a piece of dark string. A black bead knotted onto the end caught the firelight and gave an ominous wink.

Stevie swallowed. She had no idea what any of this meant, but the cork and needle gave her pause. If she wasn't mistaken…

She fingered one of her ears. They were already pierced so the worst that could happen was they would thread the bead through one of her preexisting holes. Right?

Right?

Was that needle even sterilized?

Matt's hand covered hers and squeezed. 'Relax. It's not for you.'

'Thank heavens.'

She glanced around and noted that none of the women's ears were pierced.

What was the needle for, then?

And the men…

One by one, she looked at them. Every male older than about thirteen years of age had at least one ear pierced. Maybe they were combining two ceremonies into one. She glanced around for a young initiate who might be going through a rite of passage.

The girl stopped in front of Matt with a shy smile, and the medicine man stepped forward. Stevie's lungs whooshed out a shocked breath. Surely they couldn't mean to pierce one of his ears.

'Matt,' she whispered. 'What are they doing?'

One brow cocked. 'Only *adult* men can go through the tribe's wedding rituals.'

'I don't understand.'

'Don't you?'

She blinked as awareness slowly took hold. 'That's crazy. Anyone in their right mind can tell you're a man.' As soon as the words left her mouth, hot color rushed into her face and she hurried to explain herself. 'I mean, you have chest hair and… everything.'

His lips twisted. 'Thanks. I think.'

'This is ridiculous. You're not going to let them pierce your ear.'

'Unless I'm marked as a man, I can't marry in this tribe.' He sent her a smile that made her shiver. 'You're the one who insisted on going through with this.'

'But that was before I knew they were going to punch holes in you.'

'It'll heal.'

'How can you be so blasé? What if the needle's not sterile?'

'It is. I ran it through our autoclave on the boat this morning.'

All this because of her stupid insistence on sticking around. She should have let him run while he'd had the chance.

The medicine man motioned for him to stand.

Stevie shot to her feet. 'Pierce my ear instead,' she said in loud Portuguese.

A moment's stunned silence followed her outburst, then rough laughter broke out among the male tribe members. Even the medicine man's normally expressionless eyes crinkled around the edges.

She didn't see what was so funny.

Matt turned to her. 'They think you're demanding to wear the pants of the family. That you want to be marked as the man of our union.'

If her face was red before, it had to be crimson now. 'I was just trying to help.'

He smiled. 'Trust me. You're not. But you are blushing up a storm.' His fingers slid across her steaming cheek. 'I like it.'

Turning away from her and facing the cluster of males, Matt lifted his chin. 'The role of man is mine and mine alone. I will care for my wife.'

His assertion didn't offend her; she knew the men expected it of him. What did bother her was the way her heart responded to the firm words. It softened into a pile of mush and threatened to lie down at his feet. She stopped it before it had a chance to embarrass her.

They're only words. He doesn't mean them.

Stepping forward with a cloth, the medicine man dampened it with something and then handed it to Matt. The sharp tang of rubbing alcohol stung her nose as he wiped down his own ear in preparation for the piercing.

He was doing this because of her.

She shook her head before her eyes could even think about misting over. No, he wasn't. He was doing it to continue the work here.

Don't get any ideas, Stevie. This man isn't on the market.

And neither are you!

The sterilization done, Matt handed the cloth back to the medicine man, who set it aside and took up the needle and cork.

This couldn't be happening.

Matt tilted his head to the side and allowed the medicine man to slide the cork behind his earlobe. If the needle had looked wicked before, it now looked positively evil. Stevie noted there was already a black dot on Matt's ear marking the correct spot. She hadn't even noticed it before, but it had to have been placed there earlier. Before the ceremony even started.

And he said he'd already autoclaved the needle.

Which meant he'd known this was going to happen all along. He'd probably seen the ceremony countless times before. Was that why he'd tried to talk her into leaving the village with him?

Maybe she'd forced him into a situation he hadn't wanted. It wasn't like he was the type of man to voluntarily sport an earring.

The medicine man raised the needle, and Stevie couldn't stop herself. She slid her hand beneath Matt's. If he was going through with it, she was going to make sure he knew she was here. His fingers tightened around hers just as the needle speared through his ear. To Matt's credit, he didn't flinch. But she did.

When the bead was threaded through and tied off close to his ear, she soaked another cloth with more alcohol and allowed the liquid to dribble over the fresh wound. 'I'm sorry. I had no idea this was going to happen.'

He sucked in a quick breath as the sting hit. 'The work I go through just to marry you.'

She watched as the medicine man handed the implements back to the young girl who'd brought them in. He then took a palm frond and touched it to Matt's head three times. Then he met her eyes and nodded for her to bow her head. She did and the frond brushed her crown in the same way it had Matt's.

When it was done, a cheer went up. The women started dancing, and the pipe with the curling smoke began making its rounds again.

That was it.

In the tribe's eyes, they were officially married.

For better or worse.

Catching sight of Matt's freshly pierced ear just before the men dragged him away with jubilant shouts, she had a feeling things were leaning toward the latter.

Tiago walloped Nilson on the back, sending the smaller man reeling a few feet before they both laughed and took off after the group of male revelers—probably already half-high from the fumes given off by that stupid pipe.

Hmm. Matt's eyes *had* seemed different, the icy blue irises shoved aside, overtaken by the black centers. Of course that could have been caused by the unholy terror of finding himself standing next to her while the medicine man voiced his grim decrees.

She'd experienced a few misgivings herself.

One of the women headed her way with a spray of velvety purple flowers. Stevie tried to smile, but the growing knot in her stomach made it difficult.

'These are to help your marriage bed.' The woman ducked her head when a couple of giggles rang through the clearing.

'To help my…bed?'

Please, God, don't let anyone try to give me any feminine wisdom about my so-called wedding night.

'Yes, it counteracts the effects of the *ayahuasca*.'

Stevie frowned. 'Ay-a-skwa?'

More giggles.

'Yes, it is what your husband smokes from the *cachimba* pipe. A man cannot…perform his duties while under its influence.'

Her eyes widened. She assumed this 'duty' didn't involve winning an easy hand of poker. Lordy, how was she supposed to answer this one?

She didn't try. She simply held her hand out to accept the flowers the woman offered. The ones that promised to transform her new husband from impotent pothead into lover extraordinaire.

Except he'd said he hadn't inhaled. And if these flowers contained some kind of natural aphrodisiac, who knew what could happen? Even as she said it, she pictured a toxin working its way through her skin and reaching her bloodstream. Her fingers tingled, the sensation slowly spreading—moving up her arm in a delicious wave.

Stop it! It's just your imagination.

Her teeth came down on her lip. But what if it wasn't all in her mind? Matt had said the pipe contained a hallucinogen. So what did the flowers contain?

'Will they make me sick?'

The woman gave a smile filled with secrets. 'No. They will make you happy. More than you dreamed possible.'

The tingle spread to her chest, her nipples tightening under the onslaught, before moving to her abdomen and then lower.

She snatched open her hand, sending the flowers tumbling to the ground.

The woman simply scooped them back up and held them out.

Her brain tripped into action, hoping to find a way to refuse to touch them again. How humiliating would it be for Matt to come to the tent and find her all hot and needy, unable to fight her own impulses. 'I—ah…'

'She is shy,' the woman explained to those around her, with a soft laugh. 'That is okay, *doutora*. I will place them on the bed for you.'

'Thank you.' Her breath exited on a relieved hiss. Let them all believe she was embarrassed. Better than having them realize the truth. That she'd suddenly pictured those sensual petals scattered over their bed and her lying among them. Naked. Waiting for Matt's arrival—performance-impaired or not.

Excusing herself, she went to check on Belini and the new baby. She found them both asleep, the woman's mother dozing on a mat nearby. How precious that tiny baby looked sprawled across Belini's chest, the girl's hand securing her tiny charge. She could understand now why Matt had seemed indifferent as to whether the baby lived or died in the beginning. It was a defense mechanism to help him cope with the tragedy of his past.

She moved closer, placing her palm carefully on the woman's forehead, feeling for fever. Cool and dry.

A good sign. Her fingers moved to the baby's back. Also cool, the infant's breathing remained slow and steady. As she watched, the tiny mouth puckered, lips moving in rhythmic twitches.

Nursing in his sleep. Another positive sign.

As if sensing the slightest shifting of her child's weight, Belini's lids parted, blinking sleepily. When she saw Stevie standing there, her brows came together. 'The baby, he is okay?'

'Oh, yes, he's perfect.'

She knelt down next to the young mother and took one of her hands. 'How do you feel?'

'Better. Still weak, but better.'

'That's normal. You need to get a lot of rest.'

Her mother's voice came from nearby. 'I will help her.'

'I'm glad,' said Stevie, who found herself missing her own mother all of a sudden. 'Well, I just wanted to make sure you were okay. I'll let you sleep.'

Belini nodded. 'Thank you. For everything.'

As Stevie ducked out of the tent, she ran smack dab into a hard masculine chest.

Matt.

Large hands came out to steady her, holding her against his body, while the scent of some exotic smoke drifted from his skin...his clothing.

Ayahuasca. Viagra's biggest foe.

She swallowed. Except Matt didn't appear to need a little blue pill. Or a magic purple flower. The man was doing fine all by himself.

His voice rumbled over her head, the low, sexy tones winding around her like silk threads. 'I've been looking for you.'

'You have?'

'Umm-hmm.'

The hand on her back shifted an inch or two, and it took the shock of warm skin-on-skin contact to remind her of the serious lack of fabric across that area of her body.

'May I ask you a question?' he asked, as if he hadn't noticed the wave of heat that scorched through her.

'Q-question?' Yikes. Was it one she could answer without making a fool of herself? 'Is it personal?'

'Yes. Very.' His chin came to rest on her hair, and something in her melted, her body swaying a little closer to catch more of that hypnotic scent.

'What is it?'

'The flower petals in our hut.' The words carried a strange intensity. 'Who scattered them on the bed? You...or someone else?'

CHAPTER THIRTEEN

WHY had he asked her about the flowers? Maybe he'd gotten a few more whiffs of the *ayahuasca* than he'd realized. But when he'd entered the ceremonial hut expecting to find plain, bare-bones quarters and had encountered, instead, a lavish scene, he'd stopped in his tracks, his blood turning to sludge in his veins.

Baskets of fruit and bread lay scattered on oil-rubbed tables of varying heights. An offering to the gods? Or a gift for the lucky couple?

He'd glanced to the side, following a trail of light. Hundreds of natural candles surrounded a creamy white hammock, whose intricately braided fringe brushed the ground. The flickering glow bathed the bed in mystery. Intimacy.

And those petals.

Everywhere.

He found himself yearning for something that had nothing to do with breathing a potent drug and everything to do with the night and the woman now in his arms.

Except she was fidgeting.

'I…no, er, I had nothing to do with them. I think one of the women must have put them there.'

He blinked, his common sense returning with a bump. He'd hoped…

Nothing. He'd hoped nothing.

Matt dropped his arms and took a step back. Stevie's cheeks had turned the color of a fine Pinot Noir. And she wouldn't meet his eyes.

Her teeth came down on her lip. 'I don't think either of us should touch them.'

'Touch who? The women?' He had no idea what she was talking about. And this night was heading to hell in a hand basket.

'No. The flowers.' Her glance stayed on the ground in front of her. 'I think they might be spiked.'

He waited for a second, but she didn't seem in a hurry to explain herself. 'You think they're what?'

'Spiked. You know, with a drug. Like the pipe.'

'What gave you that idea?'

Stevie's face flamed even darker, her hands twisting in front of her. 'I mean, I don't have *firsthand* knowledge of what they might do…or anything.' An awkward pause ensued, then she blurted out, 'The women said it would counteract the pipe.'

'The *ayahuasca*?'

She nodded.

'So if I were under its influence, which I'm not—' although he was beginning to have some serious doubts on that front '—then the flowers would help me do what?'

It hit him. Too many tokes on the pipe, and he'd be down for the count. On his wedding night.

Something about the whole ludicrous situation—the wedding in their honor, his pierced ear, the *ayahuasca,* an aphrodisiacal flower flung across his bed—struck him the wrong way and he started laughing.

'What's so funny?' Stevie demanded, her brows coming together.

He cleared his throat, getting himself under control with some effort. Maybe he should try to lighten the atmosphere a little. 'Are you sure you didn't touch those flowers? Maybe I should take your pulse.'

Her eyes widened, and she stumbled back a step. 'That's ridiculous.'

He suddenly realized why she was so embarrassed and flustered. She *had* touched the flowers, and they'd affected her in some way. He wanted to drop his gaze and see if he could note any changes. He was a doctor, after all. He should examine her medically.

Right.

'It's okay, Stevie. No harm done.'

'Of course not.' Her eyes met his for the first time since they'd run into each other. 'But we need to get them out of that room. Just in case.'

He forced his lips not to lift. 'We'll sweep them onto the floor with a leaf. It'll be fine.'

Matt's smile quickly faded at the thought of them in that tent. Alone. With 'spiked' flowers.

Flowers or no flowers, spending the night with her would be like walking through a pit of glowing coals.

Painful. And not just for his feet.

Several hours later, he was still awake. From across the darkened hut came the slow, steady sound of Stevie's breathing. It mingled with the hum of the jungle just beyond the mud walls of the simple dwelling.

He looped his hands behind his head and tried to make out the thatching of the tiny hut's roof. With the candles snuffed out, it was too dark to see anything more than shadows. This particular hut had been made for guests and weddings, so the weave was tighter than most of the other dwellings. Not a single shaft of moonlight made it through.

It should be a blessing that he couldn't see her sleeping.

But somehow the murky interior just fed his imagination all the more, and he was afraid when he did fall asleep, his dreams would take up where his thoughts left off.

If there was a hell, it couldn't be much worse than this. He wasn't even touching her, but he could feel the softness of her skin beneath his hands, catch the fragrant scent from her hair as she turned her head to smile at him. See the growing need in her eyes…

And there you had it. Pathetic lust from a pathetic, lonely man who should have better things to do.

Like check on his patients.

Which was what he intended to do. Then he'd go and spend the rest of the night on the boat. In his own bed.

Hauling himself to his feet, he couldn't resist creeping closer to the double-sized hammock where Stevie lay. Just to make sure she was okay.

She was. He could barely make out her peaceful features in the dark, softened by the filmy netting that covered her sleeping area.

He closed a tiny gap that had opened in the mosquito netting, before turning and heading out the door, hoping no one spotted him as he made his rounds across the village. Scraping the hair off his forehead, his wrist brushed something hard in the process. The bead in his ear.

Proof he was a man.

Absurd.

And yet Stevie had leapt to her feet, willing to take his punishment for him. Something about that had touched him deeply. In a spot that hadn't been touched since...Vickie

He shut his eyes. He was fast approaching a line he'd drawn in the sand four years ago. One he'd sworn he'd never cross again.

The quiet tones of Vickie's voice echoed in his head, whispering that it was okay to let go. It was time.

No. It wasn't about letting go. It was about the whole lifestyle. About making choices for himself that didn't involve putting another person at risk. Matt intended to keep things the way they were.

He'd been alone since his wife's death. And unless he wanted to give up helping these people, that's the way it had to stay.

When he got back to the boat, he unlocked the door to the exam room and took down the medical reference. Maybe he needed to remind himself what could happen when you gave in to selfishness.

Opening the book to the section on dengue, he touched a finger to his wife's flowing handwriting, his eyes misting. He blinked to clear them and forced himself to read. To keep reading, entry by painful entry.

But as he got to the last line, Vickie's gentle voice was right there.

Reminding him that he had a new wife now. And that he'd better not blow his chance.

Warm fingers touched her cheek. 'Wake up, sleepyhead. Time to rise and shine.'

Stevie wrinkled her nose. It was much too early to be morning already. Besides, she'd been up half the night, waiting for Matt to come back from wherever he'd gone.

But he hadn't.

Until now.

Her lids parted, and she encountered Matt's blue eyes, now crinkling at the corners. Laughing at her.

Oh, God, she must look a wreck, while he looked…

Amazing. Good enough to eat, piece by gorgeous piece.

Dark hair, slicked back off his broad forehead, was damp from a recent shower. The spicy scent of soap fused with the woodsy fragrance of nearby cooking fires. Once the mixture hit her nostrils, she had to force herself not to breathe it deep into her lungs.

She sat up in a rush, running trembling fingers through her hair before yanking the whole mass back and tying it into a knot. She willed him to leave until she could at least wash her face and brush her teeth.

Crouched down beside her, he seemed in no hurry to move away. 'How'd you sleep?'

Swallowing, she pulled her gaze from his only to spy the discarded remains of the flower petals on the ground. Time to lie. 'I slept just fine, thanks. How about you?'

'Passable.'

Okay, so that made two of them who were spinning wild tales of fiction, because he'd never come back to their hut last night.

Unless he'd slept in someone else's.

A lump clogged her throat. For all she knew, he had a woman in each village waiting to satisfy his every need. Just like her ex-fiancé's lover had been.

She could have sworn Matt was different than Michael. Loyal.

He'd been close to kissing her last night as they'd stood in front of Belini's hut. Until she'd opened her big mouth and somehow killed the mood.

Which was a good thing, right? Especially since she had no idea where he'd gone after he'd snuck out of their room.

Somehow, though, with Matt still kneeling beneath her stretch of mosquito netting, she felt a loss she didn't want to examine.

Dropping her hands to her lap, she racked her brain for something else to say, but he beat her to the punch. 'Belini's better. I checked on her this morning. And the other patients are getting stronger. We should be able leave within the next day or two.'

'Really? You think the worst has passed?'

A glimpse of something resembling sorrow flashed through his eyes and was gone. 'I hope so.'

'Me too.' She caught sight of his earring and winced before reaching up to touch the bead. 'Speaking of the worst being past, how's your ear doing?'

'Good. I doused it with alcohol this morning and...' His words faded away. He reached up to grab her wrist and turned it upside down.

'Hey, what are you—?'

'Hold still.' He stared at her arm, tilting it to and fro before rubbing his thumb over the tender flesh of her forearm.

Her stomach flipped as the calloused pad did wonky things to her insides.

She had no idea what he was doing. But she liked it. She had no intention of stopping him.

Had the man been rolling in those flower petals while she wasn't looking? If so, she wasn't going to complain. He leaned closer to her arm, and her lips parted as she wondered if he was going to kiss it.

'Damn it to hell,' he whispered.

Taken aback by the rough words, she blinked.

He hadn't moved from where he knelt, but the stroking had stopped. It was as if he were paralyzed in that one spot, unable to move.

'Matt? What is it?' He was blocking her view, so she couldn't see what he was so upset about. Was her arm smeared with dirt? Blood?

At her words, he sat up straight, and her limb came into view.

She dragged her eyes from his face and peered at her arm, trying to focus. What was going on?

When his thumb rubbed the spot again, she realized it was a bit itchy, like she'd been bitten…

Dread circled her insides, spinning an icy web of fear. She was in a village surrounded by dengue fever patients. And rising on her arm, looking angrier by the second, was a mosquito bite.

CHAPTER FOURTEEN

'WE DON'T even know if it was an *Aedes Aegypti* mosquito. It could have been one of any number of species.'

The stiff set of his lips didn't soften. 'It doesn't matter. We're leaving. Now.'

Standing on the deck of the medical boat, she'd been trying to get through to him for the last hour. 'Matt, be reasonable. A hospital can't do anything for me unless I'm symptomatic. So even if the bite is from a dengue carrier, the incubation period can be up to fourteen days. We'll have finished treating all the patients in the village by that time.'

A muscle worked in his jaw. 'Median incubation is four to eight days.'

'Still plenty of time. I'll take precautions not to spread it to anyone else.'

'It's not anyone else I'm worried about.' His eyes closed before reopening and fixing her with an angry glare. 'Why weren't you wearing repellent?' He dragged a hand through his hair.

'I did! At least during the day, but I don't like the stickiness or the smell at night. Besides, I had the net around the bed.'

'And you'd left a huge gap in the seam. I had to pull it closed before I went out to check on our patients.'

He was being absurd. 'The gap wasn't big. It was tiny. I didn't even see it until you—'

'You were awake?'

She licked her lips, realizing she'd been found out. 'Yes.'

'Why didn't you say something?'

She shrugged. 'What was I supposed to say?'

There was no way either of them could answer that, and she knew it.

'We should have left when the medicine man issued his warning. Or when I knew Belini was improving. Going through with the celebration last night was a mistake.'

'There was no choice. Belini could have died during labor. Her baby could have died. Midwives can't perform emergency surgery.'

He swore again. 'Do you know what could happen if you contract this?'

'Yes.' Wanting to reassure him, she touched his arm. 'I promise you, I'm not taking this lightly. I know what this disease can do. I've seen it.'

'So have I.'

'Oh, Matt, I know you have. And I hate that I'm the reason those terrible memories are resurfacing.' Her eyes moistened. 'But I want to stay. I *need* to stay. Just for a few more days. Please let me finish this.'

He stared at her for several long minutes, and then his attention shifted to her arm, which he'd insisted on slathering with antibiotic cream and covering with a waterproof bandage. Gripping her hand, he shook his head. 'I don't like this.'

'As soon as the last of our patients is in the clear, we'll leave. I promise.'

'This is all just so...' Unexpectedly, his palm cupped the back of her neck, his fingers warm and gentle as he gazed down at her. 'I owe you an apology.'

Expecting yet another argument, his words took her by surprise. 'W-what?'

He smiled. 'When you first showed up at the airport, I thought you were another down-on-your-luck medical practitioner looking to get out of the rut of your particular specialty. That you wanted to do something adventurous. Prove yourself to the world. But you're not just another washed-up doc, are you?' With gentle pressure from his hand, he drew her closer. 'You're the real deal. You're more interested in these people than you are in yourself.'

Guilt hit, hard and swift. If he only knew the real reason she'd come, he'd know she was a fraud. She *had* come here out of self-ish motives. After all, what could be more selfish than taking a job to get away from a cheating fiancé? From a hospital that no longer wanted you?

But something had changed over the course of the last two weeks. She'd grown to love the people of these villages. It was like a part of her she hadn't known was missing had suddenly dropped into place. A perfect fit.

And Matt…

Was something she didn't dare think about right now. Not when he spoke to her with something akin to admiration in his voice. An admiration which made her feel…valued. Special. Things she hadn't felt in a very long time. And there was more. Something lurked behind his eyes. A tenderness she didn't dare try to decipher.

She swallowed. 'I'm not as noble as you're making me out to be.'

'Are any of us?' He glanced around as if making sure no one would overhear them and lowered his voice. 'When I saw that bite, I—'

'I know.' The shadows in his eyes were almost more than she could bear. He was so close, and both of them were scared, lonely and hurting, right now. What would it matter in all eternity if she just leaned forward and…?

Before she realized what she was doing, she'd closed the two-inch gap that lay between them and touched her lips to his. He flinched, whether in surprise or rejection she wasn't sure. And she didn't have time to figure it out because a second later his palms slid up her arms, then cupped her cheeks. Tilting his head, he kissed her back, stepping closer until she felt the hard press of his chest against her breasts. Her nipples reacted immediately. Tightening with need.

Heaven. This was heaven. As was the firm, insistent pressure of his lips. The moist touch of his tongue as it slid along the seam of her mouth.

'*Mmm.*'

Okay, so she hadn't meant to say that aloud, but so what? And Matt didn't seem to mind, if the hand now applying steady pressure to the small of her back was any indication.

And, oh, yeah, there was that reminder that this man could rise to any occasion. She inched closer, relishing the shudder that rippled through his chest when she angled her hips just so.

She opened her mouth to let him in, and he didn't waste any time. A low growl rose in his throat as his tongue slid against hers, pressing hard and deep. A hand to the back of her head held her in place, not giving her a chance to retreat. As if she would.

Having this man drive her crazy was something she could get used to. So used to.

His thrusts held a desperation that intoxicated her—a focused intensity that weakened her knees and robbed her lungs of breath. He seemed to know exactly what course he was setting, and Stevie had no intention of trying to divert him from it.

Fisting her hands in his shirt, she fought to keep her balance as she maneuvered a set of emotional rapids, navigating around treacherous stretches of whitewater. One wrong move, and she'd slip beneath the surface.

Who cared?

Incredible. Maddening. That's what this was. And her need grew stronger with each heated stroke of his tongue.

Even with Michael—during their most intimate lovemaking—she hadn't experienced anything like this.

Never this amalgamation of ecstasy and dread that terrified her, yet made her crave more of the same.

His mouth left hers and trailed slow moist kisses down her neck. She shivered, his name coming out as a husky moan she couldn't contain.

He stopped, his lips still pressed to her throat.

She waited for him to continue, and although his breath rasped in and out as if he'd just run a marathon, he didn't move.

No!

He couldn't mean to stop. Not now. Not when everything inside of her screamed for him to lay her down on the deck and finish what he'd started.

What *she'd* started. Her eyes fluttered open as the gravity of what she'd done filtered through her foggy brain.

'I don't have anything on board.' The whispered phrase left a moist imprint on her flesh.

'Anything?' What was he talking about?

'Condoms. The ones in the first aid kit have been around forever. They're too old to be safe.'

'Oh.' Her face heated, then she remembered something. 'What about the ones in the health kits?'

'Gone. Tiago passed the last of them out to the villagers two days ago.' He paused. 'Are you protected?'

She hadn't exactly planned on having sex as she traveled down the Amazon, since she thought she'd be working with Tracy. And a two-year supply of the Pill seemed like one more thing to have to drag around with her and remember to take.

Besides. There was the 'no planned sex' thing.

'No. I'm not.' The words came out as a croak.

He raised his head to look down at her before pressing his forehead to hers. 'God. Sorry.'

For what? Being out of condoms? That he was having to stop? Just what the hell was he sorry for?

'It's nothing,' she forced herself to say.

The hands on her arms tightened, before he released the pressure. Released her. 'Right. Nothing.'

She tried to detect regret in his words, but his tone was strangely void of emotion. 'We're under a lot of stress—the outbreak…the wedding celebration.' She rubbed her bandaged arm. 'We weren't thinking rationally.'

'And now we are.'

She jerked her glance to his face. He might be, but she wasn't so sure about herself. 'Of course.'

He was silent for several long seconds, then he turned his back to her and looked out over the *Rio Preto*. When his voice came, it was firm. No sign of any of the turmoil she was battling inside. 'You have four days. Then we leave.'

Four days later, Stevie had no signs of dengue, neither were there any new cases in the village. The outbreak was over. At least for the moment. And hell if Stevie hadn't somehow talked him into continuing on to their next planned stop. As if she was certain she was in no danger from the illness.

Or from him.

He'd expected her to at least want to go back to Coari to be examined at one of the clinics. And he'd have used that time to make a quick run to the nearest *farmácia*.

Just in case.

But Stevie seemed sure of her own ability to resist temptation. To resist him.

That very thought made him want to growl a few choice words into the warm breeze. He settled for mouthing them under his breath.

'You are okay, Mateus?' Tiago's voice came from beside him on deck.

'Fine.'

'Why, then, are you still sleeping in the dining hall? Did you fight with Miss Stevie?'

His fingers tightened on the rail. 'No, I did not fight with Miss Stevie.' Whose bright idea had it been to allow the village to throw them an honorary wedding ceremony? He should set his crew members straight and tell them the ceremony had been a fraud, but he was afraid word might make its way back to Belini's village and offend the chief. So he kept his mouth shut.

'Then why—?'

Matt held up his hand to stave off the question. 'I didn't need any distractions, especially now.'

'Ah, I see.' The other man smiled. 'She is a very beautiful woman, no?'

His attention jerked to Tiago's face, a strange wave of anger and possessiveness coursing through him. 'Yes. As is your own wife.'

'Of course. I didn't mean to offend.' There was nothing in his crew member's demeanor that indicated he was interested in Stevie. Which made Matt feel like a first-class cad.

'You didn't offend me. I'm just worried.' He decided to tell

Tiago part of the reason for that worry. 'She was bitten back at the village.'

'Bitten?' His eyes widened. 'By a mosquito? You think she might catch the sickness?'

'No.' But even he could hear the doubt behind his negation. And if he could, then Tiago definitely heard it.

Sure enough, the man crossed himself as if warding off evil. 'Surely God would not see fit to take two...'

Probably realizing he'd said way too much, Tiago allowed his words to fade away, but Matt could fill in the rest of the sentence: Surely God wouldn't see fit to take two of Matt's wives.

That was exactly the reason they should turn this boat around and head in the opposite direction.

Except he'd promised Stevie he'd trust her judgement.

Like he had Vickie's?

She's not really your wife, Matt. She's a colleague, nothing more.

Even as he thought the words, his fingers went to the bead in his left ear.

'She will not contract the illness. Have faith.' Tiago gave his shoulder a quick squeeze before he left to go about his work.

Have faith.

At one time those words would have awoken something within him. But not any more. His faith had failed him before. He wasn't sure he could risk his heart—or Stevie's—to the whims of a silent deity.

Not this time. Because the second she'd kissed him while standing on that deck four days ago something inside him had shifted.

First in his body. And then in his heart.

Until he could figure out how to crush the emotion...or at least hold it at bay...he needed to make sure he didn't put her in any more danger.

CHAPTER FIFTEEN

'I TOLD you, I'm not leaving. I signed on for two years, remember?'

Stevie kept her eyes on the small boy she was treating, smearing antibiotic lotion onto the child's cut and reverting back to Portuguese. 'See there? It didn't hurt at all.'

Even though she hadn't glanced at Matt, she could feel his glare searing the back of her white T-shirt.

'It's the easiest solution. The villagers at Tupari will continue to think we're married, even if you return to the States. So far none of the other villages have questioned your presence or our relationship. And with you gone, there'll be no need for the crew to wonder whether or not that wedding ceremony was the real thing or not.'

She rolled her eyes as she sent her patient on his way. It wasn't like Matt had gone to great lengths to fool anyone. He was still sleeping in the dining hall. They hadn't touched since that fiasco of a kiss on the deck a week ago. 'All we have to do is tell them the truth.'

He moved around to stand in front of her where he towered over her. She suddenly regretted her precarious perch on the log, but she'd wanted to be at eye level with the child she'd been treating. She'd had no idea Matt would bring up this subject.

Again.

Her mosquito bite had faded to a tiny bruise, and there'd been no signs of illness. Eleven days and counting. In another three or four, it would be safe to assume she was out of the woods.

At least as far as Dengue was concerned.

'I didn't want Nilson or Tiago to say anything to the villagers. Neither the medicine man nor the chief would take kindly to being lied to.'

'I know how much of a hardship all of this has been for you.' The waspish words were out before she could stop them. She stood, just to show him she wasn't afraid of him. Or maybe to show herself.

They'd set up a makeshift clinic in the large cooking area of the village they were currently visiting, a place where anyone who needed medical attention could find them. The neat dirt clearing was the size of a basketball court, and the true heart of the tribe. With people constantly traipsed through the clearing on their way to one place or another, it made having this kind of discussion difficult, which was why they'd switched to English. To Stevie, it seemed rude, like they were whispering secrets about those around them.

Tiago and Nilson were busy scrubbing down the deck of the *Projeto Vida*, so they were safely out of earshot. The only witnesses to their argument were a few women who knelt a short distance away, beating cassava roots that would later be turned into a type of flour. Without special attention to preparation, the roots contained a toxin powerful enough to kill. Her and Matt's raised voices had piqued the interest of the small group, causing a couple of the women to glance their way. Stevie balked at saying anything else, even in English.

'Can we continue this discussion another time?' She nodded toward the women. 'They need to concentrate on what they're doing. I, for one, prefer not to be the cause of the whole tribe dying of cyanide poisoning.'

Matt's glance flicked to the group. 'Let's go down by the river.'

Before she had a chance to respond, a woman came up to them, holding a baby in her arms. The worry on her face caught Stevie's attention immediately, as did the infant's thin cries. Stroking the baby's cheek, Stevie tried to soothe the child while gauging the temperature and moisture level of her skin. 'Is your baby sick?'

'Yes. She cries and refuses to nurse. And today she began to vomit.'

Matt moved forward and eased the swaddling back from the baby's forehead. 'No fever.' He glanced at the mother. 'When was she born?'

'Two days ago.'

Stevie held out her arms, silently asking to hold the child. The mother hesitated, glancing from one to the other.

'It's okay,' Stevie said. 'I just want to look at her. I promise I'll give her back.'

Once the child was in her arms, she rocked her gently, a frightening sense of déjà vu shooting through her as the baby refused to be comforted. Just a few months ago she'd held an infant very similar to this one and listened to the anguished pleas of his parents as they'd begged her to save their child. In New York, Stevie had had access to the best equipment modern medicine could buy. The only thing she'd lacked had been the hospital's permission to operate. This time no hospital stood in her way, but the boat had rudimentary facilities and if the problem was serious…

Was one situation any better than the other?

She crushed the painful memory and glanced at Matt. 'Do we examine her here or on the boat?'

'Let's start here.' He motioned toward the stool. 'You can lay her across your lap and undress her in her mother's presence.'

While Matt asked some questions, Stevie listened with half an ear as she unwrapped the blanket. The first thing she did was check the wadding between the baby's legs. Slightly wet, but no sign of feces.

Next, she used her index finger to compress the skin on the baby's arm and examine the color. Normal and pink. No sign of jaundice or compromised blood flow. Closing her eyes, she sent up a quick prayer of thanks.

She continued down her mental checklist, her glance traveling down the baby's chest and over the abdomen.

Distended.

Palpating lightly, she encountered firm coils of bowel on the left side. Possible obstruction. She glanced up at the mother.

'Has she had a bowel movement?' she asked in Portuguese.

The mother tilted her head. 'I do not understand.'

Matt changed the wording and re-asked the question.

'No,' the mother said. 'There's been nothing.'

She switched to English. 'I want to take her aboard. I think she may have an obstruction.'

Half expecting Matt to interfere or try to take over the case, he did neither. 'How do you want to handle it?'

'If she hasn't passed meconium yet, there could be a plug. A simple saline enema could resolve the problem. If not, we'll have to look at some more serious possibilities.'

'Okay. Let's do it.'

Her eyes widened. And that was it? No arguments? No waffling? She waited a few seconds just in case, but nothing came. He was letting her follow her instincts. So different than Michael's reaction would have been.

Carefully rewrapping the infant, she stood and tucked the baby against her shoulder, turning to explain the situation to the mother. 'Can we take her on the boat? You can come with us.'

'You will not hurt her?'

'No, I promise. I'm hoping she'll feel better very soon.'

The whole process took less time than Stevie expected. Within thirty minutes, just as she'd hoped, the warm saline did the trick.

'Thank God,' she breathed to herself.

Matt, who'd stayed by her side throughout the procedure, laid a hand on her shoulder, giving it a quick squeeze. 'Good work. You were right.'

The warmth of his hand, along with his easy praise, sent a shiver of longing through her. She wanted to stay right here and relish this moment—to take it deep into her heart. But she still had her patient to care for.

Quickly cleaning the baby, she leaned down to kiss her tiny cheek. 'You're going to be just fine. Grow up big and strong for me, okay?'

As if understanding exactly what Stevie said, the child scrunched up her face and let out a cry. Not of pain this time. But if Stevie was interpreting the sound correctly, she was hungry.

Famished.

She handed the baby to her mother, who put her to her breast. Rooting around for a second, the infant soon found her target and latched on. Sounds of vigorous nursing filled the air around them.

'She eats.' The mother's eyes met hers. 'If you had not been here to help…' Her voice trailed away, and she stroked her daughter's head.

Matt left the room, shutting the door with a quiet click. As much as she wanted to follow him, she knew she had to make sure the baby and her mother were going to be okay. She waited for the infant to finish feeding, then checked her over once again. The baby's abdomen had already lost much of its bloated appearance. 'I'll have Tiago take you back to shore, but I'd like to check her again tomorrow. Make sure you find me.'

'Yes, I will.'

As soon as the dinghy left for shore, Stevie went looking for Matt. Probably not a wise move, but knowing his wife had been pregnant when she'd died changed things. Once she knew he was okay, she'd go back to her cabin and try to get some sleep.

She found him in the dining room, hunched over the table. His hammock was already strung up for the night, but he was still dressed. He looked up as soon as she entered, and the question she'd been about to ask died in her throat.

His face…dear Lord, *his face.* The man was in agony.

She hurried over to him. 'What is it? Your neck?'

'I'm fine.' He stood, and only then did she notice the open medical reference on the tabletop. At the sight of familiar slanting handwriting, her heart sank. She hadn't noticed the book's absence from the shelf in the infirmary as she'd worked on the baby.

'Oh, Matt. Don't do this to yourself.'

He shook off her words with an irritated lift of his left shoulder. 'What I'm *doing* is my job.'

'And yet you want to send me away and keep me from doing mine.' She motioned to the book. 'It all makes sense now. I think by reminding yourself of the terrible things that happened to your wife, it'll be easier to force me to leave.'

She took a step forward, tilting her face until she saw the brilliant blue of his eyes. Those eyes that made her insides quake every time they met hers. 'Don't you see, Matt? I can be an asset to your work. There may be women in some of the villages who won't feel comfortable talking to a man, but they'd be okay sharing personal health problems with me. Yes, the conditions on the boat are difficult, given the space constraints, but we can make it work. Can't you see the benefit of having both a man and a woman on the team?'

'You're making a good argument, but—'

'But nothing. I'm right and you know it. I've yet to hear you say anything that convinces me otherwise.'

'It's not that I don't think you're capable.' A muscle worked in his jaw. 'You've proven time and time again that you are. But if something happened…I don't want to be responsible.'

'Happened. You mean to me?'

He nodded.

Stevie put her hand on his forearm, the action bringing her a step closer. Something told her his need to get rid of her went far deeper than he was letting on. 'What happened to your wife wasn't your fault, Matt. As awful as it was, she chose to be here. With you. It's what she wanted.'

The muscles under her hand bunched until they became a solid mass, hard and unyielding. 'I think you should leave my wife out of this.'

'Someone needs to make you see the truth.' She released his arm so she could slide her fingers down the rigid line of flesh in his neck. 'The problem with your back, did it begin after your wife died?'

'None of this is any of your business.' He reached back and gripped her wrist, pulling it away from him.

Before he could drop her hand, she twined her fingers around his and held on. 'You want to get rid of me because of what happened to your wife. I think that makes it my business.'

'No. It doesn't.' Despite his words, he didn't walk away from her, didn't wrench his hand from hers. But there was an awful despair in his eyes that tore at her. He'd lost his wife and baby to a disease that claimed lives every year along the Amazon. What right did she have to minimize what he'd gone through?

None.

But she wished with all her might she could make his pain go away. That when he looked at her he didn't see a potential disaster, but a potential...

Her lips parted. Oh, God. What was she thinking?

This was a man who'd never gotten over the loss of his wife. A man who might never look at a woman and see anything other than heartache. Why else would he insulate himself from any female contact, outside those he treated in the villages?

She was a fool to think that would ever change.

That she would even *want* it to change. Hadn't she already slogged through one disastrous relationship and come through on the losing end? Did she really want to jump into one she knew from the onset was doomed?

No.

Yes.

'Stevie?'

Her eyes watered unexpectedly, and she tried to blink away the moisture, but it was too late. The second her lids slammed shut, two tears squeezed from between them and tumbled down her cheeks.

'Oh, hell.' He wrapped an arm around her and pulled her against him, until her cheek was resting against his chest. She could hear the thunderous beat of his heart as it pumped blood through his body, the sound sure and solid beneath her ear. The sensation made her even weepier, and she gritted her teeth to force the tears down her throat.

His fingers filtered through her hair, until he reached her scalp and rubbed in soothing circles. 'I don't know why I said that. You're right. None of this is your fault. And it's not really why I've been trying to find a replacement.' His voice rumbled beneath her cheek.

'Why are you, then?'

His fingers paused for a moment, before taking up where they'd left off. 'You don't want to know.'

She tilted her head to look up at him, but only got a close-up view of the bottom of his chin. There was a small scar she'd never noticed before. She longed to touch it, but didn't dare. 'I do want to know.'

'Trust me on this one.'

'If knowing will help me change your mind…'

'It would. That's what I'm afraid of.'

'I don't understand. What are you afraid of?'

His chin moved to and fro as he shook his head. 'I can't tell you.'

'Then show me. Help me understand.' Her hand went to his face, her thumb tracing the sharp angle of his cheekbone.

'Don't.' The low rasp of his voice slid through her like silk.

The whole world shifted. The solid press of his body was no longer comforting, but deadly. Her brain searched frantically for something that would anchor her to reality, but found nothing but longing.

Need.

Aware she was treading on dangerous ground, she touched her lips to the scar on his chin. 'Where did you get this?' she whispered.

'What?' The fingers in her hair had long ceased their exploration and lay tense and still against her head.

'Your scar. I never noticed it before.'

'Surfboard.'

Stevie took a moment to digest this. The man who was afraid to live his life had once braved ocean waves? 'You used to surf?'

'No. A roommate left his board near the door of our dorm room. I tripped over it in the dark, and it caught me in the chin. Six stitches.'

She smiled. 'Ouch.'

'Stevie?'

'Yes?'

'I think you should move away before I do something we'll both regret.'

Her heart tripped a couple of beats. 'Are you sure about that?'

'That I'll do something I'll regret?'

'No. Are you sure we'd *both* regret it?'

His fingers fisted in her hair and used gentle pressure to tilt her head back. 'Are you saying you wouldn't?'

She licked her lips. 'Are you saying you would?'

He slowly shook his head back and forth. 'No.'

'Then, if neither of us would regret it...'

His head lowered until his mouth was a prayer away from hers. And she was praying like mad.

'Not here,' he muttered.

He took hold of her hand and led her back to the bedroom, closing the door with a click.

With her heart hammering in her chest, she pressed her back against the solid wooden surface.

Please don't back out this time.

He answered her silent plea by propping a hand on either side of her head, and without touching her anywhere else leaned in and placed a hard kiss on her mouth. She immediately tried to wiggle closer, only to have him swear and lean his forehead against hers.

'Damn. No protection, remember?'

Stevie should care. Really she should. But at the moment all she wanted was his mouth back on hers. The kiss had been way too short and intoxicating to end so quickly. She'd worry about the rest later.

'Tiago's married, isn't he? I saw a ring. Maybe he has something.'

'He does have something: five kids.' Matt gave a soft laugh.

'Oh.'

'Yeah. Oh.'

But instead of moving away from her, he edged closer, sliding his cheek across hers, the slight rasp of his beard sending a needy shiver through her.

'Do you trust me?' His lips brushed the sensitive flesh of her ear with each word.

The breath whooshed from her lungs, and she had to replace it before she could manage to answer. 'Yes.'

'I won't put you at risk. I promise.'

The only thing at risk right now was him if he didn't put his mouth back on hers immediately. 'Stop talking,' she ordered.

'So bossy.' His low laugh softened the words, while his hands slid down her arms until they reached her hips. Fingers biting into her flesh, he brought her against him, until she felt each hard inch of him.

Heavens. There was more of him than she'd expected.

Wrapping her arms around his neck, she stretched up on tiptoe, hoping to find his lips, but he leaned just out of reach. The tantalizing slope of his mouth shifted into a crooked grin. 'Not until you say something.'

'What?'

'Say you like it when I kiss you.'

'You know I do.' Her fingers pushed into his hair, hoping to force his head down, but it was like trying to drag a two-hundred-pound anchor across the ocean floor. Impossible.

'I don't know.' He moved an inch closer until their breaths met. Mingled. 'So say it.'

'Matt, please.'

'Uh-uh. Say the words.'

'I like it.'

'You like what?'

She squirmed against him, an answering smile coming over her when a groan erupted from his throat. 'I like that I can make you do that.'

'Hell, woman. You have no idea what you might make me do if you keep that up.'

Her eyes widened. 'Oh.'

'Yeah. Oh.' He held her hips still. 'It's been a while.'

Leaning down, he tugged her lower lip between his teeth and

stroked his tongue across it, sending a wild electrical charge through her before he backed off again. She almost screamed with frustration, fisting her hands in his shirt and giving him a quick thump in the chest. 'Stop it.'

'Sorry. There are just so many delectable spots. I can't decide where to start.'

'Anywhere. Start anywhere. I don't care.' Neither did she care that the words came out a panted plea.

'In that case…' His nose brushed the line of her jaw and tipped her head to the side. 'I think I'll start here.'

He kissed her throat, his lips warm and sure. 'Your neck drives me crazy. So long. So delicate. You don't know how many times I've wanted to run my tongue along this line.' He demonstrated in slow motion, wringing a strangled moan from her.

'Or how many times I've wanted to bite you right here.' His teeth nipped at the joint between her shoulder and her throat and then stuck around to suckle the spot before moving an inch to the right and repeating the action.

Sweet heavens. She'd wanted him to shut up and kiss her, but the lush explicitness of his commentary made her imagination run wild. Her nipples tightened even as they wondered when he was going to include them in his little soliloquy.

As if privy to her thoughts, his hands slid beneath her shirt and swept over her ribcage until he reached her breasts, covering them with his palms.

She heard him suck down a breath. 'Damn. This should be illegal.'

'What should?'

'Going braless.' His thumbs scraped over her sensitive peaks, and her eyes fluttered closed at the raw sensations he sent spiraling through her belly. 'But I like it.'

He shoved her shirt up and over her head, tossing it to the side where it slid down the wall with a whisper of sound.

Her senses were running so hot that while the air around her must have been warm and balmy, the soft breeze that brushed against her torso seemed chilly. And empty.

She wasn't cold for long, because Matt's mouth soon took up

where his hands left off, tugging at one of her nipples and stroking it repeatedly with his tongue.

Whimpering with need, she burrowed her fingers into his hair and held him against her.

He obliged by biting down, and she arched against him, her legs threatening to give out when he held her captive with his teeth, lapping at the most sensitive spot with his tongue. A terrible, awful wave went through her, and she tugged at his hair, needing more from him, not wanting to wait another second. 'Matt.'

He answered by covering her lips with his, crowding her against the door with his body. Her tongue speared into his mouth, showing him the only way she knew how what she wanted from him. When his hands slid over her butt and cupped the backs of her thighs, it was as if they were of one mind. She parted her legs and allowed him to lift her onto his hips where that hard ridge of flesh hit just the right spot.

Something in the back of her mind registered that she still had on her slacks. Her panties. But he was pressing into her and releasing with rhythmic strokes, while she mimicked the timing with her tongue. No way was she going to stop and argue what now seemed like a minor point. There was plenty of time.

Plenty. Of…

Matt suddenly added another exquisite layer, sliding deeper between her thighs, her tortured flesh screaming *Yes!* when he picked up the pace, even as her mind warned her it was too soon. Too many clothes still lay between them. And, God, he was right there…pressing…grinding…groaning that it was okay…

Her head went back, mouth tearing from his as an orgasmic wave like nothing she'd ever encountered roared over her, tossing her end over end. She screamed, the sound impossible to contain, before his mouth covered hers again, trapping the remainder of the shriek. All the while, his body continued to move, not letting up until he'd wrung the very last spasm from her. She went limp in his arms, shaking as she held onto him for dear life.

He kissed her softly, again and again, murmuring how beautiful she was, how much he'd needed her to come for him.

Fragments of reality returned, a splinter here, a scrap there, taking over the mindless pleasure she'd just received. Her brain registered several things at once: the roughness of Matt's shirt against her sensitive nipples; the fact that she still had on most of her clothes; that he'd kept his word and not put her at risk.

And that he was still hard.

So very, very hard.

She blinked. Surely he'd already…

Her eyes met his, saw the stiff set of his mouth as he tried to smile at her, and she knew.

He hadn't.

'Matt. Put me down for a minute.'

He did, visibly wincing as her body skimmed over his.

This wouldn't do. Not at all. Stevie was all about fair play.

Okay, so that was a lie. The reality was that his still-raging hard-on was getting under her skin. All over again.

She slid her hands to the front of his jeans, searching for the button.

'Don't. We can't.'

A slow smile tilted her lips. '*We're* not. I am.'

The button on his jeans slid through the hole with a pop, and Matt shuddered as she tugged the zipper down his length.

'Hell, woman, if you keep doing that, I won't be able to stop.'

Sliding to her knees before him, she hauled his pants down in one quick motion, releasing him to her viewing pleasure. Her hand wrapped around him, and she leaned closer, watching his eyes darken as he realized what she was about to do. 'Well, now, Doctor. That's exactly what I'm counting on.'

CHAPTER SIXTEEN

MATT stared out over the dark, silent river, and though his feet remained anchored to the deck of the boat, the uneasy sensation that had kept him up most of the night persisted.

Something inside him was in danger of slipping beneath the surface of the *Rio Preto*—never to be seen again—drowning, held down by a piece of unbreakable cording. Even as he railed against his fate, he was powerless to fight it. Nearby lay more of the same strands, undulating to and fro, like slender filaments of seaweed just waiting to ensnare his foot if it ventured too close.

Stevie was still in her hammock as far as he knew. And he wasn't about to go in that room to wake her up. If he did, another treacherous strand would loop around him.

Even now he could feel the warm heat of her mouth as she'd enveloped him, her eyes never leaving his as she brought him to the edge of oblivion.

And hell if that memory wasn't enough to make him hard.

He gripped the handrail. Last night he'd miscalculated his willpower, and although they hadn't consummated the union—he knew himself well enough to know things weren't going to end there.

It was time to decide. He needed to do one of two things. Either pick up a package of condoms so he didn't have to wonder any longer what it would be like to slide into her depths and lose himself inside her. Or get Stevie off this boat and send her home before he got in even deeper. He cringed at the wording.

Just how strong was he? Could he send her away?

It was the smart thing to do.

But no one had ever said he always chose the wisest path. And it wasn't the first time a woman had swayed his decision.

Just look at what had happened to Vickie. He closed his eyes, his hand clenching the rail tighter. If they'd just gone back to the city when he'd wanted to, there was a good chance she and the baby would be alive today.

But they weren't. And Stevie was. Alive and healthy, and she'd come to Brazil for all the right reasons, unlike some of the doctors who had come through before her.

As if he'd summoned her, he sensed her come up behind him just before she appeared in his peripheral vision.

'You okay?' She stood alongside him at the edge of the deck.

Her question brought a quick smile to his face. He should be the one asking that, not her. He'd practically sent her crashing through the solid door of the bedroom last night. He'd noticed a bruise or two on her hips as she'd undressed, where his fingers had gripped her flesh. He'd fled the room soon afterwards.

'I'm fine.' He swallowed. 'About last night, I—'

'If you're going to apologize, save it.' She tossed her head, sending a couple of loose curls flipping over her shoulder. 'We're both adults. We both wanted what happened.'

Oh, he'd wanted a whole lot more than what they'd done, and he couldn't trust himself not to take it—all of it—which was why he'd turned around and headed back to Coari first thing that morning. Before he did something he really would regret.

'Okay. No apologies.'

She peered up at the sky and tilted her head. 'Wait. Aren't we headed in the wrong direction? I thought for sure I'd…persuaded you to keep me on. For a while at least.'

He frowned at her choice of words. Hopefully the persuasion she was referring to had to do with the pretty little speech she'd given in the dining room and not to what they'd done last night.

'We're out of health kits. I decided to go to Coari to pick up some supplies.'

It wasn't a lie. Not completely anyway. Belini's village had taken up a huge chunk of time. As soon as he made a decision about whether to keep Stevie on the team or drop her off once they arrived at the city, he'd head back down the river and make the rest of his stops.

'What about the baby? I told her I'd check on her today.'

'I saw Tiago when he came back to the boat. He said the baby had another bowel movement on the way to shore. He should be fine.'

'I'm so glad.' She paused. 'Since we're heading back, would it be possible to stop at Tupari? I'd like to say hello and check on Belini.'

'I'm sure things are fine. I can radio Tracy and ask if she's heard anything from the tribe.'

She frowned up at him. 'Surely we can spare a couple of hours. We haven't passed the village yet, have we?'

'No.' But he didn't want her stepping foot in Tupari as long there was the slightest possibility that any dengue infections were still active. She'd dodged the bullet this time. But what about the next?

Anger welled up inside him. *Send her home, then.*

If he couldn't separate his heart from his head, he needed to be man enough to do something about it. He couldn't continue to be paralyzed by fear. If that meant never working with another woman—which had been a decision Tracy had taken out of his hands this time—then he needed to make it clear he'd leave *Projeto Vida* if she went against him again.

'What are you thinking about?'

He shrugged. 'About how long it'll take to get back to the city.'

Laying a hand on his arm, she slid it down a few inches until her fingers encircled his wrist. 'Please. I'll never forgive myself if we pass by the village and something happens.'

The what-ifs worked their evil magic. Only this time he could do something about them, rather than let them play mind games on him. 'Fine. We'll stop. But only for an hour or two.'

'Thank you.' She smiled up at him, reaching on tiptoe and pressing her soft lips against his cheek. 'You won't regret it.'

He already did.

Nilson's voice came from behind him. 'Tiago just radioed. He's asking when you'll be back for him.'

'Back for him? I thought you said he came back aboard last night.' Stevie stared at Matt, her expression puzzled.

'He returned to the village early this morning. It's his tribe. His wife and children are there.'

'I didn't realize he was from one of the…' She tilted her head. 'Why didn't you wake me up?'

Not a chance. He'd been half-crazy at what he'd let himself do…at what he'd let Stevie do. He was afraid if he lay in that room with her until dawn, he'd finish things between them. So when he'd told Tiago he wanted to head back to Coari, his crew member had stared longingly at shore. Matt had realized that by cutting their visit short, Tiago's time with his family would also be cut short. So he'd told him to take a few days of vacation. The fact that there'd be one less person to chide Matt if he decided to leave Stevie behind hadn't played into his decision at all.

'It was early. I thought you'd like to sleep in for a change.' He turned to Nilson. 'Tell him I'm not sure of the exact date. But I'll radio a few days ahead of time. He won't lose any pay.'

Nilson shrugged, clearly at a loss as to what was going on, but he left to do as Matt asked.

Once the man was out of earshot, Stevie leaned against the rail and faced him. 'Well?'

'Well, what?'

'You didn't stay in the bedroom last night. Then I find out Tiago has gotten off the boat without a word. I didn't even have a chance to say goodbye to him. Now we're suddenly on our way back…' Her eyes widened. 'That's it, isn't it? You're running away. Because of what went on between us.'

'I told you we needed supplies.' He took a step closer. 'That includes condoms. Has it even dawned on you what could have happened? If you had made the merest suggestion that we…' He jabbed at the air with his index finger, unable to use the strong word that came to mind. 'If you'd climbed on top of me, I wouldn't have stopped you.'

'But I didn't.' She smiled. 'You didn't seem to mind what I did instead.'

He gave her no answering smile. 'That's not the point. I can't trust myself around you.'

'That's funny, because I distinctly remember you asking me if I trusted you. I did.' Her brows went up. 'I still do.'

He gave a harsh laugh. 'Haven't you heard? A man will say anything when it comes to sex.'

'Some might. But you didn't. You kept your word.' She reached up and touched his ear. 'The man who did this to save a pregnant woman's life doesn't say things he doesn't mean. That man keeps his word, no matter what he has to sacrifice.'

He shook his head. 'I'm not that noble, Stevie.' His hand sifted through the loose locks of her hair before tangling his fingers in them and holding her in place. 'I wanted you last night, and I took what I wanted.'

'I wanted it too, Matt. You make it sound ugly, like I had no choice in the matter.'

'It shouldn't have happened.'

'Maybe. But it did.' Her lids lowered until he couldn't read her thoughts. 'It happened, and I liked it. I seem to remember you asking me to say those very words.'

His chest contracted. How could he not remember? Every second was etched in his mind forever. He'd never wipe the memory away no matter how hard he tried.

Which begged the question. Why make her leave if it made no difference in the end?

'I remember.' He smiled, conceding his heart had already made the decision, even if his mind refused to admit it. 'But we still need condoms. Just in case there's a next time.'

Stevie blinked, then laughed, the sound a rainbow mixture of sunshine and rain. 'That's really why we're tearing back to *Coari* like a bat out of hell, isn't it?'

'I already told you, we're out of health kits.'

'Right. Health kits. With a side order of condoms.' She sidled up to him and wrapped her arms around his neck. 'I was afraid you'd decided to get rid of me.'

A wave of guilt rushed over him, but he ignored it, focusing on the soft press of curves against his body. 'Did you?'

There, not really a negation of her question. Not quite a lie.

'I did.' She sighed and nuzzled his neck. 'I'm glad I was wrong.'

He allowed himself one quick kiss before taking a step back, physically and emotionally. 'I think it's better if we don't shake our fists at fate just yet. Not until after we've reached the city and solved at least one problem.'

'You're the boss.' She blinked. 'But I do want to stop in and see Belini. Just for a minute or two. Deal?'

'Deal.'

'Thank you.' Her palm slid over the top of his hand, her pinky catching his and holding on. 'Are you positive you don't want to come back to bed for a while?'

The sensual promise in her voice made all kinds of interesting possibilities kick to life in his skull. But he'd lectured himself on this very thing a half hour ago. Better to wait until his head caught up to his heart before wading past the shallow end of this particular pool.

'Not a good idea under the circumstances.'

She grinned and released him. 'Okay. But don't say I didn't offer.'

The sassy swing of her hips as she headed off in the direction of the bedroom made him have second thoughts.

But who knew what the next few days might bring? The decision of whether to keep Stevie on or not might already be out of his hands. She'd overheard him ask Tracy to find someone else. It would be easy to shrug his shoulders and pretend he'd had no choice in the matter.

Wouldn't it?

No. But sometimes it was better to leave life-and-death decisions to someone else. Matt had found that out the hard way.

The view as they came around the bend in the river made Stevie's heart soar. Her lips curved as she spied several children playing while their mothers washed clothes nearby. Three fishing canoes bobbed against the slow-moving current, the men busy gathering food for the day.

Normal, mundane activities. And compared with what they'd found the first time she'd set foot in this village, it was nothing short of a miracle.

She turned to Matt, who stood nearby. 'They look good. Healthy.'

'They do. But remember we're only staying for an hour or two.'

'Thank you. I just needed to check, you know?'

'I know.' The warm smile he sent her put the final touch on a perfect day. Stevie couldn't have asked for a happier ending to what might have been a tragic tale. She scoured the shoreline. 'I don't see Belini yet.'

'She has a new baby to tend to. If something was wrong, we'd know it by now.'

They passed by one of the fishing boats, and Matt called out greetings. The man aboard nodded back, but he was busy hauling in his net. Small fish flipped and tussled as the water quickly drained through tiny holes, until there was no liquid left.

Stevie looked closer, admiring the fine, tight weave. Strange, most fishing nets had larger holes, didn't they?

'Hell.' The muttered word from beside her made her glance at Matt's face. His jaw was tight as he watched the villager dump the entire load of fish into his boat.

The next canoe in the group did the same, the net featuring an identical narrow weave. It looked so familiar.

She realized why and gasped in shock and dismay. 'They're using the mosquito nets we brought.'

'So I see.'

'But th-they can't. They need those so they don't have another outbreak.'

So much for her perfect day. She sucked down an exasperated breath, then realized she was probably overreacting. It was only two nets after all. The third boat was still using the standard fishing nets, from what she could see in the distance.

Just let it go, Stevie. It's no big loss.

Nilson came on deck and helped them set anchor, before lowering the dinghy in the water. Stevie's excitement returned when she realized how much they had to be thankful for. The fact that the men were fishing was a good sign. It meant everything was okay in the village. At least for now.

Matt leaped into the small boat and then helped Stevie get in. Sitting down, he rowed with strong strokes that emphasized his powerful tanned biceps—a fact that Stevie swore she only noticed in passing—and soon had them on shore.

Leaving Matt so he could locate the chief and announce their arrival, she hurried toward Belini's hut, only to find it empty. Not even the mosquito netting they'd hung was in evidence. Surely she hadn't… A momentary wave of panic hit her before she wrestled it back down.

You're being ridiculous. It's a good sign, not a bad one.

Belini was well enough to leave her house, something she hadn't been able to do the last time she'd seen her. Stevie stepped outside the dwelling and, after stopping to receive several excited greetings from some of the other women, asked if anyone knew where Belini was.

'Perto do rio,' one of them answered.

Strange, Stevie had just come from the river. Had she missed seeing Belini somehow?

She glanced around and spotted Matt in front of the chief's hut and decided she'd better pay her respects as well.

'You are well?' the man asked.

'Yes, very. And you?'

'The village is again healthy.'

Stevie nodded. 'I'm so glad.'

'Your husband is making you happy?'

A sudden rush of heat poured into her face. She'd almost forgotten these people thought she was married to Matt. But this was one question she could answer without lying, because she had been happy for the last couple of days. 'Yes.'

Matt stepped over to her side. 'She wouldn't let me pass Tupari without stopping in to see how the tribe was doing.'

'I went to Belini's hut, but she wasn't there.'

'She's washing vegetables by the river.' The fierce pride on his face was unmistakable.

Matt took her arm. 'I'll help you find her.' He nodded to the chief. 'I'm sorry we can't stay for tonight's ceremony.'

'Next trip,' the man said.

'Of course.'

As they strolled back toward the river, she inhaled deeply allowing the fragrant clean air to rinse her cares away. If paradise existed, this had to be it. 'What ceremony are we missing?'

'Another wedding. I didn't think you were up for a repeat of the last one.' He grinned down at her and fingered his earring. 'I don't know about you, but I haven't fully recovered from ours yet.'

Stevie laughed. 'You're just afraid of getting high from that pipe again.'

'Oh, so it's only me who had trouble, is it? I seem to remember a certain flower that—'

'Ugh. Don't remind me. Let's just find Belini before we're roped into staying the night.'

They reached the river just as the woman in question came out of a stand of trees, the baby wrapped in cloths and strapped to her chest. As soon as she saw them, she dropped the bundle of vegetables she was carrying and ran to Stevie, gripping her in a hug so tight Stevie feared for the baby's well-being.

'You came to visit! I knew you would!'

Stevie slanted Matt a triumphant I-told-you-it-was-the-right-thing-to-do glance as she pulled away from the embrace. 'How's the baby?' She bent closer to see the child. Wide-set eyes, retaining the typical blue cast of all newborns, seemed to stare back at her. 'He's so beautiful.'

'His name is Stevie.'

She straightened quickly and stared into the face of her newfound friend. 'What?'

'You and Mr. Matt save his life. My son will keep a part of you for always.'

Matt squeezed her arm. 'It's a big honor. I've never heard of them using a foreign name for a child.' He'd spoken in English so no one could understand except her.

Unable to stop herself, she leaned forward and kissed Belini's cheek. 'Thank you.'

The other woman ducked her head and placed a hand on her infant's dark, satiny head. 'I pray his path will be similar to yours. That he will be strong and help others. That he will find a suitable mate…just as you have.'

Stevie bit her lip, the lie she and Matt were perpetrating pressing in on her. 'If he has even half of his mother's qualities, he'll be a wonderful person.'

Bending to pick up a white mesh bag filled with green vegetables, Belini smiled. 'Will you stay for the evening's celebration?'

'I'm sorry. We can't. We have to get to Coari.' Now that she knew the people in the village were well, she was as anxious as Matt to reach the city—and to buy those 'special supplies' he'd mentioned.

Belini knelt beside the water and dunked the satchel, allowing the water to fill the bag then lifting it to let the liquid filter through the small holes.

Small holes. White netting.

Recognition swept through her, and her heart sank. 'What are you doing?'

Belini glanced up at her. 'Doing?'

'Is that the mosquito netting from your hut?'

The woman smiled. 'Yes! It is perfect for washing vegetables, is it not?'

'No, it's supposed to be—'

A hand on her arm stopped the rest of her exclamation in mid-sentence. Matt gave a silent shake of his head.

They said their goodbyes while Stevie's anger grew. Everywhere she looked, mosquito nets were being repurposed for other tasks: hanging sacks used to drain the liquid from home-made cheeses and yogurts; small squares used to scrub the bottoms and sides of cooking pots… And she'd even seen one being used as a hair ornament, of all things.

As soon as they boarded the *Projeto Vida*, she turned all that pent-up frustration on Matt. 'How could you stand there and watch them use those nets for other things without saying a word? Without letting me try to explain why they should keep them hung over their beds?' She wanted to scream in fury that all their attempts to help had been for naught. No one in the village felt the slightest hint of guilt. Not even Belini, who'd rambled on and on about how perfect those vital nets were for straining vegetables.

Vegetables! Not a single word about how they'd possibly saved lives in that village.

God, it was like she was reliving her job in New York all over again. She'd tried to talk her ex-fiancé into making policy changes at the hospital that would improve their ability to treat poorer patients. She'd been hobbled at every turn. And when she'd dared to bypass the system and save a life, she'd been shot down—her career stalled and possibly in ruins as a result. So here she was in Brazil, trying to do what she couldn't in New York.

But at least there she'd been allowed to speak her mind.

Matt hadn't given her the chance to say anything back at the village. Not once.

'Those nets could have prevented an epidemic like the one we just witnessed.' She stalked forward, balling her fists and planting them in the center of Matt's chest, only to have him seize her wrists and hold her in place. In the back of her mind she was aware of Nilson quietly vacating the room, probably horrified at her outburst. But she didn't care. If she was going to stay here, she was damn well going to express how she felt about this particular subject.

'Calm down.' The order was soft, but there was a line of steel underlining the words.

'Why? So we can get a call in six months saying there's been an outbreak of yellow fever? That Belini and her baby have died?' She tried to jerk away from him, but he held her in place. Her only option was to glare up at him.

'Do you think you're the first person to pass out mosquito nets to these people?'

'No, of course not.'

His grip on her wrists loosened and he rubbed his thumbs over the chafed skin. 'Once the immediate threat is over, there's always some other danger lurking in the background. A famine. A torn fishing net. Some other need that's not being met. Their lives are ruled by the here and now, not by what the future may or may not hold.'

'Why bother trying to help, then, if nothing ever changes? I came here to make a difference, not to have my efforts tossed in the wind.'

Was she talking about Brazil or her work in New York? Maybe they were one and the same.

'We do what we can to educate them. That doesn't include changing their culture or turning them into 'us.' We have to let them make their own decisions.'

She sagged against him, suddenly exhausted from the barrage of emotions she'd fought all day. 'And if they never make the right ones?'

'Then we've at least given them viable options.'

'You're okay with that? With patching up holes but never treating the root cause?'

'I do treat the cause. I provide them with some of the tools necessary to make changes—just like you did with the netting. It's up to them to use those tools in the way they see fit. We can't force them to do anything.'

Stevie gazed at him. Most of the doctors she'd been around were problem solvers by nature. What kind of man was able to spot the problem, figure out a solution, and then stand by in silence while that solution was ignored?

An extraordinary one.

One she could—Stevie swallowed hard—one she could grow to love with very little encouragement.

The muscles of her throat tightened. One she'd already grown to love.

No! She'd just been engaged to another man a month and a

half ago. A man who'd abused her trust in the worst possible way. There was no way she could have fallen in love with someone else so quickly.

Unless she'd never really loved Michael in the first place. But she'd agreed to marry him—had wanted to be with him. How could she not have loved him?

Rebound.

These slippery, elusive fits of emotion had to be the result of feeling rejected. Unloved.

Even as she thought the words, her heart pitched them to the side. This had nothing to do with her and everything to do with the man whose heart she could hear beating beneath her cheek.

Just as she started to pull away, horrified at the wishy-washiness of her emotions, she spied Nilson in the doorway.

She eased away from Matt, nodding toward the crew member.

'Mateus, Miss Tracy is on the radio. She said she needs to speak with you immediately.'

Stevie's heart leaped to her throat and all kinds of dire predictions swirled around in her head. Another outbreak? Something worse? She could still hear that heated cellphone conversation between Matt and the *Projeto Vida* director right after her arrival. Had Tracy found a replacement for her? Had she decided she didn't want a—what had Matt called it?— 'washed-up doc' sullying her organization's reputation?

No. Surely Matt was the one who made those kinds of decisions, and over the last day or two he hadn't seemed nearly as anxious to be rid of her as he had been.

Her mouth twisted. Yeah, why would he be when she was willing to sprawl flat on her back at the first crooked smile he threw her way?

He wasn't like that. He'd tried to resist what happened as much as she had. And he certainly could have taken it to the next step and then washed his hands of any responsibility.

Instead, they were on their way to buy condoms.

When he tensed and released her hands, she backed up a couple of steps.

'I need to get this,' he said.

'Do you want me to go with you?'

He shook his head, jaw tight. 'No. Tracy and I have a couple of things we need to discuss.'

In private.

He hadn't said the words, but the inference came through loud and clear.

All her doubts and fears leapt back in place, howling and screeching for her to do something.

But there was nothing she could do but nod and let him walk away.

As soon as he went through the door, Nilson came over and laid a hand on her shoulder. 'Your face shows much worry. Why?'

She shook her head. What could she say that would convey she was fine without lying?

Nothing. Because she wasn't fine.

Not by a long shot.

CHAPTER SEVENTEEN

'STILL ticked at me?' The connection was clear enough this time that the trace of chagrin behind Tracy's words came through loud and clear.

'I was ready to wring your neck a couple of weeks ago.'

'Not any more?' Leave it to Tracy to pick up on the real meaning behind his words. Besides, she was right. He was well over his anger.

When had that happened? His mind flashed through various scenes and came up with Stevie as she'd looked at their wedding celebration—her kohl-darkened eyes giving her a wild and untamed appearance. The way she'd gripped his hand so tightly as the medicine man had pierced his ear.

'No, I'm not furious any more. In fact, I've decided to keep Stevie on the team, so you can stop looking.'

An awkward pause ensued. 'That could be a bit of a problem. I'm leaving for Coari tonight. When can you be back?'

He frowned, her words making him uneasy. 'We're actually headed there now. We should dock some time tomorrow afternoon. Why?'

'Well…' She drew the word out like an omen. 'You were so upset at me for hiring a woman that I made a few phone calls.'

'And?' Why had he insisted on Tracy finding someone else before he'd even given Stevie a fair chance?

'A doctor in London has expressed an interest in the position, and I also called Craig. We had a surprisingly productive chat. He's willing to give *Projeto Vida* another shot.'

'Craig? The guy practically had to be medevac'd out of Brazil.' What was Tracy thinking?

'Yes, well, he thinks he might have been too hasty.'

Tracy hadn't seen the look on the man's face when he'd said, 'I'm done.'

There was more to this than met the ear. 'What'd you promise him? I know he's not just offering just because he missed me.'

She laughed. 'You caught me. I promised him a month off every year.' A beat went by. 'With pay.'

'You're kidding, right?' Tracy was a female version of Scrooge. She took pride in squeezing every dollar until it begged for mercy. He couldn't imagine her giving away a month's salary.

'I couldn't get the London guy to agree right away. I started to panic. I know you, Matt. You'll eventually run Stevie off and then work yourself to death just to prove some kind of twisted point. You need another doctor on that team. You know it, and I know it.'

'There's already someone here—who I haven't run off, by the way—so let's just leave things the way they are.'

Something that was either a snort or a burst of static came through the speaker. 'Let's just leave it? I thought you were going to have an aneurism when you learned Stevie was a woman.'

'And you had no hand in that little deception, right?' He couldn't keep the dryness out of his voice.

'I know how you play when you're all by yourself. It's not pretty.' Tracy gave a quick laugh. 'I had no choice but to hire her. And as far as you suddenly wanting her to stay, I find that hard to believe. You were pretty emphatic about replacing her the last time I talked to you.'

He fiddled with his earring, wondering if he had enough time to take the thing out and let the piercing heal so Tracy didn't catch a glimpse of it. Except Matt didn't want to take it out.

How ridiculous was that? He'd allowed Stevie to think he was keeping the bead in because of the village, but that wasn't the only reason. Not by a long shot.

He decided a noncommittal answer was the way to go. 'She's working out better than I expected. What can I say?'

Silence.

'Trace? You still there?'

'I'm here. I kind of promised Craig I'd bring him back on board. Besides, there's another slight prob—'

'Well, *un*-promise him.'

She sighed. 'I'm not sure that's wise. Listen, I'll be there in the morning. We can discuss it then.'

'Why not do it now, over the radio? Or by e-mail…I'll have access once we reach the city. There's no real reason for you to come up here.' Especially when he hadn't sorted out everything in his head.

'This is something that should be done in person.'

A chill went over him. 'Are you firing me?'

'Of course not! What on earth is wrong with you, Matt?'

He ran a hand over his neck, the pain that had receded over the last week returning as his muscles tensed. 'Nothing. We probably won't be back in time to pick you up from the airport.'

'That's okay. I'll hire a car and meet you at the boat. Same docking site, right?'

'Right.'

As soon as he signed off, he headed back up to the deck, where he stared out at the water. He caught his reflection in one of the few pieces of chrome still attached to the boat. A flash of something caught his eye and he leaned closer.

The polished bead in his ear. Wouldn't Tracy love that? He could hear the questions already.

Questions for which he had no answer.

Take it out before she sees it.

Even as he fingered the bead, ordering himself to untie the knot holding it place, he stood there like an impotent fool.

What was wrong with him?

You'd think he was taking off his wedding band. He glanced down at his empty ring finger. It had taken him losing the ring in the river to get him to finally acknowledge his wife wasn't coming back. He'd searched the water for hours afterwards, but had realized that it was gone. Forever.

Just like Vickie.

To take the earring out of his ear would be like losing Stevie, too, and he wasn't ready to do that.

Not yet.

Maybe not ever.

Damn Tracy for coming to see him. Now of all times.

He had this niggling pain in his gut and knew exactly what it meant: he was in trouble. Big trouble.

As much as he told himself that Tracy calling Craig was his own doing, and probably for the best, he just felt like giving someone a pounding.

And that someone was him.

She couldn't see Coari. Not yet. Matt had told her they'd be there within the hour, and that Tracy would meet them at the dock. At this point the longer it took to arrive, the better.

Despite her best efforts, worry had chewed several holes through her insides. First Matt had said they were rushing back because he wanted to buy supplies. Supplies that included condoms. The implication was that they'd be making love again. Then he'd returned from having a private conversation with Tracy, and the anticipation that had been building between them fizzled. Whatever he'd discussed with his supervisor had him worried.

His easy smile had disappeared. As had the intimate little touches she'd come to cherish.

As soon as breakfast was over the next day, he'd dismantled all evidence of his sleeping arrangements, claiming it was normal preparation for docking. Nilson, however, wasn't tearing around his quarters, getting ready to disembark. Neither did Matt ask her to take down her hammock.

She sighed. But at least he hadn't asked her to pack her bags. So she'd stubbornly left everything in her room. Until she was told otherwise, she planned to continue her work.

The boat motored around a bend, and there it was. Coari.

From this distance, the reddish-beige buildings seemed orchestrated to match the muddy color of the river. If not for the small strip of green along the water's edge, she'd swear the water had reached up and kissed the small city, leaving its own indelible mark.

This was the place she'd first set eyes on the *Projeto Vida*. The SUV Matt had used to pick her up from the airport was still parked in the same spot, a powdery layer of dust now coating the surface. It seemed like a lifetime ago she'd sat inside the vehicle, staring in dismay at the decrepit medical vessel.

The freshly glossed finish on the deck winked up at her, and she half smiled. Even without that minor improvement, she now saw the boat with new eyes.

As they drew closer, she noticed a woman stood at the dock, waving. Even from this distance, Stevie could tell she was beautiful. Long dark hair hung just below her shoulders with a fringe of bangs framing a delicate face. Where her own body was lean, almost tomboyish, this woman was the epitome of a pin-up girl. Voluptuous. Curvy.

A bombshell.

No man in his right mind could help but notice her.

A twinge of something ugly whisked up her spine. Maybe Matt preferred women that were soft and lush.

She mashed the jealousy back down. That was ridiculous. When Matt stood beside her, giving the woman on the dock a half-wave of acknowledgement, Stevie tried to summon up some enthusiasm. Unfortunately, she found very little to work with.

'Are you ready for this?' His voice, still full of tension, warned her something was very wrong.

'I'm not sure. Are you?' She glanced up at him, her eyes instinctively seeking the bead in his left ear. There it was, still on display. Relief swept through her along with a strange sense of ownership. Surely he knew he'd have to explain why he was now sporting an earring.

It would have been easy for him to take it out and hide what had happened between them.

But he hadn't.

'We'll soon find out,' he muttered.

The second they reached the dock, Tracy hurried over to greet them. Matt leaped the short space between the boat and wooden planks and enveloped the woman in a warm hug. Stevie swallowed, grabbing the handrail to ease herself across the gap. Hopefully the boat wouldn't lurch, sending her careening into the water.

Matt released the woman and secured Stevie's elbow, steadying her as she tried to get her land legs back under her.

'I don't think you two have met in person,' he said. 'Tracy Hinton, this is Stevie Wilson.'

Tracy smiled, leaning forward to kiss both her cheeks in the Brazilian fashion. 'I've heard so much about you.'

'You have?' Stevie and Matt spoke at the same time, and she couldn't suppress an answering smile.

Tracy laughed. 'Yes, but the reason for that will come soon enough. Tell me about your trip. Was the dengue outbreak as bad as we feared?'

'Worse.' Matt proceeded to give Tracy a quick rundown on the village, looking at Stevie from time to time to fill in the blanks. She noticed he made no mention of the wedding ceremony.

As if the other woman read her thoughts, she raised her brows. 'Aren't you leaving out one crucial detail?'

Dull color crept up Matt's neck. 'Not sure what you mean.'

'Your ear, silly.' Tracy reached up and fingered the new addition, moving closer to study the bead. 'How did this come about?'

Something about the easy intimacy between the two of them set off warning bells in her head.

Matt seemed to hesitate. 'It's just—'

'Gratitude,' Stevie interrupted him, turning to give him a fake smile. 'Don't be so bashful.'

She turned to Tracy. 'Matt saved the chief's daughter, and the village was so grateful they marked him as one of their own during a special ceremony.'

Okay, it wasn't the entire truth, but she suddenly didn't want this woman to know what she and Matt had been through...what they'd done. She didn't want Tracy knowing about the *ayahuasca* pipe or the magical flowers.

Or about the night they'd shared.

She had no idea what Matt and Tracy were to each other, and the thought of being cast the part of naïve fool—yet again—made her cringe. For all she knew, these two could be lovers.

Tracy tilted her head and studied Stevie. 'Wow. Matt's been working this river for twelve years. It's about damn time he had something to show for it.'

His eyes met Stevie's, and something sizzled just below the surface. 'You're right. It's about damn time.'

Her palms tingled, and she pressed them against her slacks to dull the sensation. Was he talking about the villagers, or about her…and him?

'Well,' said Tracy, breaking the sudden silence, 'I have a couple of rooms reserved at the *pousada*.' She smiled at Stevie. 'And I have a surprise for you.'

'For me?'

Tracy nodded, only to have Matt speak up. 'If it's regarding what we discussed on the radio, I need to speak with you privately about that.'

'That's fine.' She strolled toward a grey Land Rover. 'Let's wait until we reach the *pousada*, okay?'

Stevie was relegated to the back seat, while Tracy and Matt sat up front and discussed *Projeto Vida* business. She had no idea what surprise Tracy had in store for her, but unless it included a deep tub and a jar of scented salts she didn't much care. Even a normal shower with plenty of hot, clean water would be enough to satisfy her at the moment. Leaning her head against the headrest, she allowed her eyes to close. Exhaustion crept over her bit by bit, until the road bumps melded together into a constant drone that lulled her toward the edge of consciousness.

'Stevie, honey, wake up.' Her eyes flickered open, and she caught Matt sliding onto the seat next to her. He smiled and brushed his fingers across her cheek.

Where was Tracy? The front seat of the car was empty.

Wait…had he just called her 'honey'?

She shook her head, trying to clear it. 'Are we here?'

'Yep. Tracy's gone in to get the room keys.' He glanced toward a simple white building on the right-hand side of the car. 'Once we're settled, I'd like to go for a walk. Just the two of us. I have something I need to tell you.'

Was this it? The big let-down?

Stevie bit her lip. 'Is it about Tracy?'

'Tracy?' He frowned. 'No. It's about us.'

'About us? So you and Tracy aren't…?'

'Aren't…?' His brows went up. 'Good God, no. She's my sister-in-law. Vickie's younger sister.'

Shock rolled through her. 'I had no idea.'

He eased out of the car, taking her hand to help her out as well. 'There's no way you could have. I didn't expect you to be here long enough for it to matter.' He sighed. 'There's a lot we need to talk about, but it can wait. We have plenty of time. That is, if you're serious about sticking around. If not, now's the time to speak up.'

Hope began to build in her chest. It sounded like he *wanted* her to stay. 'Yes. Of course I'm serious.'

They went into the hotel and found Tracy on the phone. She smiled at them and passed two sets of keys to Matt.

He grabbed a pad and scribbled something then shoved it towards Tracy. She scanned it, then gave him a thumbs-up sign before turning back to her call.

'Where are we going?' Stevie asked as Matt pushed through the door, towing her behind him.

'Where do you want to go?'

'I noticed Tracy rented separate rooms for us.' She hesitated. 'Would you think me forward if I said I wanted to go back to yours?'

'No, because I was thinking the very same thing.' He smiled down at her, his blue eyes darkening. 'But, for both our sakes, we need to make a side trip first.'

* * *

They came out of the drug store with a tiny bag, the pink tint to Stevie's cheeks doing a number on his heart.

'Are you sure you're okay with this?' he asked.

'Definitely. It was my idea, remember?'

He gripped her hand as they rounded the corner, heading back toward his hotel room.

'How are we going to explain to Tracy why we're not joining…?' Her voice faded away, and when he glanced down, he saw her eyes had gone wide, the green irises turning a stormy grey.

She released his hand, and at first he thought it was because Tracy stood on the patio of the hotel. Then he noticed she was deep in conversation with a tall man in a business suit. Stevie stopped in her tracks just as Tracy and her companion turned toward them.

Strangely, when the man gave them a brilliant smile and strode toward them, Stevie stumbled back a step or two, a couple of garbled sounds erupting from her throat.

Before he had a chance to ask her what was wrong, the man reached them. He bypassed Matt altogether, stopping in front of Stevie. When he bent and dropped a kiss on her open mouth, anger roiled through Matt's system. His hands fisted and he started to move forward, but Tracy appeared at his side, her fingers gripping his forearm and holding him in place.

'I told you I had a surprise for her.' She kept her voice low. 'He's the CEO from Stevie's hospital. He flew in from New York yesterday.'

CHAPTER EIGHTEEN

CEO? Since when did chief executive officers kiss their employees on the mouth?

He shook free of Tracy's restraining hand but remained where he was, not sure what was going on. Had Tracy called Stevie's former boss and asked him to come?

The man leaned back and surveyed Stevie with a raised brow. 'My God…look at you.'

Instead of laughing, like she might have done with Matt, Stevie's hands went to her shirt and straightened it self-consciously. A sliver of apprehension lodged in his gut.

'What are you doing here, Michael? I told you we were through.' She seemed dazed, as if his appearance had been the furthest thing from her mind.

Through? What the hell was she talking about?

'I came to talk some sense into you. I had no idea our little argument would drive you to do something so extreme.' One side of his mouth curled up in a half-smile. 'I can see I'll have to make it up to you for a good long time when we get back.'

A sick sense of dread began pumping through Matt's veins.

'You don't have to make anything up to me. I'm not going back.'

'Of course you are. I mean, look at this place. It looks just as bad in person as it did in the medical journal's help-wanted ad.' He chucked her under the chin, ignoring the fact that she ducked away from his hand. 'Doctors Without Borders it is not.

We sat in bed and laughed over the pictures of this…operation, remember?'

The words 'bed' and 'laughed' grabbed Matt by the throat.

Stevie's eyes darted toward him, brimming with guilt. 'No, I…'.

It was true.

She *had* laughed—had thought *Projeto Vida* was ridiculous. And this man had been in bed with her.

The CEO of her hospital.

Jealousy and hurt swirled around inside Matt, each seeking to outrank the other.

As if realizing he'd made some kind of faux pas with his last comment, the man glanced their way and made a half-hearted attempt to backpedal. 'No offense. I'm sure it's for a great cause.' Even as he said it, he pulled a spotless white handkerchief from the inner pocket of his jacket and brushed at a spot of dust on the leg of his expensive trousers. The square of cloth disappeared back inside his coat.

'I don't want you here, Michael. How did you even find me?'

'Your doorman. Thank God you held onto your lease, you're going to need it. I had no idea you'd be willing to chuck your whole career on a whim.'

She laughed, the sound hard and brittle. 'A whim? Hardly. You made sure of that with the board of directors.'

'I overreacted. I met with the board a week ago, and they realize—like I do—that you were merely concerned about your patient. They want you back. *I* want you back. You're too valuable a doctor to waste your talent in a place like this.' He touched her hand. 'Just so you know, I didn't cancel our honeymoon reservations.'

Honeymoon? This guy was her fiancé?

She'd mentioned being involved with someone, but she'd said it was over. The words 'engaged' and 'fiancé' had never come up in the conversation.

A sinking sensation spiraled through him, and his fingers tightened around the sack containing the new package of condoms—and what he'd thought was a new beginning. He glanced at Tracy and read the pity in her eyes.

She knew.

'You were engaged?' he asked Stevie. 'Why didn't you tell me?'

She'd let him do things to her. Intimate things. And what she'd done to him… He closed his eyes, trying to block that particular memory.

'It was complicated,' she said. 'But you're right. I should have.'

Complicated.

The woman knew personal details about his life. About his marriage. And he suddenly realized how little she'd told him about her past.

The other man's eyes narrowed, maybe sensing there was more here than he realized. 'Stevie and I had a slight disagreement. Most couples do at some point.'

'Maria was more than a disagreement, don't you think, Michael?'

A tightening of lips from the other man was the only sign that her words had hit a nerve. 'I made a mistake. That's something we can discuss later. In private.' There was a definite emphasis on the last two words.

'There's nothing to discuss.'

Tracy, clearly uncomfortable with the ugly turn this little re-union had taken, glanced at Matt and tilted her head, indicating they should move away. He was having none of it.

Instead, he took a step toward the couple, noting the way Michael edged slightly in front of Stevie, blocking Matt's access.

'Is this why you came to Brazil?' he asked her. 'Because you had a falling out with your hospital and your fiancé?'

'No.'

'Yes.'

She and Michael spoke at the same time, but their answers were poles apart.

'Which is it, Stevie?'

'I ran into some trouble with the board at my hospital, but

that's not the only reason I came here. I'd been thinking about it for a while.'

Her ex fiancé let out a laugh of disbelief. 'Is that so? We've been engaged for two years and you never once mentioned coming to Brazil.' He turned to Matt. 'I'll tell you why she came. Her hospital privileges were suspended for refusing to follow hospital protocol.'

'Michael, please don't do this.'

Matt swallowed. She'd lied. About everything. She'd said she came to Brazil to 'make a difference'. The truth was, she'd been tossed out of her old job and had needed another one pronto. *Projeto Vida*'s desperation in that series of ads must have come through loud and clear.

The ads she and Mr. Smooth CEO had laughed their heads off at. *Projeto Vida* was Matt's lifeblood, and she'd ridiculed it.

A wave of nausea almost brought him to his knees.

Another thought hit. This man was the CEO of the hospital where she worked, and she'd slept with him.

The condom package whispered an accusation. She'd slept with one boss—what was to keep her from sleeping with another? She'd been worried about him sending her back to the States. Could she have led him on? Reeled him in with those big innocent eyes and that sexy accent?

What had she said?

I thought for sure I'd...persuaded you to keep me on. He swallowed. She had persuaded him. He'd been this close to telling her that he...

The solution came to him in an instant.

He turned to Michael. 'Your timing worked out perfectly. Tracy has someone who's interested in Stevie's position.' His glance clipped Stevie's, but he found he couldn't quite meet her eyes. 'You knew we were looking for someone else. The boat just isn't built to house both male and female doctors. And you saw what happened with Belini's tribe.'

Stevie's lips parted. 'Oh, but you said—'

'I know what I said.' And he'd been wrong, on so many counts. But he was about to undo all those mistakes in one cruel cut. 'The doctor who was here before you has decided to come back. We gave him that option, and feel it's only right we keep our word.'

'What? When did this happen?'

'Tracy told me about it on the radio yesterday.'

'Yesterday. And yet today you were willing to let me…' She motioned to the sack he held and a soft glitter of tears washed into her eyes. 'Oh, God.'

He almost cracked. Almost told her it was all a misunderstanding. But as she wiped a trickle of moisture from her left cheek, Michael put his arm around her and pulled her close.

Matt's resolve stiffened. How long before she decided Brazil wasn't for her? A month? A year? She'd eventually miss the career she'd had in New York, he was sure of it.

Better to allow her think he was a bastard and get it over with than watch her walk away later, trampling his heart beneath her feet. 'Can you manage your things, or would you like Nilson's help?'

A long silence ensued. Part of him hoped she'd argue with him…tell him she wasn't going anywhere. Instead, her chin went up, and she met his gaze, her face a study in angry defiance. 'Don't worry, I'll have my stuff off the boat within the hour.'

'I appreciate it. Let Tracy know if you need help booking a flight out.' With that he turned on his heel and headed in the direction of the hotel bar. He needed a drink. The stronger, the better. As he reached the door, something made him stop and glance back. Her eyes were still following him. Needing to make his point perfectly clear, he raised his brows and tossed the bag from the drugstore—along with all his hopes—into a nearby trashcan. She'd get his meaning.

They were through.

He didn't need her.

He didn't need anyone.

Matt endured the playful punch to his arm with gritted teeth and a sour stomach.

'Admit it. You couldn't live without me.' If Craig only knew how close he was to having that grin wiped off his face, he'd

stop his incessant quest for praise. 'I did a beautiful job sutur-
ing that little native girl's arm, didn't I? The scar will hardly be
noticeable.'

Little native girl? Of all the condescending, ignorant…

Tiago, fresh from his forced two-week hiatus, stepped nervously between the pair. *'Calma, Mateus.'*

Calm down? He was perfectly calm. He glanced down at his
balled fists and frowned. Uncurling them, he forced the tense
muscles to relax. His hands weren't the only body part feeling
the strain. His neck had been killing him for the past few days.
What he wouldn't give to have Stevie's magic hands smooth
away his pain.

She's gone. It's what you said you wanted, remember?

He forced his mind back to Tiago. 'How's Nilson?'

'He's on the deck, fishing for our lunch. But he said you will
not keep him from the real work much longer. He claims you are
stealing his manhood by giving him jobs fit for an infant.'

While Matt had agonized over that mosquito bite on Stevie's
arm, no one had had any idea that Nilson had also been exposed
to dengue. And in the end it had been his crewmember who'd
fallen ill. With Tiago still at his home village, and Stevie's abrupt
departure, it had been Matt who'd nursed Nilson during the long
nights when the fever had caused tremors so strong, two of the
man's teeth had broken. It was Matt who'd strapped Nilson's arm
to the metal railing of the examination table to hold it still while
he'd inserted tubing for the saline drip. Yet even while Nilson
had quaked and moaned in pain, he'd insisted he wanted to work,
his pride fierce even while he'd lain weak and helpless.

Something about the experience had brought Stevie to mind.
What if she'd been the one…

Matt shook his head to clear it. 'Nilson still needs a few more
days to recoup his strength. Tell him he's too valuable for me to
lose.'

Even as he said it, he noticed Craig studying the inner surface
of his arms yet again, rubbing at something, his teasing attitude
long gone.

'What are you doing?' Matt asked.

'That man could still be contagious. I can't believe you let him stay on the boat with the rest of us. He should have been quarantined.' He sniffed. 'If I had known he had dengue before I got on that flight, I would have delayed my trip.'

This time it was Tiago whose jaw tightened. The two crew members had been with *Projeto Vida* from its inauguration, twelve years ago. Tiago wasn't going to stand by while Craig whined about exposure as if Nilson were nothing more than a disease vector.

Matt stared the other doctor down. '*That man* has a name. I'll thank you to use it.'

'Of course, I didn't mean anything. It's just that when Tracy called me the second time, she sounded almost desperate, said you'd had another doctor leave unexpectedly.' He shrugged. 'I guess I'm not the only one who had trouble adjusting to life on the Amazon.'

Except Stevie hadn't had trouble adjusting. She'd thrown herself into the job, never balking at the rough conditions, her compassion toward Belini and her baby…toward everyone…had been boundless. She'd cared enough about their well-being to get angry—really angry—when they'd cut up the mosquito nets and used them for other things.

While he'd freaked out over her mosquito bite, she'd been the voice of reason, insisting on finishing what she'd started.

Matt swallowed. And he'd been stupid enough to send her away.

Ah, hell. He'd been an idiot. A fearful, insecure half-wit, scared out of his mind of losing another woman he cared about.

That's why he'd jumped at the chance to get rid of Stevie. And why he'd allowed himself to believe that Brazil had been a last-ditch effort to save her career. It was obvious to everyone that she liked it here. That she'd wanted to stay.

With him.

He hadn't been angry over her reasons for coming to Brazil. Or that she'd recently ended a bad relationship. No, those were only excuses. Lies. The real reason he'd wanted her gone ran deeper. And was much more personal.

Matthew Grant Palermo had been terrified.

Terrified something would strike Stevie down and take her away from him. Terrified that she'd make him fall in love with her, only to abandon him when a better opportunity came along. So he'd thrown her away, taken away her choice to stay...or to leave.

He'd been a selfish bastard.

He loved her, dammit. His fingers went to his ear. It was the reason he still had his earring in place. He was married. In heart, if not in law.

And if he *had* succeeded in driving her back into her former fiancé's arms, he would kick himself to the United States and back again.

But he was going. He had to see her. If she'd still have him.

He clapped Tiago on the back and faced his soon-to-be ex-colleague. 'Craig, it's time for you to sink or swim, because I have somewhere I need to be. You can take over for me while I'm gone. Or you can fly back to the States. Your choice.'

'B-but, you can't just leave me here alone. I just got here.' When Matt said nothing, Craig's horrified expression changed, his brows sweeping down over his nose in a scowl. 'I should have known there was more to this story than Tracy let on. I'm out of here.'

The test had worked like a charm. Matt closed his eyes and sucked down a deep breath, relishing the earthy fragrance that rose off the *Rio Preto*. 'The good news is you've helped me realize what a jerk I've been. But that's about to change.'

'You haven't exactly been a jerk. You just can't leave—'

'You are going to fetch Miss Stevie, then?' Tiago stared at him, hope shining in his eyes.

'I am.'

Craig jammed his hands on his hips. 'Who the hell is Stevie?'

'Stevie Wilson...is going to be your replacement. If I can get her to take me back.' Without a backward glance, he strode away to check on Nilson and to find his passport.

CHAPTER NINETEEN

STEVIE shoved back a strand of hair that had escaped her clip as she made her way to the patient in exam room three. Pulling the file from the holder, she gave it a quick perusal and then pushed through the heavy door.

'Hello, Mary, how's that back of yours holding up?'

She listened to the woman's progress, her eyes going to the small bump on Mary's midsection. Not quite forty, her pregnancy had been as much a surprise as the two compression fractures in her thoracic spine, the latter diagnosis sending her to the clinic where Stevie now worked. Mary was proof that even in developed countries poor early nutrition could have devastating consequences. As did the soft, cushy lives technology afforded.

Belini came to mind. Then Matt. She gritted her teeth and forced her concentration back to the woman in front of her.

'You're not riding that Appaloosa of yours at anything faster than a walk, right?' A seasoned barrel racer and equine trainer, horses were Mary's lifeblood. Her profession. Or they had been. Only time would tell if they could coax enough bone growth to stand up to the wear and tear of future competitions.

Tears came to the woman's eyes. 'It's hard.' She touched her stomach. 'It's one thing to stop riding temporarily, for the sake of the baby. It's another to wonder if this is it. The end of all my hopes and dreams.'

Been there. Done that. Had the emotional scars to prove it.

She laid a hand on the woman's shoulder. 'Let's give your body some time. The fractures have healed, but we still need to

get you into physical therapy to strengthen those back muscles.'
She smiled. 'Besides, I've been doing some research of my own.
I took riding lessons when I was a teenager. Western Pleasure.
I even have a ribbon or two under my belt to show for it.'

Mary laughed, her eyes crinkling. 'You actually rode a pea-
nut pusher?'

'A what?'

'It's a nickname. Some Western Pleasure horses are trained
to carry their heads so low they look like they're pushing pea-
nuts along the ground.'

'Ah.' Stevie did remember seeing that phrase in her reading.
She'd also read that that style of riding was no longer in vogue.
'I think you'd be surprised at how the headset has changed over
the years. Don't rule out the possibility just yet. Barrels and
Western Pleasure may be poles apart on a thrill scale, but I re-
member Western Pleasure being a whole lot harder than it looked.
And the soft, slow movements are easier on the bones and joints
than running Barrels. You'd be learning a whole new discipline.
Look on it as a challenge.'

Mary frowned as if she was considering Stevie's words. 'I'd
never thought about changing tracks. I'd miss what I did, but I
guess it's better than giving up riding all together.'

Stevie could definitely relate. She missed Brazil. But prac-
ticing in Atlanta was better than giving up medicine altogether.
And at least she didn't have to face her ex-fiancé on a daily
basis. Once the disciplinary note had been cleared from her record, she'd applied to a variety of clinics. The one in Atlanta had
agreed to take her on a six-month trial basis.

Kind of like Matt and Tracy had done. Except they'd agreed
to give her two years. Matt had given her less than a tenth of that.

It was the second time she'd been kicked to the curb at the
whim of an angry man. She had no intention of it ever happening again.

Mary glanced down at her watch. 'Whew! You must have
other patients, and I need to pick Alex up from school.' She stood
and gathered her purse, then gave Stevie a quick hug. 'Thank

you. You've actually given me a glimmer of hope. My contesting horse won't be very happy with me, but he'll get over it.'

Once Mary left the room, Stevie plunked down onto the examination stool and took a slow, careful breath. Her chest ached, but it had nothing to do with physical pain. Any time she had a few moments to herself, she thought about Matt. About Nilson and Tiago. About Belini. She worked herself to the point of exhaustion each day, trying to blot out that painful chapter in her life.

But it stuck with her in a way that Michael's betrayal never had. The fact that she'd gotten over her ex so quickly should have warned her the relationship had been doomed from the outset. She'd hoped the same would happen with her feelings for Matt. That they'd fade away as she immersed herself in new job.

They hadn't.

But it was either go on with her life or curl up in a corner somewhere. She wasn't made that way. Like Mary, when faced with difficult circumstances, she would change and adapt. Create new and more realistic expectations.

Penny, one of the nurses, stuck her head around the door. 'You have a patient in exam room two.'

Stevie frowned. 'I thought Mary was the last patient of the day.'

'She was, but someone called in a favor from Dr. Henry. Supposedly an emergency case.'

'Supposedly?'

'You let me know once you've examined him.' Penny snorted and thrust a file into her hand. 'Have fun. The guy refuses to put on a gown.'

'Just my luck. Do you mind sticking around for a few more minutes?'

'Are you kidding? I wouldn't miss this for the world.'

Stevie flipped open the chart, puzzled at the large swath of blank space. It wasn't like Penny not to be thorough. 'There's nothing on here. What's he complaining of?'

'He says he has a crick in his neck, and you've been the only doctor who could make it go away.'

'Me? He must be thinking of someone else. I've haven't treated anyone's neck since medical…'

Stevie's thoughts blanked out as memories crowded in. It couldn't be. She dropped the file on the exam table, her hands suddenly shaking.

'Dr. Wilson, are you all right?'

'I don't know.' She hurried down the hall and stopped outside exam room two. Her hands touched the door, then retracted. She forced down a couple of deep breaths.

Get a grip, Stevie. It's not him. It can't be.

Her heart didn't believe her. This time, when she reached for the door, she forced herself to push through it, readying herself for the wave of disappointment that would surely follow. She stopped in her tracks when she saw a familiar sweep of dark hair.

Propped against a wall, Matt was thumbing through the latest edition of the *Journal of the American Medical Association*. For a second, she wondered if she was having some kind of awful hallucination. She'd thought about Matt almost constantly since coming back to the States. She dreamed about him at night. Had her mind somehow conjured him up from nothing?

Then his blue eyes met hers, and she knew he was no hallucination. He was real. Here in Atlanta.

'How did you find me?' The croaked words were the best she could manage, considering the thick layer of sawdust now clogging her throat.

'Michael.'

She blinked. 'Michael?'

'Your ex seemed to take issue with you leaving his hospital. A few sympathetic clucks from me, and he spilled everything.'

It figured. 'Not very professional of either of you.'

He dropped the magazine on the counter. 'I've done several unprofessional things since meeting you. I came to apologize.'

Crossing her arms over her chest, she tried to appear braver than she felt. If he'd come out of some misplaced sense of guilt for how he'd dumped her, he could take his remorse and fly right back to Brazil.

'No need.' She motioned to the space around her. 'As you can see, I landed on my feet.'

'You didn't go back to Michael. Or to his hospital.'

'Not that it's any of your business but, no. I told you, it was over. Working with him would have been awkward. Besides, I love it here in Atlanta. I can't think of anyplace I'd rather be.'

What was one more lie?

He scrubbed a hand through his hair, and Stevie caught sight of his left ear, where the wedding bead still resided. 'I see. Maybe I've wasted a trip, then.'

Why was he here, anyway? Surely he hadn't traveled four thousand miles just to say he was sorry.

'How's the new guy working out?' The name came to her. 'Craig…wasn't it?'

Matt fiddled with the discarded magazine, his thumb ruffling the pages as he avoided her eyes. 'Yes. And he's not.'

'Really? What happened?'

His gaze came up and speared hers, the electric blue standing out against the sea of tanned skin. 'He wasn't you.'

'He wasn't…' Three small words, but somehow she must have misunderstood them. Or maybe her subconscious had placed the words in his mouth. 'I'm sorry, could you say that again?'

He closed the distance between them. 'I said, he wasn't you.' One of his hands fisted by his side. 'Nilson got sick.' The words came out in a rush.

'Is he all right?'

'He is now. He came down with dengue right after you left.'

'I'm so sorry. You said he's okay, though.' She wasn't quite sure why he was telling her this.

'He is, but I wasn't. It took Nilson falling ill for me to understand why I wanted you gone. It had nothing to do with your engagement or with your reasons for coming to Brazil.'

Her heart twisted inside her. Was that it? He was going to lay some worse transgression at her doorstep? 'I don't understand.'

'Don't you?'

She shook her head, words sticking in her throat.

'When Tracy went to get the keys for our hotel rooms, I asked if you planned on sticking around. Do you remember?'

She remembered every second, right down to the brilliant flare of hope that had erupted inside her belly. An hour later, though, he'd ground out the tiny flame. 'Yes, but I don't see what that has to do with anything.'

Penny peeked in the door. 'Everything all right in here?'

'Fine,' they both said in unison.

'Okay, then…' said the woman, her eyes wide as she let the door click shut.

Matt took one of her hands. 'When I saw Michael standing there…when he kissed you, I realized you might leave, whether I told you to go or not. Or maybe you'd decide to stay, but something else could take you away from me. Something beyond my control.'

She realized what he was getting at. 'Like dengue.'

'Yes. Only I didn't understand that at the time. I only saw a way to relieve the fear that was eating me alive, and I jumped at the chance.'

'Did it help?'

He gave a harsh laugh. 'No. Because by that time it was too late. I was already in love with you.'

'You were in love with me?' She pleaded with herself not to go down this road again, but it was no use. Her heart didn't want to listen to the very rational argument her intellect laid before it.

Because he loved her!

Matt continued, 'So, it's either live with the fear and take a shot at happiness, or live without it and be miserable.'

'And are you? Miserable?'

His hand tightened on hers. 'Every single day without you has been hell. When Tiago found out I was headed for the States, he dove off the boat yelling "Hallelujah".'

Stevie smiled at the image and moved closer, laying her hands on his chest. 'I've been miserable too.'

'Have you?'

'Yes.' She tilted her head back. 'You're not the only one who fell in love on that trip.'

A huge sigh shuddered through his frame, and he dropped a kiss on her lips. 'Thank God,' he whispered against them.

'I want to go back to Brazil.'

'What about your work here?'

'There's a trial period.'

'And if you decide you like it better here?'

She shook her head. 'I won't. Not if you aren't with me.' Reaching up, she smoothed the frown lines from his brow. 'Are you sure you can you do this?'

'Do what?'

'Live with the fear?'

He sighed, threading his fingers through her hair. 'I can't promise not to worry. I'll probably drive you crazy at times.'

'And I can't promise I won't get sick, that I won't die. But I can promise to be careful. As long as you promise to do the same.'

He fingered his earring. 'I've already made the biggest promise I know how to make. But I want to make it official. Will you marry me? Before God and everyone?'

Stevie smiled and pulled him down for a lingering kiss. 'Too late, silly. I already did.'

EPILOGUE

'Ju-Ju, you come play with me.' The plaintive cry came from Belini's two-year old son, Stevie.

June Christina Palermo, Stevie and Matt's baby girl, stepped toward the other child, her tiny feet unsteady in the sand.

Leaning back against Matt's chest, Stevie sighed. 'It's good to be back, isn't it?'

'I hate to admit it, but yes.' He dropped a kiss on top of her head.

They'd spent almost two years in the States, needing time to nurture their relationship. She'd gotten pregnant and had had June during that time. Stevie had worried the pregnancy would bring back terrible memories of Matt's late wife and unborn child, and it was part of the reason she'd insisted on remaining in the States and having the baby in an Atlanta hospital. She didn't want to put more pressure on Matt than necessary.

The time there had been good—really good—and he'd resisted coming back. But it was time. He'd needed to return to Brazil and see it with an objectivity he'd been lacking. Whether or not they stayed was a decision they'd make together. But hearing the warmth in his voice as he'd greeted the chief, she had a feeling he might not be as against rejoining the *Projeto Vida* team as he'd originally thought.

She tilted her head back and smiled at him. 'Love you.'

'Mmm. I'm glad, because if you didn't…' he nodded toward the children playing in the clearing '…she wouldn't be here right now.'

'I know.' She reached up, feeling for the gold post in his ear, her anniversary present to him last year, before snuggling closer. 'Good thing you came to your senses when you did, or I'd still be working sixty hours a week.'

'Will you miss the practice?'

'Honestly? Yes.' Her eyes swept across the clearing to where the *Rio Preto* flowed past, its current slow and easy. Alive. Free. Carrying life—and death—to the communities that lay along its banks. 'But I miss this too. How about you?'

He chuckled. 'I didn't until we got to the village. But seeing them together...' He tightened his arms around her. 'Yeah, I do.'

'Me too.' She smiled. 'It's perfect isn't it? Our life?'

Belini waved as she walked toward the river's edge, her mosquito-netting sieve filled with vegetables.

Matt gave an audible sigh that seemed to echo her own exasperation. 'No, it's not perfect. But it's close enough.'

Cocking her head for another kiss, she gave him a sassy tilt of her brows. 'That's not what you said last night.'

His mouth captured hers in a searing kiss that made her heart trip a couple of beats and took her back to the slow rock of their hammock as they'd made love in the dark of night. 'Thank heavens Ju-Ju finally caught on to sleeping in her own bed.'

They'd strung a low-lying hammock in the dining area, surrounded by a curtain of mosquito netting. The constant hum of the boat's motor and the way the bed cradled her in its arms did what rocking and cajoling had failed to do for the last two nights, lull their baby into a deep sleep.

'Do we dare hope for two nights in a row?' Stevie asked.

He nodded at Belini. 'I have a better idea. Wait here.'

Walking over to where the other woman knelt, rinsing her vegetables, he whispered something to her. Belini nodded, her eyes shooting to Stevie with a grin.

Matt returned and reached down a hand, which she accepted. But when he tried to lead her toward the village, she hesitated. 'What are you doing?'

'Remember our wedding night?'

Puzzled, she stared at him. 'Of course I do.'

'Not our Stateside wedding. The wedding they threw for us here. In the village.'

Her glance drifted to his ear, a wave of love nearly knocking her over. 'I remember.'

He smiled at her and lifted her fingers to his lips then tugged her along behind him. 'Belini offered to watch Ju-Ju for a couple of hours, and I asked some of the ladies to gather a very special flower and sprinkle its petals around the honeymoon bed.'

'You did?' A strange, shivery sensation passed through her. She lowered her voice. 'Have the men been passing around the pipe again?'

'No. But I wanted things to be perfect this time.'

As they reached the hut and he swept her over the threshold, she saw purple flowers strewn across every available surface. Wrapping her arms around his neck, she breathed in the hypnotic scent that had nothing to do with flowers and everything to do with the man holding her.

Her husband.

For ever.

'Things already are perfect,' she whispered as he leaned in to claim the first of many kisses. 'Because we have each other.'

* * * * *

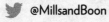

MILLS & BOON

THE HEART OF ROMANCE

A ROMANCE FOR EVERY KIND OF READER

MODERN

Prepare to be swept off your feet by sophisticated, sexy and seductive heroes, in some of the world's most glamourous and romantic locations, where power and passion collide.
8 stories per month.

HISTORICAL

Escape with historical heroes from time gone by. Whether your passion is for wicked Regency Rakes, muscled Vikings or rugge Highlanders, awaken the romance of the past.
6 stories per month.

MEDICAL

Set your pulse racing with dedicated, delectable doctors in the high-pressure world of medicine, where emotions run high an passion, comfort and love are the best medicine.
6 stories per month.

True Love

Celebrate true love with tender stories of heartfelt romance, fr the rush of falling in love to the joy a new baby can bring, and focus on the emotional heart of a relationship.
8 stories per month.

Desire

Indulge in secrets and scandal, intense drama and plenty of siz hot action with powerful and passionate heroes who have it all: wealth, status, good looks…everything but the right woman.
6 stories per month.

HEROES

Experience all the excitement of a gripping thriller, with an int romance at its heart. Resourceful, true-to-life women and stror fearless men face danger and desire - a killer combination!
8 stories per month.

DARE

Sensual love stories featuring smart, sassy heroines you'd want best friend, and compelling intense heroes who are worthy of t
4 stories per month.

To see which titles are coming soon, please visit

millsandboon.co.uk/nextmonth

JOIN US ON SOCIAL MEDIA!

Stay up to date with our latest releases, author news and gossip, special offers and discounts, and all the behind-the-scenes action from Mills & Boon...

 millsandboon

 millsandboonuk

 millsandboon

It might just be true love...

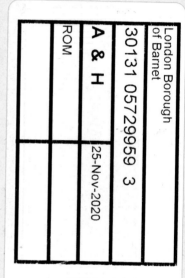

Tropical temptation
6380847